THE BIRDCAGE

Salonika, 1916: a city that is nominally neutral, but is teeming with French, British, and Serbian armies. A city seething with intrigue, where the native inhabitants are eager to make what money they can from the foreign soldiery. Welcome to the Birdcage, named after the miles of tangled barbed wire separating the city from the fighting to the North. It is the Casablanca of WWI. This kaleidoscope of nations, cultures and political ambitions shifts and re-forms around a group of English men and women, blown there by many different winds — into a world of madcap journeys by mule, motor car, and foot over the grim mountains; of U-boats lurking in the waters; of the sinister Gazmend Effendi. What is his game? Where is all the petrol disappearing to? The breathless ride is just beginning . . .

THE BIRDCAGE

CLIVE ASLET

LARGE
PRINT

First published in Great Britain 2014
by
Cumulus Books

First Isis Edition
published 2016
by arrangement with
Cumulus Books

A catalogue record for this book is available
from the British Library.

ISBN 978–1–78541–244–8 (hb)
ISBN 978–1–78541–250–9 (pb)

Published by
F. A. Thorpe (Publishing)
Anstey, Leicestershire

Set by Words & Graphics Ltd.
Anstey, Leicestershire
Printed and bound in Great Britain by
T. J. International Ltd., Padstow, Cornwall

This book is printed on acid-free paper

For Naomi

Contents

Contents

Chief Characters in *The Birdcage*

Presenting, in order (more or less) of appearance:

Captain Southall, Commander of the Kite Balloon Section, later impresario of *The Struma Follies*: "Sunny" by name and by nature

Lieutenant Winnington-Smith ("Winner"), promising artist and hopeless soldier; *in love with*

Elsie Fox, Transport Section of the British Women's Hospital, and bold venturer; *colleague of*

Isabel Hinchcliff, a daughter of the Surrey Hills, and nurse at the British Women's Hospital

Major Eglinton ("Eggie"), Scottish "Dug Out" (dug out of retirement) and Intelligence Officer

Major Otterwill ("The Otter"), Quartermaster, gardener, fatalist

Ivor Fuller ("Ivory Filler"), a Canadian dentist

Private Jones ("Twofour"), one Jones among many in his original (Welsh) regiment: rejected as *The Follies'* female lead

Private Bream ("Fishy"), of the Kite Balloon Section, a drayman in civilian life, now unlikely goose fancier

Colonel Simon ("Simple"), scholar, MP, polyglot and Man of Secrets

Gazmend Effendi, an overstuffed Ottoman, on whom Fate sits without leaving perceptible mark

General Ménière ("Manure"), representative in Salonika of the military glory of France

Joachim von Ertfurtwege ("Earwig"), German flying ace and scourge of the Kite Balloonists

Molhos Frères, restaurateurs extraordinaires, doing well out of the War

Major-General Gay, theatre-loving Divisional Commander, who begets *The Follies* when not directing the war

Compton Pauncefoot ("Footy", late Douglas Hastings), a disgraced theatrical luminary, masquerading as a soldier

Lieutenant Sandys ("Ramsgate"), Kite Balloonist and *siffleur*, late of the Pavilion Theatre, Rhyl

Captain Sewell ("Ratty"), an explosives officer who is less Byronic than he might like

Mr Bagehot ("Bigot"), Editor of *The Balkan Gazette*, and co-founder of the *Cercle des Etrangers*

Mister Desire, a.k.a. Solomon, or Vassilis: a waiter at Molho's

Ahmed (or Aaron), nemesis of Mister Desire

Rachael Pinheiros, whose beauty sweetens the chocolate at Molho Frères — sometimes known as *La Belle Chocolatière*

Captain Petrović, a young Serbian officer, in love with Isabel

Lord Sturry, representative of the Red Cross, *in search of*

Lady Sturry, organiser of a hospital in Prilep

Private Tennant ("Parsley"), skilled rider and "perfect bint"

Mrs Stalwart-Dousing, Dr Aitken, Sister Muir, Nurse Goodman ("Goody"), backbone of the BWH (three of them being vertebrae, one a slipped disc)

Sundry quondam British soldiers, turned performers in The Struma Follies; *Serb commanders and soldiers*; representatives of the Allied Armies in Salonika; and local inhabitants of the city, named and unnamed, Jewish, Greek and Turkish

1: Map of the Macedonian Front, 1916–17
from a sketch by Capt R W Southall RFC, Kite Balloon
Section, Struma Valley

"Winner sketched. The sharpened charcoal moved with precision. After some minutes, Sunny looked over his shoulder.

" 'I say, good work! They tried to teach me to draw at Sandhurst.
'A hopeless case, of course.' "

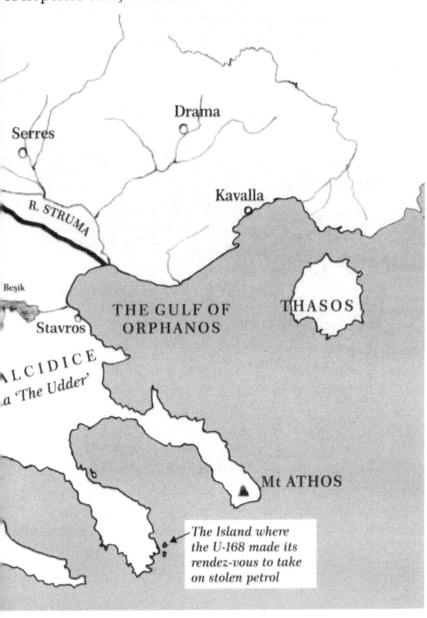

Serres

Drama

Kavalla

R. STRUMA

Beşik

Stavros

THE GULF OF ORPHANOS

THASOS

ALCIDICE
a 'The Udder'

Mt ATHOS

The Island where the U-168 made its rendez-vous to take on stolen petrol

2: Street Map of Salonika, showing the location of scenes and episodes in The Birdcage

TENTS
(French)

Citadel
(Yedi Kule)

TENTS
(British)

Rue Venizelos (formerly
Sabri Pasha Street)

City
Walls

Quarry

Tekke of the
Dervishes

Church of
St Demetrius
(Hagios Demetrios)

CEMETERIES

Rue Egnatia

Ivory's dental
studio

Hospital

Winner's studio in
a Skin Factory

Champ
de Mars

Cercle des
Etrangers

White
Tower

PORT

GULF OF SALONIKA

Spring 1916

One

The big wicker basket lurched unexpectedly.

"Steady on, you fellows," said Captain Southall of the Royal Flying Corps, who was about to climb inside. "We've got a passenger today. Wouldn't want to give him the wrong impression before he's even left the ground.

"Safe as houses," he declared in an aside. "In these parts, given the tendency of houses in Salonika to be shaken down by earthquakes or collapse under the inadequacies of their own shoddy building, safer."

The man inside the basket grabbed the rim. He was not much over five feet tall, with unruly black hair and thick glasses. His size gave the impression of his being a teddybear in a toy basket. He looked, for the hundredth time, at the enormous, gas-filled sack above him. It was shaped like a black pudding with an arrangement of three fins at the back. The balloon "nursery" had taken two days to generate the hydrogen to inflate it.

Men hauled at the ropes, and, judging his moment, Southall vaulted over the side to join his fellow aeronaut. Everyone called him "Sunny" Southall, and not only because of the alliteration. His face, burned as brown as a biscuit, opened into a smile that revealed irregular, nicotine-stained teeth. He was somewhere in his later twenties, with sandy hair and inconclusive moustache. The end of his nose and tops of his ears had been scorched by the sun.

"Yes, safe as anything, Winner," he continued in his breezy way, as the ground crew began to play out the steel wire that connected the craft with the balloon bed. "But it's recommended that you hook up to one of these things." He indicated one of the bags, shaped like an elongated champagne cork, which hung on the outside of the basket; attached to it was a harness that he gave to his companion. "Step into this." In the narrow space, Winner found that the straps of the harness developed a perverse inclination to twist themselves around his ankles. "If you should feel the need to stretch your legs and return to mother earth at any point in the voyage, all you need do is jump — from a suitable altitude of course. Gravity and the combined industry of about a million silk worms will do the rest. There's a cord which pulls out the canopy as you descend. You float down like an angel."

Winner could not see this in quite the comforting light that Sunny intended. On army papers, his name was T. Winnington Smith. Since his schooldays, he had been known as Winner, for the sarcastic reason that whatever the game being played, he invariably lost.

He had studied under the great Tonks at the Slade. Socially, the Slade years had been difficult for him. He was not like the other students. He did not conform to their rowdy bohemianism. Fervour and austerity, the Bible and Bach, long walks by the estuary in clothes that had been made by female relations — such was the stuff of his home life and, despite the patriarchal dominance of his father and his mother's excitable evangelism, he had no desire to escape it. He loved the tumbledown, pargeted Essex village, and the brown sails that he could see from the upper windows of the family house as the barges made their way up the river. While his fellow students looked forward to evenings of pleasure at the Café Royal — and other places he did not like to name — Winner wanted nothing more than to be carried eastwards to the mudflats.

Now, like Sunny, he was a member of the British Salonika Force, and about to take wing. He had never previously had occasion to leave what, from the perspective of the balloon basket, he felt increasingly inclined to call terra firma. "You don't attach yours, I notice," he observed, wondering if Sunny didn't trust the device.

"No time for it at the moment. Besides, I'm a regular. I can hook on quickly enough if need arises." Winner strove to look nonchalant, but failed. "I've jumped hundreds of times," Sunny rattled on reassuringly. "Well, that's not strictly true. Twice, actually. Was perfectly all right. C'est la guerre, as they used to say in France. But there'll be no call for it today, touch wood," he tapped the willow of the basket's side. "Because this Kite Balloon Section, which I have the honour to command, is made up of the right sort." He looked over the edge of the basket, which had now risen to fifty feet above the ground and gave a cheery wave. "Everything A1 this end," he shouted. "You can let out faster now." And then to Winner said, "Each one of them as keen as mustard."

It was an hour after dawn. A couple of the soldiers wore white, cork-lined helmets, against a sun that

5

would soon gather strength. All had discarded their tunics. The capacious seats of the khaki trousers rose halfway up the backs of their wearers. They were the men to whom the Army had not been thoughtful enough to issue shorts.

For the most part, the Section's job was done; those who were not on the winch could stand back, hand shading their eyes, and watch the ascent of the immense vessel, a leviathan of the skies, appearing to seek its own gaseous element, as it rode and strained on the wire.

Winner hardly noticed the process of levitation. It did not feel that the basket had gone up, rather that the earth below it had mysteriously receded and suddenly was no longer there. Then he found himself at a sufficient height to gaze out over the Vardar plain, still rosy and soft-shaped in the morning light. Beyond Lake Doiran rose the mountains. He traced the course of the river, an uncertain line that frayed into a tangle of sometimes broken threads as it reached the marshes beside the Gulf. That was fifty miles away. Beside it, dimly visible to the naked eye, lay the city of Salonika, surrounded, on the landward side, by what looked like a tiara of barbed wire and machine-gun posts. An eagle swept by, its pinions spread.

"Beautiful," Winner murmured, as he took in the wonders of Nature.

"Yes, it is, isn't it?" returned Sunny. "Fabulous aeronautical craft, like something out of Baron Munchausen's adventures — completely silent, if not, perhaps, wholly invisible." Sunny laughed at his own joke. The size of small thundercloud, the balloon could hardly be missed in an otherwise clear sky. "Only this glorious twentieth century of ours could have evolved it. You'll be amazed how much you can see from five thousand feet up. I'd rather be in a machine, naturally, but it's difficult to take up more than one person, and besides those crates do shake a bit. Not so easy for the observer. Better to be stationary, all things considered. That bunch of bananas at the back stops us from whirling around like a cork with every gust of wind, as we might in an ordinary balloon."

"I meant all this," said Winner, indicating the points of the compass by jerking his head; he didn't like to let go of the support he was holding. "This landscape, the mountains."

Sunny looked at him doubtfully. "Looks pretty much like sandpaper to me. I prefer Warwickshire. The cricket season will be starting soon." The launch complete, he took a pipe out of his pocket and filled it with tobacco. "Don't worry," he said, in response to a look from Winner. "Perfectly safe. I mean, the gas bag is ever so far above us, no chance of the flame catching it. And actually they're quite difficult to set alight. You'd be surprised."

"Will we really reach five thousand feet?"

"Lord yes. Ten possibly. Don't worry, though. We've got sheepskins in case it gets nippy."

The balloon bed from which they had launched, a dry gully, was far below them now. The men looked like the lead soldiers which, a present from an uncle, had formed some of Winner's few boyhood toys. (Not that he had been allowed to play with them by his parents; they thought that toy soldiers promoted aggression.) Only the soldiers of the Balloon Section were not resplendent in red and blue. They were dingy specks of dun-coloured chaff. Who would have imagined that war could be like this?

For a short time Winner had been on the Western Front, where the cacophony of the guns was so colossal that you did not just hear it — force waves hit you in the stomach, which could be nasty if you had recently eaten. Men kept their mouths open as they went past a battery in the maelstrom preceding a push. From there, his Division transferred to Gallipoli. But Winner had not gone with them; the great Tonks had not forgotten his protégé, and having the ear of other great people in London, some of them in the military, had arranged to have him transferred out of the county regiment to which he had rashly volunteered and into something appropriately vague, where he could apply his artistic talent to the depiction of Allied operations. "The man is practically a midget," Tonks had told the Field Marshal, held captive as he sat for his portrait, "and no earthly good to you. He's almost permanently in a trance. Rather more of a danger, I would say, than an asset — was always falling over easels in the life classes and came in for no end of abuse. Promising talent, though." He stood back from the canvas, before applying a judicious dab of vermilion to the Field Marshal's nose. "We're working on a plan for more artists go out and make sure the whole shooting match is properly recorded."

So here Winner now was, being lifted heavenwards. Save for the creaking of the hawser, they were in the serenity of the Blessed, as though raised by an oversized, oiled-canvas angel.

"Are you hearing me? Good." Sunny, pipe clamped in one corner of his mouth, was on the field telephone. "Make sure you have the tea ready for our return. We're starting to feel a breeze. By the way, where's Bertie? Good show. Robert. No, I know you're not Robert. R for Received. I can tell you weren't in France, signallers used it all the time there. Out. It means put the bloody receiver down." He raised his eyebrows. "Now, where's Bertie?"

Sunny looked up, looked down, straining his eyes. "Should be along in a moment. Our escort. He's just been making a delivery to the HQ. They're short of coffee."

"Really?" questioned Winner. "I thought we had plenty of coffee."

"We do, the Boche don't. One of our chaps caught it behind the enemy lines and found they didn't have any coffee in their mess. As you rightly observe, we have plenty. So they dropped a streamer on us with a message from him. You know what a streamer is? A box with half a mile or so of ribbon trailing behind it. Bertie's just dropped a streamer on them, containing coffee and our compliments."

"Is that how the war goes on here?"

"Oh yes," replied Sunny. "For us. We're all gentlemen."

"Officers?"

Sunny eyed him wonderingly, as though Winner's naivety were becoming eccentric. "Of course. Same thing. We have to maintain the civilities."

"But you do shoot them down sometimes?"

Sunny now looked aghast. "Good grief, you bet we do. That's the whole game."

At the bottom of the basket lay a couple of sheepskin jerkins, a guncase and a knapsack. "Now," Sunny continued, "on the subject of civilities, we are provisioned for refreshment, I believe. What can I offer you?" He opened the knapsack. "I have — let me see what they put in — a loaf of bread and a bottle of indescribably vile brandy. Shall we start with the indescribably vile? I know it's a bit early but it might settle the nerves. Not that I'm suggesting you have any. If we see any edible avian life on the way down, I'll pot it with the shotgun; something to serve up in the mess." He paused. "Better than shooting up a flight of geese with the Vickers on my Camel, as I tried on a dull day over France. The bird I winged managed to expire behind enemy lines. An unexpected bonus for Fritz."

They drank the brandy in silence. Detached from their fellow beings, in the innocence of the upper air, Winner felt that they were approaching a mysterious holiness. The sense of immanence grew on him. He did not share this with Sunny, whom he put down as the sort of man who would be better at tying knots or changing a bicycle tyre than intuiting spiritual presences.

Sunny busied himself with his field-glasses. "Wonderful lenses, these. Do you see over there — well, you probably can't, but take it on trust: there's a Bulgarian camp. Tents all neatly lined up, hardly anybody about yet." He picked up the telephone and crisply uttered some co-ordinates. "This will wake them up," he chuckled. A minute later, a plume of earth and rock rose from the edge of the camp, and the boom of a gun reached them. A tent was blown over. Dot-like figures could be seen erupting from the other tents. Sunny spoke into the mouthpiece, adjusting the range. The second shot fell short; the gunners had made a bracket. The men in the camp were in chaos. From the balloon, it looked as though they had stirred up an ant's nest.

The third shot landed in the middle of the tents, lifting half a dozen of them into the sky. Mules ran wild. The gun settled into a steady rhythm of fire. Sunny laughed. "Pretty good reveille for them, what? That should make a picture for you."

"It seems so far away," mused Winner.

"It is," replied Sunny. "That's the beauty of it."

"This must be how God sees the world."

They were up very high now and could see beyond the first ridge of the mountains. Winner found a block of paper in his rucksack. It was not wet, as his paper so often had been in France. But his fingers were almost too cold to grip the charcoal; the line jumped as he made his sketch. But he was excited by the unfamiliar angle of vision. Everything looked so different. He remembered the words of the Colonel who had commissioned him as a Second Lieutenant before leaving England. "You'll want to show things from our side."

Winner had thought that self-evident. "Of course, sir. The British side."

The Colonel gave him a patronising look. "Our side," he replied drily. "The officers."

Winner looked about in a kind of ecstasy. It was as though he were beside the Creator Himself, surveying the divine train set that He had made for the joy of it. He was excited but terrified. You could create by destroying. How easy it would be for Winner to alter everything by throwing himself out of the basket. Physically he would be extinguished. Then what? The Judgement. The thin air was making him light-headed. He felt suddenly weary.

The excitement of the ascent stopped him from noticing that temperature had dropped perceptibly. He pulled on one of the sheepskins.

"What a country to draw," he exclaimed. "It seems to be one confused heap of mountains. Besides, I don't really like to let go of the basket."

"You get used to the altitude. Refreshing, I call it. Shall I tell you what I like to do while I'm up here?" He produced from his pocket a triangular piece of pottery, about the size of a pasty. He put it to his lips and blew. The notes that came out of it were haunting, like an ancient hymn, or the wind blowing across the marshes.

"An ocarina," explained Sunny. "Local instrument that I picked up."

To Winner, it seemed perfect. "Those sounds — they express the weirdness of it all. Being thousands of feet above the ground, being in Macedonia. So you play it here, as an invocation to the Divine Being?"

12

"Not exactly," confessed Sunny, puzzled. "I play it here because the chaps in the Section can't stand the noise. Keep telling me to shut up."

As more of the plaintive notes vanished into the wind, Winner sketched. The sharpened charcoal moved with precision. After some minutes, Sunny looked over his shoulder. "I say, good work! They tried to teach me to draw at Sandhurst. A hopeless case, of course."

"They tried to teach me to fly," Winner responded; he did not dilate on the experience. "These mountains are impossible, chaotic."

"They do go on rather. One ridge after another. And all the while, our friend the Bulgar is busy digging himself in. Fortunately, we can get above Johnny B, by means of the kite balloon. We provide the eyes. Our brothers in the Gunners provide the HE and together — well, you saw how they scuttled around their camp just now. That's what this war is: observation combined with high explosive shells. Aviation and artillery. The infantry simply isn't in it, except to suffer in their funk holes, poor sods. I say, I'm most awfully sorry; I forgot you were infantry for a moment."

"Not any more."

"That's well for you." Sunny swept the panorama with his field glasses. "Of course, we're all in it together to a certain extent. Stuck on the Vardar, a million miles from hot water and proper beds. I was one of the first out here. The Greeks arrested me for wearing a uniform, this being a neutral country. The French officers had changed into civvies. So like them. That's all finished now. They wouldn't have enough prison space if they locked up every officer who's here. Sometimes I stare down at Salonika just to imagine the joy of being there."

"What does Salonika have?"

"Girls."

Winner mused. "I came out on a ship that was full of nurses."

Sunny lowered the field glasses and looked at him with a kind of wonder. "Where are they now?"

"I've no idea."

"You must find out and introduce me. Ah, I hear a machine. Bertie returns."

Sunny's hearing was good. The plane was a long way off and hardly audible, let alone visible. Sunny took Winner's sketch. "Yes my artistic skills are round about zero. I could do well enough with a camera," he sighed, "as long as it had a decent lens, but we don't have one out here. Add it to the list of the other things we don't have on this Front. Petroleum essence for one. Another reason for preferring the dear old hydrogen balloon to a plane. Mind you, it wouldn't do," he said, reverting to photography. "Too hot, you see. The gelatine on the glass plate melts. I can't vouch for the new-fangled bendy thing — film. Never used it."

He turned the field glasses from the mountains to the farmland below them. "You see that village. I'd be glad if you would make a sketch of it for me. I say, I'm not perfectly sure that is Bertie."

Very high up and against the sun, Winner could hardly make the plane out. "Doesn't sound like one of ours," puzzled Sunny. "Or look like it. Blimey."

14

Without taking his eyes off the aircraft, Sunny reached for the telephone receiver. But as he did so, the apparatus began to ring. And before he had even picked it up, a white puff appeared in the sky, followed by a bloom of others.

"Hello," shouted Sunny, his equable temperament for once showing signs of being ruffled. "I know it's one of theirs and," as white puffs of anti-aircraft fire opened like cotton flowers in the sky around the basket, "I can see the Archibald has started. They've missed him by a mile. Wind us down, and quickly." He banged down the receiver. He had forgotten to say "Out." He scrabbled on the floor. When he was standing again, he held a shotgun in his hands.

For Winner, as he thought about it afterwards, the next two minutes constituted a lifetime. First a *ratatatat* of bullets crackled in the sky above him. He was in no immediate danger of being hit; they were going far over his head. But he instinctively crouched down in the basket, making himself as small as he could, wondering what would happen when they punctured the gargantuan floating paunch that was the kite balloon. How could they have missed?

There was the beat of a propeller. Suddenly, an aircraft appeared very close to the basket. It had been diving on the kite balloon, and firing on it. Now it was so close that Winner felt that he could almost touch the German airman at his controls. Sunny gave him both barrels.

"Glad I brought this," he muttered, as the enemy plane wheeled away from them. "I thought there might

15

be something to bag. I didn't expect Fritz." He leant over the side over the basket, calling: "What about the coffee, you swine?"

The plane was climbing again, through what seemed like a meadow of thistledown, each tuft of which was an exploding shell. The anti-aircraft gunners were making the most of their opportunity: they could not fire when it was too close to the kite balloon. As the *Albatros* climbed, it turned, and then the bulk above the basket blotted it from view.

"It's having another go," shouted Sunny. "Damn."

Winner had been right to think that the German could hardly miss such a vast target; indeed the airman had already ruptured the skin in a number of places and gas was leaking from the balloon. But this loss was barely significant. To bring the balloon down, he needed to set it alight. So far he had failed to do so, which, for him, was bad luck. One of the machine-guns, firing from the upper wing, was loaded with tracer shells, made to explode like fireworks. Now, on this second pass, his bullets not only ripped through the canvas but ignited the gas. A small flame appeared on the top of the balloon. It was as though a gas ring had been lit. This flame was followed by a couple of others, which spread across the surface to join up. Sunny hurriedly hooked the cord to his parachute.

"Time to get out. Now. You first. Quick about it."

Staggering to this feet, Winner seized the ropes that attached the basket to the undercarriage. Initially this was to steady himself, but he found, in this shocked condition, that they gave a sense of security. He did not want to let go.

Sunny took his wrists and shook them until Winner released his fingers. Above them, what had been the kite balloon was, in a leisurely but purposeful manner, developing into a single mass of flame. He roughly pushed Winner to the edge of the basket, where he hesitated, like a boy at the water's edge who does not want to rush launching himself into an alien element. Sunny heaved at his torso, tipped up his legs, gave a final shove and Winner was over. Events were then beyond their control. Winner found himself to be released from the world. Was this death? He fell and kept falling, and then stopped with such a jerk that he nearly spun out of his harness. Sunny fell past him; Winner saw Sunny's parachute open. He, meanwhile, found himself suspended in mid air, snagged somehow, caught — as he thought for a moment — by the hand of God.

But that wasn't it. A glance showed that his predicament had a quite practical explanation.

The long straggle of Winner's chute, as it left the case, had caught on the hawser that connected the balloon with the ground, wrapping itself around the steel. For a dreadful moment, he hung there, his stomach sick with the knowledge that the wire could not stay up by itself; when the gas in the balloon was consumed, it would fall. Down would come baby, basket and all. It was a ridiculous position to find himself in; it would be talked of as a terrible but comic death. His contemporaries at the Slade would expect no less. Life had cast Winner as a well-intentioned incompetent, who could never progress beyond the duffers' teams at school, and had subsequently buried himself in his own artistic obsessions. He could hear his father, general manager of an ecclesiastical outfitters, saying: "I'm terribly cut up, of course, but the boy never could be trusted to screw on the top of a fountain pen without injuring himself. God moves in mysterious ways."

But the mountain wind determined that Winner's end would not come in that manner. Like a flag wrapped round a flag pole, the parachute unfurled itself. Winner's fall resumed. But the canopy remained limp. Perhaps the strings had been tangled.

White on white: Winner found himself enveloped in white cloth, as though a demonic maid had decided to make him into an enormous bed. He was next to Sunny. He had hit his parachute. "Sorry." Winner apologised by instinct. "Couldn't help it."

Sunny shouted back: "Not your fault."

Above them, the heavens turned orange and bright and scorching, like a second, bigger sun. Winner gazed up into it. It could have been the eye of God: a sublime eye but not, perhaps, an angry one, because Winner found himself turned on end. There was a painful tug at his groin, where the harness was fixed. He was not tumbling any more. He was still falling, but in an upright posture, and falling less fast. A glorious billowing expanse of whiteness had opened above his head. He breathed. It was the first proper breath he had taken since he had been bundled out of the basket. He gulped in oxygen. He was alive.

It was not the end of the flames. As he floated down, something passed him. It looked like an enraged fury, and it smelt of singed fabric. But no, it was not the fury — or the remains of the kite balloon's basket falling to earth — that made that smell. He looked upwards and saw that the parachute, his saviour, was not the pristine white that it had been a moment ago. One side of it had turned monkey brown. Where the basket had hit it, it was starting to char. The brown deepened in hue. A hole opened up.

But then Winner glanced down again. Trees. An olive grove. A farmhouse. Familiar things that were solidly on the ground. Ants' nests, butterflies. And within a blink of an eye he would be reunited with them. He was going to meet them. Very soon, within seconds. Faster, due to the hole in the parachute, than he may have liked. He bent his knees.

He landed in a field growing tobacco. The floppy plants, strung to poles, did something to soften the impact, but not enough. White silk was everywhere, as though he had been pitched into a drawer of de luxe underwear. He heard something crack that might have been his leg. "Buttonhooks." It was his mother's strongest expletive. He passed out.

Two

Winner swam upwards, through the primordial black depths of unconsciousness, into light. For a while, shortly before he opened his eyes, it was the light of heavenly beings, shining radiantly, with iridescent wings. He was sorry to leave them. They were replaced, when his eyelids separated, by a sharp angle of white canvas, buzzing with drowsy flies. What was he doing in a tent? His eyes hurt, so he shut them again. Then they sprang open, almost theatrically. He sensed he was not alone.

Two women in grey dresses, with white starched caps on their heads, stood nearby, regarding him with an appraising his eye. They seemed familiar, but they were not his sisters.

"He's woken up, Miss Hinchcliff," said one of them, softly. Her cap, Winner noticed, sat crookedly on her dark curly hair.

"Yes, Elsie," replied the other, taller and bossier. "You had better fetch the doctor."

Winner thought he should say something. "Did you see the angels?" he asked brightly, in a voice unlike his own. "They had wings like kingfishers." He closed his eyes again. It had been an effort, and he was not sure that he had sounded the right note.

The doctor spoke in a practical voice. "Do you know your name?" she asked him.

She was a woman, which was odd for a doctor. "Where are we? Yes, that's right: in Greece." She had fine, almost translucent skin and the air in which she moved suggested rose petals. The scent was like a cool breeze in the heat. Winner wondered why he was wearing pyjamas.

"Angels?" reflected the doctor. "The angels around here don't have wings." She smiled briefly.

"Now, can you move your arm? Your leg? I'll have to examine you. Nurse Fox, take these bedclothes off." Elsie hurried forward, blushing. She had not belonged to the hospital for long.

As the doctor probed Winner's knee, in ways that seemed calculated to give him greatest pain, he looked around him. He occupied an iron bedstead, one of a row of ten, each neatly made up with starched linen. All the others were empty.

The sides of the tent were rolled up, and outside Winner could see other tents — big long white ones and smaller round green ones. Some had been arranged in groups of four with walkways in between. Pairs of grey-uniformed nurses passed briskly along the paths. It had the air of a convent. He became aware of an absence. There were no men.

"Nothing actually broken," pronounced the doctor, with an air of disappointment. "But you may have cracked something. We'll put a cast on it. You'll have to stay where you are for at least a fortnight."

"Oh," exclaimed Winner glumly. The doctor swept out, taking the taller of the nurses in her wake.

Elsie, the dark-haired nurse, waited until they had left and then came up to him. "When I saw you, I nearly screamed."

"Did you?" responded Winner, without giving the impression that it was an unusual reaction.

"I mean, because it was you. Of all the people to fall out of a balloon and come here. I thought you was dead." She put the bedclothes back over his knees. "I was almost as scared as I'd been on that ship. You're our first patient, you know. It's probably why she wants to hang on to you for so long."

"I don't suppose you have my spectacles?" asked Winner. She gave them to him. "Good. I wanted to see you."

When the heavy black frames were on his nose, he smiled into Elsie's eyes. They seemed to be like brown woodland pools, caught by the light. One of them winked at him. "I'm meant to be transport but when I saw it was you, I got them to allow me onto the ward. I thought you'd never wake up."

They had met on the requisitioned liner that transported them and several hundred other personnel from Liverpool to Salonika. It was one of the fastest in the White Star fleet, and as big, it seemed to Winner, as the whole of his Essex village; the funnels rose taller than the church steeple.

The more adventurous of the nurses, Elsie being among them, longed to explore the vessel, but most of it was off limits. It was a disappointment: the ship was new and a paragon of modern technology. The British Women's Hospital was similarly progressive in spirit. Women performed all the necessary duties. They could do without the male sex. In fact, as the nurses quickly discovered, they would probably have to.

As the niece of an earl, Isabel Hinchcliff had been given a cabin on an upper deck; she was, so to speak, one of the gods. Elsie's cabin was an airless Nibelung space just above the water-line which she shared with three other girls, whose exclamations of wonder at the

22

dimensions and ingenuity of the ship could not conceal the anxiety that all of them felt at making a sea voyage in wartime. The destroyer escorting them from Liverpool had left them after a day.

The word submarine, meaning a type of boat, only entered the language at the beginning of the century, but after little more than a decade and a half it was now in everyone's vocabulary. To Isabel, a warship that did not show itself, in a manly fashion, on the surface of the sea, but sneaked along underneath, seemed to typify the Teutonic capacity for dirty tricks. She would not admit to being frightened. She had been brought up to believe that it was unbecoming to display emotion in public. No such inhibition prevailed in Elsie's cabin. The girls there were forever scaring themselves with rumours of periscopes having been seen, and uttering little screams.

Between lectures on wound dressing and sessions of Swedish drill, the nurses were allowed breaks on deck. It was during one of them that Elsie spotted Winner, sketching. "Only charcoal? I like colour. I thought you might have painted the waves."

Winner blinked at her. "Not these ones. Tollesbury Flats on the Blackwater — there's my idea of the sea. This is too blue."

Elsie turned the pages of the sketchbook. "Is that what you're fighting for? Tollesbury Flats." Her tone was faintly mocking.

"I'm not fighting for anything. I'm an artist."

Isabel Hinchcliff heard the remark. She looked around for the person who made it, and saw a diminutive man whose face reminded her of something she had once made in an arts and crafts class; the untidy mop of hair might have been wool.

"In uniform and not fighting?" She spoke as though to a stationmaster who had given her the wrong ticket.

"Art is important too, surely, Miss Hinchcliff," put in Elsie.

"Only, in its proper place, Elsie." Her words seemed to make further discussion impossible.

The proper place was more likely to have been found in Isabel's life than Elsie's. Isabel's family dwelt in realms of light — or more specifically, the Surrey Hills. Her father, whose energy as a barrister made such radiance possible, returned from London every evening to refresh his soul with the view that opened out beyond the pergola of old roses. Mr and Mrs Hinchcliff were rich enough to afford a sense of higher purpose. They chaired local committees, supported village associations, spent their leisure hours gardening, making music and cultivating beauty. Art was practically worshipped. As were dogs, horses, brightly feathered birds which sang in cages, fancy chickens, even, in a more ambiguous way, the foxes which sometimes killed the chickens, and were in their turn chased across country by the hunt. Art and animals ruled Isabel's life.

Elsie's childhood had taken place in London's Mile End, in a succession of terraced cottages, each one of which seemed damper and more crowded than the last. Isabel would not have recognised it as a childhood at all. There was no distinction between being little and being grown up, in Mile End, beyond size. You were treated the same, barely educated and expected to work. Elsie's father was a docker. She only saw him on days he was out of work. Then he sat morosely in the kitchen, which was also a parlour and for some of the children a bedroom, talking about strikes and the Docker's Tanner. When he was in work, he spent his leisure and pay in the Wharfinger's Arms.

Elsie wanted better. If she did not know how to get it, she had at least seen how not to miss it. She had avoided marriage, or contracting the sort of relationship her mother had entered into, which entitled her to be called "Mrs" without the official sanction of the church. Women produced children. They slaved in the house. They slaved in other people's houses, for extra money. They did other things for extra money too — anything to make ends meet. Elsie was sharp enough to get out.

At fourteen, a neat, curly-haired girl with brown eyes, she worked in a match factory. Her long hatpin became a weapon of defence, although she usually managed to- avoid the vicious cat fights that broke out among the coarser girls. At eighteen, she had gone to a department store, where women worked from early morning until late at night and promotion depended in large measure on willingness to do special favours for the man who owned the establishment; Elsie, ready with her hatpin, was not promoted. Instead, for the last two years, she had been a servant in a Tolstoyan community in Worcestershire. The opening had come through one of the lectures she had heard at the Toynbee Hall.

The Tolstoyans wore loose, formless garments, some of which, as could be plainly seen, they made themselves. They dug the vegetable plots with their own hands — and those of gardeners who understood about spades, not to mention the difference between weeds and young carrots. Great stews of the resulting produce were served at meals, which everyone, family and servants alike, ate around the same table, with the servants generally sitting in silence. Somebody's child was christened Amour Libre, which, it was explained to Elsie, meant Free Love: a concept that she found strange, having noticed that there was generally something to pay for it.

Like the others, Elsie was expected to spend some of her day labouring outside. Fresh air and stews had their effect. Her features no longer looked pinched. Her bobbed hair, sun-darkened skin and bold, dark eyes marked her as unconventional, but competent: a young woman who had taken command of her own life.

Such was the spirit of equality that pervaded the home in which Elsie worked that the son of the family started to read to her. He was at one of the Varsities. It was a hot and, for him, idle summer. The hatpin stayed in its drawer. However much Elsie's employers rose above convention in other ways, they did not do so in this one. She lost her place. It was, fortunately, just at the time that Edith Stalwart-Dousing was recruiting for able young women to serve in the BWH. Elsie was just the sort that Mrs Stalwart-Dousing was looking for.

Her references were overlooked. Fabianism and female suffrage more than made up for their absence.

Isabel ensured that Elsie's first conversation with Winner did not last long. But the pair had been thrown together on the day of the great submarine fright. Winner had been in his cabin when — BOOM! — a tremendous roar reverberated through the huge ship. His first thought was that they had hit an iceberg, which was unlikely in the Mediterranean. Rolling off his bunk, he hurried into the passageway. "Torpedo," said a soldier, as he barged past him. Winner clattered up the steel staircase onto deck. There, soldiers and nurses were crowded into a general melee, out of which order had yet to be formed.

The first person Winner met there was Elsie. She had been separated from the other nurses. "That noise was the gun," she told him. "The sailor on look-out thought he had seen the top of a submarine."

"I'd better get my sketching things," Winner had said.

"Why?"

"In case we sink."

"You won't need them if we sink," she said, suppressing an uncomfortable feeling of panic at the possibility that they might.

"No. They'd get wet."

After a moment he added, without great conviction, "I don't suppose we'll sink."

Fear made Elsie talkative. She rattled on about "rinking," an activity that involved strapping wheels to the underside of your feet. Winner could not picture himself skating on wheels. Elsie was modern. At the Front it would be her job to drive one of the Ford ambulances. She — a woman! Her narrow shoulders were strong.

And yet Winner also pitied her. For Elsie, Art was a blank.

Eventually, the ship steamed grandly into the Gulf of Salonika, at the bottom of which, half hidden by a billow of translucent mist, lay Salonika itself. The decks were again crowded with spectators. Some of the men on board complained loudly at the captain's absurd decision, taken after the submarine scare, of steering a zigzag course. It added to the journey time, but look, here they were: the ship had arrived safely. That being so, the soldiers were keen to dispel any thought that they might, at some point, have been scared.

Three

The word they all used to describe Salonika was "picturesque". On one point of the bay stood the White Tower, a cylindrical keep with battlements that might have come from a toy fort, surrounded by an outer wall, also battlemented, that was adorably known as the *chemise*. One of the girls, who had been reading a guidebook, said that the White Tower had previously been Red, due to the blood that was shed there during its days as an Ottoman prison, and they all shivered to think of the horrors that had gone on there. From here the bay swept around in a crescent, to the port. The town itself scrabbled up — or perhaps it would be better to say, cascaded down — a hillside, the wooden houses all wibbly-wobbly, as Elsie put it. The houses were different colours — pinks, blues and yellows — making what, in her diary, Isabel called "a joyful maze of colour." On the top of the hill was a castle. Minarets pricked up from the skyline as though they were spears, wanting to pierce the great blue balloon of the sky.

On the quayside, the nurses sat on their suitcases. The RAMC captain who met them had not been able to find a motor to take them to the *Grand Hotel Excelsior Olympique* (latterly the *Hotel de l'Orient Splendide*, and whose name was even now being updated to the *Hotel des Deux Armées Glorieuses*). They were reduced to watching the unloading of stores. New piles of crates were being added to the piles that were already there. The wait was a long one.

Winner, who got ashore later that morning, viewed the quay with distaste. It was not like the salty, barnacle-encrusted quays he knew at home, having been built rapidly, by engineers of the Franco-British armies, on a scale that dwarfed the existing port. No rust, no dents. Their work reminded Winner of a steel vice.

Behind a towering wall of crates he found a sentry, surreptitiously smoking a cigarette. The soldier sprung to attention, but read the address Winner gave him with slow, uncomprehending eyes. "Can't help you, sir. Never been to Salonika, sir."

"Isn't this Salonika?" asked Winner, with a dreadful apprehension that he had landed at the wrong port.

"This is Salonika, sir. Our quarters are in the Birdcage, sir."

Winner did not understand him.

"It's what they call the defences, sir: we're caged in, see, by a bloody great encirclement of barbed wire, sir. Tweet, tweet, sir." He flapped his arms sardonically. "Like dicky birds, sir: keeps us in, keeps Johnny Bulgar out. There's a whole other city inside it — made of tents. French tents, Russian tents, Italian tents and the leaky ones, sir — those are our tents, sir. But you don't want a tent, sir; you want a street. A private ain't allowed into Salonika, sir."

Winner's spirits lifted when he saw, high above the quay, momentarily suspended in mid air, a motor ambulance in a net, looking for all the world like a potato at the bottom of his mother's string shopping bag. A crane had plucked it from a lighter and was now depositing it on land. Nearby Winner could see, sitting on their luggage, some young women in grey.

Elsie, bored by waiting, was glad to spot Winner, hurrying towards her.

"They want me to drive one of them Fords across the City," she said, in a contemptuous voice intended to conceal any anxiety. "Want a lift?"

"I don't know where I'm going."

"Me neither," announced Elsie. "Expect I'll get there though. Get around the corner, behind that sentry box, and wait for the Ford. You can hop in the back. Make sure Miss Hinchcliff don't see you. She'll be in the passenger seat."

That two ladies might brave Salonika without a male escort was beyond the RAMC officer's comprehension. "I know what it's like with you motor girls, if I may be permitted the phrase." Isabel, who was somewhat beyond the point at which she considered herself a girl, drew herself up. "Very twentieth-century. But it won't do in Salonika. We're practically medieval here. The Mohammedan ladies go veiled."

Mrs Stalwart-Dousing had heard the remark. "Captain," she informed him, with the emphasis that the nurses already knew well, "this is a Women's Hospital, and it has been formed to relieve men of some of the duties that women can do, in order that the male of the species can serve his country at the front. We can drive ourselves. We shall drive ourselves. We shall not have your kind assistance when we leave Salonika. We do not need it, in this instance, while we are in Salonika."

"This isn't Haslemere," the Captain protested.

"If one can drive in Haslemere, one can drive in Salonika," rejoined Mrs Stalwart-Dousing.

Isabel might secretly have agreed with the Captain. Nothing, however, seemed to rattle Elsie Fox, although even she must have been more nervous at the wheel than she seemed, because the Ford had only gone a few yards — just past the sentry box — when it juddered to a halt, before lurching forward again. "Slow and steady," Isabel advised.

They struck out along the new road that ran from the quay along the waterfront. On it they became part of a human tide that, unlike the salt variety, flowed both ways at the same time. Theirs was the only motorised vehicle. The better class of the population travelled in open *gharries*, pulled by two or even three horses abreast. Clattering over the cobbles, their drivers flew between carts dragged by oxen and donkeys. They swept past mules that were piled so high with carefully balanced heaps that, in some cases, only their hoofs were visible. About a hundred school girls in white collars and straw hats waited in a line, giggling. Elsie, in her organising way, found it hopeless. "What a silly way of doing things, just a jumble," she muttered. She wanted to get on.

The slow pace suited Isabel. There were so many people to see and exclaim about. The whiskered Greek men wearing tasselled caps, skirted jackets and tights, with bobbles on their shoes. The straight-backed Jewish women in richly patterned dresses, heavy with necklaces, their heads covered with lace, their hair in bags embroidered with fake pearls; or their men wearing long robes and flowerpot-shaped hats. "That fellow, with the donkey — good heavens, he is a butcher: the board on the side of his beast has bits of animal hanging from it: quite grisly." Isabel's enthusiasm for new sights had to be made at full volume for her voice to reach Elsie above the noise of the motor.

To the eyes of the newcomers, the Muslim women looked like mobile bolts of black cloth — generously sized bolts, some of them. Behind one walked a young woman, evidently a bolt's daughter, in a close-fitting skirt. She wore high-heeled boots which Isabel did not think were the best thing for walking across cobbles.

Adding to the colour of the local population were the troops. A group of *tirailleurs* from Senegal, in orange hats and baggy trousers, were followed by what, to the British women, appeared to be Chinamen in coolie hats. A detachment of Russians, immense fair-haired men, with square beards and open shirts, marched by, ten abreast. They seemed like the living embodiment of the endless Steppes.

"It looks like the chorus of a comic opera," observed Isabel. Elsie had never been to the opera, comic or otherwise, but felt confident in replying, "Very rumty-tum."

The officer at the front of the Russians, seeing two women in the cab of the Ford, shouted a command and the head of every man in the column swivelled towards them. They went past at the salute. Isabel wished she had a veil to pull over her face. It was dusty and hot, and she felt very conspicuous. But the BWH uniform of long, dove-grey dress and starched white cap had no veil. It was wartime; some things had to go by the board.

Elsie was far too determined to become flustered. Isabel had been brought up too well to show it. But both women felt acutely conscious of being a centre of attention. In different ways, it was novel for both of them. Isabel had been protected, Elsie did not expect to be noticed.

"It seems to me," said Isabel, who had been given a roughly sketched map, "that the base lies directly on the other side of the town. So the quickest way would be through the centre."

"But the Captain said that we couldn't."

"The Captain," announced Isabel, "is a man. Men love to protect us, the dears."

That had not been Elsie's experience of the opposite sex, but she said nothing. Isabel directed her to turn into a street that would lead into the heart of the town.

The buildings were modern and rather less oriental than Isabel had hoped. But beneath heavy awnings their fronts were open. Out of the shops spilled charcoal, lemons, clay pitchers, melons, grapes, wine, pomegranates, brass bowls, sheep and cattle bells, knives and swords spilled onto the street. A man with blue spectacles struck a hammer onto an anvil, making sparks fly. Another sat cross-legged on a table, making sandals. There were lathes for sale, and sweet pastries. Seated on a box of brushes, a shoeblack implored passing foreigners with the cry: "Shine, Johnny; Johnny, shine, shine, shine."

"It's just like Petticoat Lane," observed Elsie.

"Or the Bazaar scene in *Kismet*," responded Isabel, having thrilled to it a couple of seasons ago at the Garrick Theatre.

The way ahead was blocked. A mule, overladen with a cargo of vegetables, had slipped, and sprawled there, like a knitted toy, unable or refusing to get up. Its owner, a portly old farmer, in baggy trousers strapped at the knee, still wearing the cloak in which he had set out early that morning, sought to stimulate the beast by the traditional means, and was lashing it. Surrey, as Isabel had experienced it, was an idyll of rose gardens and country churches, into which man's unkindness to other creatures did not visibly creep. Her spirit rebelled against the sight of cruelty. Without considering the strangeness of her position, she marched towards the man with the cudgel. "You will kindly desist from that now," she commanded. "I have never seen anything so despicable. The poor animal is suffering." Not speaking English, the mule owner looked at Isabel, flushed with anger, and smiled sarcastically, baring the long teeth that lay below the points of his even longer white moustache. He raised his cudgel again. "Oh you unspeakable man, how could you?" She felt tears forming. The cudgel came down. She grabbed at his arm. The man turned on her with fury. He was making to put to the cudgel on her.

A voice from behind Isabel called out, and his arm fell. Isabel looked round to see an impeccably dressed man in a high white collar and necktie, wearing a straw boater; a red cummerbund showed to perfection around his ample stomach. Around the wrinkles of his darkly hooded eyes played an expression of what might have been amusement. The eyes themselves looked as unfathomable as two shiny black olives. A beard, after the neatly barbered George V or Nicholas II style, framed Cupid's bow lips of almost feminine pink. The mule driver, muttering, went to see about the fallen load.

"Thank you," said Isabel.

"My dear young lady," the man's English was surprisingly fluent, "I see that you have come here, on an errand of mercy, only to be confronted by the daily horrors of this benighted country. You are one of the British ladies who have just landed, I think."

"Yes. How did you know that?"

"It is my business to know everything, insofar as such a thing is possible in this absurd town. I am a spy." He paused to enjoy the moment. "Dear young lady," he continued when his effect had been made, "do not look alarmed: it is so much more congenial if everybody puts their cards on the table. There are mine: face up. Incidentally, I hope that you and the other angels who have come to relieve the sufferings of war enjoy vegetables." He indicated the mule driver who had taken the baskets and panniers off the mule and was carrying them to the Ford.

"What is he doing?"

"I have bought his produce. I perform few acts of charity myself, but this is one I could afford; it seemed the best way to resolve what could have become a distressing scene. Not only does it spare the mule but will allow you to make soup for the wounded."

"But I couldn't accept."

"But you must accept. It would offend me greatly if you didn't. Besides, when I said I was a spy, you mustn't think that I am sneaking around, in an underhand way. I am a native of Salonika, like Mustafa Kemal Bey, who has been giving you British such trouble at Gallipoli. He was also born here."

Isabel felt that she was being patronised, as well as teased, but was sufficiently grateful to ask stiffly: "To whom am I obliged?"

"My name is Gazmend Bey, but please don't bother to remember it. These Ottoman names are so difficult for a civilised person such as yourself. Here is a card."

He handed over a piece of white pasteboard, elegantly printed. "We shall certainly meet at Molho's."

He bowed and was about to walk on, when he had an afterthought. "By the way, Mademoiselle, if you are going to the street where the other hospital ladies have been installed, it lies on the other side of the square. But I don't advise going that way. Let me show you an alternative route."

Isabel firmly declined his offer.

"But please, not the square," he continued. "I could easily escort you, if you would allow me, promising, of course, not to murder you on the way. I know what a suspicion foreigners have of us, and rightly. We're all brigands beneath the skin."

Isabel, feeling that the conversation had lurched into uncharted waters, hurried back to the Ford. Elsie was waiting for her behind the driving wheel. From his position in the back of the ambulance, Winner had used the hiatus to make a sketch of her. He worked quickly.

"You may drive on, Elsie," announced Isabel. "I think that villain of a mule driver was a Turk. Did they put the vegetables in the back?"

"I did that," Elsie replied hurriedly. She had not wanted Winner's presence to be discovered.

"Mind you, if they're Turkish vegetables," declared Isabel, "I won't eat them."

"What nationality was the fat man?"

"He was sweet." The Ford rolled forward. "He said we should avoid the square, but it is the quickest and simplest way. I wasn't going to let us be led around the back streets by a foreigner."

The Ford edged forward, behind a lemonade seller who had chosen to occupy the centre of the street and was shuffling forward, clinking his glasses; those that were not in his hands were set into holes on a kind of shelf suspended from his neck, which made him look like a bar on legs. A tight knot of young Jewish men in soft beards and fur-lined robes dispersed grudgingly, being clearly of the opinion that vehicular traffic should take second place to conversation.

Winner, now seated like a spirit of harvest amid a cornucopia of vegetables, looked in astonishment as the canvas at the back of the van was pulled open. A boy started to climb in, but saw Winner. Winner was so startled that he nearly shouted at the boy. Instead the pair stared silently into each other's eyes for a moment — long enough for Winner to notice that his black eyebrows were exceptionally fine and that a dark growth disfigured the side of his nose. His cap was decorated with sequins. The boy rode for a few seconds on the step of the ambulance. When the Ford passed an alleyway, he jumped off. Lifting the canvas, Winner saw that he was being chased by figures in strange uniforms whom he had no difficulty in identifying as policemen.

Then the Ford was in the square. Isabel looked around. Pink and yellow, the plaster façades tried to appear sober, but an irrepressible tipsiness broke out, like hiccoughs, in balconies, striped awnings and flagpoles. Viridian shutters closed the windows.

"Have you ever seen anything like it," exclaimed Isabel.

38

"Not in a hatful of Sundays," returned Elsie, abstractedly. She was thinking not of the architecture but of the crowd.

"Packed so tight, a fellow could waltz on their heads," observed a cadaverous individual, whose yellow-grey skin suggested that he might have been exhaled as a gas from the marshes outside the city, before solidifying inside a morning coat.

He was the Editor of the *Balkan Gazette*. He had come to Salonika during the Balkan Wars and had not fared well in its climate. His greatest achievement was to have founded a club, the *Cercle des Etrangers*, on whose balcony he now stood. "Always the same on band days."

"The German band, isn't it?" remarked Captain Sewell, of the Royal Engineers. He was a sharp-nosed, wolfish-looking young man, whose hair had already retreated half way from forehead to back of skull; this, he maintained, was the result of wearing an army cap at all times and so should be regarded as an injury suffered in the course of active service.

"Every nation under the sun is here, including the enemy," groaned the Editor. "As long as they don't stray into Wagner."

"I say, though," exclaimed Sewell. "There's a Tin Lizzie over there. A British ambulance — on a band day!"

"It'll never get through," said a Canadian dentist who had joined them. His name in the club was Ivory

Filler, a variant of the Ivor Fuller which appeared on his passport.

"This should be fun," replied Sewell. "I'll open a book on it. Come out here, you fellows," he called to the members inside. Gambling was one of the officer's principal relaxations. The other was pursued in a district near the railway station. Both were expensive.

"I should say," judged the Editor, as he lurched towards the door — it was too hot for a man of his constitution to remain outside — "that they'll run out of fuel before they get out of square. You know how little is to be had out here. When will people learn that the correct mode of transport is a mule?"

Sunny Southall stepped out of the French windows. He surveyed the square. "Excuse me one moment," he said, disappearing.

In the front seat of the Ford, Elsie had lost all patience with foreigners. "It's more crowded than Epsom Downs on Derby Day. Have you brought some knitting, Miss Hinchcliff, or a good book?"

Her humour was lost on Isabel, who felt that their position was very unfortunate. It exposed the BWH to comment, which would upset Mrs Stalwart-Dousing. Furthermore, she and Elsie were stranded in the middle of a crowd of men, colourfully dressed and often foreign — yes, as she looked around, her opinion was confirmed: the crowd was entirely composed of men, every one of them foreign — which upset her. A young officer was addressing her now. It was very distressing. "Mademoiselle," he said in French, "allow me to assist you." He seemed courteous. Isabel thanked him. Elsie understood from his gestures that she should restart the motor. A soldier was ordered to turn the crank handle.

The officer saluted, gave Isabel a card and strode off.

"I think he's going to part the waters of the Red Sea for us," gasped Elsie. "We'll be able to go through like Moses."

The band came down from its stand, with some encouragement from a detachment of soldiers. They formed up in front of the lorry and struck up a martial air.

"They're playing us out. Oh goodness, this is too embarrassing," lamented Isabel. "I'll die."

"Give over. It's a lark, this is. We've got our own personal guard of honour." Elsie was not prone to self-consciousness. The vehicle nosed forward.

"I admit it's rather fine."

At that moment Sunny ran up and jumped onto the running board on the passenger's side. "Captain Southall, Royal Flying Corps," he announced. "I thought you might need help."

"How sweet of you," replied Isabel. "But I'm afraid you're too late. The role of knight errant had already been filled. By Captain," she looked at the card, "Petrović, of the Serbian army."

Sunny saluted as best he could without falling off. "A Serb? His uniform appears to be French," he noted stiffly.

"Is that what it is? Just my shade of blue."

Sunny dismounted. He did not exactly sigh, having inserted a pipe between his teeth. But the Serb seemed to have got in first. "Hope to see you at Molho's," he said.

Sunny followed the ambulance like a mourner behind a hearse, until it reached its destination. There the canvas of the Ford was thrown open and Winner climbed stiffly out, over the vegetables. An aubergine tumbled to the floor. Seeing a superior officer, Winner saluted. "I've just arrived in Salonika," he explained. "I'm an artist."

To Sunny that seemed to account for any amount of peculiar behaviour. "You'll need to report to your senior officer," he suggested.

"Yes," replied Winner, searching his pockets, "I've got the address on a piece of paper."

"No need," pronounced Sunny. "There's only one place he'll be at this hour. Follow me."

Winner took his leather officer's valise from the van. From a window, Elsie waved at him. She had in her other hand a page torn from a sketchbook. Surreptitiously Winner waved back.

Sunny's loping pace made no allowance for a short man struggling beneath heavy luggage.

"What do you think of these streets?" he asked without turning his head. "Our friend the Ottoman was struck by a fit of modernising about the dawn of the century, and thought he'd turn this compost heap of a city into Paris. Notice the gas lamps, the boulevards — one of them's lined up on Mount Olympus. Needless to say, he ran out of puff. The new *quartier* stops here, on this bit of flat where the city walls used to stand — a

42

relic of Byzantium, now demolished. The streets on the hill are just as foetid as ever. Here we are at the club."

Sunny threw his hat, cane and gloves onto a table and bounded up the wide staircase. Winner dropped his valise in the hall and trotted after him like a Jack Russell.

Most of the shutters of the big club room were closed against the Aegean sun. This did not seem to have protected the furniture. It had suffered some rough usage at the hands — or trouser seats — of boisterous British officers since 1915.

"Major Eglinton is Intelligence," observed Sunny, taking stock of the room. "He is, however, asleep."

A waiter brought glasses of beer. "The man you need is Simple — or as you may know him from the paperwork, Major Simon. I don't see him. That's Simple for you: you can never tell what he's up to. Comes and goes, does the honourable member." Seeing that Winner did not understand the allusion he explained: "He's an MP, you know. When he makes a speech in the House, his notes are in Turkish. Terrifying amount of brains. Don't let it worry you, though."

An introduction was made to the lupine Captain Sewell. "New, are you?" he said, hoping that this tousled Lieutenant might be a betting man. "You'd better come with me to the railway station. I'm told that Madame Elektra has some lovely new girls." Sewell had wanted to be one of the hard-living cavalry, but his grammar school education stood against him scaling those social heights.

"Is Madame Elektra the station mistress?" enquired Winner. Sewell guffawed.

"Don't be viler than you can help, Ratty," said Sunny, steering his new friend towards a sofa on the other side of the room.

"Do you call him Ratty after *The Wind in the Willows?*" asked Winner.

Sunny shook his head. "Obviously Sewell corrupts to Sewer, and Sewer suggests Rat. Furthermore, in his case, it's spot on."

Sunny had not moderated his voice.

"Don't listen to him," Ratty called. "Come and enjoy yourself. We'll start the evening at Molho's."

General Ménière of the French army came in and saluted the room. The French always saluted; the Greeks liked it. "Molho's? Half my officers are in love with the girl who makes the chocolate there."

The Editor turned a yellow eye on him. "Hello Manure. They're wasting their time. She's almost certainly Jewish, in which case, married for years. More than half Salonika is Jewish," he informed Winner. "Officially, this was the second city of the Ottoman Empire — can you imagine it? This flea pit. Really it's the Metropolis of Israel. Everyone knows that. Everyone here. But you've just arrived so you don't. In England, nobody has heard of Salonika — or cares. And who can blame them?"

Ivory Filler broke in: "Shall I tell you the trouble with this town, Bigot?"

"Bagehot," the Editor corrected. "Please don't say vice, you Canadian puritan."

44

"Boredom. I'm bored, you're bored, the people out there in the square are bored — must be, or why would so many of them pile out to hear a wretched band oom-pahing away, a German one too. You're reduced to pursuing what I may say are unhygienic practices around the railway station."

"How can you be bored, Ivory? Your skills are in constant demand," observed Sunny.

"I'm busy," admitted the dentist. "Soldiers can't fight when they have toothache — and good Lord, you Brits have some cavities. Deep as mine shafts." Men began uneasily feeling their jaws. "But there must be something beyond work."

One of the company then spoke the words so often uttered by British officers quartered for any time in foreign parts. "We could organise a hunt." His eyes shone with what he took to be the novelty of the suggestion. "There were a dozen Masters of Foxhounds on the ship to Lemnos. That was before Gallipoli. We had a dinner and each one of them blew the horn. Grand times. I wonder how many of them are still alive? One of them was hit on the head by a shell a week after we arrived. Part of his face landed next to my boot."

"Steady on," complained another officer, whom Winner had not previously noticed in the penumbral gloom. Conversation should not be allowed to degenerate. No shop talk in the Club.

Ivory resumed. "Okay. So maybe a few of you can find the horses and chase some poor terrified creature — let's say, to be generous, that provides entertainment

45

for fifty men. Do you know how many are out here? A hundred thousand at least. Isn't that right, Eggie?"

Major Eglinton stirred himself from the depths of a low armchair, where, since waking, he had been occupied by trying to swat a mosquito. "I'm afraid I can't share that sort of information." The Major spoke with a discernible Scottish accent; his family owned spinning mills in Lanarkshire. "Classified."

Sunny took the opportunity to present Winner to the Major. "You must be the new security wallah," observed Eggie. "We don't need your services, you know. This is a tight ship."

"I'm an artist, sir."

"Good grief, whatever will they think of next?" He picked up a copy of the *Balkan Gazette*. "My one ambition is to lead my regiment into battle," he muttered. "But they stick me in Intelligence. What good did Intelligence do anyone?" He rolled up the newspaper and struck the arm of the chair with it. It provoked a small cloud of dust; the fly escaped. "Place is teeming with spies but most of them have every right to be here. The German attaché counts every paperclip we unload."

The more Winner heard about Salonika, the more he wanted to shake it off like a contagion. "I want to go to that Upcountry of yours," he said to Sunny. "It sounds pure."

Sunny adopted a kindly look, as though he were prepared to indulge a man who had plainly taken leave of his senses. "Well, well. Can't say I'd ever thought of it like that but you're an artist. To see it properly, you

46

need to get up into the sky. Fortunately I can help you. I'm Royal Flying Corps, Balloon Section."

"Glorious!" exclaimed Winner.

"Steady on."

They left Salonika the next morning, on a course that took them up into the heavens then precipitately back to earth. Back to Elsie.

Four

"It's perfectly all right," Sunny was saying as he filled his pipe. It was four days after Winner had arrived at the hospital, and he sat, wearing flannel pyjamas and dressing gown, in a wheel chair, his plastered leg projecting stiffly in front of him. "I'd been worried by that Hun pilot — Earwig, or possibly von Earwig. I mean, it seemed a bit thick coming over while Bertie was executing his mission of mercy with the coffee. But it's perfectly all right. Turns out that Bertie had engine trouble on the way back and had to put down. Earwig wasn't to know that he couldn't come to our aid, so no lack of sportsmanship there. Vexing all the same — I mean, regarding your leg; you being, so to speak, our responsibility. How does it feel?"

"Itchy."

"Can't be ants. The ones around here are too big to have got under the plaster. You've suffered a garshly wound. They should give you a hero's welcome when you get home."

"I ought to be walking before long."

"Lord, man, why the hurry? Plenty of men would give a thousand pounds to be in your shoes. Not that you're wearing any at the moment. You're surrounded by girls."

The fact had not escaped Winner. For the past week, he had been watching the nurses from the position of his bed or his wheel chair; in their grey uniforms they looked like doves. They erected the tents that housed the different functions of the hospital without any of the shouting, banging or coarse language which would have accompanied the same operation, if carried out by troops. Winner's ward, made of four tents connected by passageways, was called Newnham. Others were Somerville, Girton, Lady Margaret Hall.

There had been a boy, dressed in a boxy sheepskin jacket and wearing an embroidered cap; he had glimpsed him one morning, between sleep and waking, as the lad passed noiselessly by his tent. Winner had seen no other male.

The tents had been pitched in a meadow, speckled with wild-flowers. Fat green crickets sprung from the grasses as Winner was wheeled through them. Nearby was a grove of gnarled olive trees.

One morning he had been woken by what sounded like the rattle of a machine-gun — bah-ha-ha-ha. He found that next to him was a sheep. It could have been Mary's little lamb in the nursery rhyme: its fleece looked as white and manicured as though it had been prepared for an agricultural show, and there was a ribbon around its neck.

Then Isabel Hinchcliff appeared, in a state of untypical agitation. She had been given charge of the kitchen, over which she presided with an air of calm authority. Only today she was flustered. "There you are," she said, with affected severity with which one might address a child or a hospital patient.

"Of course," replied Winner crossly. "I can't move."

"I didn't mean you," she said. "I was looking for Snowball. A sheep."

"What for? Chops?"

"Chops, indeed! I bought Snowball from an old crone of a farmer's wife," she explained. "She's adorable; I washed her. (Snowball that is.) I'm sure the wounded soldiers will find her cheering." Isabel, at twenty-nine, had reached that point in life where she was in danger of becoming soppy about animals.

Winner had seen wounded soldiers and was not sure that they cared about sheep. He offered to draw the animal. "Sheep may safely graze."

"She'll graze safely as long as you don't tell on her to Mrs Stalwart-Dousing. She said Snowball wasn't allowed onto the wards."

"You'd better watch out for that gypsy boy." She looked blank. "He looked like a shepherd."

"There are no men here, Lieutenant."

"I saw him."

"You see things other people don't." Her manner dismissed the inconvenient, as it was often dismissed from the Surrey Hills.

The fluffy, beribboned sheep seemed to personify the idyll of life in the BWH. It was as though the nurses had come to a land of peace and plenty, which their own presence, for Winner, made even more pleasing. Elsie gathered a posy of wildflowers for him to paint. She reminded him of his sister Maud, who married a missionary.

Only it was not a land of peace. In the mountains, sporadic combat never stopped, even in the bitterest months of winter. It was now Spring: another fighting season would begin. A Serbian offensive was expected soon. The wards could not remain empty for long.

Sunny's pipe made gurgling noises as he got it going. "It's a bit of luck for me, of course," he said.

"What is?"

"Your being here."

"I don't see it."

"Come on, man. Without the excuse of visiting you, how could I get to meet the girls. As it is, it will be next stop Salonika."

"What on earth for?"

"For a vermouth at Molho's, followed by dinner and cabaret at the White Tower . . ."

"You make it sound," Winner sought for a word that sufficiently expressed his disgust, "cosmopolitan. I like it here."

Sunny looked incredulous. "You haven't spent much time upcountry. Chaps have to stick it for months together, being stung by every conceivable kind of insect, while the sun blisters the skin off. Then three days' leave in Salonika. Lord, it's better than cosmopolitan."

"You don't have any leave."

"But I have to make a report about the kite balloon, and you have to meet your commanding officer."

"No I don't. Not yet anyway."

"You do. You're essential. You'll have to go with a nurse to look after you."

"Don't be ridiculous."

"Wait there. I'll square it with matron."

Mrs Stalwart-Dousing was in the sanitary department. She was a handsome woman, with a head that, with its strong features and far-seeing eyes, might have modelled as a prophetess by Rubens: not highly groomed, the natural tendency of her grey hair to escape from its chignon being exaggerated in the wilds of Macedonia, but with soft and rosy skin. She had been one of the first women to sit the Tripos examination at Cambridge — unofficially, since women were not accepted as members of the University.

With her was Sister Muir, bird-like and nervy, who concentrated too hard on her responsibilities to smile much. To her apprehensive imagination, the dangers of the expedition loomed very large.

Isabel was there too. "I saw you in the square," exclaimed Sunny, "in Salonika. Amazing bit of luck to meet you again here."

Isabel did not seem to think so. "I don't recall." She had not told Mrs Stalwart-Dousing about the embarrassment that she had brought on the Hospital by allowing the ambulance to become stuck in a crowd of foreigners.

Mrs Stalwart-Dousing was discussing the disposal of waste. "The greatest danger to the whole operation is dysentery," that formidable organiser pronounced. "The dryness of the land makes the disposal of human waste a serious matter. When the operating theatre begins work, there will be amputations."

"We shall need quicklime," asserted Sister Muir.

"I'm not sure that burying with quicklime wouldn't preserve the tissue, rather than destroy it," returned Mrs Stalwart-Dousing. "I propose that we construct an incinerator to burn the limbs."

That gave Isabel an opening. "Mrs Stalwart-Dousing, that is exactly the subject I wanted to see you about."

"Severed limbs?"

"Wood. They're been making furniture out of it, the doctors need it for splints. We have to get the laundry running." "It's our only fuel and we don't have enough. I must have some for the ovens." Isabel was in charge of the kitchen.

Sunny saw an opening. "There are no trees in Macedonia — it's well known. Except olives of course, and you can't cut down those. Salonika, however, is awash with wood. As it happens, I have to go there. So does Lieutenant Winnington-Smith. Lend me a couple of your nurses and the job's done. Miss Hinchcliff of course must be one of them."

Isabel by no means took this for granted. "Certainly not."

"I'm sorry to be presumptuous, but you do, emphatically, need wood. How else will you get it?"

Mrs Stalwart-Dousing looked at him, as she looked at most things in life, severely. "I shall enquire into this and give you an answer in due course. I suppose it might be possible for an expedition to be made tomorrow."

Sunny tried not to smile too broadly. The long famine, as regards female company, might soon be over. As he left, another tactic came to mind. "Grand hospital you've made here, but you should get some drainage channels dug." He appeared to consider for a moment. "I might be able to help with that. I could send some men over."

"Captain Southall," returned Mrs Stalwart-Dousing, with lofty emphasis, "I know nothing about drains, but I do know that we won't take any help from your men. They are needed for other duties."

"I only thought, perhaps, for the heavy work. It would save them lounging around."

Mrs Stalwart-Dousing frowned. "Captain, I have seven women doctors, eighteen trained nurses, four trained cooks, one dispenser of medicines, one sanitary inspector in the shape of Sister Muir, a female evangelist who can act as chaplain and fourteen orderlies, including chauffeurs. All competent and hard-working women. We can look after ourselves." If they were all of the same stamp as Sister Muir and Mrs Stalwart-Dousing, Sunny thought that quite possible.

"My husband is fighting in France," she continued. "So are my brothers. The more that we can do to reduce the demand for manpower — and I mean manpower — the sooner they shall be home."

She glared at Sunny over her spectacles. "And if your men are of the lounging variety, I advise filling their time with drill. There are no men here, and we don't need them."

"I'm a man," observed Winner, who had got a nurse to wheel him up.

"I don't count you, Lieutenant. You are a patient." As she left, her eyes were affronted by the sight of a white sheep coming out of the dining tent. "Miss Hinchcliff, I saw that sheep wandering into Newnham earlier this morning."

"But Mrs Stalwart-Dousing, it's such a dear, and we were just saying how much good it would do Lieutenant Winnington-Smith."

"We are a hospital, not a pet sanctuary, Miss Hinchcliff. No sheep."

Isabel was distraught. Sunny quick-wittedly saw a solution. "Let me buy Snowball from the Hospital. You can acquire another animal and serve it up if you must. I'll take friend Snowball back with me this evening."

"Would you?" The tears that had been about to fall stayed glistening on her eyelids. Sunny thought he had never seen more beautiful eyes.

"I'd regard it as a sacred trust. I have always loved sheep." Sunny hoped he had found the way to her heart. "So that's settled: we go to Salonika tomorrow."

Winner remained silent. Sheep, shepherds, the gypsy boy he had seen that morning . . . Some trick of his mind had summoned the likeness of the youth who had tried to get into the Ford on his first afternoon in Salonika. Only the boy at the hospital carried a gun.

Five

Next day, Sunny rose before dawn. He always did. Once the sun was up and striking the canvas of the tent it would have been impossible for him to sleep. With day came the flies.

The Balloon Section was now bivouacked in a gulley, green with fragrant juniper bushes; it was difficult to spot from the air.

"The car is ready?" he asked his batman, Shakes. "Good."

Sunny threw himself against the leather upholstery of the motorcar and the vehicle bumped its way cautiously over the deeply rutted tracks. Dumpling-shaped bushes cast long shadows. Filled to the brim with melted snow, the river Vardar as the British knew it — the river Axios to the Greeks — looped lazily across the plain, as though to hurry would risk indigestion.

Sunny was a practical man. As a member of the Royal Flying Corps, he would take whatever the Army threw at him, however fantastic, while in a personal capacity finding what enjoyment and solace he could in a strange land. He fully expected the coming day to live up to the promise of the early morning landscape.

But peace did not reign in the Hospital. Two remarkable events had taken place in his absence, which had caused, in respect of the first, excitement and, in respect of the second, consternation.

The previous evening had given an unfortunate prominence to Nurse Goodman. Goody wore skirts at the knee, and was generally thought to be too "smart" for her own good. It may have been to redeem a good opinion with the others that, when somebody noticed a hole — not much bigger than a badger hole — in the side of a hillock, Goody had taken the lead. The hole appeared to have been man-made. When they shouted into it, their voices reverberated around what must have been a sizeable void.

"Come on," said Goody. "Enough fussing. Someone's got to go in."

"You can, if you like," said a pink-faced girl with yellow hair, acutely conscious of the likelihood of spiders and millipedes. "I dare you."

Goody accepted the challenge, inserting her feet into the opening, then wriggling the rest of her body through. "Ooh," she exclaimed as the last of her disappeared from view and she found herself sitting on a hard and clammy floor. Behind the opening had been a drop of several feet.

"What can you see, Goody?" they had called after her.

"Nothing. It's pitch black."

Somebody lit a match. Goody screamed. At her feet was a skull.

Later, Elsie was one of the pair of nurses who reported the finding to Mrs Stalwart-Dousing. "A skull, you say? The chamber must be a tomb. What is it like?"

"White, Ma'm. About the size of a turnip."

"Not the skull, the tomb."

"Dark and clammy. She said it smells of compost."

"Well, you'd better ask Nurse Goodman to come to me."

"We can't, Ma'm. She's stuck."

When extracted with the aid of a knotted rope, Goody was sent to get washed, before being confined to her tent. This prevented her from sharing the second artefact — of no very ancient date — that she had found during her entombment with the authorities. But she mentioned it to Elsie, as the latter escorted her to the deceptively named bath house — a tent that did not contain any baths, only a row of tables bearing enamel bowls and jugs. "There was a bottle down there and — well, some other things."

"So somebody uses it."

"Must do," returned Goody. Then she impulsively said, "look," and thrust out a thick wad of drachma notes.

"Goody," exclaimed Elsie. "Wherever did that lot come from? It looks ever so much. You won't keep it?"

"I intend to. Who'll know?"

The Goody episode had, by the next morning, been eclipsed by an even greater drama. Mrs Stalwart-Dousing informed Sunny of it as soon as she saw his car enter the hospital. "Captain, I cannot send a vehicle for wood, however much there may be to be had. Our motor spirit has been stolen."

Sunny, with his longer experience of Macedonia, took the news in his stride. "What were the guards doing?"

"There are no guards."

To Sunny, this statement was more astounding than the theft. A group of women, however educated and well-intentioned, were vulnerable to heaven knew what outrages. It seemed inconceivable that they could be so foolish as to sleep without armed patrols.

"It was in drums. They were so big that it never occurred to us that they could be taken."

"Fortunately," Sunny was able to reassure the lady, "I have fuel. I had imagined going in the staff car but a Ford could bring the wood back." Sunny wondered if they would find any. "Meanwhile, my driver stays."

Mrs Stalwart-Dousing sniffed. "We are quite able to protect ourselves, Captain. Sister Muir has a revolver."

Sunny shuddered at the thought. "I'll order him to mount guard all the same."

Winner, in recognition of his foot, occupied the back of the ambulance, the canvas sides wound up, while Sunny, Isabel and Elsie squeezed onto the bench in front. Elsie edged, at a cautious speed, onto the road that ran — if so vigorous a verb might be applied to it — beside the river Vardar, towards Salonika. The nurses talked excitedly about the robbery. To Isabel, it seemed little short of sacrilege that a hospital should have been despoiled. "I hope our tents are safe while we're away," she commented.

"There's more than possessions to worry about," remarked Elsie. Really, she thought, a clever woman like Isabel could be daft at times.

Before 1915, the road had not been little more than a track, so conscious of its unsuitability for wheeled transport that it faded into the landscape — indeed, it could do nothing else, being largely composed of stones and compacted earth. It was not used to carrying more than mules, horse-drawn carts and flocks of sheep; motor vehicles were unknown. Sometimes the road carried no traffic at all. The scrubby plains through which it passed belonged, by long established tradition, to a different world from that of Salonika. The seaport made a show of being, in parts, modern. The plains were immemorial. Little had changed since the days of St Paul. Salonika folk would never have crossed them alone or unarmed.

But the war had been bad for brigandage. Roads which robbers had previously had to themselves were now crowded with vehicles at all times of the day and night. The Ford contended with motor lorries, staff cars, pack animals and ammunition caissons, hauled by teams of eight horses. The brigands had turned to other sources of income, such as stealing from the army or smuggling contraband. Some, their pockets chinking with Allied payments, formed a ruthless guerrilla force known as the Komitadji, one of whose roles was to stop couriers from taking messages to the enemy. Skulls found in hiding places did not always belong to the ancient world. Barely had the ambulance gone quarter of a mile before it stopped for an ammunition convoy. This was followed by a straggle of hirsute individuals in casually-worn khaki trudged past. "The Greek Muleteer Corps," Sunny scoffed.

Holes the size of ponds opened up under the weight of traffic. Vehicles frequently broke down or got stuck. A bullock train might be needed to pull out a lorry or heavy gun. While it did so, everyone behind had to wait.

"We're building up for a show around the lake," observed Sunny, as they moved on. "Strange expression, that. Makes the attack sound like a form of entertainment being offered by a Swiss hotel." Winner put away his sketchbook; he had been drawing the shepherd boy he had seen in the Hospital. No one else admitted his existence. Under the barrage of scepticism, Winner was beginning to doubt his own memory.

"When does it start?" asked Isabel.

"Any time now. They can't fight much during winter. Mountain tracks are bad enough at the best of times, but impossible for guns and ammunition convoys after heavy rain. You might not believe it now how much it snows up there. It's snowing now. Down here, it's spring and the campaigning season has started."

The scene changed as they approached Salonika. First, they came upon outposts dug into the banks of earth, or fabricated from sandbags: they were roofed with "wiggly tin," as the army called corrugated iron, and manned by teams of machine gunners who waved when they saw the nurses. The machine gun nests were succeeded by trenches, gun pits and the dense entanglements of barbed wire that gave the Birdcage its name. "There's so much of it," said Isabel. "It goes on and on."

"Does it remind you of wool?" wondered Winner. "Balls of wool in my mother's knitting basket."

"I wouldn't like to untangle it," replied Elsie.

And then they were in the midst of a gigantic camp site. Neat tows of tents, organised according a logic that must have meant something to the military mind, but was inaccessible to the occupants of the Ford, stretched in every direction. "Tents everywhere," Winner marvelled. "Tents, tents, tents."

60

"Think of the canvas," said Elsie. "You could make a right old painting if you stitched it together."

"A painting as big as the sky." Winner suddenly broke into a hymn. "Love divine, all loves excelling, Joy of heaven, to earth come down."

This was where most of the British Salonika Force was accommodated, a monotonous wasteland that had been personalised with names from home. The line of tents forming Pall Mall led to Trafalgar Square. Between the tents were dumps of stores.

Winner asked for directions to brigade headquarters and the quartermaster's office, but most men barely knew which country they were in, let alone how the part that their unit happened to have occupied temporarily related to any other. They might as well have been on the moon. An officer pointed them along a track, apparently the same as all the other tracks that went between the tents. Sentries presented arms. They turned into a palisade. In it was a hut that looked like a cricket pavilion, with tubs of geraniums on the verandah.

The quartermaster's desk was spread with ledgers, chits and correspondence, organised into neat piles. Behind it, Major Otterwill had the faded, pernickety look of a mathematics teacher who had risen to being deputy headmaster at a minor public school, which had been precisely his career before joining the colours. He was a fussy man. His uniform bulged in the manner of one whose occupant generally took second helpings of steamed pudding.

The officer looked up, his pencil suspended over a ledger. "Is this a social call?" he asked irritably, as Sunny came into the room. They knew each other from England. They played cricket for the same romantically named club. "I'm trying to provision an army." Then, noticing the nurses, he struggled to his feet. "You find me, ladies, engaged in an endless task. Behind every column of soldiers is a column of book-keeping. This is a war of supplies, you know. The men also have to be fed."

This was not quite Isabel's idea of military spirit. "It must be a great challenge," she said, with some sharpness.

"It is. You know, in France, they're fighting a modern war in a modern country." The quartermaster had begun one of his lessons — a habit from school which officers, who resented it, did not challenge: such was his power to apportion or deny army stores. "France is crisscrossed with decent roads; they have some good farmers, growing sensible crops. They have factories, forests. Look around you here. We've brought the Allied armies to a wilderness, which, in normal times, struggles to sustain a population of goatherds. If you could feed soldiers on a diet of olive oil, oranges and wine, our problems would disappear. Unfortunately, they want bully. They also want shelter, transport, fuel, horses, oats, uniforms, sun helmets, quinine — that's without even beginning on the armaments and ammunition. Look at these chits, all from commanders who would win the war if only they could have a few more tins of this or crates of that. Everyone in Salonika is an Oliver Twist: 'Please, sir, can I have more?'" He smiled ruefully. "I tell them, as I tell you, that every cabbage, every pair of socks must come by ship."

He ran a hand over his brow with the anxiety of one on whom the fate of an army depends. "But I needn't tell you ladies that," he said, brightening for the benefit of the fairer sex, "you yourselves will have come by ship. Which one was it? Comfortable I hope."

"Extremely comfortable, thank you," replied Isabel. It had been comfortable for her. "Except that some people thought we were bothered by a submarine. Overheated imaginations, I expect."

Submarines were the quartermaster's bête noire. He puffed out his cheeks. "Such a lot of supplies have been lost to them. And people too, of course."

Winner, polishing his spectacles to mask his frustration, was emitting a series of exasperated squeaks, the sound of which was something like a Pyrenean marmot. As a Second Lieutenant, it was not for him to question the wisdom of a Major responsible for provisioning a whole Division; but the presence of Elsie steeled him to do it. "Excuse me, sir, I appreciate that you're hard pressed. But are there really no odd pockets of stores that haven't been accounted for, or are apportioned to a battalion who doesn't need them?"

The quartermaster could see which way the conversation was trending. Quartermasters had often risen from being sergeant-majors. He was not one of them. It pained him to disappoint, and so often he had to. "Can I offer you one of these?" From a pocket of his tunic, he produced a silver pillbox containing small, intensely flavoured sweets. "I recommend them. They came from Paris." It was the Otter's way of sugaring the pill. "Slack? Very little, alas. *Mi dispiace*." Italian, he felt, was such a civilised language.

They explained the Hospital's need for wood.

The Major smiled ironically. He put his fingers together, preparatory to a lecture. "Timber is an interesting question at the moment. Militarily we still live in a wooden world. You would not have thought it, perhaps, given the amount of metal and HE we chuck around. But in some ways we're as reliant on trees as Nelson was. The Birdcage, for instance, is practically a new city. Oh dear yes, it all needs wood. Another bonbon? I find them awfully good."

The pillbox did its round again.

"I'm told that a single army in France can consume thirty thousand trees in one day. Whole trees — trunk, branches, the lot. Most of it goes underground. Your simple request for a few sticks of wood touches on a fundamental principle of the war. The Royal Flying Corps think this is an air war. The Artillery would have you believe it's about guns. I say it's a war of supply. We feel it particularly in Salonika. Our front is ninety miles wide. A modern war, fought in conditions that would have struck the Duke of Wellington as antiquated."

"But it must be just as bad for the Bulgarians and Germans as for us," declared Isabel, indignantly.

"They have a railway — goes all the way to Berlin. The Bulgarians are in their own country. Or the one next door." For a moment, the Otter looked grave. He brightened. "On another subject, I don't suppose you came with any seeds?"

"Seeds?

"I am trying to make a garden here. You've no idea how difficult that can be."

"How can you think of gardening?" exclaimed Isabel.

"I assure you, I think of little else. I don't just grow flowers, you know. Vegetables too."

"Gardens take a long time to grow."

"Who says we won't be here a long time? I rather think we shall be. In fact I hope we are."

"Don't be preposterous, Otter," exclaimed Sunny.

"A sudden exit would mean something awful and bloody had happened. Our role is to sit the thing out. We must *threaten* to attack, so the Boche reinforces the Bulgar. But actually attack? I sincerely hope not."

"Why so?" asked Isabel, aghast at the Otter's lack of gallantry.

"Because we would get nowhere. Untold numbers of men would die to no purpose. All my stores would go in a flash — though naturally I'm trying to keep as much as I can back. Your hospital wouldn't be nearly big enough to take the wounded. At present, it's stalemate. Have another bonbon while they last. I'm expecting more from France."

Isabel waved the sweets away.

Elsie accepted, suspending the bonbon in her hand while she said: "Major, you don't have no timber. But it ain't timber we're seeking — just ordinary wood. What happens to the crates that I can see out there? One of the crates contains a motorcycle. There are ammunition boxes, trays of vegetables, hundreds of them."

"We re-use some of them. The rest . . ." He called an orderly. "What happens to the crates that we've broken up?"

"We piles them on a bonfire and sets light to them, sir."

"Bravo," clapped Sunny.

"God does provide," exclaimed Winner.

Elsie put the pastille in her mouth. The Otter returned the box to his pocket. "Well, ladies," he smiled, "when would it be convenient to collect it?"

"This afternoon," said Isabel. "As soon as we've got some more petrol."

"Petrol? Oh yes. Good luck," replied the Otter. "Can I tempt you to a pastille?"

Six

The commander of the Unterseeboot 168 scanned the horizon through his field glasses, looking for smoke. They had been having a tedious time of it. The crew had not seen action for days. It was all very well doing band practice, but since the band was principally composed of the gunnery officer, a Graz house painter in civilian life, whose sole instrument was the mouth organ, its repertoire was limited. And the submarine was only sixty-seven yards long. The gymnastics club might as well have been dancing on a drum.

Smoke from the good Welsh coal that fuelled the British navies would reveal the presence of a ship. Once spotted, he would close in on his prey — a deadly unseen presence, like a bacillus or perhaps a god. Until then, it was just the gramophone. A dolphin played around the U-boat, its back forming a silvery arc as it rose from the water, flanks dripping. Still no smoke could be seen.

He could wait. He still had the time to wait. Time meant fuel. The U-Boat, designed to sneak around coastal waters, did not have large fuel tanks: they would have to be replenished soon. On the other hand, he did not have to find large quantities of petrol. It could be supplied in drums rather than tanks, or even in cans. There were people from whom he could buy it. God bless the Greeks for their neutrality. The French and British were, naturally, furious at this aspect of the free market. They were doing everything they could to stop petrol being supplied. Still, he knew where it could be had. There was a place; he had dates on which to go to it.

Meanwhile, U-168 could stay out for another couple of days. It would be enough. He would see the smoke soon. It would be from the *Marquette*. Then he would strike.

Gentlemen, This is Molho's

Seven

Red plush, gilt carving and mirror glass; chairs by Thonet drawn up to round tables with marble tops. This was the international style of Paris, London, Vienna, Budapest, Turin ... and *Molho Frères*. The café was like the wayward child of one of Europe's great metropolitan cities which had run away to find itself lost among the wooden streets of Salonika. There it seemed a little overdressed. The *Frères*, one of whom was bound to be found in the establishment that bore their name, were similar: cosmopolitan, pomaded, looking endlessly surprised that they were not in a more imposing city. Although the pre-war café had been very different from its present manifestation, the Molho patriarch had nevertheless followed Jewish custom by sending his sons to the other cities to improve their chances in life. One brother could help another. If Istanbul disappointed, trade might be better in Trieste. One by one they had been called home. For café proprietors, Salonika was the place to be.

Only part of the café lay inside. To enter it, you had to squeeze past tables that spilled out onto the pavement and sometimes into the street, one of the busiest of the city. Whereas the interior was brightly lit to show off the novelty of the electric light, the mood of the terrace was softer: shaded, beneath vines, by day, mysterious, with the twinkling of candles, by night. Men who stayed inside usually had a half-acknowledged desire to watch the chocolate maker at her craft. Her profile was precisely that of a bust of

Queen Nefertiti which German archaeologists had recently found in Egypt.

Custom at Molho's had been nothing much before the War, and some of the Salonika community might have doubted the family's wisdom in investing so much in a concern whose takings were a thin silver stream, not a golden gush. Salonika, Pearl of the Aegean, was a merchant city. Although it contained some prosperous families, they did not like to spend two piastres where one would do. A merchant would take a coffee, clicking his worry beads as he did so; it would last all morning. The Jewish matrons, who rewarded the good behaviour of their offspring with cakes, allowed only one drink each, and left no tip. Once the French and then British arrived in 1915, however, the tills rang merrily. The café was always full. Its doors opened to yawning officers, newly arrived on an overnight sleeper train from upcountry, and wanting breakfast. Men with sagging spirits and red eyes looked in for a mid morning refresher. Aperitifs were served before lunch, tea in the afternoon, cocktails at sun down. Dawn might be breaking as the last of the previous night's tables were cleared and the rats took undisputed possession of the kitchen. Their reign, though, was short. Molho's had barely drawn breath, let alone closed its sleepy eyes, before the lock turned in the door and a flat-footed waiter began to clatter the coffee pots.

In choosing Molho's as the place to begin an evening in female company Sunny showed no originality. Officers of all the Allied nations regarded it as *de rigueur*. Not that everyone was lucky enough to have a nurse to take. Others went in groups, or by themselves. The atmosphere encouraged conversation. A French artilleryman might be observed noisily exchanging ideas with a member of the Russian cavalry, or an Italian transport officer, none of whom spoke the other's language, so that communication took place only through gestures and imitative sounds, the cavalryman turning his chair into a mount and striking his thigh with an imaginary whip, the officer of the artillery making a dumb show of exploding shells. Molho's inspired feelings of good fellowship. To the polyglot military force, its international character gave a connection with the larger world — the one that existed beyond the confines of the Birdcage, the one to which they would go back after the war. They could feel at home at Molho's, when so much of Salonika was strange.

Or so it was with the more sophisticated officers, the ones — and there were many of them — who ordered their uniforms from West End tailors, towered over malnourished Other Ranks and generally bloomed with the healthy pink sleekness of prosperity. No clothes hung well on Winner. His uniform had quickly become a collection of bulges and creases, which seemed only to have a distant kinship with the sartorial elegancies on display at Molho's. Short, swarthy and heavily spectacled, he seemed less of a god than an imp.

In London, Winner had not been a Café Royal man. He said he could not afford it, but that was only part of the story; had he been as rich as Croesus, he would still have preferred to hurry home to his village beside the marshes.

Isabel would enjoy Molho's, Winner imagined; by Salonika standards, it was smart — too smart, perhaps. She was clearly not a young lady to go to such places in London, with their overtone of actresses and the demimonde; but this was wartime. Salonika was different. Molho's was like a kind of club for both sexes, if such a thing could be imagined. It was perfectly above board. She had been brought up to enjoy company.

Elsie was, of course, a different quantity, but she came as part of the package. She was the part that Winner felt more comfortable with. She had not been to the Café Royal; of course not — you could not expect someone in her position to have gone anywhere. That, too, was the extraordinary thing about wartime. Isabel and Elsie were now sitting at the same table. Winner protectively showed her to a place next to his. He tripped over the leg of a neighbouring chair while doing so.

The men had a little money in hand. In comparison with the golden coinage of England, the grubby drachma notes seemed laughable, disgusting. Like other soldiers, they did not understand, or care very much, what they were worth. It hardly seemed to matter in this foreign town.

Winner surveyed the scene through his spectacles, blinking. He did not feel part of it. "This is unexpected," he heard Isabel say, "for Salonika. I almost feel I'm on the stage."

74

"Is it as bad as that?" asked Sunny. "We could go to the terrace, if you're dazzled."

"I meant the uniforms. Those must be French *chasseurs*, enjoying their Vermouth. And what about those bejewelled specimens?"

"Russians," returned Sunny. "Fanastic, aren't they? That morose table is a group of Serbs — always so gloomy. Unlike the Italians."

"The little Greek officer doesn't come off well by comparison — I say, the man in black with the long beard must be an Orthodox priest."

"Our khaki looks rather drab."

Winner perceived Isabel turning to him. "As an artist, don't you find the foreigners charming, Mr Winnington-Smith?"

To him, the room might have been an effusion of highly coloured mist. "Very," he said laconically.

"Do see that beautiful creature making chocolate," continued Isabel in a stage whisper. Winner turned and peered at the chocolate girl, then hurriedly turned away, not wishing to appear rude. He did not know that the girl was thoroughly used to being watched with frank and sometimes insistent observation by officers. "Her hair almost comes down to her waist," continued Isabel. "I'm quite envious of it."

"Imagine coming here every day," exclaimed Elsie. To her, Molho's was like one of the London gin palaces with which her father had been familiar, only less beery. Nor was there the same volume of noise. There was, however, an undeniable excitement to it.

"What?" reproved Isabel. "Making chocolate rather than nursing!"

"I didn't say I wanted to." Molho's was not for the likes of her. "Mind you, we've got no patients at the hospital now that the Lieutenant has left," continued Elsie cockily. "In addition to which, Miss Hinchcliff, we've run out of petrol. We're stuck." The fuel from the staff car had sufficed for the journey down to Salonika, but the Ford had used more than expected and it did not seem there would be enough to get back. They needed more, and had found it was not so easy to get.

Isabel found Elsie almost impertinent. She did not seem to know the rule (applicable to servants as well as children) about being seen and not heard. Elsie was there on sufferance: opinions were neither expected nor desired.

"Look," she exclaimed, "there's that funny Turkish man who helped us on our first day." From across the room the funny Turkish man bowed. He had been talking to Ratty. The latter, seeing the nurses, came over. Winner could not feel warmly towards him: he had the face of a cunning predator.

"Good evening, Sunny. Lieutenant Winnington-Smith," he continued after being introduced to Isabel and Elsie, "you're here as an artist, aren't you? Painting away while other fellows fight — eh? If you need a subject, there's one for you over there." He indicated the chocolate maker. "Paint her and I'll buy the picture. A souvenir of Salonika," he laughed, showing his teeth. Winner loathed him.

"Would she sit for me?"

"If she says yes, you could make a fortune selling introductions. Half the boys in Salonika would like to make her acquaintance."

"Would they, Captain? Would they really?" It was Elsie who said this. She struck Ratty as being somewhat intense, and not perhaps, quite the thing at Molho's.

"Why, yes," he smiled. "In fact," he said to Winner, "I'll back you to do it."

Appalled, Winner looked at him open-mouthed.

"Ratty," said Sunny, "try to behave like a gentleman."

Sunny had touched a nerve. Ratty looked daggers at him. "Not very gentlemanly to leave the ladies without drinks," he sneered. "Waiter!"

No waiter had come up while he and Winner had been the lone men; Ratty seemed to draw waiters to him by magnetism. One hovered now. He wore a black tie, black waistcoat and a stiffly laundered apron that stretched almost to the ground.

"*Monsieur désire quelque chose?*" asked the waiter.

"Ah, Mister Desire, is it you? Yes, I desire champagne. We call him Mister Desire because that is what he always says. Monsieur desire . . . etcetera."

"No wine for me, thank you," said Elsie.

"You've probably never had any. A little won't hurt you," replied Ratty.

"I lived with a family who drank wine and we ate together. I would prefer a cordial." It came in a long-stemmed glass which seemed to contain a bottled essence of summer.

"You're an independent woman," Ratty did not make that sound like the ideal state.

"There are vineyards here," observed Sunny hurriedly, as his glass was being filled. "I saw them from the balloon. The countryside looks like a quilt. Fields of melons, and tobacco, and little farmyards."

Ratty was not the most nimble-minded of men and ignored Sunny's attempted distraction. "That girl making chocolate could have half the room at her feet, just by raising an eyebrow. There's a boy in the kitchen, they say, who is being driven crazy by her. Proximity to such loveliness is too much for him, poor fellow."

"Won't she notice him?" wondered Isabel, alive to the possibilities of romance.

"Only to show her unmitigated scorn. Imagine — a goddess like that to be courted by a kitchen boy. It would be like Cinderella in reverse. Mind you, half the French cavalry are said to be similarly smitten, although possibly with less honourable intentions."

"Only because of the way you carry on, wanting what you can't have," frowned Elsie. "Passion takes over and you lose control of yourselves. You think you're strong but I call that weak."

Ratty despaired of Elsie. "Who's the cockney sparrow?" he asked Isabel privately. She thought it would be poor taste to reply, even if Elsie did seem to have been putting herself unnecessarily forward.

The Turk materialised at the table. He was a fat man, and as fat men sometimes do, moved lightly on his feet. They had not noticed his approach. His smile seemed both jovial and world weary, as though he had seen through the superficies of life and was determined to laugh at whatever came up from beneath. "My dear ladies," he purred, "I knew we would meet at Molho's."

"You've met already?" said Ratty, with little friendliness in his voice.

"I had the honour of helping these angels of mercy out of an absurd difficulty, the sort you could only find in a town like this. What is Salonika? Is it Ottoman, Oriental, Greek or Jewish? — nobody can say. The streets stink and strangers who have the honour to visit us are exposed to all manner of bêtises. It is now a garrison. What will it be tomorrow? Who knows?"

"You should know, Mr Bey," said Isabel. "You said you know everything."

"Not the future. Let us hope the future, for all of us, is more civilised. We will then be done with these confusing Turkish names. It should be Mr Gazmend — or Gazmend Bey, although local people are kind enough to use Gazmend Effendi. We have no surname, only what you might suppose to be a Christian name, except of course one is Moslem. It's in every respect preposterous, I agree."

He bowed, and was on the point of leaving. "But even so," he added as though it were an afterthought, "the city has some beauties. You must allow me to show you the cemeteries. They are extremely large and, on the whole, peaceful. Salonika does death well, I think. You see, it has had practice at it. People are always dying." He pulled from his top pocket a perfumed handkerchief.

Isabel interrupted his retreat. "You could tell us, perhaps, whether a hospital ship is expected from Alexandria. My cousin may be on it."

Gazmend turned. He looked grave. "Ships come and go. Their movements are secret. If she is dear to you, I hope she arrives safely. It is a bad time for shipping. Very bad. I pray your cousin will not be unlucky."

"Where will you do your praying?" scoffed Ratty with barely concealed dislike.

"In the mosque, of course," returned Gazmend Bey. "Or on my prayer mat. Our religion requires us to show respect to Allah and pray five times a day. Not once a week. Yours is the more convenient arrangement. You see, I must go home now. I hope that your once-a-week God looks after you, Captain, until we meet again." He smiled at everyone, bowed again and left.

"Tell us, Captain," demanded Isabel. "Who is that man?"

"Some sort of functionary, or he was under the old regime. He waxed fat, and you could say that he remains fat, although without the comfortable sinecures. They went when the Greeks took over, but he's like Salonika itself: he manages to survive revolution, war and earthquake. Not even the mosquitoes have got him, worst luck. He purports to be the Bulgarian consul — I don't quite see how but he must be Bulgarian as well as everything else. He also lends money, I believe."

"How can there be a Bulgarian consul?"

"We're at war with Bulgaria but Greece isn't. Yet."

"I rather like him. He has charming manners."

80

"Oily."

"He strikes me as being the essence of the Orient. He seems to move in a cloud of exotic scent."

"The man's a blood-sucking leech."

There was a small commotion as the door of the cafe opened and through it walked what Winner could only regard as an apparition. She was tall and thin-faced, her height being exaggerated by her hair, which was piled on top of her head; on top of the hair was a hat, and on top of the hat, waving like a flag above a castle battlement, was an ostrich plume. Her lips were very red, her *décolletage* was very low. Dress was too crude a word for the garment of which the *décolletage* was — or was not — part: it was like the scales of a fish, shimmering and tight of fit. She did not walk, she flowed.

General Ménière, whose companion this fabulous creature was, pulled back a chair and — having saluted the room in all directions — received the fur stole that draped her otherwise bare shoulders; he was rewarded with a look of disdain, as though she was bored by the company, indifferent to the table, wearied by the waiters attempting to discern what refreshment would most tempt her appetite: indeed, tired of the human race. Discouraging though this might have seemed, other men would willingly have exchanged places with the General, and Manure himself seemed wholly content.

"Miss Lola di Bonza," noted Sunny. "Or it could be Mademoiselle, or Signorina: her origins are, so to speak, fogged."

"What an absurd name," observed Elsie.

"Foreign names so often are," agreed Sunny. "But it isn't the name that attracts people to Lola di Bonza's performances. She's on the bill at the White Tower tonight," he added, "I believe."

"What does she do?"

"She dances," said Ratty. "She comes from some eastern country. Her dances are supposed to be those of her homeland: she was taught them by a princess."

Sunny raised his eyebrows. "I can only say that it must be hotter over there. They're not the sort of dances one could imagine a British princess teaching anyone. If they did, they would wear rather more clothes."

Winner growled, as though about to speak. He did not say anything but exchanged a glance with Elsie. To his mind, that dreadful woman was a grotesque. An image flashed into his brain: the Angel of Death sucking men's souls out of their bodies. "Completely false, every stitch on her," he muttered.

"Every stitch? Not many of those," remarked Isabel. Wanting to enlarge her experience of the stage beyond that of the Godalming Theatre and infrequent trips to the West End, she asked innocently: "Can we go afterwards?"

"Very difficult to get tickets, I should think," replied Sunny quickly. He coughed. "Besides, you wouldn't want to."

"Why wouldn't we?" asked Elsie indignantly. "Please don't stand in the way of our education, Captain. We would love to go, wouldn't we, Miss Hinchcliff?" Isabel frowned at the familiarity.

"I couldn't possibly," Sunny blustered. "You see, her costume, when she's dancing, is — how would you put it, Ratty?"

"There isn't one."

"Ahem, no. She is in fact naked."

"We're nurses," Elsie reminded him. "We have to get used to seeing the human body in all sorts of conditions."

Sunny glanced, despite himself, at the lustrous exotic, who, despite an almost vanishingly thin waist, seemed to extend — undulate might be a better word — over a bigger area than that usually allotted to a single individual. She was like an eel that will not stay in the basket. "I really don't think we'll get tickets," he said firmly.

"Good," said Isabel. "I have decided against."

There was a clicking of heels next to the table, and Winner looked up to see a Serbian officer. He was a young man, rather wild as to his hair, with a downy moustache and wire-framed spectacles; he might have been a poet or a composer. But his eyes belied his youth; they looked weary, with the deep exhaustion of someone who has spent years living in tents — fighting, moving on, bivouacking in ravines, retreating over mountains. He wore a uniform of horizon blue. Winner had a sudden desire to capture the wistfulness that was about him in paint. "Captain Petrović," exclaimed Isabel. "What brings you here? I thought you were on the front."

"I am organising some munitions. I go back tonight. Meanwhile, I come here to remind myself of the life that, for my country, has disappeared forever. We danced when I was a student in Belgrade. Now Serbia is a land of ghosts. We have to recapture it for the living." He smiled sadly. "How dull I'm being. All this talk of the war."

"What else would you talk about?" asked Elsie.

"Anything you like," said Ratty. "Let's stay amused, if we can."

"I'm sorry for you," pronounced the Serb gravely. "You don't know why you're here. We, on the other hand, do know why we're fighting. It's a sacred duty. Our land. Our families. Our history. Many of us have died in the effort to preserve them, and many more will. Till perhaps there are no more of us left."

Winner peered intently across the room. "I would paint that woman as Salome." There was no need for him to say which woman he had in mind.

"She has fascinated Manure at any rate, although he wouldn't make a good Herod," replied Sunny.

Ratty noticed that a new figure had joined Lola di Bonza's group. "I'm not sure about the Austrian next to him."

"The tall one, dressed like a band master? He has Herod's face."

"Why is an Austrian talking to a French general?" asked Isabel.

"The magnetic attraction of our Salome, I should say," explained Sunny lightly. "He's entitled to be in Salonika, the same as anyone else. Only I wish he wouldn't come to Molho's. He has a bad reputation. You know what the Austrians have been doing to civilians in Captain Petrović's country. Isn't that right, Petrović?"

Petrović, though, had already left the table. A slight young man, he was crossing the crowded room purposefully towards the Austrian.

"What's he saying to him?" wondered Isabel.

"Captain Petrović's as black a kettle," observed Elsie.

"The Serb army had a terrible time on their retreat through Albania," Sunny told her. "There won't be many men to go back to Serbia, assuming that Serbia still exists at the end of the war."

"But those men who do return," flamed Isabel, "will be . . . ," she searched for an adjective, "fine."

Winner was not sure they would be very different from other men. Often it was the finest who died.

"Look, they're going outside," noticed Isabel.

"I feared the argument was becoming *ad hominem*."

"A duel? But it's the twentieth century."

Ratty stood up. "I suggest we follow them. It should be as good as anything at the White Tower."

They left the table. "I say that Captain Petrović is fine," asserted Isabel, warmly.

Outside the men were arguing noisily. "I wish I had better German," said Isabel. "The only words I know come from opera."

Sunny thought it could turn into an opera very soon.

Petrović had a revolver at his hip, the Austrian wore a ceremonial sword. Although Ménière and his entourage were attempting to restrain the protagonists, the fiery argument seemed to be on the point of erupting into personal violence. It was, to the French, an absurd situation. Representatives of opposing nations fought each other on the battlefield, not on the streets. It was ridiculous that the two sides should ever meet, but that was Salonika: a ridiculous place. It could not be helped. One had to get on with it as best one could.

One of the Molho brothers strode out of the door, immaculate in evening dress and glossy hair — too immaculate to Winner's eye. The Molho's had acquired, in the short period of the café's prosperity, a habit of command. They were essential to the well-being of the officer cadre. Walking between the protagonists, he threw out his hands, palms outwards. Jewelled rings glittered on his fingers. "Gentlemen, what are you thinking of? This is Molho's."

The Austrian, accepting that to scuffle with a Serb would compromise the dignity of his resplendent uniform, spun about and re-entered the café. Isabel watched Captain Petrović stride purposefully away into the night.

Eight

Next afternoon the commander's luck changed. The pristine cartridge-paper sky became sullied with a charcoal smudge.

He ordered the submarine to dive. Underwater it was immobile, but lined up on the target, which he now fixed in his periscope. He knew he could not be spotted in the failing light. The kill would be almost too easy. The ship looked majestic against the declining sun, a splendid, sleek lion moving across its element with a grace that seemed effortless, but was an expression of great power. He, though, was the big game hunter. He ordered number three torpedo to be released.

On the deck of Her Majesty's Troopship *Marquette*, a nurse looked intently across the Bay towards Salonika. It had just come into view. She was pleased to be getting there early. The nun-like Red Cross ship, painted entirely white except for the huge scarlet cross, on which she ought to have travelled had been delayed; paperwork not ready, she had heard.

It was a glorious evening, too hot to be below decks. The movement of the ship made enough breeze to flutter the pennants on the masts and cool the skin of the nurses, unaccustomed to the fierce sun. She gazed into the immensity of the sea, and remembered her Keats:

> The moving waters at their priest-like task
> Of pure ablution round earth's human shores . . .

As she looked into the depths, she saw the shadow of a shape, the size of a big fish but regular, black, following an undeviating course . . .

The torpedo struck amidships. The crew scrambled to launch the lifeboats. As the ship listed, one lifeboat fell directly on top of another, crushing some of the women in the first one. Another lifeboat began to sink as soon as it hit the water. From the U-boat, the commander could see the *Marquette*'s gun, silhouetted clearly against the sunset. He had to be careful of it. Its crew might, fanatically, still be at their station. He considered moving into the dead ground which the gun could not hit, in order to deliver a coup de grace with his own guns; it would have been almost an act of mercy, to finish off a wounded beast.

It was not necessary. The *Marquette* was not only carrying a cargo of grain, a quantity of vehicles and animals, and a fully equipped field hospital, but the twenty-two officers and five hundred and eighty-eight other ranks of the 29th Division Ammunition Column. The explosion was so spectacular that the U-boat commander regretted that he was the only person to get a good view of it.

The remnant of the *Marquette*'s shattered hull reared up and seemed to vibrate in a death spasm. Within a few minutes, it had disappeared. A couple of lifeboats could be seen flailing, in their attempt to hoist sails and rescue such few survivors as there were, amid the oil and wreckage.

The commander thought of his children in Pula. They would be hungry if this war went on. Each time a ship was sunk, the British, who thought they ruled the waves, came a little closer to being hungry too. That was good. The U-boat surfaced. It had nothing to fear, but fuel was low. It slunk away from what had become the grave of the *Marquette*, towards a rendezvous on the coast.

Nine

The wooden portico was shaded by giant eaves. Some tiles had fallen from the roof and a slogan in Greek letters had been daubed on the cracked and peeling walls.

"I apologise for bringing you here. I see already it was a mistake," sighed Gazmend Effendi as he ushered them in. He was wearing a white linen suit, cut large, the brightness of which made his hair and beard seem all the more like a raven's wing. A spotted handkerchief was tucked into the breast pocket. On his head was a red fez. "I should have taken you to the Fortress of the Seven Towers: unfortunately it has been turned into a prison, thereby reversing its original role of keeping undesirables out of the city by locking them up inside. The other monuments of the city are, so to speak, jewels scattered amid the ruin and detritus of the old town; the noise and stink would have been too much on a hot day. We have an interesting *hamam*, the Baths of Paradise, which offers peace for an hour or two. But not for mixed company."

"This spot is certainly quiet," observed Isabel.

Winner laughed. "Graveyards are."

Between the grey tombs, some of their tops carved with turbans, grew an unkempt tangle of cornflowers, dandelions and tall grasses. "Couldn't somebody mow the lawn?" wondered Isabel.

Gazmend chuckled. "This is not the British Empire, Miss Hinchcliff. Even if the people of this benighted city believed in the virtues of order and tidiness, they would be nobody to put them into practice. Alas, there is only one dervish left in the monastery and he is old."

Winner wandered to a low wall and took his sketchbook out of his pocket. His presence disturbed a robed figure who appeared to have been asleep in the shade of a tomb. He walked slowly off, adjusting a pair of pebbleglass spectacles — obviously of the modern world — that contrasted with the ancient dignity of his turban. With a few deft strokes of the charcoal, Winner sketched him.

Gazmend led Isabel, Elsie and Sunny towards some buildings. "Once," he told them, "centuries ago, an important man, who was exiled from Constantinople, took a stroll here and fell into conversation with a hermit, who happened to be living in the branches of a large tree. The hermit very tactfully prophesied that the man — Ahmed Pasha was his name — would return to power. When the Pasha did so, he endowed a *tekke* — a monastery as you would call it. Alas, the dervishes have drifted away. The cemetery has even been defaced. This has all happened since 1913. But on the whole, it still provides a satisfactory refuge from the city. One can breathe."

"Not everybody breathes," observed Sunny.

"No, not the dead," accepted Gazmend.

Isabel paused to inspect a disused fountain. A lizard ran across the dry basin. "Salonika is a medieval city," she ventured, thinking, perhaps, of the drains.

"Medieval!" cried Gazmend Effendi, raising his hands in a show of incredulity. "My dear lady, far older than that. Haven't you seen the Arch of Galerius?

Galerius was a Roman Emperor. He had a palace here. The city already had five or six centuries under its belt even then. Then came Byzantium. The Ottomans are newcomers, conquering in 1430. Are! I should have said were. Now they've gone, for the present at least. Oh, Salonika is old. And naturally, like everything old," he added, "it has grown to be rather disgusting, like a dog with bad teeth and fleas."

"When our steamer came into the bay, I thought Salonika looked beautiful."

"Yes, of course. That's the right distance to see it from, with a sea breeze blowing. I know what you're thinking of: the golden crescents — *alems* — on top of the minarets, the domes of gilded lead, the winding streets, the libraries even, when you get to know the place better. But we cram into those wooden houses, and live on top of each other. That's why they knocked down the city walls. They were like a corset, squeezing the bowels of the city into a circumference it should long have outgrown. Only, like the feet of a poor Chinese lady, the old town cannot expand to a reasonable size, simply because the restraint has been removed. The streets are perfectly intolerable — unless, perhaps, to someone like our artist friend who paints watercolours and likes to see people in strange hats and robes. I wear my fez specially for him."

"Do you live in the old city?"

"With all the howl of the wild dogs at night? I'd never sleep. A few decent villas exist on the outskirts, and I occupy one of them. We have large families, you know. Many children, several wives. Before you ask about the latter, I can tell you that I have four. That's the maximum; my allocation has been used up. A pity, because, as a prudent man, I would prefer to keep a place vacant. One never knows when a good wife will come along. They are, though, an expensive luxury, like keeping a stable of horses."

"You can't say they're like horses," Isabel expostulated.

"Not as expensive as that," agreed Gazmend, "but bad enough, I can assure you. My youngest wife is the worst, but then she is also the most beautiful." He sighed. "What can one do?"

"I have no wife at all," remarked Sunny. The image of a red brick villa on the edge of a Warwickshire village, geographically in the dead centre of England, flickered into his mind; he had bachelor rooms there, near the bicycle works.

"Bring the woman that you would like to be your wife here, and I promise you that the effect will be instantaneous."

Sunny turned to Isabel. "What do you think of the view? Enough to make a lady submit to the pleas of her lover — and agree to marry him?"

"Not this lady," declared Isabel firmly.

Gazmend Effendi waged a finger in correction. "It isn't the view that has the power, my dear guests. It is the proximity of death. There are so many ways to die in Salonika. Remembering mortality quickens desire. We have only so much time left. Not enough!" Gazmend winked at Sunny. "Don't you find that, Captain?"

Sunny did not like being winked at by foreigners. "Soldiers sometimes feel that they have more than enough time in Macedonia. Too much in fact."

"Yes, indeed," said Isabel briskly. "We ought to be back at the hospital."

Gazmend assumed an air of concern. "I must detain you no longer."

"You aren't detaining us. We can't go. We need petrol."

Gazmend considered. "Petroleum is a scarce commodity. It can generally be obtained somewhere — most human wants can be satisfied in Salonika, if you know where to go — but the price is already high. It will go higher. People will make big profits from petroleum. While running," he concluded, "certain dangers."

"Who has the petrol?"

"That," replied Gazmend smiling "is one of the mysteries of Salonika. Would you like me to help you find some?"

Before Isabel could answer, Winner rejoined them. He found the city too unsettling to sketch. "I can't understand this place," he said abruptly. "It feels so ambiguous. What are its loyalties?"

"Let me explain it. The Greeks — if royalist — support Germany. There are Republican Greeks . . . but we don't talk about them since Mr Venizelos was sacked. The Turks, those who are left — you know, thousands departed after 1913 — support the Sultan. The Jews send their children off to trade in Vienna, Budapest, Prague — their sympathies are with the

Central Powers. Only not everybody belongs to those simple classifications. Edges are always blurred in the Balkans. You can be a Moslem, without being a Turk."

Sunny scratched his ear with the stem of his unlit pipe. "So, in short, nobody wants us here."

"On the contrary, Salonika couldn't be more pleased to have you. This is a city of dealers, traders, merchants. Look at how much the armies are spending. Salonika would like you to be here forever."

At that moment, the sound of a distant but immense explosion rumbled across the waters of the Gulf. They looked out to sea. A dark plume stained the perfect blue of the late afternoon sky. The smoke was rising fast. At the bottom of it was a ship. They watched as, with terrible speed, one end of it slipped below the surface of the water. Then the hull rotated about its axis, as though in a toy theatre. "That ship!" exclaimed Winner in amazement. "It's sinking." The bow rose out of the water and approached nearer and nearer to the vertical. It then disappeared from view.

The horror of it held them stupefied.

"It happened so quickly," said Elsie. "Before our eyes." The disaster had taken little more than ten minutes.

"Allah bless the souls of the people on that ship," murmured Gazmend.

"Some people would have been saved, though?" stammered Elsie. The shock had made her lose control of her voice.

Sunny looked grim. "I hope they could launch the lifeboats. I see a sail, but only one." A shroud of smoke from the explosion hung where the ship had been. Other ships in the Gulf were turning course and making their way to the spot to look for survivors.

"I can't believe that it should have happened like that. Right in front of us," cried Isabel. "As though we were the audience — helplessly watching. Helplessly." She burst into tears.

"We are all helpless," said Gazmend, "in the hand of God."

Elsie spoke slowly as though the explosion had physically winded her. "Which ship was that?"

"Even I do not know that," replied Gazmend gently. "Ship movements are kept very secret. All I can say," he added softly, "is that with every ship that is sunk, prices rise. Yes, Salonika is happy for your armies to stay."

The Myrrh of St Demetrius

Ten

Not all Salonika had seen the catastrophe but all Salonika had heard of it. It was Friday evening: the start of the Sabbath, when most of the shops closed and the city became glum. People usually spent the Sabbath indoors. On this Friday evening, groups congregated on the streets to share their news, their opinions and their horror. Molho's remained open; it always did. Sunny urged Isabel, Elsie and Winner to go there. What else was there to do? Isabel, however, resisted. She could not bring herself to frequent a resort of pleasure when her mind had become focused on a single, obsessive thought — the tragedy that they had witnessed that afternoon. Was Gwendolyn on that ship?

Light was falling as they walked past a decayed Roman arch, the sides of which were covered in marble reliefs of battling horsemen. "You may be mistaken," Sunny had tried to reassure her. He received no reply. She had a lace trimmed handkerchief in her hand.

That morning, Sunny had himself become a horseman. Or rather, he had reverted to a previous horse-owning state. After the usual amount of haggling, he had succeeded in wresting Storm, whom he believed to be a paragon among equines, from a cavalry officer in need of forty pounds to settle debts. There seemed to be little point in having command of a staff car in a land without the fuel to run it on, and to a one who loved horses, the old ways had a romance far beyond the glamour and novelty of motors. Now the memory of this triumphant purchase had been superseded by

99

the horror of watching a ship sink. Even he was subdued.

"A bell is tolling," observed Winner. It reminded him of the funeral bell at his Essex village.

The street filled with a gaggle of local people, one of whom, a shopkeeper by the look of him, carried a cross. Winner was fascinated by the long-bearded priests. They wore black headdresses and long robes. One swung a censer so vigorously that a flame leapt out of it; incense rose in perfumed clouds. Another priest carried, raised high, a large picture. "St Demetrius," remarked Winner, who had studied the local iconography. "His bones are said to gush with myrrh. You can see the grooves on the side of his sarcophagus."

The priests chanted, their voices deep and resonant.

"What are they doing with St Demetrius now?" asked Elsie.

"He's the protector of the city. A warrior saint."

The procession shuffled past, until only a few stragglers were left. A mild commotion was caused when a corporal from the RFC cannoned into one of them. "Extremely sorry, sir. Wasn't watching the road, sir. I was looking for somebody, sir." It was unlikely that the elderly gentleman who had been knocked into the gutter understood the apology. Corporal Bayley was still saluting when the old man was put back on his feet to resume the ceremony, leaning on the arm of a friend.

"Bayley," exclaimed Sunny, recognising him. "Good heavens, man, have you been in a fight?" One side of his broad, drayman's face was badly grazed.

"Not a fight, sir. I was running, sir. Fell over. I was that keen to find you, sir."

"Well, what do you want?"

"Excusing the lady, sir, the kite balloon was brought down again, sir. Lieutenant Wren has been killed, sir." Sunny groaned. Bayley paused for effect. "He died quickly, sir; that's the one mercy of it. He fell from thousands of feet up, straight down on the hard earth. Dead as a nail." He paused. "It was awful to see him, sir. Landed on his feet, sir, so his hips were pushed out of his shoulders."

"Thank you," said Sunny. "No need to go on. Earwig again."

"Earwig?" Isabel could not see how earwigs could bring down a balloon.

"Von Earwig, the German ace," Sunny explained. He turned to Bayley: "Why no parachute?"

"Lieutenant Sandys inspected the body, sir. Thought he'd been shot in the neck before he could hook up, sir."

Every chivalric fibre in Sunny's being was offended. "That's an outrage!" he exclaimed. Gentlemen of the air did not intentionally kill other gentlemen of the air, certainly not when they were observers in balloon baskets — the equivalent of sitting birds which no sportsman would consider fair game. He turned to Isabel. "I'll have to go back," he said grimly.

"Let us return with you."

"I can't. I'll be on a horse."

It was now dark. As they spoke, the street, which had been empty a moment before, began to fill again. For a moment, they thought it was another religious procession. But the crowd was more agitated than the gloom-filled followers of St Demetrius had been. The number of people quickly grew. It was as though the street was indeed an opera stage and the chorus had come on. But it was for a different production. They were of all ages. They were hurrying, sometimes running. As they charged onwards, they cast backward glances, so that some of them stumbled or bumped into each other. They were fleeing something. It appeared to be in the sky.

All that Winner could see was the beam of a searchlight, not searching the sky but fixed, presumably on some object that was out of sight. Guns were firing — he knew the sound, they were Archibalds. Then for a moment a huge silver shape filled the air above the houses, as it moved slowly but purposefully forward. It filled their view, vast and from beyond this world, like a portent.

There were screams from the crowd. It was bigger now, as though the whole of Salonika had turned out onto the street. "Zeppelin," cried somebody. An old woman with a stick hurried past them with an uneven gait. She was followed by a group of men, one of them in his nightshirt. They were running. "They're in fear of their lives," said Isabel, startled.

Winner, Sunny and the nurses moved with the crowd. "Might as well go down to the harbour and see the thing," shouted Sunny. He and Isabel reached the harbour just as the Zeppelin passed over the White Tower. There was an explosion. "It's dropping bombs."

The crowd shrieked and began to stampede. It surged back to where Winner was still hobbling with Elsie. It was impossible for Winner to keep his place against such a human tide, and he found himself in reverse motion too. He was worried someone would tread on his damaged foot. "Here," he called, and seized Elsie's hand. "We must stay together." Never before had Winner been part of such a flux of people. It was like the end of a football match, when the terraces emptied and a packed mass of people shuffled out of the ground. Only these people were not shuffling but running.

"Up here." Elsie had to shout to make herself heard. With Elsie sheltering him, they detached themselves from the road leading down to the White Tower and took a path leading up to the cliff. They could hear the guns of the ships firing. "Miss Hinchcliff was right; they were running for their lives."

"They were. Stupid lot, aren't they? They would have been better to stay at home."

"But the bombs?"

"Only a few. I think the airmen wanted the ships, not the town."

"Doesn't seem as though they've hit either. Look."

Somewhere beyond the inky blackness of the harbour, a sheet of light was illuminating the sky.

"It's on the marshes," said Elsie.

"They must have shot it down."

They found their way, more calmly now, along the clifftop. The framework of the great airship could be seen clearly silhouetted against the fire. It looked like the skeleton of a whale.

"Where are Sunny and Miss Hinchcliff?" asked Winner.

"Don't know." She had not intended to escape Isabel but was not sorry to have done so. Isabel was nice enough, in an older-sisterly kind of way; but she belonged to the employing class, and they never let you have a moment to yourself.

"Should we find them?"

"Let's watch the airship burn. What a sight. I call it," she said, in imitation of someone else, "fine."

They were still holding hands.

"It's wild up here. I used to walk on the cliffs when the hospital arrived in Salonika. This was where they put us up."

"I shall make a painting of the conflagration. It's like the fire of hell."

"Strange, on this warm night. Look at the stars. They're bright here."

"There are so many strange things about this War. Everything is confused. People are muddled up here, all the nations together. And if it weren't for their governments, they would get along well enough."

"Is it hopeless?" Elsie looked for certainty. It was a quality she identified in Winner. Winner, uncertain in his relations with people, although completely absorbed in his art, might have been surprised if he had known this. He saw in her the boldness that he lacked.

"We must hold onto each other."

"Yes."

"Death has passed over us."

She did not say anything.

"Shall we go back to the harbour?"

"Not yet. There's a hut here. You can kiss me if you like."

Winner did like.

"Stop now, please. I want to concentrate on the night. On us. On being together. It's a moment that won't last."

"We must make it last forever."

"No moment does that."

"I have something to give you," said Winner. From his pocket he took out a pebble. It was purple. It had been polished by the sea. Through it ran a stream of gold.

"That's beautiful."

"Just one of thousands of pebbles. Millions."

"It's our pebble. You see things that other people don't. You can kiss me again now."

They stayed in the hut, whispering to each other, as the dogs barked, and hushing when the feet of the sentries could be heard crunching past. The moment lasted as long as the night.

Eleven

That night the dentist could not sleep. The air was hot, and he was not alone in the room. He had tried everything he could think of to combat the bugs. They seemed to disappear into the plasterwork of the walls, to be exhaled again after he had extinguished his lamp. Organic was the best word for the houses of Salonika. Their wooden shapes resembled some of the wrinkled, shapeless ancients, in their sack-like clothes, who sat on their steps: sagging, prolapsed, unable to hold themselves upright, bowed where they had once been straight. In the stillness of the night one could hear these dwellings groan, as though complaining at the indignities that long life had heaped upon them. They creaked as one walked up the stairs. And they were alive.

The camp bed — he had instructed the people from whom he rented the rooms to remove the old bed and bedding that had been there originally — smelled strongly of camphor. He had stitched lumps of it into the bedclothes — balls of naphthalene too, whatever the risk of anaemia. He might have been locked into an old lady's wardrobe. The sheets had been liberally dusted with Keating's powder, "quite harmless to animals but unrivalled in destroying FLEAS, BUGS, BEETLES, COCKROACHES & MOTHS." No claim was made for its destructive power over lice and mosquitoes, which was just as well, because they certainly were not killed. Over his bed was a mosquito net. Its iron supports had been rubbed with paraffin. He had taken the camp bed to a hospital laboratory and had it sterilised in the hot-air oven. He had steamed the bedding. But still the bugs came. Each night he slept with an electric torch under his pillow. He would switch on the beam and stab the larger of the unwanted guests with a hypodermic needle.

He lay in bed, listening. Salonika nights were never silent. The barks of the guard dogs, coming from different points of the compass, created a polyphonal effect, teasing Ivory's spatial imagination. Donkeys brayed. Cats fought. A sentry in heavy boots marched in the square. These discordant noises had become almost homely by their familiarity. The last guests to depart from a party in the local Socialist Club were talking and singing. The Greek songs sounded unpleasantly like the drone of a bagpipe. Their stopped, but not to go away. "Johnny, you like our singing?" they called out.

"Rotten," replied a gruff voice.

"What that, Johnny? You say nice?"

Soon there would be the cockerels, then the call to prayer.

Ivory fought his way out of the mosquito net. He opened the shutters. The air was still warm, but cooler than the interior of his room. Moonlight streamed in. At last the roisterers were going home. Too late, he thought bitterly. He was up now. He could go back to bed, but would he sleep? He thought not.

Only that afternoon Major Eglinton had come to him. As he clutched the arms of the wooden dentist's chair, waiting for Ivory to probe his mouth, words came in an almost hysterical rush. At the front — Eggie had just been there — a raiding party captured three Bulgarian soldiers. Waiting to be questioned properly or sent down the line, an officer's assistant who was a Serb had battered each of them on the head with a club. Barbarism. Eggie, though, seemed to approve.

Funny how even the toughest campaigners could fear having their teeth seen to. The sound of the drill made them blanch, even faint sometimes. Eggie was as dry as a walnut shell. The king of the Dug Outs, they called him. Dug out of retirement. He had fought in the Boer War, fifteen years ago. Fiercely, if you listened to him. Yet he was one of the worst when it came to The Chair. Fortunately, Ivory had the techniques of modern anaesthetics at his command. He could be given gas.

There had been no gas in this stinking, medieval town of Salonika, with its vermin-infested dwellings and human depravity — bugs and buggery — until Ivory brought it. He carried the lamp of science. It would shine in the moral darkness. The creatures of the night would scatter at its approach. One source of suffering would be removed from the world.

They used gas in the trenches. Men died coughing and frothing. That was bad gas. There was also good gas, and he was the lord of it.

Teeth. They are part of the human condition. You cannot eat a morsel of toast without them, unless you soak it in tea. Yet for eons of human existence people left their teeth to rot. They barely bothered to clean their teeth with a twig or a bit of leaf. The Mona Lisa could only smile: a laugh would have revealed blackened stumps.

Nowadays, you could even take X-ray photographs. Professor Jeneau of the Sorbonne, the great expert in the subject, was at the French Hospital. They used to use glass plates. There was now a substitute called film. Altogether preferable. Flexible. Better in the mouth.

The way of the future. Ivory had a dark room in this very house. It made sense to go there now. The gentle moon could be kept out more easily than the sun.

Ivory flicked on his electric torch and shuffled in nightgown and slippers to the room from which all external light was excluded. The floorboards creaked. He slapped his neck. A mosquito died.

Twelve

Winner did not sleep either. Dawn had been breaking as he returned to his room, and the other soldiers with whom he shared it had been up long ago. Few people had rooms to themselves in Salonika. You were lucky to get a bed; a length of floor in a passageway was the lot of many. This one was as bare as a monk's cell. On entering, he had simply thrown himself onto the iron-framed bed and gone to sleep. The morning was well advanced when he woke. The others had flung open the shutters but still he slept. For some hours, sunshine had been streaming in through the thin curtain. It had given him a headache. But he was happy.

It did not take him long to remember why he was happy. He loved Elsie. He had spent the night in a hut with her, and he had done that with nobody else before. It was as good as being married. Did he want to be married? He had not thought much about it before, for the simple reason that it had seemed impossible. Who would love him? His parents obviously. Otherwise no independently motivated being in the universe had found him significant, except the dog he had owned as a boy. There were the models in the life class, some of whom could be persuaded to perform favours for money, but that was a financial transaction and did not count. Not that he had been bold enough to secure one of them: he did not spend money that way. That was another reason for not marrying. As his father would have said, he had not made his way in the world. He could not afford it.

But there was the New Testament. Love one another, as I have loved you. Love is not only a happy state, but a good one. Love in all its forms. That surely included the act of procreation, the ecstasy that unites man, if not always woman, with the Creator God — love, all-consuming love. It went with marriage. Whether it came before or after the marriage ceremony — or if there were no ceremony at all — hardly mattered. Winner barely thought about it; he did not need to. He was certain that they were one and the same.

This was the river along which the little barque, containing Winner and Elsie, was sailing. It would carry them out into the great ocean of life, together.

She had chosen him. He had chosen her. Admittedly without much forethought. The moment had offered itself. He had seen the way that God had opened up for him. Unless he had danced down the road of temptation instead. No. He would follow Elsie's lead. She had made her way in the world. It had been a hard way, and made her more knowing than him. At all events, the moment had happened. It was fact. His being thrilled to the sounds of morning.

Winner ran into the street and got himself shaved. He closed his eyes, pleased that he did not have to make the effort of conversation with the Jewish barber, who spoke only his own tongue. He would begin a painting. He would find someone who could make a big canvas. He had some studies already. He would make more. He would find a child and give him a bow and arrow, because Cupid would be there too.

Mentally he almost skipped down the road; his actual progress was impeded by his bad foot. Feeling his freshly smooth chin, he passed the church of St Demetrius. Demetrius had been a lover, as well as a soldier, before becoming a saint.

The night had been clear; they had looked out of the door of the hut and seen the stars. But haze veiled the morning sun. Even a short walk felt oppressive. His left leg dragged.

He was now at the church of St George, an ancient rotunda. Next to it was the triumphal arch raised by the Emperor Galerius, the very ruler whose men had killed St Demetrius.

Winner now regretted that he had not taken a tram, or hitched a lift from one of the lorries. Crossing the *Champ de Mars*, as the French, with their gift for phrase-making, called it — a parade ground even stonier than the one of the same name in Paris — was an ordeal. He was limping badly as he entered the tent city.

Elsie and Isabel had put up at one of the hospitals in the Birdcage, whose nurses' quarters were made out of a disused factory building. A guard on the door stopped him as he approached. "Can't let you in there, sir. No men allowed, sir." Winner thought the man leered at him.

It took some time for Winner to waylay a nurse going into the building who could ask after Elsie. She was a Scottish girl, with the fresh colouring of the Highlands. It was some time before she re-emerged to say that Elsie was not inside. She and Isabel had signed out earlier. No word had been left for Winner — none, at least, that could be found.

Disappointment was accompanied by a desire for action; but what action? As they had left him no message, it might be that they were coming back. He would wait. He did not want to do so under the sceptical eye of the guard. He drifted back towards the main hospital enclosure. It occurred to him that there would be a transport officer who could at least direct him to the Ford. "Two nurses, one fair and one dark? They've gone," that official told Winner. "Don't ask me where. I just know that their vehicle ain't here. What do you mean it's impossible? It's utterly possible. Oh I see the way it is." Winner could not bear to be joshed. He turned on his heel.

Why were they leaving today? Perhaps she had assumed that he would know. That was it, he did know. They must have gone to the quartermaster's compound. He would make his way there, somehow. But it was strange, all the same. A little dark cloud of foreboding entered his previously sunny consciousness. He thumbed for a lift.

When Winner found him, the quartermaster was immersed in ledgers and requisition forms.

"You again?" the Otter said, looking up. He yawned. "I've been at this since dawn." He aligned his pencil with the others on the desk and put the sharpener beside them. He could undulge this *farouche*-looking lieutenant for a moment or two; it was time for a break.

"It is an endless task," he said testily. "Look how much comes in. But do my storehouses and barns increase? No. It's like an ever-moving stream — supplies flow out as fast as they come in. Every atom of it accounted for. People think I've got an always-growing mountain of stuff. But there's nothing growing here, except my garden. Would you like to see it?"

Abruptly, Winner declined the pleasure. He explained why he had come.

The Otter frowned, keeping Winner in suspense. The man was an artist; he ought to have enjoyed the garden, instead of spurning it. Eventually he addressed Winner's concern. "The nurses? They may be here." He called an orderly. "Has the BWH collected the broken crates that we set aside for it? Find out then, would you?"

As they waited for the orderly's return, the Otter filled the conversational void: "I saw a nurse yesterday, a Canadian one. I had gone to the Ordnance to buy socks. I don't know what happened to mine. Socks are an eternal mystery."

Winner suppressed a gesture of impatience. This was not the time for socks.

The Otter smiled, as though to an appreciative audience. "I had only one and that was a quarter of its proper size. The nurse was buying a pair of braces and seemed to require the combined efforts of five staff to serve her. Really too funny. Ah," he said, addressing the orderly. "You have news?"

Isabel and Elsie had come early that morning. The wood, a mountain of it, had been loaded onto the Ford and they had left some hours ago.

"I'm sorry you missed them. Is there anything I can do? No? Do have one of these pastilles."

Winner absent-mindedly accepted one of the delicate sweetmeats from the quartermaster's box.

They had gone. Elsie had gone. What did it mean?

The Otter was continuing sociably. "While you're here, I could show you my little domain. A game of tennis, perhaps? The court is behind the latrine screens. We had a number of them spare and it seemed a good use. Some visitors do of course wonder why we have so many screens, assuming them to serve their original purpose; can't understand why we'd need such an imposing facility. I would like to have climbing plants. What a dream that would be. Nobody seems to have heard of flowers before in these parts. You've no idea the trouble one has in getting seeds."

Winner heard little of what he said. The euphoria that he had felt when he awoke that morning seemed now to be a mist, burnt up by the midday sun to reveal

114

the landscape of uncertainty and desolation that lay behind it.

"Finally, my sister sent some from home; they arrived yesterday." The Otter was unaware of having lost his audience. "I am hopeful that we shall soon be floriferous. *Molto bello.* I get the men to dig up the old horse lines for soil; so my little ones should grow quickly. Lovely institution for gardening, the army. I have three orderlies to do all the work while I order them about."

Winner stammered his apologies. Only a brief hour or two before, he had half feared the hectic course that his emotional life had taken, and the headlong, possibly premature fall into a state of lifelong commitment. Part of him had wished Elsie away. Now, violently, all of him wanted her back.

He had heard the Otter talking, without listening to what he said. "No tennis, thank you." He saluted. "I'll see myself out, sir. What an enormous latrine you have here."

The man was clearly, in the Otter's eyes, a little touched. "There is a postal service, you know."

"So there is, sir," exclaimed Winner ecstatically. "I hadn't thought of that."

"They've gone back to the hospital. What of it? See if writing a letter works." His tone was patronising. Winner, prickly under other circumstances, was merely flooded with gratitude. "If not, I'll see about getting you upcountry. It's not likely to be comfortable. Mind you, I expect something in exchange, young man."

"What?"

"Seeds."

His manner then changed without warning, as he remembered his administrative burden. There was no time to chat with lieutenants. "Now, if you'll excuse me, I really must get back to my desk."

An Unpleasantness and its
Consequences

Thirteen

Two days later Winner was holding tight to the banister at the *Cercle des Etrangers*. One step at a time, he mounted the staircase. It caused him some pain; the cast had rasped the skin off his leg. But he had given the club as the return address for his letter to Elsie. There had, he thought, been more than enough time for a reply.

It was after lunch. In the coffee room, General Ménière nosed a balloon glass of post-prandial brandy. Winner returned his salute. He also saluted Major Eglinton, who was reviving his constitution after the morning's toils in hot, dusty Salonika with a little Seltzer water. "We don't salute in clubs," the latter snapped.

Winner looked at him blankly. "How long does it take the post from Salonika to reach the Vardar?" he asked. Winner could only have one thing on his mind at a time.

"Have you reported to your commanding officer?" returned Eggie.

"I don't know where he is."

"He's back. I suggest you find him."

"Do you know when the letters arrive? I'm waiting for one."

"We're all waiting. We've got a job to do — fight the Bulgar. But we're waiting to get at him." To be marooned on this forgotten front of the War, in the morally offensive town of Salonika, was difficult for Eggie to bear. He could see, when he visited the front, that an all-out attack on the Bulgarians' mountain positions would be suicidal; but rather that than more festering in this sink. He assumed that most right-thinking men felt the same. "The question is, Manure, how do we keep the men fresh?"

"We are studying the same problem," acknowledged the Frenchman. "All men share the same needs."

"We thought horses might do it," pronounced Eggie.

"Horses?" Winner saw Ménière's face become a study of ironic surprise.

"Oh yes. Dukes and dustmen go to the Derby. We would have to decide how to handle the betting."

"There must be some soldiers in the ranks who used to be bookmakers — a word, incidentally, that we French have borrowed from your language."

"Good Lord, I don't mean to lay it on. We want to be sure it doesn't take place. Imagine the fights."

Winner struggled to his feet. "I heard the door. That may be the post now."

An unearthly noise wafted from the stairs. Winner recognised it as the sound of an ocarina. He collapsed back into his chair. As Sunny appeared through the door Winner cried: "You've come from upcountry, I don't suppose you've brought any letters?" Sunny confessed that he hadn't.

The conversation resumed. Sunny agreed that bored men get restless. "What they want are shows."

The Major winced. "Shows! Where I come from they're banned by the kirk."

"Frenchmen," said the General, "need women."

Sunny reassured him on that score. "Shakespeare managed the difficulty, so do we."

The General looked puzzled. "Bints," added Sunny by way of gloss.

Ménière's mastery of Tommy slang was as limited as his knowledge of the Elizabethan stage. "Very good," he murmured, sniffing his brandy. He then leant over to Eglinton and gave his elbow a shake. Startled, Eggie spilt his Seltzer water over the knee of his jodhpurs. "I like your shows. But doing is always better than looking, don't you think, Major. Eh, eh?"

"I wrote yesterday," Winner told Sunny.

The latter shrugged. "The letter might have arrived by now. Or it could get there next week, or," he filled his pipe, "never."

The General pursued his theme. "So we have arranged a service for our men. You probably know that there are some houses around the railway station which soldiers frequent? They get girls there. We have investigated the matter. They number more than a hundred."

Eggie pursed his Scottish lips. "Yes, it's a disgrace."

Suavely Ménière accepted the point. "There I agree with you. It is a disgrace that the men should expose themselves to the risk of disease in this way. The brothels lack the most basic hygiene precautions."

"They should have been closed down long ago."

"Yes. There are enough dangers to our soldiers from malaria, dysentery and the rest, without having to add syphillis to that number."

"The French disease? The British army regards it as a self-inflicted wound. The men can be court martialled for it."

Ménière sipped his brandy. "That won't eliminate the problem, merely encourage soldiers not to report it until too late. A different approach is needed."

"Shoot the malefactors?" suggested Eggie.

"That would reduce our army even further. We want to look after this aspect of their welfare as well as the other. As you know, we of the French army attach particular importance to such things."

"Like your chef, general? An army marches on its stomach, eh?"

"I'm thinking of another organ. We're arranging for *maisons closes* to be brought from France.

Eggie was unfamiliar with the expression.

"*Bordels*, red lamps, brothels."

"Good grief," exploded Eggie. "I wouldn't have imagined even the French would think of that."

Ménière took it as a compliment. "Thank you. We pride ourselves on our powers of invention. All the girls will be French — volunteers of course." A gleam appeared in Ménière's lizardlike eye. "I suspect they'll have to be hard workers, but they'll get paid."

"So completely French," was all that Eggie could muster.

"Indeed," continued Ménière, "completely French. Supervised by French doctors. The whole service provided by the soldiers' fellow nationals, in a language they can understand. *Pas mal*, I think you'll agree."

Winner dragged himself to the top of the staircase and shouted down:

"Has the post come yet?" His voice reverberated around the hard empty space.

Eggie's brick-red face was turning an even more vivid colour. "Great heaven."

"It simply solves a problem," continued Ménière modestly. "But we don't want to keep this aspect of the war effort to ourselves. Our men fight shoulder to shoulder with their allies. They share, so to speak, the same bed. Why not this bed too? The brothels will be open seven days a week. I have no doubt we would be able to occupy all the available time, but, in a gesture of fraternity, we would like to consecrate one day exclusively to the British."

"You mean," Eggie almost choked, "that, every week, our men would be free to fornicate for a day?"

"Not free, Major. They would have to pay the usual rates. But yes, a day specially for them."

Eggie leapt out of his chair. The Seltzer glass flew unregarded onto the carpet. "General Manure, sir!" His tone expressed outrage.

Ménière realised that he had put a foot wrong. But which foot? "My dear Major, let's not be hasty. It was an offer made in good faith. One day is not enough? Perhaps you're right. Let's make it two days."

Across the room, Winner was anxious about his mission to find Elsie. Sunny did his best to reassure him. "Tell the Colonel that your work must be at the front. Any day, the BWH will become part of the front. There's a push on. Meanwhile, I'm looking for Ratty."

"Whatever for?"

"He's an Engineer officer. General Gay has commissioned a delicate piece of balloon work. I don't think you ever knew Jenny Wren." He paused out of respect to the dead. "Meanwhile, I shall take in a show. Will you join me?" he asked Eggie, teasingly.

The latter would have looked shocked, only he felt that there was now no depth of human nature left unplumbed.

"You'll have to one day, you know," Sunny continued.

Eggie was saved from answering by the sound of boots clicking rapidly up the marble staircase. A moment later Ivory Filler, breathless, burst into the room. "Is Simple here? I need Simple."

"Major Simon, you mean?" clarified Eggie.

"Of course I mean Simon. There's been a murder."

"Who's dead?"

"A waiter."

The officers sank back in their chairs. "A waiter? My dear Ivory, *calmez-vous*."

"At Molho's."

"Good Lord," exclaimed Sunny, "why didn't you say so? We need Simple, and quick."

Winner asked the obvious question: "Does anyone know where he is?"

Fourteen

The dead waiter was Mister Desire. He had been killed in the kitchen of the British Salonika Force's most popular café. Officers were, by turns, aghast, stupefied and pruriently fascinated — to the point that, soon, everybody was talking about it. Everybody except Winner. He took the gloomy view that it was precisely the sort of visitation that might be expected to strike so falsely glittering a fleshpot. His mind was on Elsie. He still had not heard from her. It was as though he had found a precious jewel, only to have it stolen the next day. He needed to have word of her, to see her preferably, to be told that theirs had been more than a random encounter. It was the only idea that he could entertain. He pursued it as doggedly and single-mindedly as he pursued all others.

That afternoon, Winner's purpose was fixed. He needed seeds. Seeds were the essential precursor to getting upcountry. If he could find seeds, the Otter would furnish some form of transport. Without seeds, he faced the unendurable prospect of loitering in Salonika, waiting for a letter that might or might not have been written, might or might not have been lost in the inner workings of the military postal service, might or might not have fallen victim to a hundred and one other eventualities. Winner could not bear it. Waiting might have been the permanent condition of the BSF. To him it was intolerable.

He entered a grocer's shop. "Seeds," he almost shouted, in his high-pitched excitable voice. "For flowers."

Although the afternoon sun shone with its usual strength, the shop was a dark as a cave. It was a large shop, as shops in Salonika went, but there were so many tubs or beans, pulses, rice and other staples around the walls that the space for customers was restricted to a narrow file. The shopkeeper looked at Winner without comprehension.

Winner picked up some beans and threw them down again. Using his charcoal, he quickly drew a diagram indicating their relationship to a plant. It was becoming like a biology lesson.

Understanding began to dawn on the shopkeeper. He had no seeds in the shop. He thought, however, that seeds could be found at his cousin's house. His cousin had a vegetable patch.

The grocer scribbled a note in Hebrew characters. Translated, it read: "The officer wants seeds. He will buy anything. Don't undercharge." He gave the note to a boy.

Winner followed the boy into a side street. Immediately the architecture changed. Gone was any attempt at regularity, or at street lighting, or the symmetry of plaster facades. The wooden houses, bulging out into covered, first-floor balconies, appeared to be leaning against each other, or towards each other, as though they were a row of drunks who needed mutual support. Whoever might have been inside them could look out through fretted screens, without being seen in return. But the wormy front doors were open. Before the doors, on the steps of their houses, sat the elderly of the town, wrapped in shawls and robes, and impervious to the stink of ordure from the open drain in the centre of the street.

Hobbling on his cast, Winner would have been glad to have boots on both feet, rather than only one. The unbooted foot, with its protruding toes, had a more direct relationship with the organic matter over which they were passing than he would have wished. His guide had no shoes at all.

Beneath the ramparts of the castle was a gateway. Through it they reached a tall, white-stucco building. This, from the Hebrew writing, Winner took to be a synagogue. The boy pushed open the wrought-iron gate, but instead of entering the synagogue, they merely crossed the courtyard and entered an alley. This took them to the grocer's cousin. He was a tall man, in a long open robe; with his strong features he would have been handsome if it had not been for the lack of front teeth. A graceful gesture of his long fingers motioned Winner into his house.

Winner felt as though he had entered a cigar box. The walls of the passage were wooden and a fragrance of spices hung in the air. He was shown into a large room, whose furnishings evinced the phenomenon of double consciousness. One end was provided with modern gilt tables and chairs, of the kind that might have been bought in a department store in Vienna. Most of the opposite wall was occupied by a large Turkish divan covered in carpet and cushions. Strained by the fretwork shutters, the light made patterns on the walls. It was a moment before Winner realised that other people were already there. A man of about thirty, with intensely black hair which made his skin, as white as plaster of Paris, seem almost to shine with an inner light, was sprawled across the divan. He got up and bowed. Winner saw that the cuff of his shirt was frayed.

"I am Moise Zacut," he said. "As you see, I speak English. My neighbour and," he glanced shyly at the tall man, "friend asked me to come. He speaks French of course — we all do — but not English. This is a cousin," he said, indicating another figure, dressed in a fur-trimmed robe, who made a vague gesture of greeting, as he peered at them through spectacles as thick as bottle glass. "My neighbour thought it would help your mission if I were here to translate. You need weeds."

"Seeds," Winner corrected him

"Yes, seeds. He has seeds. You will have some coffee, in the Ottoman style — the Greek style as we should say now, being part of Greece. Or apple tea? The Turks like that. We do not drink water now. The angels who guard the water are resting at this time of year, and this gives the demon an opportunity to infect it."

Winner accepted tea. His host went in search of the womenfolk to make it.

"I am a friend of the house," the man said. "An intimate friend. I hope to be more intimate still. I am engaged to the daughter."

Winner muttered congratulations.

"I am allowed to come once a week. It is the new custom."

"What was the old custom?" Winner asked.

"Just a few times a year. In Salonika, the husband is chosen by the bride's parents. We become acquainted before marriage. We do not converse much. In my case, there is no need to converse."

"Why not?"

"Because I know she is beautiful — I can see it. I also taught at her school. Yes, Jewish girls are educated here. I teach Hebrew. Grammar," he said with a note of pride. "The principles of the language. The children do not learn it by chanting. That was the old way. Her father will give her money. We shall be happy. If we do get married."

"But you said it was fixed."

"Agreed by the family, yes."

The father returned. He took out of his robe some screws of paper and threw them on the inlaid table. He pronounced his one word of English, learnt that afternoon: "Seeds."

Winner carefully unpacked one of the miniature parcels. "Tomato," Moise informed him. Other morsels of paper contained pumpkin and pomegranate seeds. Then, with a flourish, some marigold seeds were produced. "Beautiful flowers," explained Moise.

A girl entered with a tray. Winner recognised her. Once seen, her olive-skinned face, downcast eyes and graceful figure were rarely forgotten by members of the BSF. She was the beautiful chocolate maker from Molho's. Some habitués of Salonika's leading café for Allied officers would have thought that Winner had stumbled upon a valuable fact of geography: la chocolatière's address. From the assiduity with which Moise relieved her of the burden, it was clear that she was his intended. She refused his help, setting the tray down on a faux Louis XVI table that looked too fragile to bear even that weight. From the speed at which she

129

turned to leave the room, he thought that the marriage would not happen soon.

"You see how she despises me," sighed Moise. "But why? I am a rabbi. I would bring honour on her house." He translated into Ladino for the father's benefit. The latter raised his hands in a gesture that combined frustration, anger and resignation in equal parts. He spoke quickly, before throwing himself onto a sofa in disgust. The seeds had been forgotten for the time being.

He addressed Winner. "He asks what you would advise. Do you have daughters?"

"I have sisters. Some older than me. The youngest is eleven."

"A good age to begin the search for a husband."

"She's a child."

"Too early? Marriage partners are decided by God. There is no point in waiting. We regard large families as a blessing. Why wait to begin?"

"Does the young lady agree?"

"No. She maintains she will never marry me. In your country, what would you do?"

"Let her make up her own mind," declared Winner staunchly.

The father said something. Moise interpreted. "You would not beat her?"

"No."

The young man reflected. "Money is not an issue in this case. The young lady's father has plenty to give us. As a rabbi, of course, I am a scholar. I teach. I do not take part in trade. But this is a rich community. Many Jews. It can afford many rabbis."

There followed another tirade from the father. "He says that the girl is being punished. She is being sent out to work. Let her see whether she likes it. He will cut her off, his favourite daughter, without a drachma. It is in the café of our cousins, the Molho's. She makes chocolate. Let her make chocolate all her life."

"She is a modern young woman," ventured Winner.

"Yes. Modern. There is no need to be modern in Salonika. Why? We have our history and our traditions. It's the fault of these wars. They are making us modern."

Looking around the room, Winner did not think that the modernising process had got as far as their end of the room. He sipped the hot tea. "Is there somebody else that she likes?"

"Impossible. Her parents would surely known. We have learnt something from our Mohammedan neighbours; our women cover themselves, they live separate lives."

"I would like to paint her." The father looked too shocked for Winner to pursue the idea.

He put some drachma notes on the table and the seeds in his pocket. The elaborate courtesies that preceded any departure in Salonika were still underway when the door to the house began to resonate beneath a pounding fist. Winner dropped his precious burden.

The door was opened. In the frame of it stood the Provost Marshal, accompanied by a couple of military policemen, their heavy tread betraying their previous

131

employment as beat officers of the Metropolitan Police. "We have come," announced the Provost Marshal through an interpreter, "to interview your daughter. There was a murder this morning at Molho's Café."

"We know," replied Moise. The man in the glasses, who had been writing something in a pocket book, stood up and slipped unobtrusively out of the house.

The policemen seemed to take up as much room as six ordinary individuals. Their bulk had a galvanising effect on the owner of the house who began a lamentation about daughters and what became them when they did not follow the traditions of their kind and the advice of their parents.

"Come now," the Provost Marshal was saying. "We must see the young person," — he did not call her a young lady — "and find out what she knows. She knows something, I'll be bound. If we don't see her here, we'll put her in a cell and talk to her there."

At that point a boy came into the room. It was the same boy that had guided the Otter and Winner through the old town from the grocer's shop. He handed the Provost Marshal a note. The Provost Marshal read it. His moustaches twitched. "That does it, then," he observed to himself. "Come on boys. There will be no need to interview the individual after all."

He turned on his heel and walked out, followed by the policemen. Winner bowed as courteously as he could and went after them.

The evening sun was still bright. Leaning on his stick, Winner began to make his way downhill. As he did so, a Greek officer strode along the pavement towards him. Winner stepped aside into the street, and found he had placed his cast in something unpleasant. He was fairly sure that the officer smirked. "We're allies, aren't we?" Winner called after him.

The officer stopped.

"No. You are guests here." He resumed his rapid pace. "Some guests never go home."

Fifteen

Once, Roman legions had tramped along the Via Egnatia. The road had connected the two imperial capitals of Rome and Constantinople. St Paul and Silas had taken it on their way to preach in the synagogue; the people of Salonika, the Thessalonians, got a letter. Now, the Salonika stretch of the Via Egnatia was lined with wooden booths, each crammed with merchandise. Shopkeepers squatted in front of the booths; when an item was required from their stock, they simply reached behind for it, without getting up. Winner was now limping past them.

As he did so, one of the stallholders tugged at his trousers. He looked down, angrily, to see a man wearing a turban and thick spectacles. Those spectacles; had he not seen them before? He expected to be importuned to buy something. Instead, the man pushed a piece of paper into his hand. On it were written the words, "*Cercle des Etrangers. 12.30.*" Winner looked up from the note, expecting to interrogate the eyes behind those thick lenses. But in the space of the few seconds it had taken him to read it, both turban and spectacles had gone.

It was as mysterious as it was baffling: a summons that, from its strangeness, could not be ignored. Winner had been forced to start late, after resting his foot, and now it was already approaching midday. He redirected his steps towards the club. On getting there, he sank gratefully into an armchair at the head of the staircase, overlooking the entrance.

After half an hour, he saw the turbaned stallholder come in, talk to the doorman and enter the building. That was extraordinary: natives would not normally be allowed into the club. The man disappeared into a corridor on the ground floor. Winner waited. At twelve thirty exactly, a British officer appeared on the staircase, which he ascended two treads at a time. He was a wiry, athletic-looking individual, with crisply parted hair. At school, Winner imagined, he would have been captain of cricket.

"Lieutenant Winnington-Smith?" he asked at the top. "I am Major Simon."

Winner jumped to his feet. Major Simon wore spectacles — very thick ones.

"I hope you haven't been getting bored in Salonika, waiting to meet me. It must seem dreadfully rude but I went under cover for a few weeks."

"Can I ask where you've been, sir?"

"Oh, various places. I got behind the enemy lines. For the last few days I've been in Salonika. I'm Intelligence, you know. Helps to know what the other

134

side think. You can't find that out by sitting in an office." He smiled. "But that's enough about me. I want to know about you. I own some of your work."

"Good heavens. Where?"

"At home. One of my Bloomsbury friends told me about you. I am a great admirer. Do you have any of your sketches here?"

"Only my sketchbook," replied Winner, giving it to Simon. Simon took out a magnifying glass.

"I suppose it's for your sleuthing, sir?"

"What is?"

"The magnifying glass, sir. You pick up clues."

Simple did not reply. Without the magnifying glass he would have seen only a blur. At school, a special secretary had been employed to read out the books.

"If I may be allowed to ask, did you find anything out, sir?"

Simon turned his little-seeing eyes on Winner: they were a watery shade of blue. "Oh yes. Quite a lot about how they think. They're going to starve us out. Submarines." He looked at the sketches again. "The cemetery, I notice. I was there the other day." He put down the magnifying glass. "They're Austrian though. That's something."

Winner looked puzzled.

"The Ostrich doesn't have the big vessels, which can travel thousands of miles. Only ones that operate around the coast. They're an elite force, but they need to refuel. Have you had luncheon?" Simon knocked over a table on the way out of the room.

With his bad eyesight, Percival Simon, MP, should not have been in the army at all. But the authorities overlooked the defect. He was quite simply the cleverest man anyone knew. His Oxford college made him a fellow. But college life quickly bored him. He tried publishing, writing plays, devising puzzles. Most things lost their interest after a while, Parliament included: not a place for gentlemen, he maintained. Since his arrival in Salonika, he had spent much of his time, when not in disguise, inspecting Classical sites.

"Were the seeds any use?" he said after they had sat down at a table laid with a white cloth.

Winner dropped his menu in surprise.

"The ones that you were looking for last night," continued Simon, by way of explanation. He paused for effect. "You saw me, in the house of the Jewish merchant."

"You were the man who dodged out when the Provost Marshal appeared?"

"Yes. I like to collect information. There was clearly some information to collect, given the murder at Molho's. But actually I had already made myself an intimate of the house. I wanted to know what the Jews are talking about. They're the majority of the population here, after all."

"How did you get admission?" asked Winner, astounded.

"I told him I was a cousin," replied Simon, smiling, "from Smyrna. They have so many cousins, it was entirely possible he had one he couldn't remember."

"You speak the language."

"Oh yes." (Did Winner remember Sunny saying that Simple spoke fourteen languages?) "There was no point in the Provost Marshal interrogating the girl. I had already spoken to the family. She wasn't involved in the crime. She was upset by it, though. *Barev dzez*," he said to the waiter, before ordering a local dish that was not otherwise being served.

"Your Ladino is fluent?"

"That was Armenian. Didn't you notice his amulet? The Armenian symbol of eternity. But you want to get to the BWH," he continued. "Plenty of good subjects there, I should think."

"Yes. I was a patient."

"You got to know one of the nurses? I thought so." It did not take any great penetration to deduce that might be the case.

"I don't know what's become of her. I have to find out."

"You could write."

"I have."

"Go then." Winner stammered his gratitude. "Salonika," continued Simple, "has a certain topographical charm, but it's what you can't see that's interesting."

"You don't mean the fleas?"

"Secrets."

Simple ordered coffee. "Spies. Remember the *Marquette*."

"Is that why it was sunk, sir? Because the enemy was waiting for it? Surely they couldn't have intended to sink it if they'd known that a hospital was on board?"

Simple looked at him steadily. He was touched by Winner's naivety. His own view of life was more complex.

"The ship was also carrying a divisional ammunition column."

"So that's why it sank so quickly."

"Yes. The enemy knew about it. How did they know? That's what I have to find out." Simple stood up. "But artists have their mind on bigger things."

Winner accepted the comment at face value. "I have an idea for a picture. A big one. I just need the canvas."

Simple considered the problem for a moment. "Difficult to find stores in Salonika at the moment."

"Nearly impossible," sighed Winner.

"If I were you, I'd try a ship's chandler. I'll give you a note to explain your needs." He wrote it in Ladino, Greek and Turkish.

Winner thanked him. He was about to leave when a thought struck him: "By the way, sir, you might visit Captain Southall's Kite Balloon Section. No, nothing to do with spying. Somebody has found an old tomb."

Simple looked up. "Golly."

As fast as his damaged leg would permit him, Winner left the club and went to the harbour. The sailmaker was outside his shed, watching the boats landing fish — their catch of which would soon be sold at the inflated wartime prices that had begun to make fortunes in Salonika. The shed stood amid ropes, wharves, buoys, boxes of fish and fishermen's nets.

Winner gave him Simple's trilingual note. Having adjusted his cap, the sailor stared back at him open-mouthed, to reveal teeth like the rotting posts you find on a beach, worn down by the sea. He could not read. There was, however, canvas in the shed. But pantomime gestures, intended to represent an artist painting, did not convey that he wanted it stretched onto a frame.

"I could help you perhaps." It was Petrović. The young captain bowed gravely.

Petrović translated Winner's requirement. The sail maker laughed; the Englishman was mad to want canvas stretched onto a frame but he would not let that stand in the way of a bargain. Winner lapsed into silence. The canvas would need to be sized, to seal up the gaps. He would need some rabbit hides to make glue. How many times he would have to prime that rough fabric with gesso? And could he obtain gesso in Salonika? He might have to make it from powdered chalk.

"You're an artist," observed Petrović, breaking into his thoughts. "Good. Our fight too must be recorded. For many of us it will be to the death." They strode towards the Serbian camp where Petrović had horses. "This war will create a free Serbia. My generation lays down its life."

Winner was not thinking about the meaning of his words. "Yes," he agreed eagerly, with tactless enthusiasm, "I'm painting a *Last Judgement*."

Sixteen

Every detail of the murder at *Molho Frères* did the rounds of the club, to be discussed and theorised over, by men who had little otherwise to engage their deductive faculties in Salonika. They had got the basics of the drama from Ivory. He had been there when the report of a revolver had startled the kitchen workers at Molho's. The kitchen was in the basement. Like all restaurant kitchens, it was a stern, workaday space, full of steam and bad temper, which seemed to have more in common with a prison than with the glitter of the café upstairs. White tiles, covering the walls, dimly reflected the light which percolated through windows set below road level. The noise echoed around hard surfaces like a thunderclap. There had only been one shot. In the restaurant, diners heard a scream. Of operatic volume, it emanated from the ample lungs of the head cook, a man with a face like a plucked turkey, who fainted at the sight of blood. A waiter who was just then hurrying upstairs with a tray supported at shoulder height tripped over the prostrate chef, and the clatter of soup plates and tureen reverberated through rooms that had fallen preternaturally quiet.

One of the Molhos had appeared, his urbane smile undermined, for once, by a nervous twitch, among the tables. "*Mesdames et messieurs*, continue your afternoon, I beg you. Nothing in the world to concern you. *Maestro*," he clapped his hands and music flowed once more from the band of elderly musicians to whom nobody listened. "Ahem. If there is a medical person amongst us, perhaps he could make himself known?"

In the absence of a doctor, Ivory put himself forward. "Is something wrong with his teeth," jeered Ratty.

140

Ivory followed monsieur Molho into the bowels of the establishment and through the throng of waiters standing about, like automata whose clockwork has run down.

There lay Mister Desire, stretched at full length upon the floor, beside the deal table at which the pot boy had been peeling vegetables. Ivory spared his listeners no detail of the scene. A bright red stain with a dark centre had opened up like an overblown peony on Mister Desire's white shirt. Blood was spattered over the wall, the piles of vegetables, the stone sink; more had spilled from the body onto the floor tiles where it was making a sticky pool.

"His eyes were wide open, like this," said Ivory, "and there was a gurgling in his throat. Blood started to come out of his mouth. Blood was everywhere." Bigot noted the lurid details for the *Balkan Gazette*.

"It may not have been the shot that killed him," Ivory had continued. "When he came down, he cracked his skull on a large earthenware bowl — one of those big heavy ones that you see in dairies. Pretty funny, heh? You shoot a man and he dies from hitting his head on some crockery. It was the kitchen boy who did it. He had a crazy passion for the chocolate maker. Mister Desire teased him that she would never look at him, because he was only a slave in the kitchen. Stating the obvious, you might say. He went on and on about it, and — well, you see the consequence. He got his come-uppance. I'm not sure that there isn't a moral in it. Damned if I can find it, though."

Ivory's listeners could picture the scene. The dead man. The recumbent chef. The waiters and scullions standing around as though the Last Trump had sounded. The open door through which the pot boy had made his unscheduled exit. Then Molho, rapping his knuckles on the table and saying in that Spanish language of theirs: "Come on. What do I pay you for? There are customers upstairs who need to eat." The kitchen resumes its bustle, and if some of the dishes were salted with tears or, courtesy of Mister Desire's vital fluid, coloured pink, nobody noticed.

The next part of the story had been told by the Provost Marshal, as he stood at the unlit fireplace, the shelf of which was at a convenient height for his elbow. He had removed his pith helmet, the hard rim of which had left a red weal-like mark on his forehead.

You had only to look at the Provost Marshal's boots to know that, in civilian life, he had been a member of the Metropolitan Police. He had been charged with upholding the law in Salonika, and uphold it he would. Privately, he regarded it as a Sisyphean task, given the squalid muddle of the place, with its different religions and languages. How could an Englishman understand what went on at the ends of dark alleyways or inside hulks of rotting timber buildings, crowded with foreigners? A big man, he was now sweating profusely: never was a fellow more in need of a drink or, the hint having been taken, bought so many. Suitably revived, he unpacked his findings for the benefit of the club.

If the murder had not occurred at Molho's, the Provost Marshal began, he would have left the investigation to the local police. But Molho's was Molho's. Already people with crowns and stars on their shoulders were asking how the enquiry was going. The interest was not wholly military in nature. The story of the crazed boy who had shot his love rival was as good as a novel. To have said, "the Greeks are looking into it" would not have sounded well. Another whisky and soda? That would be civil. Ta very much.

The waiter had been called Solomon Mallas. The Molho Brothers did not know much about him. It was unusual for them to employ people with whom they were not already acquainted. Generally, they chose family and friends, or Jews who came to them through the recommendation of other Jews. But they had been so busy since the Allies arrived that they needed more staff, and Solomon had been a waiter before. He said he was a Jew, originally from Athens. He was efficient, assiduous, always there. He said that he had most recently been a sailor. There was nothing strange about that. It was second nature for Greeks to take to the sea when they could not find work on land. He gave the impression of having travelled widely. He seemed to know more about Marseilles and Genoa than he did about Greece. Many people had gone away during the Balkan Wars.

The girl is called Rachael. It is a Biblical name. The Provost Marshal remembered the story from Sunday School. Jacob saw Laban's daughter coming with the sheep, he rolled away the stone from the well, kissed her and hurried off to ask her father for her hand in marriage. He had then worked seven years for Laban, been tricked into marrying Leah, the first born, then put in another seven years. The Provost Marshal had never understood why Jacob had thought it was worth the graft . . . until now. Looking at this Rachael, he could see why a man might devote the best years of his life to winning her.

Rachael, however, says she knew nothing about Aaron, except that he seems to be embarrassingly infatuated with her. Their paths sometimes crossed in the kitchen, when she got the milk for the chocolate. She does not know why he had conceived such a great love for her; they hardly spoke. She certainly does not know where he lived. Or where he might be now. Or anything else about him.

The name of the pot boy is Aaron. "The case turns on him," put in Eggie impatiently.

"Foreigners do have passions, you know," agreed the Provost Marshal.

Eggie harrumphed. He knew about the difficulty that the Latin had in subduing Nature. The *maisons closes* had arrived.

"Indeed, the French have a special name for cases of this sort," continued the Provost Marshal. "Cream passionelle." He made it sound like a pudding.

He took out a large handkerchief and passed it over his brow. "It's a sad tale. By all accounts, Aaron was — is, I should say — a courteous, well-mannered youth. It's beyond doubt that Aaron did it. As to where he is, Lord alone knows. We'll find him though."

Nobody had been interested in Mister Desire, unless it was to catch his eye in the busy café, while he had been alive. After his death, the *Cercle des Etrangers* could not hear enough about the squalid facts of his home life. The Provost Marshal fed their appetite.

His apartment lay in one of the foetid wooden streets of the old town. A little girl had opened the door to the Provost Marshal after he had pounded on it for some time — just a crack, until what the Provost Marshal had first taken to be a heap of old clothes came to life as her grandmother. She looked at his uniform and told the child to let him in. A younger woman appeared. While the grandmother had the look of a gnarled tree root that clings to a river bank and refuses to be washed away, the Provost Marshal categorised the daughter — as he assumed her to be — as a loose branch that gets swept hither and thither by the stream of life. Her eyes had a wary, hunted look; on her cheek was an aubergine-coloured bruise. The effect of seeing the Provost Marshal and his men was electric. She screamed at them to leave. She declared wildly that they could not enter the house without the permission of the man. They were not to touch anything. She had specific instructions. The interpreter explained that a man associated with this address was dead. "Dead," she queried. The idea seemed to pacify her. "Vassilis?"

"Not Vassilis," said the Provost Marshal, through an interpreter. "Solomon."

"We don't have anyone called Solomon here."

"The man was of medium height, he had dark hair."

145

"That could be half the men in Salonika."

"Part of an earlobe was missing."

She bowed her head. "That was Vassilis."

"He worked at Molho's."

"Perhaps. I don't know."

She sunk onto a chair. She was a very young woman, not the girl's mother perhaps, but her sister. She had long hair that had been dyed blonde and wore a cotton skirt. This was the look of new Salonika. But like so many people who would have preferred otherwise, she was condemned to the wooden squalor of the old town. She had no means of escape.

"Your husband was shot," the Provost Marshal told her.

"He was not my husband."

"We need to know why he was killed. We can then bring his murderer to justice. We shall begin by searching his possessions."

She looked at the Provost Marshal wildly. "No." She spat the word out with violent emphasis. "He would never allow it."

"But he's dead, Madam."

"How do I know it? What if he returns?"

"It won't take long," declared the Provost Marshal. He nodded to a man at the door and two other policemen came into the house.

The woman flew at them. The Provost Marshal restrained her. "We shall be as careful as possible and pay for breakages."

They broke nothing. Mister Desire had few enough worldly goods — some clothes, a cape, a book about tides, a few photographs of himself and more of different women, all packed neatly into a seafarer's trunk.

"What happens now to those destitute women I don't know," concluded the Provost Marshal. "It's a sad story."

The *Cercle des Etrangers* murmured agreement. The case, so fascinating because it touched a place they knew well, was, they now realised, nothing more than a grubby domestic episode, of the kind that is enacted between excitable Southern men all the time. Italian opera was full of them.

Later, the Provost Marshal went to Simple's office. "There are some things that will interest you, sir," he reported. "Aaron was only a pot boy. They gave me an address. A rented room. Bed, washstand, that was it — nothing to suggest where he is now, or even that he occupied it very much."

"I see what you mean," replied Simple, turning over a small Hellenistic bronze in his fingers. He had bought it in the *souk*. "If this crime happened spontaneously, where were the clothes, the shoes, the personal effects?"

"There was none of that, sir. We also went to Vassilis's place — Vassilis being the water also known as Solomon and Mister Desire. Searched his trunk, nothing there. We then had a hunt around for a hiding place. There was one behind one of those icons — you could see the fresh plaster. So the men nipped out and borrowed a hammer and chisel. A couple of taps and we found a secret cupboard. He'd plastered a box into the wall. These were the contents, sir." The Provost Marshal laid on the table some papers, a printed map, an envelope and a large quantity of drachma notes.

"Return the money to the woman," said Simple. "She'll need it."

He then squinted at the papers under his magnifying glass. Most of them were composed of lists. Names of regiments, quantities of stores, numbers of horses. There was also a small sheet of paper was marked with a jagged line, a dotted line, some wavy lines and a Greek cross. Next to the jagged line were a couple of irregular rings. There were a number of dates in the margin.

One of Simple's eyes was near-sighted, the other long-sighted; out of neither did he see well. The scrutiny took some time.

"Not worth getting killed for," observed the Provost Marshal, once it had concluded.

Simple held the Hellenistic bronze to his eye, as though questioning it. "No. But friend Vassilis was a spy."

Seventeen

While Simple and the Provost Marshal attempted to unravel the mystery of Mister Desire, Sunny had his own conundrum to consider. With him on the balloon bed was Ratty — Captain Sewell of the Royal Engineers. Ratty was an expert in explosives.

"It's a ticklish problem," Ratty said. They were looking at the balloon basket. It was already manned, if it could be put that way: a figure in a khaki uniform stood at the side, next to boards displaying the usual maps of different scales. The balloon had not yet taken off, but the figure seemed to loll, as though searching the dry ground of the balloon bed for beetles. "Give me two pounds of HE and I could bring down St Paul's Cathedral. Just a question of knowing where to place it. But that's in a confined space. We've experience of that sort of thing. This is different. Couldn't be more in the open. Nothing to contain the explosion. But the HE should detonate all right. Five hundred pounds should do it. I've arranged for the plunger to be concealed in the trees over there."

"A good way away, I notice." Sunny could not bring himself to like Ratty, even though he was useful.

"Even you must see the reason for that, Sunny."

"We don't wish to advertise our presence to friend Earwig?"

"Precisely. I've got a second observation post over there, on top of the hill, in case he gets around the other side of the balloon and I'm unsighted. We can talk to each other on the telephone."

"Might be glad of tin hats when this lot goes up. Only of course we don't have any out here. I suppose that's everything?"

"I assume you've told the Archies to lay off?"

"I hope that won't give the game away, but we don't want Fritz to be frightened off."

The kite balloon floated upwards. It was an hour after dawn. "How about a bet, Captain Sewell?" asked Private Bunn. He had been a bookmaker before signing up. "You're a sportsman."

"On what."

"Whether you succeeded in blowing Fritz out of the sky, sir."

"It'll have to be on tick, Chelsea."

"You already owe me, sir. What a shame. And the tortoises will be racing at three o'clock." Bookmaker though he was, Chelsea liked an officer to be a gentleman, a prime quality of which was the settling of debts.

Ratty stalked off to his hiding place. He settled down to a morning's observation: a solitary activity that allowed his mind to wander to the gypsy family with whom he would soon be united. He had first seen them near his camp. The women had dark eyes and colourful skirts — red, blue, yellow, green. One of the dark-skinned, insolent daughters was almost as beautiful as the chocolate girl at Molho's. Her brothers turned out to be rather more possessive of her than he had imagined. They seemed to expect him to marry her, before he could so much as take her for a promenade. He had offered money. They wanted a wedding as well as money — and considerably more money that he had expected. It was a tempting proposition though. What harm could there be in a gypsy marriage? It couldn't be legally binding at home. The payment might be large, but imagine the benefits. A woman of his own for the duration of the war. What figure, he wondered, could he get them down to?

They waited, but the German airman did not come.

Ratty's mind turned to the chocolate maker. His stratagem there had been foiled by his favourite waiter's demise. He had hoped that Mister Desire might have

150

opened a channel of communication. That was off the cards now. Perhaps just as well. That pot boy might have put a bullet in him, as well as Mister Desire. Still, the pot boy was now nowhere to be seen.

They were all talking about it of course. There had been rumours. The Molho Brothers had been arrested for spying. The chocolate maker was pregnant. Mister Desire was really the boy's father.

Salonika: that's where the fun was. It might be weeks before he was there again. Meanwhile, he would have to make do with the gypsy.

By midday, they had to conclude that Earwig was not to be tempted.

They began to winch the balloon down and Ratty emerged from his place of concealment. "Those bushes have an anthill," he observed crossly.

"You had no difficulty in staying awake, I should imagine," remarked Sunny.

"None."

"But if at first you don't succeed. Give it a day or two, to look casual, then try again, what?" He had every intention of putting up bobby-trapped balloons until the Earwig was squashed.

Ratty brushed an ant off his breeches. "By then I might have something to bet with."

Eighteen

It took Winner eight hours of painful riding to reach the BWH. Once there, he swung stiffly down from his horse, feeling both pride and relief. The saddle had been uncomfortable; a Serb trooper had improvised a cloth loop for his damaged foot to rest in, instead of a stirrup. As soon as the nurses saw him, they took him in hand. One dove fluttered off for a wheel chair, another flew towards the operating theatre for Dr Aitken, a third stayed with Winner in case he collapsed.

She looked severely at Petrović, as though he had been responsible for leading her patient astray. "I've not come for medical attention," Winner protested. "I'm looking for Nurse Fox. You know Elsie, don't you? She's one of the drivers."

"Then," said the Dr Aitken who came up, looking stern, "you'll need the transport department. But not until I have examined your foot."

Winner had seen her the last time he had been at the Hospital. She had an elegantly long nose and delicate skin. Her erudition seemed almost donnish. Today she smiled even more fleetingly than she had done before. She told one of the nurses to fetch a wheelchair. "Take him to Newnham," she said to the others. "Ask one of the Serbs to push him and go back to your wards." Her air of quiet efficiency had become curt.

A Serbian orderly bowled the chair over the familiar turf. Petrović went to look after the horses.

It had been so pleasant before, Winner remembered. Why had he ever left? But it was no longer the same. "There used to be no men," Winner said to the nurse beside him.

"We've got so many men now," she replied. "Wounded of course. But some of them can help

152

around the place when they are able to walk again. We're hard pressed in the wards."

The hospital had lost its air of being freshly unpacked. The grasses and wildflowers of the meadow had been trampled down to form paths. The white tents had begun to look dusty. The green tents had started to fade. There was an air of bustle. Through the rolled-up sides of the tents, Winner could see that the beds were now occupied. The big push that everybody expected had not begun, but the war in the mountains never stopped. There was a backlog of wounded Serbs to treat. A steady stream of them was being brought back in the Fords. These leathery-faced soldiers, whose immense flaring moustaches reminded Winner of a painting he had seen of Caractacus, the Ancient Briton, looked fiercer than any other breed of men he had seen.

Newnham was a different place. He did not have it to himself. Men looked listlessly up from the other beds when he was wheeled in. Those who were well enough to play cards glanced at him casually and went back to their game. One more wounded man made no difference. "Tommy, cigarette?" asked one hopefully but Winner did not smoke and he had no Woodbines to give.

Winner was left on his bed. He was exhausted after the journey but would not let himself sleep; he would find Elsie first. Dr Aitken took a long time to arrive. She found him outside the ward. He had resolved to continue his search; the doctor could deal with his foot later.

"Go back to your bed, Lieutenant. I'm surprised at you." Meekly he obeyed. "We don't have time to spend on cases like yours any more," she told him crossly.

"I fell out of a balloon," he protested.

"We're busy now," she said austerely. She began probing Winner's leg. "The worst thing is the malaria."

"Is it bad in the Serb army?"

"Heavens, no. I should think they're immune. But our nurses aren't. We've only been here a month and there are four cases already. One good thing about it is that the Serbs — the walking wounded, that is — can provide guards. We need them."

"I should think you do."

"For the stores, not ourselves. Things go missing."

Winner thought of the young man he had glimpsed from his tent the last time he had been in the hospital. Seen by him but apparently invisible to everyone else. Had he been one of the thieves?

"The Serbs won't stand any nonsense. Anyone they catch — well good luck to them." Winner was not sure whether the good luck was for the Serbs or their prisoners. He winced as she removed the cast. She felt his foot and eventually pronounced it to be well. "It will be frail," she told him. "Ask one of the Serbs to make you a nice stick. They're practical people." He felt the last remark conveyed an implied rebuke.

Winner limped off to the transport department. The lorries were kept there when not in use: female mechanics would check them over after each run. There was a pit that they could crawl into for work that was needed underneath.

154

Only one of the eight Fords was at base. A girl in overalls was checking the tyres. "You want Nurse Fox?" she replied to Winner's enquiry. "We all want Nurse Fox. If you find her, tell us about it. She's left us one driver short. You could ask some of the other drivers. They're in the dining tent."

The way to the dining tent passed the cook house. That, Winner remembered, was Miss Hinchcliff's department. She would know.

The scene that greeted him was dramatic. Isabel stood with a knife in her hand. Her apron was splashed with gore, her forearms were red and she carried a knife. Winner remembered a painting of Judith, having just cut off the head of Holofernes. He looked at her in horror.

"Good evening, Lieutenant," she said, as though nothing was untoward.

"Have you been performing an operation?"

"The blood? Yes, I'm covered in it, aren't I? I'm not sure the apron has kept it all off my clothes. Forgive me if I don't shake your hand. We've slaughtered a sheep." She cleared the table in front of her. From her expression, as well as her appearance, the sacrifice had cost her an effort. "Oh dear, a relative of Snowball I expect. Someone else had to deliver the coup de grace. I wanted to be there, though — to know how it's done for next time. One can't afford to be squeamish in wartime. I got through by imagining the poor animal was a submarine captain. If I had one of those to kill I would stick a knife into his neck without difficulty." She said it as though she meant it. "Fortunately I'm enough

155

of a country girl to know how to cut the carcass up." She caught Winner's appalled expression. "I refer to the sheep."

The sheep's head reminded Winner of John the Baptist. "I wonder if I'll be able to persuade Laundry to let me wash some extra garments this week," continued Isabel, in the bright tone to which he was accustomed. "We're limited to three items a week. Last week, I served boiled turkey in white sauce, with macaroni. So much easier to get out marks."

Winner had previously thought of Isabel as an ethereal creature, but she seemed to have become almost aggressively down-to-earth. He had not, however, come to talk about laundry. "I've been trying to find Elsie — I mean, Nurse Fox. I thought you might know where she was."

"So that was what brought you." Her look changed to one of ominous sympathy. "We don't know where Elsie is at the moment."

"But she came back with you." He was momentarily irritated by the consideration in Isabel's voice.

"Yes, with me. She did. It was kind of her." Isabel was washing her hands in a china basin, with water poured from a jug.

"Why kind?"

"I had to leave quickly. I felt I had to, at any rate. I thought Gwendolyn had been on the *Marquette*. She was." She rubbed her eyes with hands that were still blotched with red. "One hundred and seventy doctors, nurses and orderlies," she cried: "all drowned. The inhumanity of it." She sliced into a leg of the sheep

156

carcass. It calmed her. "Poor Uncle Godfrey and Aunt Vic. They were her parents." The knife was at work again. "It seems worse when it's a girl like Gwendolyn. I don't mean because I know her — knew her. Soldiers expect terrible things to happen to them. That's what fighting does. But Gwendolyn was a dear person. She was coming to help undo a little bit of the destruction. Instead she was killed herself."

The antidote to emotion was to keep busy. That was the way of the Surrey Hills. Isabel vigorously towelled her hands and forearms. "I couldn't bear Salonika another minute. Elsie came with me."

Winner wanted to ask if she had been reluctant to do so. Isabel sensed it. "Naturally she wanted to get back to her work here. But I don't think she would have wanted to leave so — precipitately. It was a kindness."

Isabel had been aware, that night in Salonika, that Elsie had been alone, until dawn, with a man, and in other circumstances she would have felt obliged, from her position of authority, to take action. She would have interrogated her and told Mrs Stalwart-Dousing what she knew. But Gwendolyn's death had eclipsed Elsie's misdemeanour.

"I can't help being awfully cut up by it," she continued, reverting to the *Marquette*. "I suppose I should say that thousands of lives are being extinguished every day, but . . ." She turned away.

Tragedy was, as far as possible, banished from the idyll of the Surrey Hills. In that well-contrived house, built in the style of a tumbledown farmhouse, although it took five indoor servants to run, voices were never

157

raised. Money procured the best medical advice. Domestic life was cultivated with the precision of a science and the intuitive understanding of an art. Isabel was unprepared for the sudden death of a loved cousin.

"I'm sorry," said Winner.

"Elsie said something about you. She was going to write, but she didn't know where to address the letter. I think she sent something to your regiment."

"And now?"

"She drove the Ford to the mountains. That's where the fighting is. I believe that it's difficult to get a vehicle up those mountain roads. They're crowded with soldiers going forward, and all the mules. Then the ambulance has to get back. Well, Elsie didn't get back." She then said something that Winner did not expect to hear. "We had become friends."

Isabel looked at him. He felt himself sagging like a puppet whose strings have been cut. "I'm sorry," she said.

Winner looked so defeated that Isabel felt she should reassure him, however little she believed in her own words. "There's probably nothing badly wrong. The lorries are always breaking down. They overheat on the steep slopes. Perhaps she has run short of fuel. We're finding that very difficult. We have to use the mules more than the motor ambulances. Elsie has nothing if not pluck. She's made of stern stuff — tougher than me."

"But one of the other Fords would have passed her."

"Perhaps it did. A message may be sitting with the transport officer, but hasn't been passed on. We are so

158

busy now. Or the driver might have gone back to the mountains without telling anyone else." Even to Isabel this explanation did not sound particularly convincing. A stranded lorry would have been a story that soon got round the camp. "Or it was taken off the main highway for repairs. They're very resourceful, the Serbs. They can mend anything. Stay here and I expect she'll be back."

"When did she leave?"

"A few days ago now. Late afternoon. I saw her before she went. She said there was just time for another run."

"How many days ago?"

"I suppose it must have been Wednesday."

"Three days."

"That's not so long — not up here. You learn to be patient."

"I'm not patient."

"You must try." Isabel turned doleful, preoccupied eyes on him. But through the mist of her own sadness she did perceive that this curious, diminutive young man seemed very anxious about Elsie. She was touched.

"You must eat something. Look, I can feed you." She gestured towards the cauldrons on the fires outside the tent. "If you've not already been disgusted by the sight of blood."

It was not that which made him decline to eat, though. He felt too distressed.

"But you should eat." The deep, certain voice behind him belonged to Petrović. Its timbre reminded Winner

159

of an Orthodox priest but the words were not solemn. "You should always eat. In the first place it is polite. In the second place, out here, you don't know when you'll next have the chance. Miss Hinchcliff, don't you think that is so?"

"You should eat too, Captain."

"Miss Hinchcliff always feeds me when I am here. So I come often. But not only for that reason."

Isabel coloured as she turned away.

"When I was young," continued Petrović, "we always had food. The village was surrounded by orchards, the peasants had gardens. Every morning I was woken by cowbells. Flocks of geese ran down to the stream. They made a noise like this." Petrović produced a convincing honk.

Isabel laughed. Winner did not.

"Cheer up, Winner. We'll find her." Petrović, though a fatalist, was reassuring to Winner. They were the same age but he was a practical man who knew about the world.

"You grew up in the village, Captain?" asked Isabel.

He laughed disparagingly. "No. Not in those houses made of sticks and mud. But our house overlooked it. It was a manor house, built by a Hungarian family. My father is a doctor. He had a big library. He liked to read books in the summerhouse. That was where his patients came to see him — the poor ones, I mean. They could not come into the house. He would vaccinate them there. He called it his temple of Aesculapius. I wonder what it's like now. Pulled down for firewood, probably."

"Aren't your parents there?"

"I don't know. Probably. But with troops billeted on them and nothing to eat."

"But all the food . . ."

"How do you feed an army? There's never enough. The soldiers take everything."

Isabel showed them a place that they could sit. There were no chairs, but a boulder lay conveniently near. "I cannot give you a table, but the wood you found for us, Lieutenant, has been put to good use already. I have trays."

The tray was not finely finished, but was good enough to carry out a couple of bowls of stew, some bread and a jug of water, which had been boiled.

While they ate, they watched a Ford arrive. Woman orderlies, wearing trousers, took out the stretchers.

"There will be more of those," observed Petrović. "This hospital will be overflowing." He cut short his gloomy predictions when Isabel reappeared. "They are like angels, these wonderful nurses. Dear Miss Hinchcliff is the archangel. She looks after the fit as well as the sick. She builds me up for the campaign. It's just as well I have to move on, or I would be as fat as a eunuch. I wouldn't like to be a eunuch though." He smiled. "I'd rather be butcher, killing Bulgars."

If asked to describe Petrović, Isabel would have called him a sweet boy. All boys that one liked were sweet. Petrović's manners were old world, and not at all rough. He spoke French. But he said strange things, sometimes. Life at the front had done that to him, she supposed. She would have liked to make him gentle again. He was a sweet boy really.

"Now, the horses are rested and I am fed. I move on. Good-bye, Winner."

"Not goodbye yet. I am coming with you."

"Don't, I beg you. What would be the use?"

"To find Elsie."

"But she'll come back of her own accord. If you go to the front, you might miss her. You're a man of sensibility. You won't like it there."

"My mind is made up."

"That's dear of you," declared Isabel. "But is it wise?"

Winner shrugged.

"Come then," said Petrović. "I go to look after the horses."

Isabel decided to see them off. "I'll walk to the lines with you, if I may." They were both of them sweet boys.

The horses were drinking at a stream. Petrović ordered them to be saddled. The men led them back. Winner hurried back to the cook house to fill his water bottle. Isabel and Petrović were left alone.

"Goodbye, Miss Hinchcliff."

"Not goodbye, it sounds so final. Farewell."

He kissed her hand, looking at her as he did so, as though from the other side of a great separation: a distant, sad look that made Isabel shiver. He put his arm round her. "Be cheerful!"

He kissed her again, now on the lips, insistently. It surprised her. He was perhaps not such a sweet boy after all. When she pushed him away, he kissed her again. It seemed such a little thing, for this man who might, for all anyone knew, be about to die. She found

162

her mouth opening. His moustache bristled against her skin.

"Don't be silly," she told him. It did not sound the right thing to say to a departing warrior.

"You will marry me?"

"I am thinking."

"Say you will marry me. It will make no difference if I am killed." He looked at her again, from the depths of a deep well of sadness. "Men and women should become friends slowly, graciously. It is natural. Now this war means there is no time. Yet our souls still need warmth. Our bodies too. The warmth of knowing we might be loved. The warmth of hope."

Isabel put on a forced cheerfulness. "If it hadn't been for the war, I wouldn't have met you."

Petrović looked into her eyes. "What was it that the gladiators used to say? Those who are about to die salute you."

"But you must not die."

He smiled. "I shall need an angel to watch over me."

He was gone.

Nineteen

Joachim von Erfurtwege climbed into his *Albatros*. The British had put up another observation balloon. The young aviator regarded it as little short of an insult that such a preposterous object should be allowed space in the sky. There had been one up the other day, but the mechanics had been working on his plane.

163

The German had been on the Western Front: a nineteen-year-old, fresh from military academy, proud to be serving the Fatherland that was, to him, rather more truly a Father than to other boys. His actual father had died when he was a child; so had his beautiful, olive-skinned mother. His mother's brother had taken him in. Joachim was a delicate boy, with piercing blue eyes; to him, his uncle seemed a coarse man, who never drank wine and owned a number of drapery shops. Joachim longed for the military. For glory. Glory would establish his rightful place in the world as a von Erfurtwege.

Glory was not to be found on the Western Front. That was a war for civil engineers, making concrete fortifications in the trenches that were impervious to shells. There was little except routine, tedium and physical misery for the soldiers — hardly worth risking one's life for.

So he volunteered for the Imperial German Flying Corps. After crashing a few planes, he succeeded in qualifying as a pilot. Macedonia, to which Joachim was transferred, was not much of a Front. German High Command may have thought that a great Allied army was being massed here, but no sign of it could be seen from the air. His role was to prop up Bulgaria, a land that was scarcely civilised. It had, however, one great advantage for Joachim. There were very few other German pilots. It was a place where he could shine.

Shine he did. When he shot down an airman behind German lines, he was sure to visit him in the field hospital, bringing cigarettes and chocolates, and if he could find any, English books. But he intended to shoot down as many of the French and British as possible. As for observation balloons, they were dangerous to attack, but he was determined to destroy every one that was launched.

The *Albatros* flew high over the Vardar plain. He could hear the rattle of its engine, but only occasionally. The plywood cockpit shook as he tested the machine guns. For the most part his ears were filled with the beating of the wind. Here came the Archibalds. The puffs of the shells hung in the air, as though they were decoration. He could not see another flying machine. The kite balloon was a slug, about to be forked by the gardener.

He could see the observer now, looking over the side of the basket. This was the sixth balloon that he had attacked. The other men thought he was crazy, but it had not been so stupid. Sometimes he had returned with a hole in his wing or tail fin, but nothing that stopped his craft flying. Repairs could be made with little more than brown paper and glue. Once, the observer had fired a shotgun at him, so that pellets pattered around the cockpit, one of them nicking his cheek. A shotgun! As though he were teal.

He was almost above it now. The sun was behind him. He tipped the nose of the *Albatros* into a dive. It was exhilarating. He began firing from a hundred metres away. He was closing quickly. Was there a flame? No. Yes, there it was. Joachim laughed from elation as, at the last moment, he swung the *Albatros* away from the target. There would be another celebration in the mess tonight. They would find some girls.

He wondered if the observer would make it safely to the ground.

Thousands of feet below the *Albatros*, the Balloon Section watched it approach the decoy. They were tired. The previous evening, the Bulgarian artillery had started to shell their position. As a consequence, they had walked the balloon to a new bed. Walking the balloon was one of the least popular of the tasks that were required of the Section. It was done when the balloon was half-inflated, so that it floated a little way above the ground. There were rings around the waist of the balloon, and from each one descended a rope. To each rope was attached a man. The men — eighty or so of them — had to tug the balloon along, while it forever lurched and strained as the breeze caught it. Greek farmers, prepared to maintain that their crops had been ruined, pursued them, issuing tirades of incomprehensible abuse.

"What if he rumbles us?" somebody asked. "Surely he can't think that we'd give it to him on a plate."

"Fritz does it by method. He's not trained to ask himself questions. You point him at the job and he does it. Yes, he's doing it now: he's diving."

Ratty, from the shelter of the bushes, strained his eyes. It might not work. It only stood a chance of working if the aircraft was within a few yards of the basket. There was an awful lot of HE up there, but the explosion could simply disperse itself in the air, like

166

a firework. A big bang, for nothing. But Earwig was unquestionably getting close.

And then he lost him. He was on the other side of the balloon. "Have you got contact?" he barked into the telephone.

"Robert. I see him. He's coming in. The balloon's alight. He's turning away. He's passing the basket. Three, two, one. Now."

Ratty depressed the plunger. The balloon, which had shown a flicker of flame on the top, erupted into a fireball. It hung in the sky like a second sun.

The *Albatros* continued under its own momentum for a moment. Then it tipped over and spiralled to the earth. The tail fin had been blown off.

The ground crew let off a cheer. Ratty strode back looking pleased with himself. They walked towards the remains of the plane. There was no point in hurrying. Nobody could have survived.

In front of them, a heavy object thudded onto a rock, bounced off and knocked Sunny to the ground. It was a huge metal disk. They recognised it as the nose plate of the kite balloon. Sunny got onto his feet, wincing from the pain in his arm.

The *Albatros* was reduced to a litter of wreckage. The pilot's body, young and slim, looking incongruously elegant in its tailored uniform, lay nearby, like a discarded ragdoll.

The jubilation left Bill's voice when he saw him. "A brave young man."

"It doesn't seem right," replied Private Bream.

"We had to do it, Fishy. Think what he did to Lieutenant Wren."

"Jenny was a sportsman. I don't think he would have liked it. We didn't play fair."

They walked quietly back to their bivouacs. On the way, Ratty accosted them. "Have you seen Chelsea? I have some winnings to collect."

Twenty

That evening, Sunny was still in high spirits. Bringing down Earwig had been like shooting a pheasant. Since few dishes tasted better than roast pheasant, he did not initially trouble himself about the regrettable necessity of killing one of the countryside's more gorgeously plumaged birds. He had his left arm in a sling but the discomfort was more than outweighed by the euphoria that still buoyed him up. Besides, his garshly wound would certainly require ministrations from the BWH.

"I tell you what," he declared to Ramsgate, "that show was awfully good."

"You mean the Earwig spectacular."

"Yes that, but I referred to the Macedons. Good name for a concert party, by the way."

It was that leisurely hour, when the sun, descending towards the mountains, scattered a last brilliance of rays across the plain, lending a honeyed intensity to colours that had looked bleached a few hours before. Sunny tipped his pith helmet to shield his eyes. He, Ramsgate and Ratty, whom Sunny, against his better judgement, had to acknowledge as the hero of the hour, were lounging on an open-sided truck that was being pulled along a narrow gauge railway by mule. The Royal Engineers had laid a light railway line — one of a spider's web of communications behind the front — and Sunny saw no reason why they should not use it for their evening out.

"They gave the Motor Transport Company a run for its money," he observed.

Ratty threw his cigarette stub onto the track. "I never saw Slip Your Clutch. Didn't it have girls?" he enquired.

"Stop!" cried Sunny, jumping off the truck. "Find that gasper, you idiot, or there could be a fire. I don't want the Balloon Section to be consumed."

"Why worry? You don't have a balloon."

Sunny climbed down and extinguished the stub. "Oh yes, it had girls. Not proper ones, obviously. Bints. There was a wonderful programme seller with bare shoulders and back. Six adorable dancers on stage. A general in the front row seemed to be quite affected."

Ratty said nothing. He was more affected by the thought of a young gypsy girl, with her smooth dark skin and grumpy bearing. He would see if he could change the bearing. He would master her like a horse.

On the mule plodded. The truck creaked. The air was scented with wild thyme. A flock of magpies made the sky above them flicker like a cinema screen.

Sunny played the ocarina. He paused when a hare bolted across the plain. His hand moved instinctively to the leather holster on his hip, to see if he could bag it with his revolver, but he decided against the attempt.

As the land breathed out the accumulated warmth of the day, he did not wish to disturb Nature's tranquillity. He reviewed the events of the morning in his mind. That had provided hunting of a different sort. He had bagged von Earwig. It had seemed, at the time, to be a sporting challenge. And yet behind his retina there remained the sight of the young airman, his body mangled. He would be given a military funeral, of course. So much was due to the chivalry of the sky. For now, the unearthly notes of the ocarina provided an improvised lament.

The chivalric code. Had his trick with the HE in the balloon basket transgressed against it? It had not been entirely square. But then what about von Earwig? He had shot down an observer. It was something that happened — on both sides — more than Sunny liked to admit; that sort of thing deserved to be punished. Unless it had happened by accident. He puzzled the question out as far as he could but without achieving an answer. It made him impatient with the mule's progress. What he needed was not self-examination but a show.

That show of Ramsgate's the night before: that had taken him out of himself. The dining tent had, with a stage made of biscuit tins, become the Balloon Section's Palace of Varieties. In it the *Macedons* had opened their evening with what the programme described as National Airs on the violin. Next, Bill Bayley performed some Original Magical Problems. The loquacious Fishy Bream acted, appropriately, a monologue. Then came a comic sketch, before

170

Ramsgate stepped forward to occupy, with becoming modesty, a low place in the batting order as a *siffleur*. As Welsh enchantress Morgan-le-Fay, Jones Twofour — so called from his number, Jones 243831, used in his previous regiment, a Welsh one, to distinguish him from all the other Joneses — wore a costume made from army-issue blankets, stars cut out of old bully beef tins and a headdress that had begun life as a knitted balaclava helmet. He modelled his act, terrifyingly, on his mother. Twofour gave as good as he got to the hecklers. Dogged persistence won respect.

They were now off to compare the *Macedons* with *Mens Sana in Corpore Sano*, as tonight's concert party was billed. It was being staged by the Army Gymnastics Corps.

The railway, intended to help the movement of heavy loads around the front line, had been laid quickly, without the Great Western Railway's regard to smoothness of bed. Wherever there was a dip, the truck speeded up, threatening to overtake the mule. Sometimes it would stop with a jolt.

"Singletree," exclaimed Ramsgate, as though it were a novel expletive. He referred to the crossbar which helped attach the mule to its burden. When the tension in the traces slackened, it fell to the floor. "It's got under the wheels. You're an engineer, Ratty."

"Off duty, old cock. Well-earned repose after bringing down the Earwig. You won't find me fixing singletrees tonight."

The Army Gymnastics Corps had come to give tone to the British army; they wore flaring moustaches and could have done good business as strong men on a seaside pier. One end of Corps' marquee had been made into an improvised stage. In front of it hung a curtain contrived from a number of ground sheets attached to a pole.

Sunny rekindled his pipe.

"Lights," shouted a stentorian voice from behind the curtain, and the hurricane lamps around the sides of the marquee were extinguished. Conversation subsided to an expectant murmur. A man on a unicycle appeared in front of the curtain and, pedalling with aplomb, drew it back to reveal a chorus of splendidly proportioned individuals, dressed in striped bathing suits. It was neither subtle, nor sophisticated; but for the audience of British servicemen, in the wilds of Macedonia, it provided the magic carpet on which they could travel far away from the lonely present, into a warm, remembered, carefree place of the mind: the longed-for land of Home.

A piano (where did they get it?) strummed. In the darkness, Sunny forgot to worry about the dead German airman. At the end of programme that included a display on the parallel bars, a trapeze act, a monologue, some tumbling involving chairs, and a solo on the mandolin, tears of delight rolled down his face: tears which said there was rather more to this world than war.

Once the lights had gone up, the mood that each man had been cherishing was dispelled, and they resumed the relations usual among British officers, embarrassed

172

by tender emotions. A tent had been set out as a bar. In it was General Gay.

"Marvellous," he was saying to the Gymnasts' CO. He had blue eyes and a fashionable drawl. "I like to see the men making an effort to entertain themselves. Good for morale. Helps reduce petty crime, too."

"Sport, sir. Very important to the men, sir, is sport. On the King's birthday, sir, they had a bit of fun. Rattling the tin, sir."

"Begging?"

"No, sir. Two men are blindfolded and tied to a stake by a long rope. One has tin with a stone in it which he rattles — hence the name of the game, sir. The other has a sandbag with a stone in it. He has to find out where the other fellow is by the rattle, and then whack him. Other fellows without blindfolds are harassing the sandbagger. Good fun, sir. Very."

Gay raised his eyebrows quizzically. "Men must have something beyond sport, though. The feminine touch, thoughts of the fireside, loved ones far away."

"We don't go in for females around here, sir. I mean, we didn't put one into the show."

"The one thing lacking."

The CO drew himself up.

"Very good all the same," Gay assured him. "Shows stop the mind dwelling on these wretched submarines. We just need to encourage more of them. Don't you agree, Sunny?"

Sunny did agree. He mentioned the success of the Kite Balloon Section's own concert party, under the expert direction of Ramsgate Sandys, formerly of the Pavilion Theatre, Rhyl.

The general's eyes gleamed as though with inspiration. "Then we must do something across the Division. A competition, what?"

The idea was greeted, as ideas propounded by generals often were, with an enthusiasm that amounted, in some of his listeners, almost to rapture.

Ratty saw a snag. "Very difficult to pull off, sir," he noted laconically. "You'd have to have concert party after concert party giving their performance in front of the judges, presumably in the same place; it would be like the ancient Olympic Games, sir."

The General's face reflected the irritation of a baby deprived of a treat. "You did well to blow up the German ace, Captain Sewell. But in the matter of entertainments, you seem to lack, if I may say so, the aggressive spirit."

It was Sunny who put in a counter proposal. "Wouldn't it answer the purpose better to have a single divisional show, sir? There would be a competitive element in that. Men could audition for it."

The general looked at Sunny, as though he, Sunny, were the Angel Gabriel and he, Gay, were the Virgin Mary. "You're quite right, Captain. I believe that your Section is without a kite balloon at the moment. Besides, we couldn't have you going up in one with your arm in that state. Experience at Rhyl? Splendid. That's just what we'll do. You're the very men to put it on."

An hour later, Sunny, Ramsgate and Ratty were making their way slowly homewards, along the railway track. "How easy is a bush supposed a bear!" quoted Sunny, keen to live up to his new theatrical responsibilities. "*Midsummer Night's Dream*, you know. Did it at school. I was Snout." It seemed appropriate to a night ride on a Macedonian light railway; appropriate too to his new role as divisional impresario. He put his pipe in his mouth with every indication of contentment. He had been charged with a task, an odd one perhaps, but a challenge. He would follow it through.

The mule plodded somnolently on. After a while, the wagon gathered speed as the track took one of its periodic downward slopes. It jolted to a halt, throwing the occupants forward. Before Sunny could say "Singletree," something cracked into the clumsy wooden edge of the wagon, against which he had just been leaning. All three men knew that it had been a shot. Without a word being said, they leapt down and opened their holsters.

There was another shot. "He's in the bushes," observed Ramsgate, indicating a dark mass whose outline looked like a blot of black ink on the indigo of the sky.

"I'll see if I can flank him," said Ratty. "Give me cover." Sunny loosed off a couple of shots towards the bushes as Ratty ran nimbly over the track. The mule let out a bone-piercing bray and kicked at the wagon. "What we shall do is this," announced Sunny decisively — but before he could finish outlining his plan, the mule had broken free off the traces and was galloping off down the track. Ramsgate ran after it, with the gait of a flamingo in St James's Park. Sunny fired at the bushes to distract their assailant. A shot whistled past him. The enemy seemed not to be interested in Ramsgate, who offered the better target.

It was not how Ratty saw it afterwards, as they pushed the wagon towards the mule — or the place that it had been last seen. "Two valorous exploits in one day," he observed smugly. "The man ran off when I came on him from the side."

"You didn't hit him though?" asked Sunny.

"Might have done," returned Ramsgate, not wanting his glory to be diminished.

They spent the rest of the journey with eyes peeled, interrogating every bush and declivity in case a gunman were hiding in it. There was no further incident that night.

"What do you think he was after?" Sunny later asked Ramsgate.

"Our wallets, probably."

"Yes, I expect so," replied Sunny. Only he had a sense that was not the right explanation. The gunman had deliberately shot at Sunny, not Ramsgate. There seemed to be only one person in his sights. Sunny had the uncomfortable feeling that it was him

The Hospital at Prilep

Twenty-One

A ceaseless stream of men and animals went to the mountains; a lesser stream returned. It was not only relative size which distinguished the two streams; the beings on their way to the mountain, although tired and perhaps travel sore, were alert and high spirited. Those who were making their way back to the plain looked as though the spark of life had been ground out of them. Their eyes were red, their heads hung and they seemed to move by dragging one leg after another by a conscious effort of will.

Winner was in pain from his foot; but he was determined, energetic and impatient. He had to master the impatience. Progress on the roads of Macedonia was never fast and rarely predictable. Under the weight of men, horses, gun limbers, mules, ox-drawn carts, motor lorries and farm animals, it sometimes became impossible to move at all. Entering the mountains, the road withered into little more than a track. Even to get onto it, to start on the ascent, took two hours, during which they rested their horses, with a jumble of other men and beasts, on the last part of the broad plain. Winner felt that he was queuing for a popular fairground amusement.

"Can you guess what I was collecting from the harbour?" asked Petrović, as they waited.

Winner hated guessing games. "Fish?"

Petrović laughed. "Fish! What would we do with fish in the mountains? Unless it was to throw at the

Bulgarian trenches in order to stink them out. No. Spring onions."

"They're a delicacy?"

"Oh yes. And Spring has barely come to the mountains yet."

"It must be beautiful in the spring."

"It is. Spring comes; the fighting starts again. My springtime is over. I was a student. I wanted to be an architect. It will be a good time for architects after the war, because so much has been destroyed. I would like to be there. It will be a great time — for once, a national style. But for the time being I am a soldier, and we soldiers expect our contribution to the soil of our motherland to be a different one. We shall manure the soil, when our bodies are buried in it."

They rode on. Winner's mind was on Elsie. Had she been laid to rest in this soil?

"We have always had to fight. It is our national character. It defines us. We fought at Blackbird's Field."

"Earlier in this campaign?"

"No, in 1389. The Battle of Kosovo."

"A memorable victory."

"No. Our army was wiped out. But we won something, and that was a great cause. Against the Ottomans, against Austria-Hungary. The same cause. It is our greatest possession, handed down through the centuries. One day — I feel it — we shall win. If not now, one day."

Despite his blood-curdling words, Petrović looked composed. He did not appear to be a violent lunatic. It would have been easy to imagine him at a symphony concert in Belgrade, or taking his sisters on sleigh rides.

180

"I'm afraid I shock you. I shock myself to say such things. My old self: the one I grew up with, before the fighting in the mountains. I have left our home, the comfortable house that my parents had — I don't know what has become of it. Are my sisters starving? Perhaps they fled. My men do not know if their villages have been burnt, their possessions stolen, their wives raped. They fight on like ghosts."

"They must be fierce ghosts."

"A good adjective. They are fierce. Their metal has been tested in a pitiless cauldron, the impurities have been purged."

From a distance, the mountains seemed to rise abruptly, as separate from the plain as a sleeping grey-backed dog might be from the green rug on which he lies. Close to, the ascent was less dramatic. A track looped itself gently around turfy hillocks, before corkscrewing, by easy gradations, into the woods above. The passage of so many men, animals and vehicles over what had been little more than a forest track had churned the ground into a quagmire. The horses had to drag their hoofs out of the mud at every step. Men would be seen, up to their knees in water, pushing on wheels, trying to propel carts out of the morass into which they had sunk. The file of men and vehicles moved at the speed of the slowest.

Winner's knees hurt, he felt as though his seat bones were cutting through his breeches, but worst of all were his thighs. He was a short man. On that broad-backed animal, it felt as though his thighs had been forced apart, so that the lower part of his body was going to split in two like the wishbone of a chicken when it is pulled. He was, however, determined not to stop before Petrović.

They emerged from the woods onto a narrow path strewn with large whitish stones. Then the scene changed, and they were crossing an upland meadow. Winner's mount kept pulling at the rein, in an effort to get his neck down so that he could nibble the sparse herbage. They splashed through a mountain stream, where the horse drank. Meadow gave way to moor.

The air grew colder. Limestone broke out in weird shapes, the sides of which were bare rock. Up ahead, men crowded away from the track, as a Red Cross ambulance approached. Winner waved it to a halt. "I'm looking for a missing driver from the BWH, Elsie Fox."

From behind the wheel, the driver — a man — replied with Cockney fatalism. "Do I know anything? In this chaos?" He laughed mirthlessly. "Good luck, Guv'nor." As a conscientious objector, it was as near as he could approach to "sir".

The ambulance passed, and Winner toiled on.

The light was failing. Men were starting to make bivouacs by the side of the road. They foraged for wood, tearing limbs from the stunted mountain trees where they could find them. The gusts of wood smoke that were soon blowing over the path smelled of home. "We'll stop here," announced Petrović. "It is dangerous to go on at night. The track gets steep and . . ." he indicated a sudden drop with his hand. "The horses need rest."

Winner had reached that state beyond pain where his legs felt as though they were made of rubber when he slid down from the horse. He tried not to stagger. The horse stretched its neck, its mouth ripping at the scant blades of grass. His back steamed when Winner removed the saddle.

"Tomorrow we go through the iron landscape," Petrović informed him.

"Ironstone?"

"No, iron. You will see."

There was no shelter on the mountainside, beyond that provided by cliffs of rock. Winner dozed, woke up, found that his muscles had become rigid through the effort to keep from shivering, and the only thing to be done was to walk around, until the blood flowed again. He had the illusion that he could feel it inching forward through his veins. At dawn, he swung himself stiffly onto the horse. Petrović saw him. "It's worst when you start the day."

They were near the summit of the mountain when the scatter of rocks was joined by another kind of debris. The ground was littered with the abandoned wreckage of war. Among the rifles, bayonets, helmets, shell cases, empty grenades, trench mortars, wire cutters of great size and strength, and dozens of rifle cartridges, were an extraordinary number of unexploded shells and grenades. "Iron," said Petrović. "A souvenir of the fighting of 1912 and 1913. And still more will be added to it."

They were now on the edge of a mountain. Below them, the valley was thick with mist. The road occupied a narrow ledge, beyond which the mountain fell away sharply. Winner could not see what lay below the milky covering of mist.

As the sun gathered strength, the mist separated into strands of vapour, through which it was possible to glimpse treetops growing on the sides of a deep valley. Winner felt his soul expand with hope.

The sun had all but dispelled the mist when Winner saw the wheel of a motor. It was a hundred feet below them, and could simply have been thrown over the side of the road and allowed to roll down. But why discard a whole wheel? It was lodged in a bush. The wheel could have belonged to a vehicle that gone off the road and crashed down the mountain until it was stopped by trees. Winner did not know for sure that it was Elsie's vehicle, or any vehicle; and yet he was sure. He felt certain of it. "Petrović," he called.

"A wheel? There are so many accidents."

"I must find out. Will you hold my horse?"

Winner scrabbled down the mountainside. If asked to do so under any other conditions, he would have certainly declined; it would have seemed a madcap thing to do, even without a weak foot. Going down, sliding and slipping, he caught hold of bushes and saplings to slow his descent. He ignored the pain.

He had been right. A Ford ambulance lay on its side in a crevice below the wheel, which must have been twisted off as it rolled down. He hated to think of what it must have been like for the occupants. There was no sign of the people who had been in it: no corpse behind the wheel. The windscreen was broken, papers that had been in the cab strewn about the floor. He reached down his hand to pick up one of them when his eye was caught by a small smooth object, purple streaked with gold. It was the pebble he had given Elsie. This had been her vehicle. Where was she now?

Twenty-Two

The Colonel's headquarters occupied the largest of the cottages in the mountain village, but was almost ludicrously cramped. The big Serb fighters were forever in danger of knocking their heads. It smelt of woodsmoke, and a smog of cigarette smoke hung beneath the wooden beams of the ceiling. The officers seemed worn out. But they made the effort of will to shape their sagging cheeks into a smile to greet Petrović cheerfully when he came in. They seized Winner's hands in their bear-like paws, addressing him in German. Winner could only stammer a good evening. He was impatient for news that might lead him to Elsie. Petrović put his questions.

The colonel looked at him sympathetically. He had white moustaches and a thick bristle of white hair on his head; what had once been a jaunty bearing had not been completely suppressed by fatigue: he must have been a resilient man. "There might have been an accident to an ambulance. I don't know. Gentlemen, have you heard about this? A British Ford off the road? No, they don't know either. If she was hurt, she could well have been taken to one of the hospitals in front of us. Perhaps Prilep."

"How do I get there?" asked Winner, after the account had been translated.

"You can't. We think it has been overrun."

"What has happened to the patients?"

"We don't know. There was a retreat. I hope they got back behind the line. I would not have wanted them to have been taken."

"And if they had been?"

The colonel looked at him steadily. "They probably weren't."

Winner wondered whether to believe him,

"But we shall recapture it," said the colonel with a smile. "Serbia shall live at peace within her own borders at last. It is what we are fighting for."

"You are fighting for peace?"

"We are fighting for Serbia. It is the same thing. When we have Serbia, we shall have peace. It will be the homeland of the Serbs. Why should Serbs fight against Serbs? It is the presence of Bulgarians, Turks, Jews — well, not so much the Jews, they don't generally fight — who are the problem."

"But what about the Bulgarians and Turks within the boundaries of your Serbia. You can't simply get rid of them."

"Why not? I assure you, the Serbs were here first. No, they must find somewhere else to live. Although it would seem that the population will be much reduced by the war. We die fighting, our families starve — but Serbia will be free."

There was a shout of approval from the other officers.

The door of the little house was flung open. An orderly stepped through, saluted and made way for a man in a fur travelling coat. The coat made its occupant look immense, like a bear. Pushed onto the man's forehead was a pair of goggles that looked like a second pair of eyes. "Gentlemen, good evening. Colonel." He shook hands. "Nobody speaks English I suppose?"

"I do," admitted Winner. "But I don't speak Serb."

"No good as a translator then."

"However, Captain Petrović might help."

The newcomer turned to Petrović. "I am going to the hospital at Prilep. Perhaps you can tell you how to get there."

"That's extraordinary," gasped Winner.

"Quite possibly. The hospital is run by my wife, Lady Sturry. She is a remarkable woman. I don't intend to leave her to the Bulgarians," he barked a laugh, ". . . for the sake of the Bulgarians."

Petrović looked at him with admiration. He translated to the others. The colonel clapped his hands. The others followed suit. Petrović summed up the mood: "We admire your courage and determination. We are sorry that you will find it quite impossible. The roads are very bad. We have no horses to offer you. We do not know what has happened in that area, or what has become of the hospital."

"All I seek, gentlemen, are directions. I have known bad roads before. I don't require horses; I have a Wolseley motor car. What has become of the hospital is the very thing I intend to find out. I am travelling as a

British subject, but under the auspices of the Red Cross. I expect that to be respected."

"You must not expect too much. You are in the Balkans."

"At all events, I intend to get to Prilep and find my wife. It has not been easy to get even here. At one point, the car sunk up to its axles in mud. It took two oxen and thirty Austrian prisoners of war to pull it out."

"I'm afraid that will have blocked the road."

"It most certainly did block the road."

"You see," said Petrović, turning to Winner, "why there are so many delays. While this gentleman's car was being released from the mud, nobody on the road behind him would have been able to move. Ammunition, medical supplies, reinforcements — all would have waited."

"I cannot be blamed for the state of the roads. My only concern is to reach my wife, and to help, if necessary, with the evacuation of the hospital to a more suitable location. I intend to do it."

The officers showed him a map. "This is the only hope," said one of them, indicating a circuitous route.

"I shall leave at dawn. Now, can you tell me somewhere that I can sleep."

The officers thought this was an amusing observation. "You can sleep anywhere you like, providing it has not already been occupied. We have no hotel here. There aren't any beds."

"This room has a fire. Do you have any objection to my sleeping here? I'll take a chair." On saying which, he drew one of the few chairs in the room up to the fireplace, settled himself in it and placed his feet on a pile of logs. He was still wrapped in his fur. Within a few minutes his jaw had fallen open and he had started to snore.

It had been agreed that Winner would accompany him to Prilep — or as far towards it as they could get. They left at dawn.

Twenty-Three

"What do you know about motors?" enquired Lord Sturry. They had descended from the heights of the mountain and were now in the northern foothills. It was the first thing he had said for an hour.

Winner woke from a reverie induced by the early hour of the morning, the comfort of the leather upholstery of the seat and the purring of the car. "Nothing at all, I'm afraid."

"So you won't be much use when it breaks down. Unless to push. Although looking at you, it might be better to regard you as a jockey and put you in the driver's seat. Perkins can push. I'll help." Perkins was the chauffeur.

From their comparative bulk, it did seem a better arrangement to Winner, but he forbore to say so. "I'm quite happy to push," he replied.

They were making for Prilep, in a fragment of country still held, they hoped, by the Serbs. Lord Sturry had announced that they would strike out towards Negotino. "We are making a considerable detour, as you'll be aware. And these Austrian prisoners keep blocking the route." They had passed several thousand Austrians since the day had begun. When Lord Sturry had stopped to talk to them, in German, he learnt that they had been given nothing to eat for two days; nor anywhere to sleep. At night, they just lay by the roadside, in the rain. "I shall have to complain about this," he declared.

"Who to?"

"You mean whom. To whom shall I complain. That's just it, I don't know. I haven't seen anyone in charge since we left the hut."

But the bedraggled stream of prisoners did not mean that the Serbs were winning. The stately Wolseley was like a liner, sailing against the tide of retreat. The first little town that they reached — a place of crumbling, plaster-walled buildings, scattered among vegetable patches — was gripped by panic. In the distance, guns could be heard. Wounded hobbled in from every direction except South, wanting, like everyone else except for Lord Sturry and Winner, to take the one road towards Greece, and that had been brought to a standstill by the chaotic volume of traffic. Sturry directed the car towards the railway station. It seemed a residuum of authority might be found there. But the approach to it was congested with stationery wagons containing stores that had to be urgently got away, so as not to fall into enemy hands. The weight of the vehicles, combined with the heavy rain, had dissolved the road surface into porridge. The Wolseley lurched into a hole filled with water. Its wheels spun.

"We're stuck, Perkins," announced Lord Sturry.

By dispensing some currency, he persuaded a man driving oxen to lend assistance. It was no use. He next organised two motor lorries to put their shoulders metaphorically to the wheel. As they were getting into position, he strode off towards the station buildings.

"We think Prilep has fallen," the stationmaster informed him.

"Won't there be a train going in that direction?"

"Oh yes, we'll send a train. We have to rescue what we can. But it won't get through. It will only pick up the men and stores that have come out. The Austrians are only fifteen miles away, we hear. Heaven knows what will become of the timetable."

Lord Sturry told him to telegraph. "There will be nobody to answer," came the reply. He insisted; the telegraph man sent the message, evidently regarding it as a formality.

The Wolseley had, with difficulty, been released from its mud bath. "We shall disable the motor," announced Lord Sturry. "Take off the distributor caps, Perkins, and hide them."

"We're abandoning the car, my lord?"

"Yes."

"Very good, my lord." Perkins was crestfallen. "And the luggage, my lord?"

"Take what we need for a few days, leave the rest," commanded his employer. "I find it difficult to believe we shall ever retrieve that vehicle, despite the precautions," he told Winner. "Be quick about it. A train is about to leave."

Returning to the station, they climbed on board. Lord Sturry positioned himself at the window. The train did not leave for another two hours. It was just as well, because the delay enabled Perkins to rejoin his employer. He was staggering beneath a leather steamer trunk.

Eventually the wheels of the train began to turn, and they rolled out of the town through a countryside which seemed as peaceful as it was possible to imagine. Peasants were out in the fields, as though war had never entered the valley.

The stationmaster had been wrong. The next town had not yet been occupied. The three men climbed down onto the platform of the station at Prilep as though they were visiting a holiday destination. There was nobody about, except a single female figure.

"Here at last," said a commanding woman in a formidable hat. "I was beginning to wonder if we'd ever see you."

"Am I very late?" her husband asked, absurdly in the circumstances.

"We can do nothing about that now."

"The hospital has not gone?" enquired Lord Sturry.

"Evidently not. I am here, as you see."

"We agreed, though, that it would be best for you to clear out. I made arrangements."

"You did make arrangements, Hector. They were admirable. I'm sorry to say that there was a flaw. The

192

entire hospital was packed and ready to move off in twenty minutes, when the transport was cancelled."

"By whom?"

"I tried to find out. Presumably they had to cart off some guns or shells or some such. We were not the priority. So we stayed."

"You've got a lot of stores here. What if they fell into enemy hands?"

"Really, Hector. You might think about your wife as well as your stores. Never fear. We have distributed the stores. The soldiers were very pleased to have them. I don't think they'd eaten for days."

"What now?"

"We wait. The last officer who was here asked me to take responsibility for the civilians in the town, most of whom are hiding in cellars. I intend to fulfil that duty. I have my nurses to consider, and the wounded who were not able to walk."

"I'll stay too."

"Hector, you will not. As a man, you could be imprisoned. What would it achieve? Go back and report to the Red Cross."

Lady Sturry could tell Winner nothing about Elsie. She thought that she might have been with them, but had been sent back as one of the patients able to travel. "I can tell you nothing more. Nor," she announced "can I offer you luncheon. The army left us the bread that they had, but it's made from maize, not wheat flour, and sodden."

"Very well, we leave then," concluded her husband. "But how?"

"It's a pity you don't have a motor," remarked Lady Sturry, with the wisp of a smile. "There's nothing on the road. Everybody has gone." She pronounced it gorn. "You'd have a clear run."

"The train may go back eventually," grumbled her husband. "We'll return to the Wolseley. Perkins, you can find the distributor caps."

"No, my lord."

"Where did you hide them?"

"I threw them in a pond, my lord."

Lord Sturry's wallet procured four mules (one bore the steamer trunk) and they began to lurch back towards Greece.

Snow was falling when they reached some newly built cholera sheds. They had already been occupied by thirty or so nurses fleeing from another hospital. The sheds had stoves in them; they were unexpectedly cosy. Winner asked about Elsie; they could only speculate that she had been sent back behind the lines. Perhaps she had lost her memory.

The nurses strongly objected to having men in their huts, and directed them to the stable. Winner heard the doors being bolted as they left. The straw of the stable was filthy. It smelt overpowering of mule. The animals gave warmth, but also kicked.

As soon as the first sickly smear of dawn appeared in a sky, heavy with grey clouds, he, Lord Sturry and Perkins resumed their journey. White with snow, the track in front of them wound up beside a wall of rock. On the other side, the mountain plunged almost vertically down to a boulder-strewn torrent. They set their teeth against the cold.

They travelled all morning, ever upwards, saying little. In the middle of the day, Perkins lit a primus stove, as the prelude to a picnic of bread, tinned sardines and coffee. "Would you like your chair, my lord," enquired Perkins, who had already spread a rug on the snow.

"Chair?" barked Lord Sturry. "I won't be lingering to enjoy the view."

There was little view to be seen. The valley had filled with cloud. "We must be three thousand feet up," he mused.

They stamped their feet to restore circulation. Thrown onto the snow, the grounds of the coffee made what seemed like a necklace of jet. Perkins packed up the primus and the journey resumed.

They had not gone far when Lord Sturry's mule lost its footing. Having thrown its owner onto the ground, it scrabbled desperately on the loose stones at the edge of the path and disappeared over the edge of the cliff. It skidded down the rock face before plummeting to its death with a ghastly and protracted bray.

"Damn," said his lordship. "Take the trunk off that animal. Does it have a saddle? Rig it up somehow. That's the end of our luggage. Winner, you'd better open it up and take some warm things. No point in leaving them here." Winner threw away his regulation cap, replacing it with one lined with fur. The trunk also contained jacket and boots of a luxury he had never previously encountered. By the time Winner had finished dressing, Sturry had moved grumpily on. The trunk lay abandoned by the side of the track.

The pass itself now appeared high above them. It was deep in snow, but their spirits lifted to see it. They were so cold that they had ceased to feel the pain of it; their bodies seemed to have become frozen to the animals they were riding. But they now had hope of an end to their endurance. Laboriously, they trudged up the last stretches of the zigzagging track.

There were some Serbian guards at the top, their faces muffled by balaclavas and high collars. One of them stepped forward towards Winner. "Petrović!"

But the officer was not Petrović. "Papers," he demanded.

Lord Sturry and the valet dug into their pockets. "I don't have any papers," confessed Winner, with a laugh. "I'm an artist, not a soldier. They didn't give me papers."

The Serb repeated "Papers," and held out his hand. Winner searched for his passport. It was in the army jacket that he had discarded.

The officer said something in Serb. A soldier came and took Winner by the arm. Winner tried to shake him off, but the grip was insistent.

"This man," exclaimed Lord Sturry loudly, "is British soldier." He repeated the identification in French and German. It did no good. Sturry and the valet, hunched against the cold, went on. "Don't worry, Winner. I shall complain to the British consul, as soon as I find him." As his mule began to descend the mountain. "I shall also mention it in my report to the Red Cross."

The soldier pushed the artist before him. Never had Winner felt so alone.

A Lesson from the Professor

Twenty-Four

In the mountains, Spring was still struggling to shrug off the memory of Winter. On the plains, the temperature was balmy. The meadows beside the Vardar were speckled with mauve-coloured poppies. Dragonflies, on long range patrol from the river, darted, hovered and sped on again. Only the enormous bloated form of a kite balloon, riding at its moorings, suggested that this was anything other than an idyllic scene. The Balloon Section lived close to Nature.

"Will you breakfast inside or outside today, sir?" enquired Sunny's batman. They called him Shakes as a delicate tribute to the shellshock that he had suffered on the Western Front. It was still evident in his unsteady hands. Sudden noises made him throw himself to the ground.

Sunny looked up from the bowl over which he was shaving. "Oh inside, without a doubt. I want to luxuriate in the amenities of my personal space."

"The absence of flies, sir?"

"I very much hope there will be an absence. The vapour worked, Shakes?"

"Seems to have done the trick, sir. No buzz, buzz, buzz, sir."

"Splendid. Then lay the table, and ask Lieutenant Sandys to join me. Our last morning in the wilds."

"Lieutenant Sandys left the camp early this morning, sir."

"Tiresome of him, when he might have shared a fly-free tent. This evening we go to Salonika, Shakes, but I don't mind telling you that my heart will, in some ways, be heavy."

Sunny had been ordered to put on a divisional show; that, it was generally assumed, could only be organised from Salonika. A few weeks ago, the prospect of installing himself amid the life and amenities of the town would have enchanted him. Since then, he had found the one thing that almost every man in the Allied armies craved: the company of women. The fount from which this blessing flowed was the BWH. He had persuaded Isabel to come to Salonika once. She would not be free to make many visits now, given the extent to which the beds were being filled and the nurses were falling sick.

And would she have gone? Sunny perceived a rival in Captain Petrović. He had what the French called *cran* — pluck. He cut a dashing figure. He was brooding and intense. Sunny was not made in that way. At the minor public school to which he had been sent, the moral code merged Christian chivalry with the Ilyad, clean living with the cult of the hero; the manly virtues did not include self-expression. He had been drilled to take victory, defeat, anything that life could throw at him, with the same unruffled equanimity. If he could, he made a joke of it. However, it had begun to dawn on him that something about his style fell short of the seriousness expected by those elements of the BWH which were dedicated to the higher life. Those elements seemed, of late, to include Isabel.

Sunny lit the first pipe of the day and cast an eye over an old copy of the *Balkan Gazette*. It was a peaceful morning. A rosy light fell on the mountaintops and he could hear the calling of turtle doves. Even life upcountry had its pleasures.

There was, however, one aspect of it which he would be pleased to forego. Coming home from the Army Gymnastic Corps' concert party, he had been shot at. Since then, his person seemed to have attracted other attentions. The guards had spotted a local man sniffing around the edge of the camp. There was nothing unusual in that; people often wanted to sell things. But he had particularly asked which tent belonged to the Captain. It may have been a coincidence, but soon afterwards Sunny had found, curled beneath his cot, a large snake. Ramsgate, with his mastery of natural history, had told Sunny it would have killed him. It was not Sunny's temperament to be paranoid, but he had begun to think that he was a target.

The rattle of crockery on a tray told him that Shakes was carrying the breakfast tray into the tent. To these sounds was added another. It came from overhead — the steady insistent beat of a propeller. Suddenly, it became louder as it approached and swooped down over the camp. There was the noise of a falling breakfast tray as Shakes flung himself on his face.

Sunny tossed the *Balkan Gazette* aside to see a BE2 bi-plane circle, then land on the flat ground next to the camp. Out of it jumped Ramsgate.

"A little surprise for you," Ramsgate laughed. "We haven't been having much luck with the kite balloons, so I nipped over to headquarters to see if they had one of these I could borrow. It took some persuasion, but they agreed to our making a reconnaissance of the enemy line. Do you know Major Simon?"

Simple was climbing out of the observer's seat in the plane. He peered around him and correctly identified a visual blur as his host. "I heard that someone has found an ancient tomb. Lieutenant Sandys offered to give me a lift."

"Not a bad machine," said Ramsgate. "What do you think?"

"I think you're in time for breakfast," said Sunny. "In," he added significantly, "my tent."

"Is that wise?" asked Ramsgate as he loped beside him. They skirted Snowball who was making the close acquaintance of a particularly succulent tuft of grass.

"You will find that there has been a one hundred per cent improvement on the fly front. We formerly had swarms. They have now, so to speak, buzzed off."

"The lifting of a plague. Did you find an Old Testament prophet to do it for you?"

"Science, my dear Ramsgate. Shakes has released a patent vapour. The flies are no more." They reached the tent. "Shakes, Lieutenant Sandys breakfasts with me."

"I thought he might, sir. I am boiling another egg, sir."

"With Major Simon."

"He shall have the last egg, sir," sighed Shakes, who had been hoping to eat the rarity himself.

Shakes laid another place at the camp table. The officers seated themselves on biscuit tins.

"No flies?" marvelled Ramsgate.

"Can you hear any?"

"It does seem to be remarkably unbuzzy."

Sunny smiled. He leant forward to pour the coffee. "Blast, I've spilt it. I felt something on my neck. I expect you have been admiring the snake skin." He pointed to the hide of a snake, quite a large one, suspended from the side of the tent.

"Is that the smell?" remarked Simple. "I wondered."

"It's drying, prior to my getting it properly cured in Salonika. I've had another turned into a lady's belt."

"For anyone in particular?"

"As a matter of fact, yes. An angel of mercy at the BWH. Something to remember me by."

"Are you leaving?"

"I go to Salonika today. Alas."

"You're becoming like Eggie. He hates Salonika. You used to like it."

"The eternal feminine leads us on, as the poet said. Or should do. Instead, I'm taken away from it by this caper that General Gay has set his heart on."

"Generals must be allowed their follies," observed Simple.

"That's a good name," returned Sunny. "We'll call it *The Follies*."

Ramsgate sipped. He put down his mug. There was a little splash. "What was that? It can't be raining."

"Not inside."

"Bloody fly."

"You bet we'll bloody fly."

"No, it was a fly. It crashed into my coffee."

"I do apologise." At that moment, a dying fly landed in the butter, attempted to free itself, accepted its fate, and lay there, sunk in the yellow dairy richness, revolving its legs.

"It is raining — raining flies."

"I think one's gone down my shirt."

"So sorry. We had better finish breakfast under an umbrella."

"Bugger breakfast."

"Quite."

"Shakes, there's a drizzle of flies in the tent."

"I'll get a broom, sir."

"Good idea. You could try beating them to death with it. Meanwhile, Lieutenant Sandys and I shall take to the Empy-rean."

"The where, sir?"

"The sky, Shakes."

Ramsgate demurred. "I can't have that, Sunny. We have a guest."

"I was imagining that Major Simon would be in his tomb. Under the ground rather than over it."

"I would be happiest there," Simple replied.

"But have you ever flown over the mountains, sir?" questioned Ramsgate.

"No," admitted Simple, not mentioning that he would not be able to see very much if he did.

"*Noblesse oblige.* The honour of the regiment. You, Sunny, shall take the controls, while Major Simon is given the ride of his life."

"What about the tomb?" Simple almost pleaded.

"The tomb won't go anywhere, sir." Ramsgate was firm, if wistful. But on these occasions, family had to hold back. "We'll run you over for it on our return."

"I assure you, it's not necessary to wait." Simple protested as much as he felt politeness would allow.

Sunny took him by the elbow. "You've got some goggles? Good. Haven't flown for a while but I expect it will come back to me. I'll give you a complete *tour d'horizon* — a glimpse of the sea, then over the enemy lines."

The early morning clouds seemed no bigger than powder puffs; the sun etched the contours of the mountains in deep relief.

Simple gazed through his goggles as the undifferentiated greenness of the plain gave way to the blue of the sea; they followed the coast for some time before turning towards the angular greyness of the mountains. It felt cold.

As a finale, Sunny flew several miles beyond the first range of mountains, trenches zigzagging across their sides. Most of the trenches were unoccupied. As long as the Bulgarians clung to the mountaintops, they would not be needed.

In his exuberance, Sunny swooped down on a Bulgarian camp. An earpiece in Simple's leather jacket connected to a rubber tube; into the mouthpiece at the end of the tube Sunny yelled, "You could chuck a bomb if you liked." It was as though they had smoked a beehive. Men scurried everywhere. Trousers were buttoned up, braces pulled on, by those who had been resting; latrines hastily abandoned. Sunny noticed that a hole, about the size of a half crown, had appeared in a wing. He looked down. They were shooting at him with rifles. He made a turn, then lined up for a dive.

Bullets whistled past; a splinter flew from a wooden strut. But from the ground it appeared that the mad Englishman was diving straight at the soldiers who were shooting. The soldiers flung down their weapons and ran for shelter.

Sunny lifted the plane back into the sky and pointed its nose towards the mountains. He turned round to Simple and made a thumbs up. Once Simple had noticed, he reciprocated. This was what war was meant to be about.

Enough was enough, and they headed back over the mountains. They came down over the BWH. Sunny had a belt to discuss. He wanted to measure Isabel's waist. It would require putting his arms around her.

Isabel had spent the morning outside the hospital, seeking a solution to the water problem. So little water was there at the hospital that the nurses' laundry was confined to three articles a week. They washed themselves using china jugs and basins, and occasionally make-shift showers, but baths with hot water had become, for Isabel, a memory from a distant world. So when she was told that, not far from the Hospital, were some mineral springs, whose cold, bubbling water collected into pools, it seemed that her daily existence might be transformed.

"They're in the woods," she announced to Sister Muir, who sat beside her in the pony trap. She indicated the direction with the whip.

"In the woods?" replied Sister Muir. "I wish I'd brought my revolver. I've got one, you know."

"Whatever do you intend to do with it?"

"Protect myself," announced the nurse. A thin, sparrow-like woman, she was in her fifties. Her anxious disposition had got worse with age. "It's a wild country."

"It is wild, isn't it? That's what's so glorious about it. Look at the flowers."

"The owls kept me awake last night," replied Sister Muir, through pursed lips. "The cuckoos never seem to stop."

By now the pony and trap had reached the path through the forest, and Isabel leapt down. Sister Muir followed more cautiously. They walked along a track that was springy with leaf mould, to a boggy clearing. People had been there before them. A way across the muddy ground had been made with sawn tree trunks. Isabel walked carefully across, followed, even more carefully, by Sister Muir. When they stopped, they were above a pool, whose surface bubbled occasionally.

"I thought you would be interested. From the sanitary point of view."

"The smell is not good."

"But wholesome," said Isabel, undaunted by the lack of enthusiasm. "Local people come here just to breathe the air. Although in a confined space it can make them faint."

"Where do they take off their clothes?"

"I don't know. I suppose we could do that here. There's nobody to see us."

"Not yet. I knew I should have brought my revolver."

"I think you should try the water. I'm going to." Isabel deftly removed her white cap, the white apron with its big pockets and her grey dress. Standing in her shift, she felt more vulnerable than she had expected. "I could always go in like this. It is so difficult to get our clothes washed."

"You wear silk," observed Sister Muir, as though it were the ultimate indulgence. "In Macedonia!" She was severe on frippery.

"It was all I had at home," apologised Isabel.

She decided against keeping the underclothes on, stripped them off and slipped down the muddy side of the pool to a rustic ladder that had been fixed there. The next moment modesty had been resumed: only her head was visible above the sulphurous water.

"I think I hear someone coming," said Sister Muir, unkindly. Isabel gasped. "No, it's only a deer."

"Join me. It's quite warm enough. They say it does all kinds of good to the body."

"Who says?"

"Captain Petrović."

"And did he find it warm enough?"

"Sister Muir! You don't imagine I would dream of coming here with him?" said Isabel, scandalised. "He told me about it. We couldn't wash clothes here, I don't suppose — they'd smell — but we could wash ourselves."

Isabel had lost her initial shyness, and now floated on the water, her toes visible as well as her head. "You should really try it."

"No, thank you."

"I'll come out then. I don't suppose you remembered the towels."

"They're in the trap."

"Then I'll have to warm up with Swedish exercises. It'll save having to join in the drill at the hospital. But it's too delicious to get out now. Won't you join me?"

"Very well, I will."

With small, precise movements, Sister Muir removed her outer garments, allowing a brief glimpse of underwear that was to a distinctly older and more utilitarian pattern than Isabel's, before that too was removed. She placed a thin leg on the ladder.

"I still don't like the smell. I like the water though," she said as she lowered her torso beneath the surface. "So Captain Petrović told you about this? He's a very obliging young man."

"He believes he is going to be killed."

"Many of them must think that. Let's hope it's not true."

They were silent. "So many people are dying," reflected Isabel. She floated for a moment. "How long do you think it takes for somebody to fall in love?"

"That depends on the person, I should imagine, and what you mean by love. Longer than you have known Captain Petrović, I would have thought."

"But doesn't the proximity of death accelerate things? Somebody said that the other day. You have worked in hospitals, haven't you? I should imagine it's the same there."

"By the time people get to hospital, they aren't thinking about love."

211

"But the men who go to war are perfectly healthy; it's just that their lives may be cut short at any moment."

"It's what they depend upon," replied Sister Muir, making circular motions with her arms in an approximation of breast-stroke.

"Meaning?"

"It's what they say. To help their wooing. Girls fall for it."

"I find that cynical." Isabel disappeared beneath the water and re-emerged, her hair plastered to her forehead and streaming.

Nearing thirty, Isabel was aware that her best years might be spent in the string section of her parents' domestic concerto, rather than as the soloist in her own. She could interview a cook, make nettle tea and organise a garden fete; she could play the piano and embroider a seat cover; she was fragrant and empathetic. Before Salonika, life had not required her to be self-reliant or to make difficult choices. In short, she had been formed for marriage, but somehow that had not come.

"Captain Petrović spends a lot of time with us."

"Captain Petrović is fine. All the Serbs are."

"One doesn't marry a nation, though. Do you love Captain Petrović?"

"I don't know. I think not. Not yet at least. But I would hate to find I was wrong when it was too late. If he really is going to be killed, that is. To find out that I loved him after he had died would be awful for everyone. Particularly for him of course."

"What would you do?"

"There wouldn't be a lot I could do."

"I mean, what would you do if you married him now."

"Go and live in Serbia, I suppose."

"That's hardly practicable. Serbia barely exists at the moment."

"Then he'd come to Surrey. He speaks very good French. So do my parents."

"It might require some adjustment, mentally speaking, by all parties."

"No worse than Frank Sewell — Ratty as they call him for some reason. He's going to marry a gypsy, he says."

"Something like that happened in Carmen." Sister Muir levered her slight body out of the water, by means of the rudimentary ladder. "It didn't end well."

The bird-woman picked up her neatly folded clothes, held them to her chest and trotted across the wooden causeway to the edge of the woods. She was followed by Isabel, looking more dishevelled than a bather by Renoir, but just as blooming. She collected her garments, dropped where they had been removed, and followed Sister Muir. Sister Muir, still damp, was struggling into her clothes. Isabel preferred to recline on the tussocky grass, hoping the warmth of the morning sun would be enough to balance the cool of the wind on her naked skin. It was not. She felt a chill, and pulled her shift around her shoulders.

She looked carefully at the ground. "There are crickets in these holes. I dug one out the other day."

"They make quite a racket."

"Not as much as the frogs."

"The frogs are appalling."

"Not appalling. Jolly."

"Jolly noisy. But I'm going to disinfect the ponds. They breed mosquitoes. Not these ones," she continued, as Isabel hastily examined her body to see if she had been stung. "They wouldn't like the sulphur. But the ponds near the hospital."

"But the frogs?"

Sister Muir smiled thinly. "They'll hop off somewhere else I expect."

Isabel said nothing. She liked the frogs. But it was true that malaria was taking a heavy toll on the nurses.

There was a movement in the branches. "That was a bear, I expect," declared Isabel. Sister Muir emitted a little spinsterish scream, before saying: "I don't believe you."

Isabel put her shift on properly, buttoned it and pulled on her drawers. "We're in the middle of Nature. Bathing has never been so delicious."

"I would prefer English plumbing. Nature isn't civilised. It's something you girls would do well to remember."

"Civilisation is at war with itself. European civilisation anyway, which I suppose is the whole of it."

They found the trap where they had left it. Isabel took up the reins. Civilisation had, in one sense, reasserted itself: in her uniform, any resemblance to a Renoir bather had disappeared. "I'm not sure that young people — the generation that's giving its best men to the war machine — have the same ideas about civilisation as the older people. For them, time's short."

"They'll find it isn't really." Sister Muir stared at the road. "That flying officer visits you, doesn't he? He's English, at any rate."

"Captain Southall? Yes, but he smokes a pipe."

"Almost all the servicemen smoke."

"He's rather a duck. Perhaps if I'd met him in England. Out here, one wants more."

"More what?"

"More everything."

"Be careful of what you wish for. You'll end up in a harem."

Isabel thought of Mr Gazmend. She giggled. "One of the sultans had seven hundred wives. I bet they fought like cats."

"Good grief. Stop at once."

Two aeroplanes were flying low over the hospital. One flipped over and flew for a moment upside down, the other nose-dived from a great height, turning as it did so and only pulling out of the spiral at the last moment.

"I should have brought my helmet."

"We're not being attacked. They're French, you can tell from the markings. Do you have a helmet?"

"I made it from a tin basin. What are the French doing here?"

"They seem to like us," smiled Isabel.

"They shouldn't give our patients a fright. It's terribly dangerous," she expostulated. "Thank goodness they didn't fly over the sulphur pools."

At the hospital, Isabel and Sister Muir saw that a flying machine had landed on a meadow. It was not, however, one of those belonging to the French. The roundels on the wings identified the BE2 as a British craft. So did the fact that next to it were Sunny and Simple.

"Major Simon," Sunny explained to Isabel, "wants to research Goody's Grave — a subject of archaeological importance. Sister Muir, could you ask someone to take him there? I can stay here with Miss Hinchcliff. A snake has entered Paradise, but fortunately it will soon be a belt." She assented. "But Simple," Sunny said, taking a piece of paper from the observer's seat of the plane, "don't forget your map."

"I don't have a map."

"This piece of paper is a map, surely. It looks just like the coast we flew over. Coves and what not. Shaped like an udder."

"Thank you," said Simple. It was one of the papers taken from Vassilis's digs.

Sister Muir produced Nurse Goodman. "The tomb was really her discovery. I'm sure she would like to show it to you."

"No time for that, now," interrupted Simple. "Sunny, would you fly me straight back to Salonika?"

Twenty-five

On the pass through the mountains, the Serb soldiers took Winner to a chapel. The interior was covered in paintings of saints and angels: huge, robed figures, sometimes with wings, invariably with haloes, stood, frozen in solemn gestures, around the upper part of the walls. The lower part of the walls were closely packed with icons in frames, or prints, including Leonardo's Last Supper. What could be gilded, had been. A sunburst in silver scattered rays above a doorway at the east end of the chapel. Here there hung curtains, concealing the most sacred of images; the importance of others was marked with what Winner took to be lace antimacassars, draped over the top of the frames.

He looked around in delight. As though by involuntary impulse he began to sing:

> Ye servants of God, your Master proclaim,
> And publish abroad his wonderful name.

A soldier shoved him and he stopped.

The chapel had been taken over as a military command post. Greatcoats and knapsacks, rolled maps and ammunition belts, had been piled around the walls. The roof space was clouded with cigarette smoke rather than incense. Behind a table, which Winner suspected had once been the altar, sat a Serb officer. He looked at Winner with hollow eyes. It was daytime, but so dark in the chapel that a lamp stood on the desk, illuminating the maps and papers that were spread on it. In the background hovered a priest in long black robes and long grey beard, the hair at the back of his head in a bun.

Winner wore only fragments of uniform. It had been supplemented with cap, boots and jacket from Lord Sturry's trunk.

The Serb captain said something. A soldier began to search Winner's pockets, producing a square of chocolate, a Bible, a sketchbook, a charcoal pencil, the scalpel to sharpen it. The Bible was handed back. Eating the chocolate, the officer turned over the pages of the sketchbook, looking carefully at those which showed landscapes. He threw himself back in his chair. His flaring moustaches were stained brown around his lips. He added to the nicotine by lighting a cigarette.

He asked Winner a question. Winner could not understand the words. They were Serbian, and his mind, like his body, had gone numb with cold. The officer said something else, this time to the soldiers, and went back to his papers. The men pushed Winner into a corner. He fell over the knapsacks. He got up again, protesting: "I am British. I am an artist." They pushed him again, harder this time, and he went back on the floor. This time he stayed there. The priest spoke to him in a language that he took to be German, but he did not understand it. One of the soldiers, wrapping himself in a greatcoat, left the chapel.

Winner looked at the frescoes for inspiration. By the dim light, the Byzantine figures appeared more than usually lugubrious. Some carried the attributes of their martyrdom. One was St George, the soldier saint, with silver sword raised against the serpent. Another figure beseeched a long-bearded God the Father, wearing a beard to rival the priest's, who had appeared in the clouds in a chariot pulled by four orange horses, with wings. The saint stood by a river; behind him were mountains. Winner felt that the saint's example was good. He began to pray.

The sound of gunfire, which had previously been distant, was getting louder. The explosions were also more frequent. St George sword arm seemed to tremble with the drama of it.

After what seemed like hours — in reality forty-five minutes — the soldier returned with a grey-haired man, also in a Serbian uniform, although he looked too old for military service. "How good to be in this holy building," he exclaimed in English. "Look! What painting!" His nasal voice had a wheedling quality. "How realistic, and yet how spiritual! Please, dearest sir, do you see? A hundred years before the Renaissance!" It was the sing-song voice of a guide. "I am soldier now," he explained to Winner, "but, dearest sir, before all this, I was a professor of English. I used to take groups around the country." He smiled in a self-deprecating way. "Professors do not get paid so much in Serbia. Now," he continued brightly, "they would like me to translate for you."

Winner was relieved to have someone who would understand him. "Tell them that I'm an English artist. I went to the Slade — that's a famous art school in London. I'm here to make a record of the war. But I had to find a friend — a nurse — who disappeared. I've been looking for her with an English lord, whose wife has a hospital. I never knew his name. He had a motorcar but his man threw away part of the engine." He continued to recite his adventures. The professor listened politely. He smiled. He always smiled.

"Wait a moment, please," said the professor, addressing the Captain. They had a brief discussion. The professor turned back to Winner: "He thinks you are a spy. Why else do you make drawings of our positions?"

"I am not a spy. I'm an artist."

"Are you a soldier."

"I was a soldier."

"But you don't have any papers."

"No. I suppose they didn't think about it."

"The uniform you're wearing, dearest sir, is incomplete."

"I've been very cold. I wore anything to keep warm."

The Captain spoke. The professor smiled as he said, "The Captain is sure you're a spy."

"Then tell him to try me. He will look very foolish. Captain Petrović will answer for me. He can tell you who I am."

The professor translated. The Captain shrugged. "There is no time. They have to move positions." At that moment a shell exploded very close to the chapel. "They can't take you with them. They will take you outside and shoot you. I'm sorry. These divine images," he waved a hand towards the ceiling, "will be the last thing you see on earth. Is there anything I can do for

220

you, any last thing, dearest sir? A letter home, perhaps? Just a short one; there isn't much time."

"My drawing things." With the charcoal, Winner scribbled a few words, folded the paper, torn from his sketchbook, and wrote "Nurse Elsie Fox, The British Women's Hospital," on the front. He thought it unlikely it would get through.

The priest came forward and said some words in a voice so deep that it seemed to come out of a cavern, rather than a human chest cavity. He made the sign of the cross and began chanting.

"Now, if you're ready, please," said the smiling professor. "They ask if you would like a blindfold. They advise it."

"But this is a mistake. I am an artist."

"A cigarette, perhaps? A cigarette can be nice, dearest sir."

Winner refused the cigarette. "Perhaps I could take your cap, dearest sir? You'll have no need of it and it looks very warm. It would interfere with the blindfold."

Snow was falling when they went outside.

"Stand here, dearest sir," said the professor. It was far from clear why this very spot had been chosen. Like the rest of the landscape, it was broken by jagged rocks. "I tie the blindfold, dearest sir. We wait one moment for the Captain. The captain is always so busy. Now . . ."

At that point, a roar filled Winner's ears. He was thrown backwards over the rocks. So that is what it is like to be shot, he told himself. He opened his eyes. He could see nothing. He thought he was dead.

An Island in the Aegean

Twenty-Six

Simple peered at the Otter from the other side of a desk piled with chits. His words and manner was blunt. "I need petrol."

"Petrol? This war is coming to be run on petrol. Can I offer you a pastille? They come from Paris."

"No, thank you. Petrol, and I'm in a hurry." Major Otterwill, thought Simple, could be an old woman.

"Quite. I could provide any quantity of warm underwear, just arrived — this of course being nearly summer. But petrol: oh dear, I'll have to disappoint somebody. You're sure?"

"Quite."

Suppressing a sigh, the Otter ordered some large cans to be brought around, from a supply intended for the Durham Light Infantry.

"Going far?" asked the Otter conversationally, as he completed the docket.

"Along the coast."

"The coast," repeated the Otter. He had been at the coal face of divisional administration since he got up, this morning and every morning for weeks past. Simple's words throbbed tantalisingly with horticultural possibilities. "As far as the Udder?" Few people got to explore the bag of land that, on a map, seemed to depend from the mainland next to Salonika and end in three teat-like peninsulas. He felt as though he was growing old in the Birdcage, and might die in the depot, surrounded by avenues of mature trees and a mountain of spiked chits, from the weariness of old age. "I wonder what the botany is like there."

"No idea."

"Of course not. You probably aren't going for the flowers. And I wouldn't dream of asking what you are going for. But I do wonder."

"Don't wonder."

"I mean about the plants. Can I show you my garden?"

"Not now."

"Down the Udder!" To the Otter's plant-hungry mind, the words had an irresistible glamour. No chits on the Udder.

"Come and see for yourself, if you like. I can't guarantee you'll be safe."

"We should to stay away from the clifftops, I daresay."

"Why?"

"Isn't that the danger you meant? One might fall down."

"One might find something worse happening if that petrol doesn't come quickly."

The Otter was absorbed by a decision. "All right," he said with the air of one taking the plunge. "I will come."

"I'm leaving as soon as I've got that petrol."

"Yes, what's happened to it?"

The orderly reported that four cans had been loaded into Simple's staff car.

"Tell the deputy quartermaster to take charge. I shall be back — when shall I be back?"

226

"Tomorrow probably. Possibly next week. I don't know. The main thing is to start."

"Yes, certainly. *Arrivederci a tutti.*"

Simple would dearly have liked to drive the staff car — or any car — himself; the ingenuity of motors appealed to him. But since every object that was further away than the flag on the end of the bonnet was to him indistinct, he concluded that, even for a physically reckless man, this would be unwise. Consequently, he sat back against the leather upholstery of the rear seat, next to the Otter. The driver steered the car west through the camps, with sentries saluting on all sides, then out beyond the endless coils of barbed wire. Almost at once, a more ancient landscape asserted itself, as though the presence of the Allied armies was nothing but a temporary aberration on a scene that had not changed for centuries.

"What are we doing exactly?" queried the Otter.

"Taking a look about us."

"Ah. Secret stuff."

Simple did not reply.

The road barely existed in places. Few people travelled it. The first stretch took them across marshes, with beaches and the blue sea of the Aegean on their right. It then cut inland. There were mountains on their left hand, above which hovered puffs of cloud. "The Allies are building roads all over Northern Greece, but this one seems to have escaped their attention," remarked the Otter. "Still moving? I wasn't sure the tyres were going to stand up to that hole." They had to change tyres three times in the course of the journey.

The road disappeared entirely in the villages, low and whitewashed, that they passed through. Yellow maize pods and bunches of red paprika hung in the windows. A veil of smoke trailed from the windows, doors and gaps. The Otter eyed the scene with distaste. "Squalor."

"Don't you find woodsmoke clears the lungs," returned Simple.

"Might mask the smell of fish, I suppose."

Simple professed a liking for the Simple Life.

"Personally," replied the Otter, "I like my club, with lamb cutlets and a bottle of claret."

They had charts of the coast. They hardly needed them: there was little choice of road. It was merely a question of calculating how far they had gone. Signposts did not exist, nor did villages display names.

"Of course, the mere fact that we're here may render the whole expedition pointless," remarked Simple. "We are effectively advertising our presence. But it was all I could do at short notice. Ordinarily I would have preferred to have come more discretely."

"In disguise, no doubt."

"Nothing too fancy. On a mule, with a scarf to cover my fair skin."

"You wouldn't want it to burn."

"I wouldn't want to reveal my chin. Not hirsuite enough. Wrong colour. I'm going to stop the car around here." They pulled off the road and into a wood. "It will cause comment but I hope we are sufficiently far from the objective for word not to travel too quickly. The driver can stay with it. He's well armed."

They walked down to the sea. The sun had lost some of its summer strength but the air was still warm. They stood at the end of a deep bay. The sea sucked on the coarse sand, like a Chinaman eating soup. In the bay, there was enough wind to fill the sail of a fishing boat. To the Otter, the landscape was all too reminiscent of Gallipoli. Sandy beaches fringed the coves, before the land heaved itself up into cliffs and steep-sided gullies. The gullies and even the tops of the cliffs were surprisingly green, even at this late stage in the year. "You know, the pines must drink in moisture from the atmosphere. How else could you explain it?" wondered the Otter. Simple did not reply. He was scanning the headland.

"There should be some sort of church here, if I'm right," he said. "I don't see it though." He gestured towards a smudge on the horizon which might or might not have been a religious building; he did not admit to the weakness of his sight.

"I don't either. We could ask someone."

"Do you have any Greek?"

"A bit rusty. Ancient, of course."

"Never mind. Mine is serviceable." Simple saw a shape moving a few yards away and correctly identified it as being human

The shape materialised into a figure of almost Homeric antiquity, wearing a triangular cap with earflaps, a kind of striped skirt and crudely made slippers. In a high-pitched voice, the shepherd confirmed that there was a chapel there. It was dedicated to St Nicholas, the patron saint of sailors. But it was far away. He never went there. Crazy people lived on the promontory. Fishermen, not shepherds.

"Do you think there will be roads?" wondered the Otter.

"No idea. I don't propose to take them. We'll find a boat. What sort of a sailor are you?"

"A bad one."

"You can sit in the back, then, and pretend to do something with the nets. Which way is the harbour?"

"Down here, I presume. You can see it."

"Yes of course."

Simple found a boat easily enough. The owner could not contain his glee at the drachma notes he was receiving — as much as he might have got for a record catch, without having to do the work. Before the fisherman pushed them off, his wife handed Simple a package.

"Smells worse than the villages," observed the Otter, wrinkling his nose at the boat.

"But think of it, you are not having to walk," replied Simple, as he busied himself with the sail. He was, reflected the Otter, one of those people who could do practical things. He wondered if it was an instinct.

The wind caught the sail. "For the next couple of hours, we shall have little to do but philosophise. You mentioned chops and claret; our fisher friend and his admirable lady have provided an almost equally Lucullan feast. Bread and wine. Good enough for Our Lord. Good enough for us."

The Otter sniffed the bottle. "It's not wine. A spirit of some kind. Smells of aniseed," pronounced the

230

Otter. He took a cautious a swig from the bottle. "Fire water," he said, passing the bottle to Simple. I'll have a smoke to take the taste away."

"They call it *ouzo*, I believe. Home-made probably and God knows what proof. Pity about the wine, although it would probably also have been filthy."

They glided across the smooth sea; having tossed the stub of his cigarette over the gunwale, the Otter looked over the side at a reef which seemed to him surprisingly close to the hull. Simple seemed to know what he was doing. The Otter stretched himself out, avoiding, as far as he could, anything overtly fishy, and dozed. Simple was tranquil but alert, always — in a sailor-like manner — finding something to do with the ropes or the sail. He put his magnifying glass to a compass. The Otter woke up as they came under the shadow of the hills. "You can see the chapel, I expect," observed Simple.

"I don't think I can," replied the Otter.

"Neither can I. Better look out for it."

"Ha, it's there, peeking out from between the trees."

"Quite so."

They beached the boat, dragging it out of the water a little distance from their objective, then climbed a gully and set off through the pine trees. They rolled down the sleeves of their shirts to stop their forearms from being scratched by the sharp twigs. They came to a halt beside the clearing that surrounded the chapel.

"You have your revolver?," asked Simple shortly. The Otter nodded. "And it's loaded?"

"Why no, it isn't. There seemed little need in my remote outpost and one worries about accidents."

"I've got some spare bullets. Might be as well to put them in."

As they approached the little building, they saw that its door was open.

"Nobody inside," announced the Otter. The interior was thickly hung with paintings, and more images appeared on the screen that separated the tiny chancel from the nave. Simple sniffed. "Petrol," he pronounced. "My word, it's strong."

Simple knelt and examined the floor through his magnifying glass. It gave him the air of a Sherlock Holmes. "They were storing it behind the altar, to judge from the trail here. I wonder if the priest knew."

"I don't see how he could have remained in ignorance."

"No. Imagine if he'd lit the candles."

"It can only just have been removed."

"Yes. Shall we take a look at the beach?"

There was a path leading down to the sea, but Simple did not take it. Instead he ran back along the path to the boat, stumbling over the obstacles that he did not see. "We'll sail around. We'll get the best view from the sea. If we stay far enough out, we'll look like fishermen, but we can observe them through the field glasses."

They rounded the headland and the Otter scanned the beach. "There's the petrol all right. A forest of tin drums. Well, a copse anyway. I can't imagine how much there is in them."

Simple sailed the craft away from land. "We've seen as much as we can for the time being. No point in making ourselves conspicuous."

"What do we do now?" asked his companion.

"We wait. Hoping that nobody from the other side of the bay comes to warn whoever it is with the petrol of our presence."

"Friend Vassilis?"

Simple frowned. "How do you know about that?"

"A murder at Molho's? It's the talk of the *Cercle*."

"I wish that of those who did the talking could have their mouths sewn up."

There was an uncomfortable silence. "Molho's, of all places," reflected the Otter. "Whatever next? The place is practically a club."

"A very good place to pick up information, for someone who kept his ears open. Men say all sort of things after a couple of cocktails."

"I suppose," posited the Otter, "what the fellow in the boat's doing isn't actually illegal. Greece is neutral, after all."

"Three things," replied Simple. "First, where did he get the petrol? Not through any bona fide channel, I'll be bound. Secondly, who's he selling it to? That we'll find out, but unlikely to be a regular household supplier, given the cloak and dagger business. Thirdly, Greece may be neutral but Salonika is under Allied martial law: a bit confusing for the locals, possibly, but I should think they've got the gist."

The sun was setting. It seemed to bleed the warmth out of the air. But still the pair waited, the Otter with revolver drawn. "Look," he whispered; he hardly needed to speak softly, given their distance from land. Simple took the field glasses although they did not do him much good. "He's loading the petrol into a boat. Shouldn't we stop him?"

"Let's see where it leads."

The man launched the boat with some difficulty, it was so fully laden. He then raised the sail and tacked out towards a small island that lay half a mile off shore. The boat was very low in the water. There was, however, no danger from the sea, which was as calm as a sleeping child. He rounded the island. Supported by Otter's observations, Simple saw just enough to know that he intended to land.

"What shall we do?" asked the Otter.

"I'll put the boat ashore on the other side of the island.

"That wouldn't be very good if he saw us."

"No."

"I mean, they might do something to the boat. We might find it very difficult to get back."

"Yes."

"I don't want to give the impression that I've got cold feet . . ."

"Not at all."

". . . but I wonder if we are taking an unnecessary risk. We could get the Navy to send a patrol boat."

"We could. But when would it get here? Besides," added Simple with an uncomfortably withering look, "we'd miss the fun. You wouldn't want that."

By now the little craft was pointed towards land. The beach was at the foot of a gully, debouching from which was a stream. They jumped out of the craft and pulled it as far into the gully as they could, so that it was partly concealed by the dense vegetation. The light was going, and the gathering shadows in the gully seemed, to the Otter, far from cheerful.

The Otter picked the bottle of ouzo out of the boat. "We might need it later. Warming stuff, if you can take alcohol that strong."

Simple nodded. He had ceased to be conversational.

They climbed up the gully, their feet alternately sinking into the soft sand or stumbling over tree roots. Pine trees of all sizes clung to the slope. Needles poked into the men's eyes and branches scratched their bare arms. At its top, the gully opened into a plateau which had been ploughed. "Not much cover," remarked Simple, making for a scatter of bushy trees on the other side of the field.

It was not a large island. But in the time they took to cross it, dusk changed into night. The sky, though, was clear, and the moon gave enough light for them to proceed slowly. They reached a cliff. "What say you we pause," suggested the Otter, pulling a cigarette out of a packet. "Don't," said Simple shortly, as the Otter fished out a little brass box of matches. "Somebody could see it. And we'd better keep quiet." They made their way along the cliff top until they were looking into a cove. Simple tapped the Otter on the arm. The Otter nodded. Below them was the shadow of a boat.

"He's waiting," whispered Simple. "A rendezvous."

"We could arrest him now. Overpower him before his chums arrive," returned the Otter quietly.

"No. Might make them windy."

★ ★ ★

After dark, the temperature dropped sharply. Waiting, the men turned up their shirt collars and tried to rub circulation back into their arms and legs. The Otter wanted to walk around to warm up but Simple would not have it. Whoever it was that was expected would have to come by water. They scanned the sea for craft, fastening their attention on shapes that turned out to be only shadows. They spent an hour in discomfort, straining their eyes. Then, from the open water, came the sound of an engine.

A small craft was approaching. But it was the vessel beyond it that excited Simple. In the moonlight the Otter could distinguish the silhouette of a U-boat.

"This is interesting," said Simple, as though to himself.

"He needs fuel, presumably," remarked the Otter. "Why here?"

"The Navy must have made it difficult for him to find a supply. Turkey has run dry. His base is too far away. He can't buy it openly in Greece; we'd be onto him like a shot. Besides, there isn't much petrol about."

"I can confirm that."

"There are some big submarines, I believe, but this isn't one of them. Doesn't have much range. Can do a lot of damage though. You remember the Marquette of course."

"All those nurses and doctors."

"Fuel is his problem. He has to resort to this sort of business."

Crewmen sprang out of the boat and pulled it onto the beach. They quickly began loading the cans of petrol into it. "What shall we do?" asked the Otter. "There are too many for two people to arrest. Besides, they'd be rescued by the ship."

Simple considered. "Otter, you get round to the other side of the cove. Go down to the beach. When they shove off, start shooting. Not at the men. I want you to hit the oil drums. And leave me the *ouzo*."

It seemed an odd priority to the Otter but he was pleased to remove the bottle from his pocket, where it had been digging into his thigh. "Dutch courage?" Simple didn't smile.

The Otter ran as quickly as softly as he could around the cliff. When he arrived on the other side, he found a problem. There was no way down to the beach. By now, though, the crewmen had loaded half the cargo. He pushed on. The cliff was steep. He was not going to jump: he would break his ankle. If he tried to climb down, he would be bound to slip in the hurry and heaven knew what would happen then. He looked around, conscious that Simple would never forgive him for muffing it. He ran, stumbling, to the end of the next bay, where the land shelved, although precipitously. He scrambled down as quickly as he could, more or less within the limits of his natural prudence. His feet slid on the rough surface, and he lost his balance. It was easier now to slither down in a recumbent position, using his feet and elbows. At the bottom, he landed suddenly in a bush full of long prickles. His adrenalin stopped him from feeling the thorn stabs.

He dashed back along the beach. He would have preferred to stick to the shadows beneath the cliff but it would have been difficult to move quickly through the loose sand. Instead, he took a line along the sea's edge, crouching low in case he was spotted by a look out on the U-Boat.

He waded around the headland. Moonlight, looking like long silver ingots, glinted on the water. He was just in time to see the boat push away. There was shouting in the boat. He had been spotted. He raised his revolver and fired. The cans made a much better target than the crew would have done. A metallic ping told him that he had hit them. He fired again. There was a crack. The men in the boat were shooting back, but, reflected the Otter, they would find it difficult to keep a steady aim in the rocking craft. They were against the moon, he was in darkness. He emptied his chamber.

He ducked down into the water. He did not want to make himself a more conspicuous target than necessary. Where was Simple? On the further side he saw a light. It reminded him for an instant of a Christmas pudding. A blue flame danced across the sands. The Germans had not noticed yet, because they were looking intently at him — or rather, now that he was almost submerged, for him — firing at intervals. There was a shout in Greek. The smuggler was pointing at Simple. The will o'the wisp was nearly at the boat now. The Germans saw the flame, just as Simple threw the bottle to which it was attached. The bottle broke in the bottom of the boat. Men were now on their feet, stamping at the flame as it spread around their boots. Simple, only a few yards from the vessel, coolly sent a

238

few more bullets towards the drums. They flew in all directions, but one hit the mark.

More petrol spilled out, pooling with the fluid that had been splashing from the holes made by the Otter's bullets. In an instant the flame from the ouzo had ignited the spilt fuel. There was a different flame now, an orange one. It flashed around the craft, catching on men's boots and clothes. Each of them flung himself over the side. As they waded ashore, the cans were engulfed in flame. The scene looked for a moment like a Viking burial, and then came the explosion. The men hurled themselves onto the surf. Only Simple, who had withdrawn to a safe distance, was left standing. A piece of hot twisted metal nearly took off his ear.

The Otter splashed toward the beach. As he did so, he reloaded his gun.

The crewmen struggled to their feet. They had lost their weapons in the scramble to leave the boat. Simple gestured with his revolver for them to raise their hands. "Gentlemen, I am a British officer and I am taking you prisoner."

Twenty-seven

The Otter emerged from the sea, his clothes streaming with water, like a figure from the Trevi fountain. He walked up to Simple. The fire from the petrol in what was now a furnace of a boat lit up the night scene. For the time being, the Otter did not notice the cold. "Quite a bag," he observed. "Three seamen, a Greek pirate and, if I'm not mistaken, a submarine commander."

The seamen were wearing fatigues. "*Kapitän?*" asked Simple of the man in uniform. He nodded.

"We had better do something," the Otter continued. "They can't have missed the blaze. A party will be coming from the mother ship any minute."

Simple addressed the seamen. "Launch the boat," he ordered in German, waving at the Greek's vessel. When they hesitated, he insisted: "*Schnell.*" Discipline had become second nature to them. In the circumstances in which they found themselves, Simple was the commanding officer. They obeyed.

Once the boat was in the sea, the U-boat commander was ordered into it, encouraged by a tap from the Otter's pistol.

"Do you think we should tie them up?" said the Otter, meaning the party on land.

"Not much point, really," replied Simple, hopping into the boat. "They'd be released in a second. Besides, we don't have time." He began hoisting the sail. The Otter gave the craft a final push seaward and himself scrabbled over the side. As the sail filled, it looked for a moment as though they would be carried towards the burning boat. The fire had subsided and parts of the hull were now smouldering; it would have done them no good to run into it. But Simple was too good a sailor for that to happen.

The breeze was good. They sped silently into the dark of the night. As they did so they saw a rowing boat cross the water between the U-Boat and the land.

240

"They must have seen us," said the Otter. "Why didn't they fire? The ship has got a machine gun on it."

"Uncertainty. They don't know for sure what has happened. For all they know, we might be going to fetch bandages."

Wind filled the sail, and the fire sank to a distant glow.

"They'll follow us," Simple predicted. "But they'll have difficulty in seeing us, with luck. Or hearing us for that matter. That's the beauty of sail: not a sound. We'll stay in the shadow of the island while we can. Curse this moon."

On the far side of the island they clung to the coast. Simple's eyes narrowly searched the horizon. The Otter, in his damp clothes, was finding the night very cold. The U-boat commander sat with his back straight.

"Simple, I'm sure you speak German."

"I do."

"I thought you would. Might you therefore," ventured the Otter, hugging himself for warmth, "ask him if he has any seeds?"

"Can't you think of anything else," answered Simple irritably.

"I find it consoling," replied the Otter, "in times of stress. It's a pity you used that spirit. I could do with some."

"I find it more consoling to feel this breeze. It's blowing for land."

"In Trieste, my father was a gardener," said the commander in English.

"Where is the submarine though?" continued Simple, without hearing him.

"He greatly admired Gertrude Jekyll."

The throbbing of a diesel engine made its way to them over the water. "That answers my question," muttered Simple. He lowered the sail. They could see the silhouette of the submarine nosing towards the little strait. Presumably the crew now knew the full story from the companions whom they had rescued. They had also deduced that the British soldiers would need to make their way back to the mainland. The boat was therefore patrolling the little strait.

"I did not know you had gardens in Austria."

"Some. Among people of quality. We recognise that England has studied the domestic arts more fully than we on the Continent. You have, so to speak, brought civilisation in such matters to a perfect state. The climate, though, is wrong for flower borders in Trieste. Excuse me." He suddenly stood up, shouted and waved his arms.

"What are you doing? You'll have the boat over."

The commander went towards the side of the boat, which was now rocking violently. Just as he was reaching it, Simple pulled him down. He brought his pistol down on the side of his head. "Your shirt," he snapped at the Otter. The Otter struggled out of the damp garment and handed it over. Simple rammed it over the commander's mouth.

"Did they hear?" whispered the Otter.

"I don't know." The commander was not struggling now, but Simple still had his hand pressed to his face.

242

The submarine chugged past.

"Look after him, will you." Simple pushed the commander's inert form onto the floor of the boat and hoisted the sail. Shirtless, the Otter began to shiver. The commander was moaning in a low voice. At least that meant he was alive.

"We might be able to sneak past them, back to the mainland, while their backs are turned," observed Simple. "If they see us, it will be hopeless. We'd have to dump our friend over the side."

"But in his present state, he'd drown."

"Yes. I don't think anybody's chances of survival would be very high. They might think we had made a bit of a fool of them. The Germanic peoples aren't known for their sense of humour. We wouldn't be taken prisoner. What would they do with us on a submarine? Damn."

"What?"

"They're turning already. They must have heard *Herr Kapitän*. I might as well have shot him and be done with it."

The Otter had stopped shivering. He was watching the submarine as it turned.

"There is one possibility, you know."

"The submarine will follow us."

"Obviously."

"Then take a course a little nearer the mainland. Then lower the sail."

"Why?"

"If we lower the sail, we'll make a difficult target. The moon will be behind them, not us."

"But we won't be moving."

"If we're in the right place, it won't matter."

"You're mad."

"We're not going to beat them to the shore. Now, right a bit."

The Otter peered intently over the side. There was an oar in the boat and he lowered it vertically into the water.

The submarine was now bearing down on them like an avenging angel.

"Here we are," announced the Otter. "Down with the sail."

"I hope this works," muttered Simple.

"Let's see what happens."

There heard the unmistakable sound of grinding metal: the awful sound of a crash that any motorist knows will cost time and money to repair. "Up with the sail," ordered the Otter jubilantly. Simple was there before him. Over the water came sounds of German shouts. As they sailed away from the submarine, which had run onto the reef, a burst of machine gun fire spattered into the water. Simple tacked. "They haven't got our range yet. We can't outrun them. Even if they're stuck, that gun will have a range of over a mile." Another row of waterspouts leapt from the water. The Otter ducked the boom as Simple tacked again.

The Otter found himself literally holding his breath. Air did not enter his lungs until he noticed himself becoming faint and he forced his ribcage to expand. He heard what he wanted to hear: silence.

"They must have decided not to bother with us. They've got problems enough of their own."

It was not until they were pulling towards the village that Simple acknowledged: "that was quite a good stunt."

Having beached the boat, they strode along to the car. The commander had recovered consciousness. He did not make any further demonstration of defiance. "There are some rugs in the motor," the Otter told him. "I should think we could all do with one. It was awfully interesting, what you were saying about Miss Jekyll. You see my mother's rather a friend of hers."

"Munstead Wood," replied the Austrian.

"Perhaps you'll get to see it," put in Simple, "now you're a prisoner of war."

"Steady on," put in the Otter. Simple, he thought, could be unnecessarily caustic at times.

They wrapped themselves in rugs. The Otter cranked the engine. "Plenty of petrol," reflected the Otter. He felt as though he had lived through a Greek drama, of the sort the Ancients put on: he was drained of emotion.

"Oh yes," returned Simple, looking significantly at the captain. "Plenty of petrol."

Twenty-Eight

Three weeks later, Winner contemplated his boots. He had begun to wonder if his feet had ceased to exist. But the rest of him, although pierced by cold, was alive. He had not been killed by the shell.

At the chapel, he had been blown onto the ground. He had lain on the ground for some moments. If he was not dead, perhaps he had been blinded. He could see nothing. His head hurt. He did not know it, but he had been blown twenty feet into the air and had come down heavily on a rock. When he put his hand to his temple, he remembered the blindfold. He tore it off. Half his clothes had gone. He was gazing upwards at the lichen-covered trunk of a thorn tree. After a moment, he used the tree to haul himself upright. He looked for the chapel. All that existed was the east wall, with the sunburst. The little building had received a direct hit. The captain must have been killed. The cap that the professor had taken was hanging from a branch of the thorn tree. What remained of the professor lay immobile against a rock. His eyes were wide open and his face wore an ingratiating grin. He was dead. Beside him, on a fragment of masonry, Winner could see part of the fresco of St George. The soldier and the priest had disappeared.

Apart from a painful rib, Winner found himself to be intact. He did not, however, have much time to collect his wits. From the vantage point of the pass, he could see Bulgarian soldiers coming up the road below. The Serbs were falling back. He moved with them. Before he did so, he stopped to pick up a cap — a Serb one. His own coat having been torn off by the blast, he took the professor's. He now bore some semblance to a fighting Serb.

"I am looking for Captain Pretrovic," he told an officer, when the group he was following had caught up with the rest of their unit. The officer looked at him with distaste, but pointed him down the line.

By now, Winner was drained of everything except a tenacious will to survive and find Elsie. Near the point he believed to be Petrović's stretch of the front, he collapsed, out of exhaustion, his head on his hands. He fell into a deep sleep.

A sergeant had woken him up. "Buttonhooks," Winner growled.

A deep voice admonished him: "Don't curse the man." He recognised the tones. It was Petrović's voice. "The sergeant didn't want you to die. You certainly would have done if you had slept there all night."

Winner struggled painfully to his feet. To his embarrassment, Petrović embraced him with Slavic warmth as a friend. Winner did not care to be embraced, but was pleased to stay on with Petrović's unit.

The unit was ceaselessly on the move. Winner's boots were, fortunately, particularly good ones, having been made by Lord Sturry's bootmaker in St James's of the best quality leather. They were also a reasonably good fit; but in the three weeks since leaving the chapel he had not taken them off. He began to fear that they had become permanently welded to his feet. But if he took the boots off, his feet might never get into them again.

Fighting, on guard duty, taking up new positions, fighting. Endlessly. Without a break. That was his new life. It was exhausting, but it was a life. He was not dead.

Whenever Winner saw someone new, he asked him about Elsie. He no longer needed a translator. The men understood the few sentences that he needed to say. The answer was always no.

One cold night Winner asked Petrović: "Can't you give the men blankets?"

"They would only throw them away. They don't want to have any more weight than they can avoid. They have to keep their packs; we insist on that. But I know that some of them are completely empty."

It was a starved landscape; the rocky skeleton of the earth poked through a skin-like covering of soil. The sound of shelling echoed almost ceaselessly around it. Before the reverberations of one shell had died down, another would be on its way.

Blankets would have allowed the soldiers some escape, and not just from the cold, thought Winner. They could have crept under them and hidden, their eyes dark, their hearing blocked against the guns; and they could have dreamt of home. As it was, they slept anywhere, wherever they had the chance. They just flopped down. It was not warming, their sleep, but cold. Dreamless.

"They're giving us steel helmets now," continued Petrović. "The men don't like them much."

"They dress like foresters going shooting," said Winner.

"It's what they're used to. They're not Tommies."

That was evident from their stockings. Each soldier had his own, knitted to a different pattern, but always with colourful tops — red roses and yellow trees, or pink roses and forget-me-nots. They were wound about with the straps of their *opanke*, or sandals, made of camel skin.

That morning Winner watched the Serbs creep from rock to rock. The Bulgarian position was formed by a ledge. As they got nearer to it, they no longer crept between the rocks but ran. The most advanced ran up to the ledge and threw grenades over it; then all the soldiers together rushed forward, crying "hourra, hourra."

Petrović was jubilant. "You saw my men. They were good. Do you have soldiers like that in the British Army? They were very good."

Winner picked some mountain flowers and laid them in an empty shell case. The new position looked very similar to the old one. "What have you gained?" Winner asked Petrović. "One mountain simply has another mountain behind it. They go on and on."

"So? We'll fight every mountain, one by one."

One day the battalion marched through a fertile valley. The day almost had the air of a festival. Word of the army's arrival had travelled, and peasant women from all along that valley, as well as some of the neighbouring valleys, had turned out to watch it pass. Mothers looked for their sons. There was rejoicing when they saw them. Men were allowed to fall out briefly to hug their parents, although they had to hurry to get back to their units again.

The peasants called out the names of those they were looking for. "Have seen Goran?"

"He's coming, Mother," the men would shout back.

"Where is Slobodan Jovanović? He's with your Regiment."

"He's coming. He must be behind us."

Winner had been lent a horse and rode beside Petrović. "I hope she finds him."

"She won't," replied Petrović. "He starved to death in the retreat through Albania. The men don't want to cause unhappiness."

Winner rode on in silence. Did they know what had happened to Elsie? Perhaps they knew and did not want to cause unhappiness to him.

It was when Petrović's unit left the front line and took up its position in the reserves that Winner found the field hospital. Before the retreat, it had been on the road that Elsie would have taken.

"Have you brought the supplies?" the doctor asked. He spoke in English. "Don't look surprised. I have lived in the United States."

"I haven't brought supplies."

The doctor did not disguise his annoyance. "What are you doing here, then? Can't you see we're busy?"

The hospital occupied a tobacco factory, which was now lined with beds. There were too many wounded for the beds; some of them leant against the wall, or lay stretched out on the floor.

"I am looking for someone."

"Don't ask me to remember whom I've treated. They come, so many of them. There's no end to it. I don't sleep. I haven't slept for months."

"You might remember. It is a nurse from the BWH. She drove a Ford."

"English?"

"Yes."

"We had an English woman, a nurse. She died."

Winner turned and walked out of the factory. It was colder in the factory than outside, where the sun was warming the crisp air. All the same he began to shiver uncontrollably.

The doctor walked past. "I'm sorry," he began.

"Thank you."

The doctor looked puzzled. "I'm sorry you didn't bring the supplies."

The Gaiety of Nations

Twenty-Nine

Winner made his way back to Salonika without any fixed plan beyond finding Simple and trying to get himself sent home. Before that, he had something to do. That was to sleep.

Winner considered himself to be a country boy. He was sturdy, if not physically tough. But his time in the mountains had almost destroyed him. He had not been fighting: he could hardly imagine the further layer of exhaustion and fear that combat would have imposed. Nor had he been in the field for months — just a few weeks. But in that period he had been forever cold, had never properly slept, had barely eaten a single satisfying meal, and had been constantly on the move across difficult terrain. These trials almost crushed him, but he had kept going, his sinews strengthened by the prospect of finding Elsie. When he heard that she was dead, he crumpled.

Few soldiers in Salonika had the luxury of their own room; the only bed that he could find was in a corridor of a grandilo-quently named, but otherwise flea-bitten hotel. But even there he succeeded in sleeping unbroken for thirty-six hours.

On waking, he made his way to the *Cercle des Etrangers*. He had hoped to see Simple. Instead it had been Sunny who hailed him. "An artist," he cried. "Just when I had need of one. You shall design our sets."

Winner looked at him uncomprehendingly. Not even Sunny's congenital buoyancy could dent Winner's settled and inextinguishable gloom. In fact Sunny's cheerfulness grated on him. But he was rudderless. In this condition he followed in Sunny's wake.

Space was precious in Salonika, and it said much for the importance that General Gay attached to the Follies that Sunny had been given an office. "Our theatrical home," declared Compton Pauncefoot, throwing his arms wide, when, after having climbed several flights of stairs, he walked into the modest space.

Pauncefoot had been, at some point, a theatre manager. He was not an obviously military figure, being afflicted — particularly at times of duty that he might otherwise have found tedious — with a condition little known to medical science, if not, some wondered, invented by Pauncefoot himself, called "distended abdomen." His abdomen had a happy presentiment about the Follies. They would mean an absence of army work and an indefinite spell in Salonika.

Sunny remarked: "We needn't worry about over-ostentation as regards furnishing." Except for a somewhat overblown impresario, an officer of the Royal Flying Corps and Winner, sunk in a torment of misery, there was nothing in the room beyond a table, a chair and a dead mouse.

Sunny looked out of the window. It overlooked Ivory Filler's dental surgery, or as Sunny privately thought of it, torture chamber. Eggie was going in there now. Sunny shuddered and lit his pipe.

Winner had thrown himself disconsolately on the chair.

"Elsie was always looking for something, you know. That was the trouble." Sunny and Pauncefoot exchanged

256

glances. They had grown used to this sort of disconnected comment from Winner. "Some people find God. She needed a cause."

Sunny had his own worries. He unfolded a copy of the order that had been sent around the Division by General Gay. It read:

From:
The Adjutant of the 76th Division, British Salonika Force.

To:
All commanding officers of the Division.

Subject:
Soldiers required for divisional concert party, and their duties therein.

General Gay requires the Division to stage a concert party at a date to be decided, but not more than two months from the date of this order. All the show's needful resources will be found from within the Division.

This includes both the performing and management elements of the production — i.e. actors, singers, musicians, designers, costume makers, lighting engineers, director, etc.

You are requested to inform your unit of the decision. Auditions and interviews will be held for the posts

257

needing to be filled. Soldiers wishing to be considered for roles in the production should apply to:

Lieutenant Sandys, Kite Balloon Section

as soon as possible.

The General particularly asks that you encourage would-be members of the new unit to come forward, and make it possible for those who are successful in the auditions to forego regular duties for the duration of the show.

Sunny had, in addition, printed a flier, encouraging men to put themselves forward. But he still had the nervousness of a host on the night of a big party — a host who knows none of his guests personally. "Do you think anyone will come?" he wondered.

Pauncefoot plumbed the depths of philosophy. "This, Sunny, is the theatre; it will come right in the end. Probably. But meanwhile, remember the key fact," he paused significantly: "we aren't Upcountry. You're younger than I am, Winner. Could you just nip down and find another chair?

Men heard the call in different ways.

On the Struma Plain, Harry Withers, batman, had just placed a cup of tea on an outcrop of rock which served Captain "Woody" Elms as a table for writing the battalion diary when the Captain threw him General Gay's order. Woody and his men had been in the front line for a fortnight. "Glad to see that the Old Man has his priorities straight," sneered Woody. "Soon he'll be organising rest cures at Biarritz — for the select few, of course." Woody's sarcasm was heightened by the listening patrol that occupied the previous night. He had lain face down for hours, without detecting any stray Bulgarian movement, but getting very stiff in the process. "I suppose the platoon commanders had better read it out at quinine parade."

The quinine ration was issued daily. "Bitter?" gasped one joker in the ranks. "It's worse than my mother-in-law."

That evening, Withers was cleaning his officer's field boots. Not all officers wanted shiny footwear on moonlit nights, but Withers would never have allowed Woody to face Johnny Bulgar in dusty boots.

"Any response to General Gay's order?" queried Woody.

"Only one man as yet, sir."

"Who's that?"

"Me, sir."

"I can't allow it, Withers. You're invaluable."

"Very kind of you to say so, sir. But the order did ask that every assistance should be given."

"Well, the most I can hope is that they won't want you. What were you as a civilian."

"*Thés dansants*, sir. I played in a trio."

"You never told me."

"You never asked, sir."

"Go to hell then."

"Thank you, sir. I'll write home for my cello."

★ ★ ★

259

George Penny, from Norfolk, was Number One in a Lewis gun team. As he cleaned the weapon, he talked. "What you have to do, see, is creep up on them," he told his Number Two. "And then wait. Wait for hours, not moving a muscle, so that you look just like a floating log. You want hundreds of them, see. Oh, it can take forever."

Number Two was filling the long cartridge belts of the Lewis. "What time do you go out, Copper?" No man called Penny could escape being called Copper.

"I told you that," he replied. "Before dawn, and it's winter, see; black and miserable. And you have to wait, your nose just above the surface of the water, until the first streaks of dawn trail across the marshes, like the fingers of a corpse. You wrap up as warm as you can, but you still nearly freeze to death."

"Then?"

"Then, flocks of them come to feed. Not just geese, see, but teal, widgeon, mallard, golden plover. All the ducks and waders in Creation."

"Well?"

"Well what?"

"Well, you're lying on the marsh or the lake. What next?"

Copper put his finger to his lips. Looked theatrically around to ensure hush, then shouted "BANG!"

Number Two dropped the cartridge belt.

"That bloody great gun goes off," Copper continued. "You only get one chance, see. But it's a Big Bertha, that gun; packs a huge lot of pellets. With that one shot, you might hit a hundred birds."

"Oh, glory," sighed Number Two. "All that rich food. Better than the chorus line of the Clapham Grand. Not to mention the feathers." He had worked in a hatters before the War.

"What I reckon is, couldn't we try something like it with the Lewis? All those birds on the marshes. We strafe them, see. Then . . ."

"Roast dinner . . ." Number Two's eyes drifted off into the distance, resting on the mountains in an unfocused way. On that day, though, the mountains themselves seemed to be out of focus. Smudged. "What do you make of that, Copper?"

Copper looked up from the gun barrel. "Looks like a black cloud. But it's not where a cloud's supposed to be. It's lower down."

"It's moving, too. Across the plain."

"Towards us."

The men fell silent. So, too, did the crickets. The mules shuffled round so that their rear ends faced towards the oncoming cloud. The atmosphere became very still, but oppressive.

"Feels weird."

As Number Two spoke those words, spurts of dust stirred at their feet. They formed into eddies like the vortex of water running out of a bath. Their eyes stung.

"Get down, man. It's a sandstorm, see."

Just as the pair flung themselves to the ground, the sky darkened and the mountains disappeared from view. They were enveloped in the cloud. It seemed to have eaten the world. Plain, mountains and the tents of the camp all disappeared within the all-devouring bowels of the cloud. There was a howling in their ears. The cloud seemed intent on sucking the breath out of their bodies, and replacing it with hot, stinging grit that stuffed their nostrils. Their shirts filled with the billowing dust and ballooned out, like the tyres of the Michelin Man. They put their arms over their heads as rocks came crashing and bounding past. Their tent was caught up and like a sheet of paper. The dining marquee was the biggest structure in the camp, a huge affair. It was whipped from its moorings and went sailing over the Monastir road like a barrage balloon. A hut made of corrugated iron and baulk timber rose up, to the alarm of the people reading and writing in its shade. When it came down again, it might have been a pack of cards, scattered across the camp: the ground, that is, where the camp had been.

Having struck and played havoc, the tornado sped on. In the few moments that it had taken to pass over the site, order had been reduced to chaos. The mules had no need to escape from the kraal; the kraal itself had been ripped up. Pots, tent poles, knap sacks, bedding, clothes, chairs, shaving brushes, lavatory seats, tins of bully, harness, wheels of shattered carts — all had been strewn across the site as though some mythical giant had emptied the contents of a dustbin over it.

When Copper and Number Two opened their eyes, they found the air still thick with dust. There was dust everywhere. Their hair and clothes were coated with it. Scraps of what had been camp life — letters, grains of rice, tufts of grass that had once been the makeshift thatch which covered huts made of baked clay — were still whirling back to earth. Number Two put out his hand and caught a paper as it floated past.

It was headed:

NOTICE:
AUDITIONS FOR
THE SALONIKA FOLLIES
A Divisional Concert Party.

The Division seeks players, singers, musicians, set designers and costume makers.

Only the best need apply

Copper blinked the dust out of his eyes, took the paper and stared at it. "Look, Number Two. It says costume makers. I know about hats."

"Hats. You're talking about hats? We've got to clean the gun. If we can find it."

"I might apply." He looked at the devastation around him. "Anything would be better than this."

Private Effingham was in Salonika. He was known, perhaps affectionately, as Burps, because his digestion often took him that way. It did so now, as he swayed downhill in company with an officer's driver and an orderly from one of the hospitals. They had met in a bar, but that was at the start of the evening. Now it was late.

The authorities, misled by Burps's waggish decision to declare his religion as Jewish, had sent him to Salonika for the Feast of Rosh Hoshanna. That they had got the date wrong did not matter to Burps He saw it as an excuse to get drunk.

On his unsteady progress through the Old Town, Burps's eye was caught by an architectural feature. These houses possessed balconies. Men sang beneath balconies. Burps felt that he should do so himself. It would be a way of thanking the Jewish family who had, considerably to their surprise, found Burps on their doorstep, with a note about a Jewish festival that would not take place for several months. They had fed him. The meal had ended with a tiny cup of very thick chocolate which he ate with a spoon. The beautiful daughter of the house made it a Molho's. She unquestionably deserved serenading.

One detail mitigated against the success of the performance. He had chosen the wrong balcony. This became apparent after its owner flung up the shutters and threw out a bucket of what Burps hoped had been water. A crowd was assembling. The singer attempted to bow his way out of the difficulty, but as he turned to leave, he felt a hand on his shoulder. It was an officer of the Royal Flying Corps. Burps saluted.

"You'd better come with me," said the officer. "Now," demanded the captain, when they had reached a street corner that was sufficiently far away to seem private, "name, rank . . ."

Burps told him, adding, for good measure, Church of England.

"I don't care about that so much, but I heard you sing."

Burps winced. "Sorry, sir. Roshshashashana, Shur."

"You have a fine voice. What did you do in Blighty?"

"Shurveyor, Shur. Before that, Covent Garden, Shur."

"Fruit and veg?"

"Chorus of the opera, Shur."

Sunny whistled. "You may be just the man we're looking for.

Meanwhile, Winner began to sketch out his sets. They would be a harmony of aubergine, gray and black.

Thirty

Eggie strode towards the club. The yellow pompoms of the mimosa trees were releasing their sweet scent. Eggie noted the scent, the sunlight, the season. He walked smartly through the double doors, sheltered by the arcade, that led to the *Cercle des Etrangers* and left the bewitching, sensory charms of late Spring to those that enjoyed them. It was not mimosa which perfumed the air of the coffee room but smoke. The plume from Sunny's pipe, mingling with the wraith of Bigot's Egyptian cigarette and the trail of a Padre Corbel's Woodbine, formed a mystic union above the low-slung leather armchairs. A monophysite, wanting to demonstrate his conception of the Trinitarian nature of God in the dispute that convulsed fifth-century Byzantium, could have found no better illustration.

"Summer's coming," Eggie observed curtly, as he walked in. "Time to close the shutters." Outside a stork could be seen flapping heavily to the nest it had made on a chimneypot. "Ah padre, I was hoping to see you."

Corbel had spent the morning making white painted crosses. They would be needed at the hospital. The marshes seemed to breed mosquitoes as big as blackbirds. He had the burial service by heart.

"Shall we go through to the back room?" suggested Eggie. "More private."

Wearily the padre rose. A rugger blue, he was the embodiment of the Church Militant, the champion of a simple and robust faith. But people would keep sharing their inner lives with him. He would as rather see their underwear.

"The dust is rising on the Via Egnatia," Corbel observed conversationally. "I never know why they won't use watercarts."

"That's Salonika," scoffed Eggie: "likes to fester in its own stink."

Eggie was then stopped in his tracks by an abomination. With soft tread, Gazmend had materialised in the room. He was not a member. He was a native. He was a Turk.

Eggie recovered himself sufficiently to speak. "This," he said slowly, conscious that the man whom he addressed was foreign, "is — a — club. Members — only. *Compris? Au revoir.*"

Gazmend ignored the implication of the last words, even though they had been spoken, for his benefit, in a foreign language. "You were talking of Salonika, my

266

native city," he observed blandly. "I quite agree. But one step at a time: congratulate yourselves that the Allied presence has suppressed the brigands. We used to go in terror of them."

"This is quite impossible," exploded Eggie.

"Not at all impossible, alas. They would capture children from the villages: it was like an education in life for which they demanded rather heavy fees, reminders being sent in the shape of ears and noses, cut from the unfortunate pupils. Persistent non-payment resulted in a severed head. It was most distressing. Now the roads carry too much traffic for them ever to be unsafe, and the brigands have a new source of enrichment as irregulars in the pay of the Allied armies. Under the skin, they remain the same cut-throats that they always were."

"It's quite impossible that you should be here, talking like this. The porter should have stopped you."

"He did stop me."

"Then how is it that you're here?"

"He let me through." Gazmend's strangely effeminate lips formed themselves into an almost coquettish smile. "I received a letter. I came to see what I could do about the kitchen."

"Are you going to cook? You've come by the wrong stairs."

"I would love to say that I could prepare a sheep's head for you. The joy of cracking it, the scooping out of the insides. Or an intestine — we eat them a bit like spaghetti. I can see your appetites are whetted, but I leave that department to my wives. It's the kitchen. The

Club wants to improve it, I understand. I own the building."

"We do want to improve the kitchen. There's a committee."

"That's something we don't have much in Salonika. We have *Komitadji* in plenty, but they're something quite different. But this committee. Who is on it?"

"I am," said Ratty gruffly.

"Captain Sewell, a pleasure as always."

"You know each other?" barked Eggie. "Whatever next."

Never in his darkest fears did Ratty imagine that Gazmend would pursue him to the Club.

"I thought you were expecting to leave Salonika."

"You were expecting, I think, that I might be required to. That would be a difficult thing for the Club, of course."

"How so?"

"I would need to collect the rent. All that is owed. You might have to leave the building. You see, the *Cercle* has an interest in my staying."

"You're trying to blackmail us," expostulated Eggie.

"Certainly not. The captain is mistaken. I remain. I have to. I am, after all, a consul."

"The Bulgarian consul. The staffs of the consulates of the Central Powers have been sent packing. Salonika may be a dungheap of spies, but we've got our pitchforks out."

"I was the Bulgarian consul, that's true. In Salonika, a man may represent more than one country. The record I believe was four. The gentleman in question used to have a different sofa in each of the corners of his room, so that each visiting trouser seat could be received by the cushion of its country. Necessarily the countries in his portfolio couldn't all be his own. I am now the Roumanian consul. The Allies are at war with Bulgaria, but Roumania has not declared for one side or the other. Yet. Your governments particularly hope that Roumania will be a friend." He smiled again, in token of the amicable sentiments they might all hope to share.

"Actually, I cannot prolong my visit here, however delightful that would be." He spoke as though they had been pressing him to stay. "Let me only discuss kitchen matters with the committee, in the person of Captain Sewell, and I shall be gone." Ratty took him reluctantly into another room. "You want the money," Ratty said wearily.

"You surprise me, Captain. Business in the Club? That would never do. You do owe me money, but another time. The kitchen can wait too." He smiled affably; Ratty looked at him as though he were a snake. "But I do have a question I would like to ask you. The Royal Engineers use motor lorries. Only in Salonika do we still go around on mules, as though Mr Rolls had never met Mr Royce. Now," he said fixing his coal-dark eyes on his victim: it was the leathery pouches around them that Ratty particularly disliked, "how do you get the petrol?"

In the back room, Eggie sat by a table. Corbel took a chair next to him.

"Padre, you've never pulled a tooth, have you?" asked Eggie. From his size he looked quite equal to doing so.

"Is that what you wanted to ask me about, Major" answered the padre, "or do you have something else on your mind?"

"I just wondered."

"I could have a go if you wanted me to." The padre looked at him shrewdly.

"Teeth are my Achilles' heel."

"I see. Continue."

"No, that was it. As regards teeth, I mean. It was a different matter altogether that I wanted to talk about."

"I thought it might be." Men sought the padre for all manner of reasons, to comfort themselves with faith, set their consciences straight, seek advice about the wife or family at home. He tried to reassure about their place in Creation for whatever time they would occupy it. There had been so many men, so many little talks, so many white crosses.

Eggie came to the point, by as direct a route as he could. "Immorality. That's why I wanted your support."

"Indeed," said the padre. "You're troubled by it?"

"Yes. I want to stop it."

"Good. Reject the flesh."

"Shows."

The padre leant forward and laid a reassuring hand on Eggie's arm. "It doesn't show."

"I mean the shows they're trying to put on. That are actually being encouraged by the Division. They're an open invitation to vice."

"Vice?" queried the padre. "How do you know?"

"I went to the dentist. Ivory. As I came out, still a bit groggy from the gas, I saw . . . I can hardly believe it, but I strongly suspect that I saw two soldiers leaving the offices of the Follies in a state of — I don't know how to put it."

"Inebriation?"

"No."

"Undress?"

"No."

"Shock?"

Eggie inhaled through hairy nostrils. "Inappropriate intimacy."

Corbel was silent for a moment, as though turning the horror over in his mind. "Not on the street?"

"Where else?"

"I'm not surprised," confessed the padre. "I have always felt that Cromwell showed much discretion when he banned the theatre. We should take this to the General."

"My feelings entirely."

They found General Gay in his office. He was an immaculate soldier, whose uniform, its light-weight fabric as close as the army could aspire to gossamer, fitted perfectly, having been made by his tailor in London, and whose leather boots and straps showed not a speck of dust. He was tall, well-proportioned, healthy, energetic and the play of his face showed a searching curiosity. Although his office occupied a barn in a farmhouse, somebody had rigged up a bookcase. There was a table on which stood the gramophone. When he stood up to receive Eggie and the padre, it was from a neo-Classical mahogany chair, bought, at a stiff price, from the Salonika bazaar.

They saluted, tea was offered. "General, it's about the Follies," began Eggie, after the usual civilities had been exchanged.

"Have you heard the latest? They say their theatre, when they find one, will be named the Gaiety — after me. Flattering, what?"

"The point is," took up the padre, "vice. We all know that the theatre serves as a licence for moral lassitude. It has done since the Restoration."

"There are no Nell Gwynns in the Birdcage, as far as I'm aware, padre."

"There are no women. Not real women. That's exactly it."

"So where does the harm lie?" wondered the General, innocently.

"In men acting as women," cut in Eggie, "and not only acting them. The crime that dares not name its name."

"Oh that," sighed the General. "Most of the boys at school grew out of it."

Corbel looked stern. "These are not boys, General. This isn't a public school."

"It's very like one, in some ways. Thousands of young men, effectively locked up together, nothing to do except sport — and no women. What follows?"

"Discipline," answered Eggie sharply. "Punishment if necessary. Under King's regulations they could be birched."

"They impersonate women because they miss them. The audience feels all the better for the tender recollection of home. They're acting. They're corporals

272

in the transport section or orderlies in the RAMC when they're off stage."

"Mightn't it be better," ventured the padre, "if the men practised drill?"

The General sipped his tea. "We're in this for the long haul. We need efficient soldiers. We also need them to be cheerful. Morale, you know."

Corbel expanded his rugby-playing chest. "You say morale. I say morals. When you take men from different regiments, different battalions, different traditions, with different skills and from different backgrounds — and they're thrown into a disorderly hodgepodge in, of all unsavoury holes, Salonika, something unhealthy is bound to result."

"There is some wisdom in your words," reflected the General.

"Rid Salonika of vice," urged Eggie.

"That would be a tall order. But I undertake to rid Salonika of The Follies."

Thirty-One

There was no doubting that it was summer. "PHE-W, it's hot nowadays," soldiers in the Birdcage told each other. Parades were over by ten o'clock in the morning. After that, the men lay around under cover, reading and sweating, sleeping and sweating, or just sweating. Upcountry, the pleasures of the season were shared with an active mosquito population, but at least the Royal Engineers built dams across the streams in the gullies to make swimming pools. There were no swimming pools in Salonika. In Salonika summer was worst of all.

Ivory Filler hated Salonika. It irked his sense of order. Cobbles. He was walking over some now — so difficult for the feet, and so noisy. The thoroughfare was an inferno of noise. Iron-shod hooves clopped, horns blared, cabmen yelled, Greek soldiers chattered in high-pitched voices, wheels clattered, in the distance growled the sirens of ships. And the populace ceaselessly gabbled, gabbled, gabbled.

Flies. They were another curse of Salonika. Well, science might yet provide an answer to that problem. He had an experiment underway. Sure, flies could be swatted, caught on flypaper, poisoned with unpleasant vapours — remedies which addressed the symptom, not the root cause. The scientific mind identified the problem as one of eggs. Each female fly could produce hundreds of progeny. By the time the loathsome insects were airborne, the battle was lost. They had to be killed at the egg and larva stage. How? By persuading the females to lay their eggs in boxes of earth mixed with beer. Ivory had set some up at home. They had been out for a few days. He was confident that, at any moment, they would be squirming with little white maggots. He would then burn the boxes. There might be a patent in it.

Pleased by the thought, Ivory smiled. He stopped smiling when he found the sidewalk, as he called it, blocked. A crowd had gathered. In it he saw Ratty. The

274

back of his jacket was damp and he seemed to be arguing. He was attempting to change money.

"I thought this would be a simple transaction," he moaned. Ratty prided himself on living high. That was expensive. He had no private income. All he received on top of his army pay was the occasional contribution from his widowed mother in Bromley, who could ill afford it. The last thing Ratty wanted was for his finances, in any aspect, to be public knowledge — particularly when the public might include Gazmend Effendi. It was one of those days on which the worst inescapably happened. Ratty became aware of a boater, a silver-topped cane and a strong aroma of bay rum.

"I see your difficulty, Captain Sewell," said Gazmend, as though having read Ratty's mind. "You think of money as being a private matter. In Salonika it is everybody's business." Gazmend pulled out a large spotted handkerchief and mopped his face. "I myself am particularly interested — and very glad — to see you in funds."

"They never last long," muttered Ratty. "What's this man saying?"

"He wonders," interpreted Gazmend, "what currency you want."

"Drachmas, of course."

Gazmend chuckled. "There's no of course about it. I recommend French francs. It's what I always use. Drachmas are only for the more sordid transactions of life. Shops. Women. Other trifles."

A man in a long robe, reminiscent of a dressing gown, tapped Ratty on the sleeve. "*La livre turque est encore d'un usage fort courant,*" he advised.

275

"One can still use Turkish pounds," observed Gazmend. "But this man — from Armenia, I think — advises Italian lira."

Ivory had heard enough. As he pushed his way to the back of the crowd, he collided with a barber who croaked: "Piastres." Into his ear, a tailor breathed the word "Lepta," as well as garlic fumes.

At the back of the crowd he found Sunny. Winner was with him. "I've been given the most extraordinary orders by General Gay," Sunny was saying. The crowd was breaking up. Winner, however, stayed where he was. He looked as though he had lost the power of independent propulsion, like a wheeled toy that a child has abandoned.

"Wants us to relocate," Sunny continued. "I say, cheer up." As he said this, the man with strong views on the Turkish pound approached him. Sunny brushed him off, but the man was insistent, going so far as to seize his elbow while, with many smiles, attempting to turn him back. Sunny made a gesture of irritation.

There was a clatter in the road. Iron shod hooves and iron rimmed wheels were striking the cobbles, as a *gharry* came trotting towards them. It was going at a spanking pace. Then the driver lashed the three horses into a gallop and they tore towards the remains of the crowd.

The flimsy carriage swung, its wheels striking sparks from the stones. Turkish Pound had a firm grip on Sunny's arm, it seemed to restrain him. Within a moment the *gharry* was upon them. Sunny, gazing, spell-bound, at this display of madness, found that he had been shoved him into the street. Taken off guard, he staggered. He was about to fall.

Winner's lethargy disappeared. He was close enough to dart forward and grab a forearm. Throwing all his weight towards the pavement, he succeeded in pulling Sunny upright. The hooves of the horses thundered by. Winner sprawled onto the paving stones. Sunny felt the breath from flared nostrils. Flecks of foam from the horses' mouths landed on his jacket. Afterwards, he had a memory of a staring, maddened horse's eye, seemingly a few inches from his own. The near wheel of the carriage flew past only a hair's breadth from his foot. If he had been on the cobbles, it would have smashed his head.

For a moment, Sunny was too dazed to do anything but stagger. As soon as he had regained his equilibrium, however, he looked furiously around him. He wanted to find the man who had nearly caused his death, but the few seconds in which the episode had taken place were enough for him to have disappeared. The *gharry* had already turned a corner and was gone from sight. Turkish Pound had also made himself scarce. "That was nearly unhealthy," exclaimed Sunny. He took a pipe from his pocket.

"Salonika is a dangerous place." Sunny looked into Gazmend's currant-black eyes. He noticed how dark the hoods were — almost sinister. He tried to light his pipe but his unsteady fingers kept dropping the matches.

Ratty was pushing a sheaf of Greek notes into his pocket without counting them. "That driver was too quick for me, or I'd have taken his number. Too busy with my transaction. That's done now. I shall go to Molho's — a good time for some conversation with the chocolate girl. Will you come with me? You could do with a brandy."

Sunny declined. He felt himself shaking.

Gazmend smiled. "I, on the other hand, have nothing to do and would willing accompany you to Molho's. You could tell me about your gypsy wife." Ratty attempted to distance himself from the incubus but they walked off together, Gazmend loquacious, Ratty monosyllabic. "While I could tell you about Denmark. Do you know Denmark? It's another neutral country, like Greece. To my taste, however, too cold." His voice eventually became inaudible.

There was only one place where Sunny felt he could recoupe his nerves. He and Winner bent their steps towards the *Cercle des Etrangers*. "Quick thinking on your part," observed Sunny gratefully. "I was nearly under the wheels of that thing. There seems to be a campaign against me. They haven't succeeded yet, but they seem to keep trying. The pot shot after the Gymnasts. The snake in the tent. Now this."

"Why you?"

"That's the strange thing. I've no earthly idea."

The *Cercle des Etrangers* provided its usual solace. Sunny's composure returned, as did Winner's. They were enjoying the peace of the afternoon from the depths of the club's armchairs when a subaltern burst in on them. He had been on the landing overlooking the staircase. The treads of the staircase, made of marble, were shallow, ensuring that the men ascending it — they always were men — generally did so at a stately pace, allowing plenty of time for them to be observed, generally unseen, by the occupants of the leather armchairs and chaise-long that were disposed next to the balustrade.

"I've just seen Ratty," he exclaimed, "on his way in."

"Nothing unusual in that," Sunny replied, "unless he was dressed, in compliment to his domestic status, *alla zingara*."

"It was who's with him."

"Give details."

"I can't."

"Then doesn't your story fall a bit flat?"

"I mean, I don't know his name. But he's not British."

"French?"

"Not one of the Allies at all."

Sunny had only just raised a questioning eyebrow, when Ratty himself walked into the room, with an embarrassed air. "Ratty," cried Sunny, "where are the spangled waistcoat, the tight trousers, the spotted handkerchief on your head. I don't see so much as an earring." He was then silent. Behind him, as cool as the fountain in his own garden, was Gazmend Effendi, his difference from the other people in the room, all of whom wore khaki uniforms, accentuated by a red cummerbund beneath his jacket.

"Good grief," said Eggie, placing his glass of mineral water on a table, but neglecting to put forward a hand. "We've seen you before."

"It is good of you to remember, Major Eglinton." Gazmend bowed. "On the previous occasion, I came as your landlord."

"Rest assured, the building is holding up," Eggie told him scathingly. "No leaks."

Gazmend bowed, as though he took this reflection on the soundness of the roof to be a personal compliment. "The plumbing, I hope, is also satisfactory. It rarely is in Salonika, and now such drains as we have are hopelessly overloaded. But I'm sorry to introduce such a subject before luncheon."

With a visible effort, Ratty asked Gazmend what he would drink. Eggie looked as though he had been blown up with a bicycle pump and his eyes were about to explode. He took him aside. "Look here," he was beginning.

Gazmend regarded them with a quizzical eye. "I hope that my presence does not disturb you."

"Me?" replied Sunny, who remembered Gazmend's courtesy in the cemetery. "Not at all. I think that Major Eglinton is perhaps going over the rules of the Club with Captain Sewell. You see, it's awkward for me to say this . . ."

"Captain, forgive me if I interrupt you for a moment. It may save time and avoid unpleasantness. The *Cercle des Etrangers* is what its name implies: a club for foreigners."

"That's it," confessed Sunny, relieved not to have to explain the point of difficulty.

"You may be under the impression that, in Salonika, I do not — how would you say it — fit the bill."

280

"Just so."

"But Salonika is a Greek city, and I am not a Greek."

"You are Turkish."

"I used to be Ottoman, but it's not that."

"Bulgarian then. Just as bad, I'm afraid."

"No."

Sunny gave up the guessing game. "So what are you?"

"I have recently found that I am in actual fact Venezuelan."

"You were born there?"

"I can't remember. I was very young."

"You didn't mention Venezuela when we last met."

"The subject never came up. It is only recently that I have got my papers in order."

Sunny looked at him sceptically. "How did you manage that?"

"There we are lucky in Salonika. We have so many people who can help with that sort of thing. It is a city of artisans. Jews mostly. Clever people. There are artisans who will make any papers you need. I also found the staff at the Venezuelan consulate very obliging. Actually there is only the consul and he is an old friend."

Eggie had finished his conversation with Ratty and stalked out of the room. "The Committee shall hear about this," he threatened. "So shall the Provost Marshal. The man is the Roumanian consul. Roumania come out for Germany."

"I have just been explaining my position to the others, Major. I'm not the Roumanian consul — a thankless task, disgusting people. I am simply a foreigner in Salonika, like yourself. Captain Sewell has been kind enough to put my name down for the club." He paused for effect. "Perhaps you'll second me. I'm sorry, don't distress yourself: only my joke. I must not be forward. As a foreigner in my own city, I don't know the rules. Not your British rules, at any rate."

"Now, Venezuela, if I mistake not, is neutral?" posited Sunny.

"Exactly that. I am like Mr Fuller, the dentist."

"He's Canadian. Canada isn't neutral."

"I apologise. I imagined that he was American. He looks so healthy and self-righteous. Not like the people of Venezuela, my own land, who are very — well, Venezuelan."

Ratty was not enjoying the occasion as much as Sunny. "I should imagine that you aren't intending to dine," he suggested.

"On the contrary, since you're kind enough to ask me, I would be delighted to eat something." He continued to Sunny: "It's so difficult to know, these days, where one belongs in the world."

Winner sought clarification: "Were you never Bulgarian?"

"Good heavens, I've hardly been as far as Nish."

"They say you were the Bulgarian consul, though."

"I was; I try to oblige. But Venezuela called to me. My own dear Venezuela."

"As a neutral, you can't be expelled," observed Sunny.

"I think not. Caracas would be most displeased. I shall sit it out. I shall observe. I shall, above all, have luncheon."

As they descended the marble stairs, the subaltern whistled a martial air. "You know that probably," he said as they went into the dining room.

"I don't think I do."

"*Gloria al Bravo Pueblo?* It's the Venezuelan national anthem."

Ivory, meanwhile, got home and collected his maggot boxes. In the brown fragrant earth, a myriad of white larvae writhed. He lit the porcelain stove, waited for the fire to catch and, one after another, dropped the boxes on the flames. Salonika was a maggot box, he reflected. If only it would also burn.

Ivory threw himself into the one easy chair and attempted to read a book. It was hot. The flies were as bad as ever.

Thirty-Two

General Gay was as good as his word to Eggie and the padre: he would rid Salonika of the Follies. To fulfil his orders, Sunny and Ratty set out for the Birdcage. They had a call to make on the Otter. Ratty had a staff car at his disposal.

"Excellent," said Sunny. "Snowball can come in the boot." The sheep followed them into the quartermaster's office when they arrived.

"Otter, old man," opened Sunny, "we need nails. Not only nails, but timber, canvas . . ."

"Damn your nails," replied the Otter.

Sunny, who had been walking nonchalantly towards the armchair, recoiled at this unexpected asperity. "No nails?"

"Absolutely none. There are dozens of men like you wanting nails. All the nails we've got are committed."

"At this point, old man, you usually offer me a jujube."

"There they are on the desk. Take one." Sunny did. "Then get that infernal animal out of my room."

"You don't seem quite yourself."

"I had Simple in here wanting petrol. Bloody nearly killed me."

"What did he do with it?"

"It wasn't what he did with the petrol. It was what he did with me. We sailed to an island to stop a smuggler and were nearly shot to pieces by a U-Boat."

"I heard about that. You came back with a U-Boat commander."

"I would much rather have come back with some *Scrophulariaceae*."

"Aren't they a medieval disease?"

"Figwort," the Otter corrected him. "I spent hours wrapped in a blanket. You've no idea what that man is like, Sunny. He nearly killed both of us. If it hadn't been for some rather clear thinking about the whereabouts of a concealed reef, we'd be at the bottom of the sea."

"You didn't let him drive the car, did you?"

The Otter gave him a withering look.

"It seems to have affected you," said Sunny, with concern in his voice.

"It has."

Sunny evinced sympathy for the quartermaster's broken nerves. Ratty did not have his reserve of fellow feeling. "The fact is, sir," he began curtly, "we've been ordered by General Gay himself to build a theatre. It will be on the Struma. There will be a camp, too. His idea is to have a divisional base for the production and performance of shows."

"Ridiculous," muttered the Otter.

"Tell General Gay, sir. Meanwhile, he wants a theatre, we have to construct it, and I must ask you to provide what's necessary to do so."

"I'll tell you what," suggested Sunny. "We'll discuss it in the garden. Snowball would enjoy the walk."

"You won't get around me like that." He paused to spear a chit on a spike. He did so savagely. "I planted a garden before, you know. Just as it started to grow up, I had to move here. That's the army for you. I went back to it the other day: nothing there."

"Rabbits?" asked Ratty, matter-of-factly.

"I hope so. They will have got fat and might then have been eaten by a hungry soldier. But I suspect it was just decay. Weeds grow up and they're too rank for the tender garden plants. Besides, this climate. What could survive the summer without watering? But it's surprising what can endure if properly cared for. Here is my kingdom. Order out of chaos and fresh vegetables every day. No number nine pills for me."

"That's just Gay's idea for the theatre," exclaimed Sunny. "Making the desert bloom."

The Otter looked glum. He picked up the pastille box and ate one of the bonbons himself. "He does know that it's quite impossible?"

Ratty laughed caustically. "I can't see how that's relevant, sir. It certainly hasn't stopped him from ordering me to do it." He paused while the Otter assimilated this truth. "So a way must be found."

The Otter looked for a distraction. "We could play tennis if you like."

Sunny looked stern. "We don't have our things."

"Let me show you the garden after all." The quartermaster stumbled out of the door.

Snowball, who had found her own way out of the office, was nibbling a row of marigolds. Sunny shooed her away.

"The whole British Salonika Force is clamouring for supplies." The Otter stopped to inspect some young fennel plants. They had grown from seeds that an old man had fished out of a jar in the Jewish bazaar. Fennel! What use was fennel when his heart yearned for *Helianthus*, Golden rod, *centaurea montana* (blue), Iceland poppy . . . "Whom do I disappoint? I have a hospital which collects the broken packing cases, to use the wood. You know about that of course. That's how desperate we are for materials. I have to husband my stores. Keep a strategic reserve. Heaven knows how much will be needed if there's a push. You can't just come and take what you like for a theatre."

Sunny took the Otter's arm, as one might that of someone recently bereaved. "General Gay said it came to him in a flash of inspiration. He was being

286

harangued by Eggie and the padre — they've rather taken against the Follies, you know. He saw that they were right. To throw together a heterogeneous lot of soldiers — different ranks, battalions, all the rest of it — is asking for trouble. Do the thing properly. Give us space, and a theatre of our own. Away, alas, from the temptations of Salonika, but that may be as well. The temptations were playing havoc with rehearsals." The Otter groaned. "Lovely things you've got here," continued Sunny diplomatically. "Are those aubergines? We don't have them in Warwickshire. Excuse me a moment." He ran over to Snowball who was making short work of the Otter's nasturtiums.

The quartermaster considered who, among those needing stores, was shouting the loudest, and who could be bluffed into waiting until further shipments from Britain replenished his granary.

"It's the submarines," the Otter continued to Ratty. "The more that the war goes on, the more we need supplies. But less and less is getting through. My latest delivery came by private yacht — Sir Thomas Lipton's. A complete new outfit for the BWH, the one whose nurses collect the wood. They'll be pleased."

"A new outfit, as in buildings, sir?"

"Yes, everything you could think of."

"A hospital is very like a theatre," observed the Engineer.

"Not really."

"But could be made so, sir. Quite easily."

The quartermaster looked appalled. "That is the most dreadful suggestion. These stores aren't even mine. I'm merely giving them house room until I tell the hospital that they're here."

"But you haven't told them yet, sir."

"Not yet."

Ratty looked at the Otter squarely. "Sir, do you know the phrase, the exigencies of war?"

The quartermaster eyed him sourly. He liked the nurses. He found Ratty offensive. The nurses were far more pleasant to deal with than the others who generally came to his door: officers from the Labour Corps, stained and exhausted by weeks of camp life and construction work, who swore brutally when they were denied. He wanted to oblige the nurses, but they were more malleable than a divisional commander such as General Gay. They could be fobbed off. There would be no distressing language. He foresaw a busy time for the pastille box.

"Think of it as a loan," continued Ratty. "Sir Thomas would hardly notice it. He wouldn't, in fact, know, would he, sir?"

"Not immediately. There will be trouble later."

"Isn't that so often the case in life?" volunteered Sunny, who had returned with the recalcitrant sheep. "What are you talking about?"

The Otter sighed. "I'll need a chit."

"Naturally."

"The nasturtiums are doing well, aren't they?"

"They were."

Sighing deeply, the Otter returned to his desk.

Thirty-Three

General Gay's theatre could not be erected in Salonika, whose urban resources were already stretched to the limit. Even the confines of the Birdcage, the encirclement of barbed wire and other fortifications that surrounded the city, were too crowded. He decreed that it should be planted, instead, on the Struma Plain, the broad territory which the Allies had recently occupied to the east of the Vardar — a land remarkable for its cypress trees, migrating birds and mosquitoes. Tents were pitched, stores organised, cookers erected, latrines dug. The settlement was soon known as Camp Follies.

The boom of the guns by day, the bullfrog orchestra at night — one was as much a part of the aural background as the other. The men could see the sharp-topped mountains, with their different pimples or Pips, occupied by the Bulgarians. But Camp Follies belonged to another world. It was not shelled. The men there felt their state to be an almost Arcadian one: simple, but in harmony with Nature. Several members of the Kite Balloon Section had got jobs as stage hands. Bill Bayley was one of them. His only complaint was the roofers. Hammering started at dawn and went on all day. "Enough to give someone a headache," he muttered, as he walked to the wash house.

Sunny came up. "Where's Bream?"

"On guard duty, sir."

"Really?"

"We have our own rota, sir. It's the geese."

289

"Oh yes, very important. Well, remind him that rehearsals are about to start."

"Those geese," sighed Twofour, as Sunny left. "Lovely little things."

"Lovely big things soon, I hope," corrected Bill.

"It was a bit of luck that Fishy found the nest. Someone else might have made an omelette."

Among all the little comforts that men managed to secure for themselves at Camp Follies, the geese, hatched from eggs, were an undoubted masterstroke. Men sacrificed their rations to watch the goslings grow. They fed them by hand. It was not done entirely through love of wildlife. It was still five months to Christmas but the soldiers looked forward to it.

Sunny still had his mind on roast goose when Seymour Lamsley sauntered towards him. His cigarette was in an ivory holder. When he had been with his battalion, he had been content to share the discomforts of soldiering. Since being made the leading man at Camp Follies, he had started to demand privileges.

"To act well, I really need sleep," he had told Sunny. "That means a tent of my own." Lamsley had been the star of such West End successes as *Lord Henry in the Pantry*, *Kiki* and *O! I Say*. Sunny eyed him wearily, wondering what his next demand might be. He soon discovered. "What are you going to do about Footy?" Lamsley asked, as man to man.

"You mean Compton Pauncefoot? I have nothing in mind."

"His ideas are antiquated. Keeps talking about trap business. I'm school of Irving, you know."

Pauncefoot himself caught the last words. "Irving! Tree! The genius of the British stage," declared the manager. "But a good show needs bints. Rows of them, in spangles and tights."

"Crusoe was alone," objected Lamsley coldly, "except for Man Friday and Ben Gunn."

Pauncefoot roared with laughter at this literalist imagination. "Oh dear, you amuse me. Too much, I fear — I must watch my abdomen. I suffer from it. We are artists, Lambchop. I need hardly tell you that. We invent."

Lambchop reflected. "Then how do you answer the obvious question?"

"Which obvious question?"

"Who is going to play opposite me?"

"How do you mean, dear boy?"

"If we are going to deviate from the story so far as to have women on the island, I shall need a leading lady. Who will it be?"

"Jones Twofour."

"Covered in spots. He's written home for tablets, but will they get here in time? Besides, he's more a character turn. We need to have a Bow china shepherdess."

"The perfect bint."

"An English Rose. Our bints would do well enough behind the bar of the Elephant and Castle, but they don't melt your heart."

As they conversed, a flock of eight geese made their housewifely way through the camp, necks outstretched;

following them was Twofour, speaking to them in Welsh. In his hand was an upended rifle, with bayonet fixed; Twofour was using the bayonet to spear any stray pages of the *Balkan Gazette* that were blowing around the camp. Sunny wanted it shipshape. Twofour's bucolic appearance confirmed Lamsley in his opinion.

"I am taking the girls down to the water, sir," Twofour called. "But I have to keep watch over them, like, sir. Some men would have them for breakfast." Lamsley put his hands together as though appealing to heaven in his despair.

Twofour moved on. He tired of litter picking, and carried his rifle on his shoulder, its bayonet decorated with a millefeuille of newsprint. There was a stream — its liquid content reduced to a few puddles — at the edge of the camp. He looked at the geese with fatherly concern as they waddled around the watercourse.

"Watcha," said a voice near to him.

"Watcha to you," replied Twofour. The man seemed to have come from nowhere.

"Are you on sentry go?"

"Only as far as my girls are concerned."

"Girls?" asked the soldier, with interest. Twofour gestured towards the gaggle. "Oh geese," he said with marked disappointment. "Do you always have newspaper on the end of your bayonet."

"It depends what the reviews say. If they're bad, I might have the reviewer as well." He smiled broadly. The other man looked nonplussed. "Not that we have been reviewed yet, but we will be. That's the theatre."

The newcomer blinked. "What's the theatre?"

"As a matter of fact, that building there. The Gaiety. After General Gay. But he's away now in . . . Hold on. Who are you? You might be a spy."

The other laughed. "I wouldn't be much of one. I am Sir Parsifal, the original Simple Fool; I know nothing."

"Pleased to meet you, Parsley. You've come to act?"

"I don't think so."

"You've got a building trade then?"

"Certainly not."

"Why are you here?"

"Because I was sent here. I suppose the C.O. will know. Where shall I find him?"

Parsley shouldered his pack and walked off. He was a young man, not tall, with a general air of softness and pinkness about him. Even Twofour noticed that he walked with a springy, athletic stride.

Sunny was outside his tent. In his hand was his ocarina. He had improved his repertoire but had suspended his rehearsal of it. Winner, black as ever, was addressing him. He was in no mood for the foolery of the Follies. He would go to Salonika and work on the big canvas he had ordered. Sunny did not seek to dissuade him.

When Winner had left, Sunny opened the letter presented by Parsley. It was from a prep school friend who was now an infantry commander in the division. It was to the point. "Heard you were treading the boards. I thought you might have use for this soldier." Sunny looked at Parsley. Even in a brief glance he could not miss the Private's bloom of youth.

"You're an actor."

"People keep asking me that, sir. But I'm not, sir."

"And you don't know why you're here?"

"I was hoping you'd tell me, sir."

Sunny looked at him for a moment. The young man's blue eyes stared confidently, a little dreamily back — he was shortsighted, but vanity forbad spectacles. A smile played on what he might almost have called, in a girl, his rosebud mouth. In a girl. Was that it? It didn't matter. In another life, Sunny would not have imagined how men looked in make-up, bustiers and skirts. But he had an idea that Parsley would come across as convincing.

He blew a few notes on the ocarina.

"Come this way. Rehearsals have already begun."

One evening, Sunny found Pauncefoot, who had missed rehearsals, in his tent. He refused to come out. "What's this Achilles business?" enquired Sunny.

"This is the end of Footy," declared the manager in a luxuriance of gloom. "No more shall his voice be heard in the places where men rehearse. They shall be a desolation, a hooting of owls, and an hissing. As the Prophet Jeremiah might have said, people will walk by and wag their heads."

"You're drunk," summarised Sunny succinctly.

"It is true that I am drunk. I am a boulevardier, a debonair personality, and debonair personalities do drink. The drink only adds to my natural gaiety. But tonight even drink has failed me. Sunny," he leaned forward blearily, "I am undone."

"Then do yourself up again."

294

"It's the fault of that boy."

"Patroclus?"

"Parsley. I tried to befriend him, Sunny. He is a nice boy, a charming boy. But he has divined my secret. What a nice boy. Clever too. I hate him."

Pauncefoot's head sank on his chest. His eyes were red.

"Pull yourself together," advised Sunny.

"He called me a fake."

"What of it?"

"He was right. My name is not Compton Pauncefoot."

"It's an unusual name, certainly."

"Not an impossible one. Only it happens not to be mine."

"What is your name?"

"Hastings. Douglas Hastings. But I got tired of it."

"No! The famous Douglas Hastings, impresario, actor-manager? Whatever happened to you? Wait I remember now. Trouble with the law, wasn't it?"

"They were nice boys too." He rose unsteadily to his feet, with a half-formed idea of tearing the clothes from his breast, prior to beatng it. He decided against doing so, not sure what the distended abdomen would make of it. "I didn't grow up in a country house with a private theatre. I come from Lambeth."

"People do," comforted Sunny.

"I was a great theatrical personality. Even you — an ignoramus from Warwickshire — have heard of Douglas Hastings. But that was while the old Queen was alive."

"Which old queen?"

"Her late Majesty, Queen Victoria. I was the King of Melodrama. Ask me about trap business: I was the acknowledged master of it. I got out of — to my shame I say it . . . out of . . . what I can only refer to as prison. The theatre shunned me. It had moved on. I joined the army. I lied about my age. You may not believe it, but I am forty-four. Even then they didn't want me."

"So how are you here?"

"Because, with the last shilling I had in the world, I ordered a uniform; a charming young tailor fitted me for it. Lieutenant's pips. When the regiment was leaving for France, I joined them. I reported to the Colonel on the ship, explaining that there had been some confusion over the papers. That was acting if you like! He said: 'Oh well, if you're here and you went to the old school, you'd better stay with us until the papers catch up.' Only I hadn't been to the old school."

Sunny considered the predicament. "The main thing is to get the show on."

"We can't do it, lamented Pauncefoot. "It needs Parsley."

"Parsley is incidental. We didn't even know of his existence until a few days ago."

"No. He's central. I love him. Everybody loves him. The division will love him. He is the beauty of the division, the nearest a male of the species can approach to being the real thing without changing sex."

"Can he act?"

"I have every confidence that he can. But does he want to? No, not for me."

"I could order him to do it."

"He wouldn't put his soul into it. Give me your revolver. I'll shoot myself."

"Don't be stupid. Let's analyse. What is it that this man wants most? Horses, I think, are his passion."

"He might have said something about them. I didn't listen."

"Men feel their privations differently."

"They mustn't in a public place."

"To some, it's being remote from their wives and family. Others yearn for the comradeship and tastes of a London pub. Parsley longs for a horse to ride."

"What follows?"

"Parsley follows. I have the perfect horse. He'll be the perfect bint."

Some days later Parsley was cantering Storm in a circle. Sunny could not help staying to watch. He had agreed to enter him for the Divisional Horse Show. Man and equine seemed to be in perfect unison. The young man lightly dismounted. "You know, sir, I'm a little nervous."

"About competing? There'll be nothing to it."

"No. The other show."

"It's only dressing up. We did it at school," Sunny told him.

"That's easy, sir. I have five older sisters. They were dressing me up all the time, sir. I loved fooling people."

"Then you're the answer to our prayers."

"But that wasn't on the stage, sir." Parsley looked troubled. "I'm not sure it would be respectable. My parents live in the country, sir. I don't think they approve of actors, let alone bints."

Sunny lit his pipe, largely to gain time while he martialled an argument. Parsley's parents would be unlikely to find out. Little of what went on in Macedonia filtered home, to the undoubted relief of much of the BSF. That, however, seemed a caddish line of argument. Then inspiration struck. "Do you know *Figaro*?"

"One of the Italian force, sir?"

"No, he's not in the army. Find out and study a figure called Cherubino. Tell me what you conclude."

Thirty-Four

The relentless, baking days of summer had been hard for the BWH, sheltered only by canvas tents; but eventually the sun showed signs of losing some of its strength. It was then that the weather gods visited the Hospital with a storm during the night.

To begin with, it seemed like an entertainment laid on for the benefit of women who welcomed a change in routine. "It is most exciting," Isabel had scrawled in her diary. "My bedclothes are soaked and the tent is waving about from side to side. Mrs Stalwart-Dousing has been round with a lantern to see how we all are." But she had had enough of it by morning. Long before dawn, the tent had blown down altogether. They had had to find what shelter they could in other people's tents. Just as they were getting up, the air was rent by a scream. A centipede had found a dry refuge in a fold of the clothes a nurse was putting on. But that was Goody; she deserved a lesson in entomology.

"Hailstones as big as marbles," Isabel had scribbled, when she had been able to find the diary, a page that was not damp, and the time to write on it.

In the morning, Isabel dressed in damp clothes, got the tent upright again and made what disposition she could of her "things." Her duties did not stop for rain. She splashed out, in wellington boots, across a few of the many streams that were trickling through the camp; over the summer, the sun had baked the clay ground to the hardness of marble. Rain was still falling in a steady drizzle. The cook house appeared to have been transformed into a boating lake. She waded about it, a sou'wester on her head. It was rather like a holiday she had once had on Skye, only without the peat fires to go back to.

Molem Vas was struggling to light the fires for her. He was a Serb with enormous moustaches. Each morning, this being no exception, the moustaches were set in a press. He got his name from the Serbian for "If you please," which is what he was always saying.

Rain had gusted onto the woodpile, and so far the damp wood had produced only smoke.

On the wards, nurses were trying to exchange soaked bedding for dry sheets, although it was difficult to prevent the new linen from brushing against damp. They stood with their feet in water, their fingers numb. The men shivered. They were a naturally stoical lot, who had endured terrible privations in the mountains. But some of them were now as weak, helpless and vulnerable as babies. Water flooded the graveyard that, with its mounds of earth and wooden crosses, "was getting bigger week by week. Isabel applied herself, as best she could without heat, to the making of tea — or rather the assembling of the huge urns and the measuring out of the tea leaves.

That morning, as Sunny rode out of Camp Follies, Parsley had run up to him. "I've found out about Cherubino, sir. Chelsea — that's Private Bunn — told me. He won at Uttoxeter a couple of years before we came out. By Figaro out of Lady's Secret. Is that what you meant, sir?"

"No, Parsley."

"I thought not. I told Chelsea the mare was Saucy Susan."

"I was thinking of Mozart."

"I haven't heard of a mare called Mozart, sir."

Sunny whistled *Voi che sapete* as he hacked through the rain to the Hospital, reflecting on a note he had received. It was from his boyhood chum, the one who, now officer, had sent him the soldier known to him as Private Tennant, to Camp Follies as Parsley.

"He seemed too beautiful an English lad to be killed. A perfect specimen. We're only doing the odd stunt now, but no doubt it will be like the Western Front in the end — so many men blown to pieces. I wanted to save something from the wreck." Sentimentalist, thought Sunny, but not disapprovingly.

All things considered, he could have chosen a better day for a visit to the BWH. "I came to see if you were all right," he exclaimed, with some truth, on seeing Isabel. "I see, however, that you are."

300

"You see we're not. We don't wear mackintoshes for pleasure."

"This infernal rain."

"Our tent blew down."

"Let me help put it up."

"Some of the patients have done that. We were meant to be getting some permanent buildings, — wooden ones. Sir Thomas Lipton sent them over. We had a go at the quartermaster. He only offered us pastilles. Most unsatisfactory."

"Did you find out what happened to them," asked Sunny uneasily.

"No."

"Just as well."

"What's that?"

"Just as well to find out."

"But we didn't find out. That's the point."

Sunny changed the subject. "I bring greetings from Snowball. She particularly asked me to say how much she's enjoying herself."

"I sometimes prefer sheep to people," Isabel said pointedly.

"I understand. She is a dear sheep. She misses you. You should come and see her. Sheep are sociable animals, you know, and we are not quite so much under water."

"I don't think Mrs Stalwart-Dousing would be keen. Not until it stopped raining."

"The rain will stop one day. Perhaps it will inspire Winner to paint a great picture of the flood. He has gone to Salonika for the nonce — a little down in the dumps, but he's all that the Follies has got by way of artistic genius."

"The Follies?"

"Didn't you know? We are doing theatricals now. Until reequipped with balloons."

"The Follies!" Isabel repeated. Her tone was not one of approbation. "I suppose we all have to find ways of forgetting the war." Sunny, she had come to conclude, could be a fool.

"Yes, the war isn't everything. I've seen enough of it."

Sunny had also seen enough of the rain. Isabel's cook house had not been constructed as an all-weather facility. Although the storm had relapsed into a steady drizzle, the puddles around the heavy cooking range were patterned with an ever-changing geometry of circles, where fresh rain was hitting them. Rain mixed with the steam from the huge copper of water that was boiling. Shakes would have a job cleaning Sunny's field boots which looked as though he had spent a day on the hunting field.

Isabel, perhaps as an indication that the visit had now run its course, began to look out the ingredients for the day's stew. (Every day had its stew at the Hospital; it was the easiest dish to cook in volume *en plein air*.) One of the younger nurses stood at the stout wooden table, chopping vegetables in the rain. "But the war," she said after some minutes, "keeps coming. I mean the wounded do. There are more travoys now."

A mule swung past. On either side of it hung stretchers, each with a wounded man strapped to it; girl orderlies trotted along beside each of the soldiers to make sure he did not fall off.

Isabel sighed. "We do seem to get the worst. We have, at the moment, an injured thigh — half of it quite blown away. We have a face with the eye hanging out, who covered Mrs Stalwart-Dousing in gouts of blood when he coughed near here. There's a Russian boy who's got no hands and is nearly blind. Perhaps it would be better if he didn't live. That's wicked of me, I know." Isabel looked unblushingly at Sunny. "So, so many."

That was the war, Sunny felt like saying. He had seen horribly damaged bodies in France — endless numbers of them, endless numbers of dead. Then he had volunteered for the Royal Flying Corps and joined the chivalry of the sky, where gentlemen duelled with gentlemen in an element that was far removed from the sufferings on earth. The gentlemen died too, but at a distance. "It's a miracle that some of them get here at all, of course," he observed.

"Because of the travoys, you mean."

"No, I meant that you've got a German orderly, haven't you? The Serbs don't seem to go in for prisoners."

Isabel felt that was intended as an aspersion which she did not want to hear. "All I know is that they fight terribly hard. They are fine," Isabel declared passionately.

Sunny thought a change of subject would be in order. He retreated to neutral ground. "Terrible weather for the time of year."

"The end of summer. The campaigning season will restart in the autumn — not that it ever stops in the mountains. We thought the summer would be our chance to reorganise the Hospital. We hadn't reckoned on the malaria, diphtheria and, typhoid cases, on top of everything else. Not to mention typhus, scarlet fever and consumption."

Sunny was thoughtful. Then he burst out: "Damn the war. I beg your pardon. I should not have sworn. We must try to forget the theatre of war. Come to my theatre at the Follies."

Sunny climbed onto Storm and set out through the rain. As he had remarked to Isabel, the horse could hardly have been better named. Isabel's reply still puzzled him: "Sunny might be an equally appropriate name, don't you think?" He was not sure it was meant as a compliment.

Isabel returned to the tasks of the morning. Molem Vas and the one German prisoner, Rudolph, carried the tea urns to the wards. The Serb patients assumed that the bitter liquid was a medicine that they were required to drink for their health; tea was unknown to them at home. The nurses, however, were pleased of the drink, and no more so than when they were working in such damp conditions. Sister Muir took a cup in the cook house. "I wish Molem Vas wouldn't wear that thing on his face. Macedonia is frightening enough as it is. They say that the Senegalese troops steal children and carry them into the mountains."

"Whatever for?"

"To cook and eat them, of course. Didn't you know? I'm glad I've got my revolver."

"You aren't a child, though, Sister Muir." Looking at her, Isabel did not suppose a trooper would find much to eat.

"I felt safer when Captain Petrović was here."

"Yes, Captain Petrović is fine."

The men she knew in Surrey did not admit that life was serious. They might be droll like Sunny, pastille-offering like the Otter or sporting like so many of them, but they saw it as their duty to shield their womenfolk from reality. Isabel had come to Macedonia to escape the satin-lined case that her parents had made to protect her. Petrović did not make jokes. He had purpose. It was alarming and exhilarating. Yes, he was fine.

"I'd feel happier if we weren't in tents," said Sister Muir. "They seem vulnerable. The wards would be so much better in huts. I'm told that last night was nothing to some of the thunderstorms you can catch in these parts." She made the extreme weather sound like a disease. "Follies!" she snorted.

"So many follies."

"No, that's where the huts have gone. There's some nonsense about the Struma Follies. Sir Thomas sent out a whole hospital, a wooden one. It's been built into a theatre."

"No," exclaimed Isabel. "He wouldn't have."

"Certainly he did. Sir Thomas is most generous."

"I mean that Captain S — whoever is in charge of the theatre would never have done something so mean."

Sister Muir looked at her as though she were simple. "That's the army. What's it made up of? Men. Of course they only think of themselves. I haven't lived on this earth for fifty-three years without learning something."

Isabel was silent. Sunny could be annoyingly frivolous but she had found him a pleasantly home-like contrast to the tempestuous and unknowable Petrović. She would have believed he could be such a merciless betrayer. She went to the wooden table and cut through a cabbage. It might have been a human head.

It was only when Sister Muir had left that Isabel noticed a Serb soldier, hovering at the edge of her kitchen. They did that sometimes, hoping for scraps. Usually she was kind to them. Today she felt wearied by Sister Muir's confidences. "*Gubi se*," she told him without looking up.

"*Dozvoli da ti pomognem*" — let me help you — replied the soldier in a soft voice. Too soft for a soldier. Isabel stared at him incredulously, before uttering the one word: "Elsie?"

Autumn 1916

Thirty-five

Isabel was driving the trap back from the sulphur pools. It was late afternoon and the low sun seemed to be brushing a golden varnish over the autumn landscape. Beside her sat Elsie.

It had been difficult at first. There had been so much for Elsie to tell: that Isabel felt she should have told. But the sheer volume of experience seemed to inhibit Elsie. It remained tightly packed up, like the neatly folded contents of a trunk that she did not want to disturb. She could not dig down to the bottom and create chaos. She was, therefore, reserved, and Isabel felt hurt. That first day, Isabel had served her food, petted her, and would have shouted out so that all the nurses could come running; but Elsie did not want that. She ate her food like a soldier. Molem Vas looked on, his waxed moustache working up and down to convey different states of astonished bafflement.

"Don't call them," Elsie had ordered. "I don't belong here any more. I am a private of the Serbian army."

"But how?" Isabel was more than curious. Part of her was horrified by what Elsie had gone through. The other part was somewhat in awe. For a sheltered young lady, serving on the Macedonian front was brave enough, but nothing compared to Elsie's experiences. Society had given Isabel a position of implied authority over Elsie, a working girl; but the working girl had done so much more.

"It's not unknown for a woman to serve. You always said the Serbs were fine."

Isabel had enough tact not to press her. "You can sleep in my tent," she told her, "like before. There's room. One of the other girls has gone sick. People are always going sick now."

"Won't Mrs Stalwart-Dousing think that odd?"

"I would have to tell her, of course. The others too, I suppose. Serb soldiers aren't usually allowed."

"No," replied Elsie, without laughing. "I see that, Miss Hinchcliff. Perhaps I should move on."

"I won't let you do that." Now that she had got over her initial amazement, she could look properly at the young woman who had become more to her than just another nurse, and who was still surely special, but so changed. Her face was thinner. Elsie had always struck her as something of a terrier: small, lean, active, prone to nip. The army uniform could never have fitted her very neatly but it now looked too bulky for the frail body it contained.

"I don't think I could. I'm too tired."

"You would be. You've come back from the dead. You need to be nursed. We do that here, you know." Elsie had turned her brown eyes on her. They now looked so big in her gaunt face. They looked distant, as though the real Elsie was somewhere far away.

A smile flickered. "I remember. Seems so long ago that I left."

Isabel found Elsie some clothes, Molem Vas was sent out of the cook house and Elsie exchanged her soldier's uniform for that of a nurse. She washed as best she could, using the jugs and basins of the wash house. Then she slept.

Mrs Stalwart-Dousing had to be told of Elsie's return. "I thought she was dead," she had exclaimed. "Why ever didn't the girl get a message to us? I shall write to her people; they will be relieved. They will have assumed the same thing. I am happy that she has come back, but I cannot say I am pleased with her. What is her story?"

"I don't know her story," replied Isabel truthfully. She did not mention that Elsie now thought of herself as a soldier, not a nurse. "I'm not sure she has any people."

Mrs Stalwart-Dousing looked regretful. People ought to have people, although she could not exactly say that it was anybody's fault if they did not. "That Lieutenant, the artist, found the ambulance. She must have hit her head in the crash. Another one for the sick ward, I suppose."

But Elsie avoided the sick ward. Dr Aitken examined her, and pronounced her to be very weak, but not otherwise ill. Elsie preferred the tent. So did Isabel. And it was there, one night, as they lay alone, that she began to talk.

"It was dark on the road," she said suddenly. "Have you seen the roads in the mountains? They ain't roads at all, just tracks — the ground all chewed up. Sloshy. You can't see a thing in the dark. The lights on the Ford ain't much stronger than candles. It was a narrow track and the land fell away very sharp. I took as much care as I could. Can't tell you how wet it was. Raining like no tomorrow. It must have weakened the edge of the track. One moment I was going along, rain gusting into the cab, barely able to see a thing, but moving forward, even though the wheels were slithering. Then the wheels weren't slithering no more. We just sort of tumbled. I don't remember the rest, as far as the accident goes.

"They found me down there, I suppose. Must have done, because then, next thing, I was in a field hospital. Didn't know what was going on because nobody spoke English, with this big bandage round me head where I'd hit it. I could only hobble around. I just wanted to sleep. I didn't sleep much. I was on a ward with soldiers, who kept crying out because of their wounds. I don't know what happened to the nurse who was with me in the Ford. I think she must have died."

"I believe she did."

"I've seen so many people die. Suppose we all have."

She fell silent, and for a while Isabel listened to the noise of the bullfrogs. She thought Elsie had fallen asleep, but after some minutes she took up her tale.

"It must have been the nearest hospital. Or the best equipped. But it was in a forward position. I was there for two days when it had to pull back. It was a near thing. The hospital must have waited till the last moment. They probably didn't have orders. That happens sometimes. There are so many things for the commanders to think about that they forget about the field ambulances and hospitals. I was all right. I could walk. Not very well, but enough to move. They were very anxious I should get back. I was a woman and they didn't want the Bulgarians to get me. So I went back with the retreat. Some of the hospital couldn't move.

Those of us who could get along somehow did the best we could. You know, the Bulgarians don't spare anybody they think is a Serb."

She drank some water and went on. "The hospital was on a plain. We managed to get into the mountains, where we were safe. Safe enough anyway."

"You must have been scared."

"Ought to have been, but I think I am more scared now. I didn't know what was happening, really. Don't think anybody did. I was all right. The orderlies had worse cases to look after. People did what they could for me, but I'd had a knock on the head and I didn't speak a word of their language. I just followed the crowd I was with. I lost the other patients. I was with soldiers. They shared their food with me, not that I wanted to eat. I started to live as they did. I didn't know how to get back. Then the fighting began. Nobody wanted me around. But who had the time to look after me? When we were attacked, I had to do something. I made myself useful by filling cartridge cases and carrying ammunition to the front. It's different, the fighting in the mountains. They don't have trenches. They run from rock to rock. I have always been a fast runner. It was painful at first, but that wore off after a few weeks. It wasn't much use running in a nurse's uniform so I found some breeches. I dressed as a soldier. Not a very smart soldier, but the Serbs ain't the Guards. They're a homespun lot. They liked me. They said I brought them luck. I was their mascot."

Isabel looked at her through the layers of the mosquito net. There was a bright moon outside and the tent was not absolutely dark; but she more sensed than saw Elsie's unmoving silhouette, lying like a marble effigy on a tomb. "Weren't you frightened?"

"What of? I was frightened of the enemy. I didn't want to be captured."

"But you were alone. A woman."

Elsie considered for a few moments. "I'm tired," she said. "I think I'll sleep now."

Isabel let her go to sleep. She wanted to ask about Winner: whether she should write to him. She wanted to ask Elsie about a lot of things.

The next burst of confidences had come when they bathed in the sulphur pools. "This would have seemed the greatest of all luxuries in the mountains." Elsie could not swim but she was rejoicing in the freshness of the water. "A bath, oh it's heaven . . . Warm underclothing, too: they need it more than guns."

"Go home and start a campaign."

"England? I don't think I'll go home. I'm not sure I should even be here."

"You don't mean you're going back? asked Isabel.

"What choice have I got?" She disappeared beneath the water. When she re-emerged, she shook the water droplets off her short hair and declared: "They are the most wonderful men I have ever know."

"Good heavens. You sound like Goody."

"Not in that way. But honest. They take what comes, whatever it is. Don't complain. That is something about

314

this war. You find out what people are like, what they can do. I wouldn't have thought any of them could have survived the conditions in which we have lived. But they do, Miss Hinchcliff. They laugh and joke and sometimes manage to get a drink — an alcoholic one, I mean — but not often. You should see how cheerful they are. A tin of sardines, you'd think it was the food of the gods. Tinned prunes for afters — what a slap up feast that makes of it. And they might be dead the next day. Some of the best and kindest are dead. You should hear them when they hold a ceilidh, the ones who are alive I mean, obviously. They don't call it that, they've a Serb word for it. Lasts all day, with special dances. The men dance with each other, in a line. They are real comrades." She hummed a Serb melody. "Now I am one of them . . .

"They're all sorts. We've a soldier as used to be a ship's steward. He speaks ever so many languages, all like a native. So I've somebody to talk to. And he's teaching me the lingo. I'm an honorary man. My own tent to change in, that's all. It's funny. I insist on doing all that they do. Therefore a lot of shouting gets aimed in my direction. I can survive that. I have before. Don't know if I can survive the cold of the winter, though we'll see."

They left the pools. The evening was cool, so they dressed quickly. On the trap, Isabel remarked. "But you are still a woman. A lone woman."

"If I had been an unprotected Bulgarian peasant girl, I don't know what would have happened. They're no better or worse than other men in that respect. But I've

315

become one of them. They wanted something to love I suppose, in the same way that they make pets of birds and even rats if they can take them. Not that they loved me at first. I daresay. But they wanted to take care of me. They were lambs. Protected me like I was their sister. They have very little food. I don't know how they fight on those empty bellies. But they always managed to find something to give me, otherwise I would have starved. They did come to love me, but in the same way that they loved each other. They showed me how to shoot a rifle, how to take cover, the meaning of the words of command. We're all brothers. Common purpose. Comradeship. I grew up in a city, in a big family — there were so many of us, crammed into our little house; there wasn't time to be close."

Isabel touched the horse with the whip. "Still, you aren't a man."

As the trap jogged into the hospital, they saw horses. "Captain Petrović is here," exclaimed Isabel. Without a word, Elsie jumped down and hurried to her tent.

Petrović had been looking for them. He came up to the trap. His uniform, although worn as neatly as ever, was splashed with mud. "I am so pleased to see you again, Miss Hinchcliff."

"You will eat with us?"

"No, I only have a few moments. Precious moments. I do not know how much time we shall have together, so I have written you a letter." He handed her a small envelope. "I shall wait most anxiously for the reply."

He called his orderly and prepared to leave. Before he did so, Elsie ran up. She was wearing her Serb

316

uniform. She saluted. "Reporting for duty, sir," she said.

Isabel called after her: "Elsie, you must write to Lieutenant Winnington-Smith. He loves you."

Thirty-Six

Elsie was in the mountains. A holidaymaker would have thought that the scenery amid which she now moved was glorious. They would have admired the pair of pine trees that had chosen that spot to raise their tall heads. To Elsie, the mountains seemed anything but picturesque. She was called Fox, and now she was living like one. All day the soldiers laboured, sweating, under the autumn sun. As soon as it was dusk, the heat disappeared from the air. It was very cold in the night, in a trench that was little more than a slit in the ground, with stones and sandbags piled up in front of it. Ground sheets were stretched from the rocks and thorn trees to make rough bivouacs. They had only their greatcoats to provide warmth. If they slept, it was only because they were so exhausted that they could do nothing else; but they would wake up, every hour or so, shivering.

Nothing was permanent; the squad of ten men, a *decetina* as it was called, was always on the move, always fighting, even at night.

Not all the men liked having a woman in the *decetina* at first. They thought she would need looking after. Elsie quickly showed that she was not that kind of girl. She was small but tough, and a quick learner. She could soon fire a rifle, as well as speak some words of Serbian. She did not complain about the thirst that she felt during the day, as their waterbottles ran dry, or of the heavy pack that she carried. When the field battery got into enemy hands, she ran down the hillside with the men, yelling the "hourra, hourra" war cry, before they all took what shelter they could behind rocks. They stayed there all day, husbanding their water by taking no more than sips. When they retook the battery with the help of another regiment, they flung themselves on the ground beside a pool and lapped like animals. It was the most exciting day of her life.

It was a proud evening when Elsie was chosen to go on patrol. At sunset, the field kitchen sent cauldrons containing stew and black tea, both cold by the time they reached the *decetina*. It was not much of a preparation for a night, which, to Elsie, would be a sleepless one. They would go out just before dawn, the moment when the human frame is at its least resilient — when a sentry is least likely to spot an attack.

She felt as she did when she was rinking. Sometimes the skates took off by themselves and she had a rush of panic, which turned to elation if she regained the upper hand. She was having a rush of panic now. It might turn to elation, or she might be killed.

Elsie's boot struck a rock as she climbed out of the trench and she thought the whole valley must have heard it. They crouched low. It was difficult to move quickly in that position because of the weight of the

318

canvas vest that they had strapped onto her. It was sewn with pouches, each of which contained a grenade.

There was no barbed wire it in the mountains. Nor had the landscape been cut up by artillery fire. The lush pasture reached almost to Elsie's chin as she stooped. Each step released the scent of herbs. It was a wet night, which made the grass slippery. But no moon or stars shone down on them.

They stopped. They could hear the Bulgarians talking. Elsie looked intently, through the darkness, at the corporal, to be sure she was acting correctly. She could hear, more than see, that he was unbuttoning the pouches on his vest. She did likewise, carefully lifting out the grenades. The corporal touched her arm. This was the moment. He stood up and lobbed his grenades. A moment later he had another in the air. Elsie hurled hers as far as she could. There was a dull thud. The talking stopped. There was an explosion, followed by another.

They were running back, listening, bending low. Behind them, a rifle was fired. It hit a rock. The next shot dug into the ground in front of them. They zigzagged. Other shots followed, but they were climbing up to their own trenches now and could not be seen. In a moment, Elsie was back over the stone wall, being hugged by everyone who was there. She was elated.

"What did you hear?" asked the sergeant.

"Groans," said the corporal, looking annoyed.

"Pity," replied the sergeant. "Bad luck."

"Why?" asked Elsie.

"Groaning and swearing mean that you've just hurt them. The top of a finger perhaps — somewhere sensitive. It's when they don't groan that you know they're dead."

Elsie was not sorry to have heard groans. The outing was exhilaration enough. She did not know that she wanted to kill anybody, although perhaps she had.

Or perhaps she had not. When morning had broken and breakfast — more cold stew and cold tea — had arrived, the corporal called over the ship's steward to translate. He listened, nodded and swapped the sort of glance that men do exchange when they talk about feminine weakness. "The next time," he said to her kindly, "remember to take out the pin."

The kindness hurt.

Elsie's colonel had his headquarters in a cottage. "So how is my little squirrel today?" he beamed. Elsie was guaranteed to amuse him. His white moustaches twitched. "Not tired?"

"A little tired."

"What? You aren't a soldier. Not a Serb soldier. You should never be tired."

"I am not tired," replied Elsie. The truth was that she could hardly stand.

The colonel did not look at her as an example of femininity, but as a curious specimen of natural history and a very good joke. Miss Fox! A squirrel, not a fox, he had said on hearing her name. "Why do you do it?" he asked her, as he always did. "It isn't your homeland that's been occupied."

"I thought you needed my help." The colonel's laughter shook the roof beams. A piece of soot was dislodged and floated down onto his cropped head. It was, though, the best answer Elsie could give. She was far too exhausted to examine her motives further. If she had not been, she might have considered that she needed a purpose. She had always sought for one. For some people, it came in religion. There had been no religion in her upbringing. Instead she had found the Toynbee Hall, Tolstoy and the BWH. And now the Serb army.

The colonel often sent for her in the evening. The slim figure, in the rough, muddy uniform that did not fit her, was a delight to him. Her hair had been cropped; it made her brown eyes look bigger. The Serbs were used to strong women but here was a prodigy: someone who chose to live like them, when, for many Serbs, their greatest wish was to escape the harsh rule of poverty.

This evening he told her to go to the town. He would give her money. "Enjoy yourself for a week. There will be nothing doing here. It is going to be exceptionally quiet. You'll be bored." He smiled kindly beneath his moustache. The ship's steward translated. Elsie saluted.

As Elsie was leaving, the colonel said to the other officers in the room. "Some fierce fighting is coming up. Her *decetina* will be in the middle of it. It would be such a pity for our English squirrel to be killed."

Elsie turned. "I refuse to go," she announced. "The steward has been a good teacher. I understand Serbian now."

The colonel laughed until he had to wipe his eyes. When Elsie had gone back to Two Trees, he said: "What a shame."

Thirty-Seven

"It's against Nature, Sister Muir." Sunny had been reduced to speaking to Sister Muir because Isabel refused to see him. He had made rather a friend of that matron, in the hope that she would occasionally speak well of him to Isabel. "The natural condition of a Macedonian summer is lassitude. The grass wilts, the beasts seek shade — only the BWH ignores the clear message of the wild. Miss Hinchcliff says she's too busy to talk."

Sister Muir looked at him as though he were a pet dog and explained in simple terms: "That's because we're rushed off our feet. I don't think Dr Aitken has left the operating theatre for a month. Then our nurses keep falling sick. Mrs Stalwart-Dousing has gone to Salonika to organise more quinine and see the medical people there. I shouldn't be talking to you. Nurse Goodman came onto the ward today wearing a silk blouse."

"There was the Divisional Horse Show. Miss Hinchcliff was there and she cut me."

"I would have known what to do about that blouse if there weren't so many nurses on the sick ward." Sister Muir sounded half cross and half fretful.

"Have it laundered?"

"A silk blouse, Captain, means only one thing. It means Salonika. I should send that one home. She's young. She ought to be under her parents' eye. I can't stand in for them any more. It was one thing on the ship coming out. I packed them off to bed before they had a chance to become too friendly with the ship's officers. No time for me to do that now. And we need every pair of hands we can get, even Nurse Goodman's. Salonika!" exclaimed Sister Muir, as she rose to her feet. "I don't know where she gets the money."

"Miss Hinchcliff doesn't need to be supervised, yet she still won't see me."

"Cheer up, Captain. Storm won the Divisional Horse Show."

That was, indeed, a comfort. After the race, Parsley confided: "Cherubino, sir. A boy played by a woman, who has to disguise himself as a maid. Is that the one you meant, sir?"

"Yes, Parsley."

"As long as I don't have to sing, sir."

The excitement had already liberated his thespian personality. Sunny told Sister Muir that she would soon see Storm's rider perform on, literally, another stage. "And for that, your nurses don't even need to go to the Gaiety Theatre. Entertainment has come to them."

Sister Muir looked at him suspiciously. "In what form?"

"The Struma Follies. The greatest thing to hit Macedonia since the invention of High Explosive."

"Here!" It was only one syllable that Sister Muir uttered but she filled it with enough meaning for a thousand. Her mouth opened, she looked like a cod on a quayside.

"That's right. Mrs Stalwart-Dousing specially requested it."

"Are you sure?"

"She isn't here, I suppose?" asked Sunny with assumed innocence. "Pity, or you could've asked her yourself. I have her letter somewhere. Can't quite put my hand on it. 'My dear Sunny,' it begins — that's what people usually call me, you know. 'We are bereft of amusement among the thorns and thistles of the Vardar. Come and cheer us up. Your old friend depends upon it. S-D.' I came ahead on Storm. The troupe follows on mule carts. We shall take over the dining room after luncheon, in the hours it won't be needed before the next serving."

"It seems very strange that Mrs Stalwart-Dousing should not have mentioned it to me."

"You know how it is: she's been terribly busy. So have the Follies. I squeezed her in, so to speak. All too soon I have to abandon my command at the Gaiety. New kite balloons are in prospect. But look! The company is already here. Have you met our manager? You've probably heard of him from England. Compton Pauncefoot."

Pauncefoot kissed Sister Muir's hand; Sister Muir withdrew it sharply, as though she feared ravishment. "I can't describe the suffering on that mule," he began volubly. "But I am prepared to undergo the torments of Hades — not a million miles from here, incidentally, according to the Ancient Greeks — in pursuit of my

324

art. Spectacle. Some trap business. Soon your patients will be dancing a jig. But oh, my distended abdomen. I'll leave it to science in my will. It should be exhibited in a museum of medical horrors."

Sunny smiled ingratiatingly at Sister Muir. The colour of his irregular teeth had not been improved by pipe-smoking. "Show opens at three o'clock."

Sister Muir bustled away to the wards, too busy to notice the sound of the carpenters. In the dining hall, Lamsley was saying: "I shall enter stage left. Pause for reception. Did somebody remember my costume?"

As a *coup de théatre*, the Follies' appearance in the Hospital was a great as anything on stage. The Hospital was astounded by their advent. Nurses, weary from weeks of monotonous routine, excitedly discussed their rotas, so that as many of them as possible could go, while leaving the wards adequately staffed. Sunny had brought every member of the company that he could find, plus a detachment of Royal Engineers provided by Ratty. There were two hundred and fifty men. In record time, a stage was erected in the dining tent. At three o'clock, everybody who could spare themselves from other duties, including Sister Muir, was in the tent. Sunny was insistent that Sister Muir should not miss the show. The sides of the tent were lowered. The show began.

Immediately the curtain had gone up, another performance was put in hand. This, however, was outside the tent, under the command of Ramsgate Sandys. Only fifty men were required for the entertainment. That left two hundred to begin rapidly and as quietly as possible to dismantle the hospital. Nurses protested. They were politely overruled. Ramsgate assured them that he had been given full authority by Mrs Stalwart-Dousing. Most, being so short-handed, felt they could not leave the ward to seek reassurance from Sister Muir. The few who did found that the entrance to the tent was guarded.

The show lasted longer than any that the Follies had so far mounted. Lambchop mercilessly ad libbed, delighting in an enthusiastic audience. Twofour appeared and reappeared through Pauncefoot's traps like a jack-in-a-box. Parsley, in character, could have taught Nurse Goodman something about coquetry.

By six o'clock the applause was wearing thin. By seven, even the most stalwart of the audience was wondering why they played without an interval. At seven ten, it finished. "Very good indeed, Captain Southall," said Sister Muir. "Quite took me out of myself. But if I may make a suggestion: next time make it shorter. You have quite upset the hours of the hospital. Supper should have been served at six."

It was dark when the audience came out. The nurses, having been away so much longer than they expected, almost ran to their wards. But where were they? The tents had been taken down. Every one of them had been moved. "Sister Muir," demanded Isabel, "is it true that Mrs Stalwart-Dousing authorised the complete removal of the hospital. It is now sited on a slope."

"It is certainly not true." The voice was not that of Sister Muir. It came from Mrs Stalwart-Dousing, who had arrived back at the hospital after an arduous journey from Salonika, which had left her tired and hungry. "Explain the meaning of this, Captain Southall."

Sunny had been prepared to meet wrath. "Mrs Stalwart-Dousing, beautiful evening. How nice to see you. Good trip?"

"I require an explanation."

"Madam, we are now in the autumn season. The winter approaches. I could not, simply could not allow you to continue operating the hospital on this pernicious site. I resorted to a ruse. I have moved it to a more propitious location. My men — I have over two hundred of them — are digging proper drains as we speak. I don't anticipate your being pleased. Not immediately. I am confident, however, that you will look on the matter differently in a few months' time."

"On what authority did you do this?"

"On nobody's but my own."

"Captain Southall, I have seven women doctors . . ."

"I know, if I may interrupt you. Trained nurses, trained cooks, a dispenser of medicines, and so forth, not forgetting the female evangelist — you have them all. What you don't have is a civil engineer."

"You are a civil engineer?"

"No, I have a bicycle business. Southall's Cycles. Customers' hopes never deflated, unlike some of their tyres."

Mrs Stalwart-Dousing clucked disapproval.

"My father, however, is one of the largest contractors in the Midlands. Laying out hospitals is, to the Southalls, more natural than sneezing. I saw at once you had chosen the wrong place. I have put it right. I should have done so before. I incurred your displeasure

— and the displeasure of a person who is dear to me — through an unfortunate association with Sir Thomas Lipton's huts. They were intended for your hospital; they were turned into a theatre. Not my fault, but I could not leave you to another Macedonian winter as you were. I expect," he added wisely, "no thanks."

Mrs Stalwart-Dousing considered the matter. "The new plan may have advantages." She was a pragmatist.

By sunrise the next day, the work was complete. Isabel paused before the cookhouse. It was more substantial than the old one; wooden planks served as bridges over the ditches that had been dug to either side. She remembered the last winter, spent miserably in wellington boots and sou'wester. Inside she found an envelope; she recognised the handwriting as Sunny's. The letter read: "I did this for you."

Thirty-Eight

There had been an unexpected consequence of the Hospital's removal to a new site. One of the slopes that the soldiers had used in repositioning the tents contained Goody's Grave. The men had been unaware of it, except as a letterbox-shaped opening in the ground, until they saw somebody starting to climb out. Seeing that the surroundings were not as quiet as he had expected, being occupied by two hundred or so men with canvas and guy ropes, the individual beat a hasty retreat. But he had shown himself enough to be seen.

Sunny regarded the opening, rather as though a fox had gone to earth on the hunting field. "We could dig him out, or send in a terrier. The terrier might get the worst of it, though, if he's armed."

"Molem Vas wants to go in with a carving knife," declared Ramsgate. "There's another possibility, though: we could smoke him out."

Disappointed of his mission, Molem Vas stood over the opening with a kitchen knife in his hand while soldiers collected some brushwood. They got a fire going and pushed some of the branches into the hole. There was no response.

"I expect he's stamping it out," judged Sunny.

"Might work better if we close up the hole," advised Ramsgate. "The smoke couldn't escape."

They waited until the twigs had almost burnt through. In that state they could be crushed underfoot, but not without releasing quantities of smoke. "Prepare to block the earth," ordered Sunny.

Ten minutes later, when the opening was cleared, they could hear coughing. "Come out," ordered Sunny.

"No good," considered Ramsgate. "We'd better administer another dose."

They did. This time they left it for longer before reopening the tomb. They listened. "I can't hear anything," observed Sunny. He shouted into the chamber. His voice echoed. "I'm going in."

"For heaven's sake, don't think of it." The voice was that of Mrs Stalwart-Dousing. Much as she disapproved of the manner in which Sunny had acted in redesigning her Hospital, she had come to approve of him. He had been right; the drainage was improved. "Nurse Goodman got stuck."

"So we'll dig him out after all."

"Oh dear, that will disappoint Major Simon. He wrote me a letter. He was so hoping to see an interesting archaeological discovery. You'll reduce it to a building site." She put on an air of resignation. "You do realise you've probably killed him. The embers will have consumed all the oxygen."

Sunny organised digging operations, removing the earth from the top of the mound. Then he called for crowbars. He took one himself and thrust it beneath a stone that formed part of the roof. But from inside the chamber came a sudden, echoing report and everyone jumped back. "That bullet went within an inch of my leg," Sunny exclaimed. "He's evidently not dead." He applied his crowbar from a more secluded position. Other men took places around the stone. It must have been a huge slab, but slowly it rose up. The opening began to gape. Molem Vas hopped around it like a Chinese guardian spirit, his knife at the ready.

"Heave," ordered Sunny.

There was a loud crack. Sister Muir screamed. But it was not a gun. The roof of the tomb had collapsed. The stone had split. "Quickly, get digging," ordered Sunny. "There's someone under there."

The men worked as fast as they could, but the stone had extended far under the canopy of earth. All that it supported, as well as some of the side of the hillock, had collapsed into the tomb. Eventually they reached the floor of the tomb; on it they found a young man, little more than a boy. He wore a sequined hat. There was a birthmark on the side of his nose. They pulled him from the rubble and Dr Aitken took his pulse. She bent her ear to his chest. "I'm afraid he's dead," she said. "Crushed by the rocks. So young too." She closed his eyes.

Over the boy's shoulder was a canvas bag. There also found some money, some bread and a rifle.

Sunny took the boy's cap and pushed it into his pocket, as he examined the contents of the bag. "I'll have to tell Simple," he observed.

"A boy has died and you only think of archaeology?" replied Mrs Stalwart-Dousing severely.

Sunny chose not to hear her.

Next morning, Simple was in his office. There was a knock on the door and Eggie strode in. In his hand was a fly swat, made of a piece of forked wood with some muslin stretched across it. "Seen one of these? Bought it for a shilling, must have cost a farthing to make." He brought it down smartly on Simple's desk and examined the surface. It was smeared with what had been a fly.

"You could set up a factory. However, I prefer Rosemary."

"Eh?" queried Eggie. Who was Rosemary?

"I rub it on my skin. Or Pennyroyal. It's what they use out here."

Eggie frowned. Simple would go for the native solution. Aromatic herbs did not appeal to the Scotsman. Sensualism. A train of thought led him to

Lola di Bonza. It was why he was there. He had something to report. "That dancer," he could not bring himself to mention her name. "I decided to take steps." The swat swished and another insect was flattened.

That dancer. Obviously Lola di Bonza. Eggie did not need to say. An image of Lola, as Simple thought of her, rose like an insistent water nymph from the waters of Simple's mind. Deep and, for the most part, unvisited waters. It was not a new image. He had been a young man, travelling. Segesvár — that was the Hungarian name — was an unshaven sort of town, its colourful façades tied up like a bundle of rags by the medieval fortress walls. The Austrians called it Schässburg, the locals Sigişoara, the English nothing at all — nobody at home had heard of it. There had been a theatre there, a hotel. "Did you ever see her perform?" he asked Eggie.

"Yes. At the Hellenic."

"Of course. I heard something about oranges."

"Good grief, have you ever been into one of those halls? Staggering amount of noise. Subalterns in uproar. I only went to observe."

"That doesn't explain the orange."

"Ah that." Eggie inspected the underside of the fly swat, on which a number of insect corpses were spread-eagled. "As a matter of fact, one landed in my lap." Eggie coughed. "An orange. Can't describe what was going on. Some Second Lieutenant being lowered out of one of the boxes by his ankles. You would have thought they'd want to see the performance. Not that it was worth seeing. I think the Cycling Beauties were on

332

stage; lassies doing trick turns on their bikes. Big girls, some of them. Wore tights." He paused. Simple appeared not to be listening. "Well, the orange struck me. I sent it back with good measure."

Simple did not say anything for a moment. Eggie wondered about him. Then, suppressing a sigh, Simple returned to the present. "General Gay mentioned it."

"Very unfortunate. Military police came in just as I was returning fire. They saw me, not the subaltern. They, erm, escorted me out. The General, however, quite understood."

"Young men letting off steam, he said. Only of course you aren't so young."

"No I'm not."

"No."

Segesvár. It must have been ten years ago. Simple had seen Lola at dinner. She was not so famous then and her beauty required less art to assist it. He had gazed at her with adoration. Only she was with an admirer; she always was. But their eyes met.

It was the one time in Simple's life that he had been sorry not to be rich.

"Of course, when the General went into the auditorium," Eggie continued, "the theatre had gone quiet. I suppose it was the Military Police."

"Unless it was Lola. Miss di Bonza I should say." Her performances had that effect.

Eggie considered the point. "Afterwards I explained to the General how noisy it had been before he arrived. Not sure that he got the point. Said you could have heard the bullfrogs croaking on the Struma Plain if you'd got sharp enough hearing. But by then that nixie was on."

On a corridor of the hotel in Segesvár, there had been a bathroom. That said something for the hotel; Segesvár was not oversupplied with bathrooms.

Simple walked past it. Or he had intended to. It was evening. The door had been flung open, and short-sighted as ever, Simple walked into it. Out of the bathroom — as though, in memory, from a cloud of steam — came Lola di Bonza, wrapped not in a dressing gown but in a full-length sable coat. First she laughed; it was a deep, intoxicating laugh, but natural, unlike the manner she put on for the public and her admirers. Then, seeing that he had gashed his forehead, she caressed his brow. That also seemed natural.

"Was it my fault? It was, I know. I shall give you something to make it better. Come with me." And he followed her into her bedroom, filled with as many exotic and heady blooms as a conservatory. "From my lovers," she said.

Simple banished the scene from his mind. "You were in exuberant spirits."

"Not at all. I'd met that devil, Ratty. Celebrating having shot down an *Albatros*, he told me. I'd have thought it would have been bad luck. It was my bad luck. You know Ratty. Too much champagne. Too much of everything. Only so much I could do to say no."

"I can imagine."

Simple had not said no in Segesvár.

"You're only a boy," she had told him. "You may never see me again." She threw open her sable coat.

She wore nothing beneath it. "But you'll never forget me."

He had never forgotten.

"General Gay watched the di Bonza woman," continued Eggie. "Actually sat through the performance. I left. Waited outside. Told him what I thought of it too."

Eggie had found the show almost as informative as it was shocking. Never, in fifteen years of married life, had he seen Mrs Eglinton undressed. The removal of the undergarments was preceded by the donning of the nightdress. Congress had been known to take place: their children were the living proof. But of the whiteness of her flesh, the abundant snowfields of her breasts, the marmoreal smoothness of her buttocks, he knew nothing. They were as forbidden to his sight as the other side of the moon. Lola di Bonza put everything — breasts, buttocks, belly, thighs, fur — on public view, sheielded only by ropes of jewellery and swags of veil that served to emphasise more than conceal.

"Nothing but a *fornicatorium*," was how Eggie dismissed the Hellenic Opera House. He would have liked to follow ancient precept and anathematise Lola di Bonza in public, denouncing her from the pulpit of a Protestant church.

"What did the General say?"

"Thought she soothed the military mind. Made a joke about oranges — Nell Gwynne, she was an orange seller apparently. Not sure he got my point. But it wasn't that woman's performance I was worried about. The she-devil has been worming secrets out of every man that she met. I've put an end to that racket. The Provost Marshall has arrested her."

"I know."

Simple would know; he always did. "That woman's a spy," Eggie continued. "A lot of information has been seeping through to the enemy. She's at the root of it, mark my words."

"At the root of it," Simple repeated. "*Radix malorum est femina. Cherchez la femme.*" Eggie wondered if Major Simon had finally gone barking.

No, Simple had not forgotten the whiteness and softness that had been vouchsafed to him in Segesvár. She was like Rubens's mistress — he had looked at the painting in Vienna — turning in her fur as though it were her own sex. Lola was slimmer though.

Eggie wondered about Simple. Was he losing his grip? Fortunately one of them had focus. "Damn her," he said, "and good riddance."

Simple locked the image from Segesvár back in the treasured compartment of his memory from whence it came. Might was well leave it there after all these years.

"Let me explain Miss di Bonza's role in our operation. She was, until arrested, a marvellous conduit of negative intelligence. General Ménière made special use of her — for that purpose, I mean. All the things that we really wanted the enemy to believe, but weren't true, we fed through her. She was of course a spy; she got paid for her services — her espionage services. What she didn't know was that she was really working for us without realising it. She wouldn't have cared, as long as she got the money. She's useless now. By getting her arrested, you've spoilt the game."

"Your game's too subtle for me," replied Eggie. "When I see a whore, I have her locked up." He brought down the fly swat sharply on the table next to him. "Missed."

Simple looked with distaste at the fly swat. "Next time, try Rosemary."

There was a knock on the door and Sunny entered. "Who's Rosemary?" he asked.

"The herb, of course," replied Eggie as he left.

Sunny reported the events at the tomb. "Pity the site couldn't be properly excavated," said Simple. It would clearly be a day filled with regret.

"Never mind about the tomb. I wanted to show you this." He gave Simple the bag that the boy had been carrying over his shoulder. Simple took out a yellow envelope and peered inside. "What is it?"

"I believe," said Sunny, "it's that new thing for cameras. Film."

Thirty-Nine

Sister Muir came into the cook house of the BWH carrying a hat box. She placed it on the table, next to some turkey gizzards. "Would you mind if I sat down for a minute?" she asked. "I'm not feeling so well."

"Please do," said Isabel. "It's a warm day for autumn." She indicated the one chair to Molem Vas; he chased off a cat. His moustache, as was usual before lunch, was hidden behind the press which kept its waxed points in condition.

"I can show you my cage," she continued to Sister Muir. "I watched the man collect the willow. He then had to boil it to take off the skin. It's for my hoopoe. Captain Southall brought him for me. I call him Hugh."

Sister Muir was silent. "I'm sorry. You were speaking."

"About Hugh's cage. They're always doing something, the village people. Knitting, or spinning, or working on the fields — the women, that is. The basketmaker was male."

"That's why I have my revolver."

"To shoot the basketmaker?"

"Because they're always doing something and you don't know what it is. Half of them are gypsies."

"I rather like the boys, don't you? When they're galloping the horses. And the women — what's the expression that Frank Sewell uses? That's it, they tone so well."

"He was going to marry one, wasn't he?"

"He said so. I hope he didn't. Tone can't be the sole basis for marriage — not that sort of tone, anyway. Tin, possibly. Not tone."

"I would have thought gypsies had plenty of tin. They're tinkers."

"You're taking me literally. By tin I meant money. Anyway, the point is: they aren't playthings."

"No. That's why I've got the revolver."

Sister Muir, elbow on table, leant her head on her hand. It was such an uncharacteristic gesture for the self-disciplined woman that Isabel wondered if she should not see one of the doctors. "No, I'll be fine. I just have a headache. Still, it made me think."

"Don't think if you have a headache. It will make it worse."

"What if something happened to me?"

"What sort of thing?"

"Anything. I wouldn't want it under my bed."

"Nothing will happen to you under your bed."

"The revolver's there."

"Then you needn't worry about things happening under the bed."

"It would be on my conscience."

"That would depend on what you did under the bed."

"I don't think I should leave it there. You've always said that. So I brought it here."

"Inside the box? I thought it was a hat." Isabel placed a cup of tea in front of her.

"No, it's the revolver. I felt I should stow it safely, in case something happens."

"It's not loaded, is it?"

"I don't think so. Can it matter?"

"I'd rather it wasn't."

Sister Muir lifted the hot enamel mug to her thin lips. "Gordon didn't tell me. Gordon, as you know, is my brother. It was the last thing he did for me before crossing the water — it's rather precious, as a result. A memento. I didn't see him again."

"Poor man. Where was it?"

"What?"

"That Gordon was fighting."

"Good heavens, why do you think he was fighting? He's far too old to be in the army. It's his revolver from the last war, the South African one. He went to Mull but the weather was so bad he couldn't get back to see me off. He did give me this, though. I feel rather light headed. Do you think I should take it out of the box. He did show me how to fire it but I've probably forgotten."

"Perhaps Molem Vas could help."

"A foreigner? No fear. I'll handle the weapon myself. Here it is."

She lifted it carefully out of the case. "I think the bullet goes in here. I wonder how you get it out." She peered at the chamber. "I do feel a little giddy."

There was a loud sound, as though a dinner gong had been struck by a member of the Army Gymnastic Corps in a confined space. But more than that, Isabel noticed — there was a percussive quality to it. She wondered why she was lying on her back on the floor.

The bullet from the gun — Sister Muir had accidentally pulled the trigger — passed through several objects: the side of the box, a Bible left by the female evangelist which Isabel never had time to read, both sides of a copper cauldron and Isabel's arm. Sister Muir screamed, then fainted.

"I haven't been killed, have I?" asked Isabel, rather dazed. "At least I'm in the right place. This is a hospital." She laughed slightly hysterically.

340

Molem Vas was already kneeling beside her, when Dr Aitken ran in. He had removed his shirt and was winding the sleeve round her arm. "Molem Vas, do get dressed," she told him. "Look after Sister Muir."

Sister Muir opened her eyes and looked at Molem Vas's face, the lower half covered by the moustache frame. She closed them again.

Two orderlies ran in with a stretcher. "I hope," said Isabel faintly, "that this won't delay luncheon."

The Little Squirrel at Two Trees

Forty

In Salonika, Winner had found a studio in the skin factory. It was big enough for his huge canvas. The painting would be a *Last Judgement*: God looking down on the world from a great height, the height that Winner had himself reached in the kite balloon. That terrible moment, the *Dies Irae* — the day of wrath — when the trumpet would sound and the dead be woken from their graves, some to join the angels in Paradise, others to be dragged down into the pit of Hell. It had been in his mind from the beginning. But there would be more Hell in this picture. It was the Hell that he was suffering.

He would use material from his sketchbooks. He leafed through one of them. It was the book that he had in his pocket on the morning he went up in the kite balloon. The early pages showed the men of the Kite Balloon Section at tasks around the balloon bed. There was Bill Bayley at a rope, Jones Twofour at the hydrogen valve, and the kite balloon itself, too big to fit on a page, just parts of its underbelly, brooding over the landscape like a black incubus. He had sketched Sunny, in a few lines, preparing to get into the basket. The next pages showed the drawings and sketches he had made of the panorama that opened out when they were airborne. The mountains, in heaps — he had drawn those at Sunny's request. The scale was awesome. He knew now what it meant to be a soldier, ant-small, trying to fight your way from ridge to ridge, or trying simply to survive. The idea that it might be possible to cross those mountains now seemed insane.

As he looked at the drawings, the conditions of making them came back to him. It had been cold, and he had not liked to look down. But he had made himself. The next pages bore rapid notes of the farmland more or less below the balloon, spread out like a coloured map. He had enjoyed the novel angles that it had given him. The vineyards, the yards, the farmhouses, the animals. But this was a detail that had surprised him. He had meant to ask Sunny about it. A pattern of circles in a farmyard. They looked like oil drums, but how could that be? Then he had jumped from the balloon and the thought had gone out of his mind. He had not looked at the sketches while he was in the BWH. They made him feel queasy. He had shut his books away before going on his quest to find Elsie.

But now that he looked again those circles puzzled him. He would send the drawing to Sunny. No, he would himself go to Camp Follies. He was meant to be designing some sets. And so Winner hitched a lift with an Artillery limber. It was a bone-rattling form a transport, and the dust of the journey got in his throat. It tooks two mugs of tea before he could speak without coughing.

"That day was strange, wasn't it? When we went up in the balloon."

"Yes. We got shot down." Sunny remembered it clearly.

"Not that. Just before the German airman appeared. I was sketching. Here is the page."

Sunny sucked on his pipe. "I'd seen something odd."

"I think I know what it was. Look here — pile of drums."

"Yes. Strange thing to find on Macedonian farm." Sunny scratched his ear with his pipe stem. He had entirely forgotten about the oil drums until Winner's sketch had prompted his memory; but he would write to Simple. Just a note to say that there was a farm upcountry, which might have been storing petrol. Simple could investigate further.

"Very nearly unhealthy, that parachute jump," he continued. "But some good came out of it. We met the nurses."

"Yes." Winner did not sound as happy as Sunny expected.

"You liked Elsie Fox."

"Yes." Winner was unaccountably morose.

Sunny tapped his pipe on his heel. "Have you seen her?"

"She's dead."

"Good heavens, no. You must have heard? She came back."

Winner jumped to his feet, knocking the canvas of the tent and upsetting a pile of books. "I must go to the BWH at once."

"You forget dinner, Winner."

"No time. Can I borrow your horse?"

Forty-One

It says much for Sunny's good nature that he agreed to loan his precious animal to Winner. Sunny was not convinced of his horsemanship; and he was right to be fearful, although it was not so much Winner's riding that let him down, as his ability to navigate across country in fading light. Macedonia had no signposts; in any case, he could not have read the script; and he did not have a map. There were no roads, only tracks for horse-drawn carts and sheep.

The plain seemed deserted. The villages and farms were half ruined. He did not know what reception he would get if he knocked on a door. He might be knocked on the head. Storm was a valuable animal. He continued in silence.

Winner stopped by a copse, wondering if he should bivouac. He heard sounds. Gleeful sounds, accompanied by splashing, and some words in a language that was not Greek and not English. It seemed an unlikely spot in which to hold a bathing party. He dismounted, tied Storm's reins to a tree and crept forward. Actaeon must have felt rather similar when he spied on Diana.

He inserted his body between the branches of the copse until he could see the pond. There were two men in it. They had left their clothes, or some of them, on the bank. They were up to their knees in water, but they were not washing. Every so often they would make a dash to the bank, flap their hands and fall back laughing.

Winner was not sure who these people were but it seemed prudent to Winner to inspect their belongings.

They were undeniably vulnerable in their present condition, but they might have been armed. Quietly, he crept around to the piles of clothes. They consisted of uniforms and boots. The men were still in their underwear. Were their uniforms Bulgarian? Was it Bulgarian that they were talking?

Among the kit were two pistols. Winner removed one of them from its holster. They were too busy with their game to hear him do so. They were so startled when he introduced himself that one of them slipped into the water.

They raised their hands, mouths open. They were men of his own age, and might have looked quite dashing, with their shocks of hair and rich moustaches, if they had not been dressed in waterlogged long johns. "*Qui êtes-vous? Bulgare?*" One asked.

"English," replied Winner.

They looked at each other in relief. "*Nous sommes français*. French."

Winner glanced down at their uniforms. There were no obvious distinguishing marks.

"Aviateurs," continued one of the men. "Airmen."

"Where's your craft?"

They pointed to the other side of the wood from the one Winner had entered by.

"Why are you in the pond?"

"*La chasse aux grenouilles*. We look for frog."

Winner found that two flying machines did indeed stand on flat ground outside the copse. "We land. We feel on-gree. We look for frog," explained one of the airmen. Out of the pond, the man was seized by a fit of shivering.

He removed his sopping underwear, dressed without it, and took a sheepskin-lined jacket from his plane. One of the planes had run out of fuel. They were planning to spend the night there, with the idea that the functioning plane would collect some fuel and fly back with it in the morning.

Winner was hailed as a major benefactor when he produced some rations from his saddle bag, along with his bivouac sheet. Although foodless, the Frenchmen had wine. Together they pulled enough fallen wood out of the copse to make a bonfire.

It was easy for the young men to establish common ground. They talked about girls. The Frenchmen began by extolling the wonder of the British nurses. There were also the Canadian nurses to consider: on the whole, the primmest of the field. The French nurses were low class, peasants and working girls. The British nurses represented the via media. Only that afternoon the aviators had, on their way to making a patrol, diverted to the skies over the hospital where Isabel worked. There they had spent twenty minutes making acrobatic turns. They had been cheered by the Serbian patients. The nurses were far too busy to watch. English women, said the airmen, could be rather cold.

"Women! I tell them that my father lives on the *Champs-Elysées*, surrounded by servants," laughed Jean-Christophe. "When he's really a station master from Bordeaux."

Winner told the story of Elsie, and his attempt to find her. They were enchanted.

350

"She is a Serb soldier?" asked Jean-Chirstophe incredulously. "You and I, we shall fly to Serb headquarters. The very first thing. My friend will ride your horse."

Winner was almost ecstatic with gratitude. To fly to the mountains tomorrow morning would save a long agony of riding.

By way of thanks, he went to his saddlebag and then into the copse. The Frenchmen followed him. A ray of light leapt from Winner's electric torch. An astonished frog, fat as a diva, which had recently been serenading the pond with its croaks, sat immobile. Winner threw his cap over it. Within moments Jean-Christophe had impaled the amphibian on his knife point. A dribble of blood ran down the blade.

"*Joli coup*, Johnny," he exclaimed.

Winner felt sick.

Forty-Two

In the mountains, the airmen found Elsie's Colonel. He and some other offices were studying a big map. The air of the cottage that was being used as the headquarters was heavy with smoke and exhaustion. The Colonel could do nothing but express his regrets about Elsie. "My little squirrel?" he mourned. "She is not here. Nor can you get to her. They're fighting. It's very hot at Two Trees." He put his finger on the map, sighed, then straightened his back. He talked strategy to the other officers in Serb. It was clear that the outlook was bad. The enemy might break the line at Two Trees, unless fresh reserves were thrown in; but there were no reserves to be had.

Winner did not care about the front as a whole. Elsie was in danger. The men's faces said as much, without need of translation. "I have to get to her," he burst out.

Jean-Christophe knew Two Trees. "That will not be possible," he told Winner solemnly. "We'd be shot down. Besides, there's nowhere to land the machine."

Coffee was brewed and Jean-Christophe took a cup. Winner staggered outside, into the crisp mountain air. He could hear gunfire.

It would take hours, days, to reach Elsie by foot. He might never do it. It seemed hopeless. If only Jean-Christophe had agreed to take him. By plane, she might be little more than an eye blink away, if he could find her. He had, though, a better chance of seeing her from the air than from the ground. Jean-Christophe's plane stood in the meadow. It took him only a matter of minutes to run over to it. He dodged between the network of wire struts and wriggled into the cockpit.

Winner had attempted to fly before, when hoping to join the Royal Flying Corps. The RFC were not so particular about height as the rest of the army. An instructor had shown him the controls. When the plane overturned on landing, it had been mutually agreed that a brighter future awaited Winner in another branch of the services. But he thought he could remember the principles. He put on the Frenchman's goggles. An obliging Serb swung the propeller and removed the chocks, the engine leaped into life; its roar, with the beat of the propeller, annihilated any other sound. The plane bounded, bumpily, over the meadow and rose into the sky. Take off, he recalled, had gone well the last time.

The land fell away. He was off the side of the mountain. Air rushed at his face. Puffs of ack-ack: he must have flown over the Bulgarian line. He quickly gained height. After a few minutes, he had left the front line behind. He was high over enemy territory. The air was very clear and very cold. He felt as cold as he had been with Lord Sturry. It was not snowing, but the sky was lurid. Below him, what should have been a beautiful green valley, dotted with trees, looked as though it had been covered by a sickly film. Against clouds that were the colour of overcooked liver, the curvaceous spire of a church shone out, as it caught the sun, as though it had been lit from within. It rose above a wooden village. Beside the village was the railway line that went all the way to Berlin. Winner glanced to the right. A less welcome sight came into view. A German plane.

Instinctively Winner turned away, diving steeply, but the German was on his tail. Holes began to appear in the papery wings of the plane. The airman was shooting at him. Winner tugged on the stick. The plane abruptly turned. In front of him was a mountain. He had lost too much height to fly over it. He kept turning to evade the pursuer. The side of the mountain was suddenly very close. The manoeuvre appeared to baffle the German, who thought that Winner was on a collision course. Winner succeeded in turning a full circle, stampeding the cattle which had been grazing placidly in a meadow, until his craft appeared within a few feet of them. Then he flew low along the valley floor. The German plane, now in front, was itself circling to get behind him again. Winner disregarded it.

The valley wound back into the mountains. Flashes, followed by bangs, came from the hilltops. Field guns. He must be going back towards the front. By the looks of it, he would have to cross it again; the German airman was coming up fast behind him. On the mountain top in front of him, he could see Bulgarian soldiers, some in reserve, others crouching behind rocks. Shells were falling on all sides, but the anti-aircraft guns had not picked him up: they were facing the other way. On the summit of a hill stood some horses. Their riders were looking intently at the battle through field glasses.

Later, Winner could not have said whether he had intentionally chosen the line that he now took. It owed something to his desire to evade the German plane. There was also an element that was involuntary, due to his low flying skills. Perhaps sudden inspiration also played a part. Whatever explanation he later chose to adopt, it was unquestionable that the men that he saw were Bulgarian officers. They were wholly unaware of his presence. Winner flew very low to the ground, and came up on them, shortly behind their horses' tails.

The effect was remarkable. The horses reared and flew forward. A couple of the officers were unseated instantly. Another plunged over a crag. The rest were stampeded towards the line. They galloped between the rocks. These were some of the best horses in the Bulgarian army. They had been trained to charge. They charged now, however much their riders tried to pull them up. The officers must have been superb horsemen to stay on for as long as they did. One fell as his horse leapt a fallen tree. A horse came down, when it wounded its foot on a piece of jagged shell. It was like the Grand National.

Of Elsie's *decetina*, only the ship's steward, Elsie herself and two others were still fighting. The rest were injured or dead. As the colonel predicted, it had been, in the military sense, hot. There was no time to analyse thoughts or feelings, let alone nurse regrets; but Elsie knew that she would soon die. "What we need," said the steward, "is a miracle."

Elsie was about to say that she did not believe in miracles when she heard the thunder of hooves. Peering cautiously from her rock, she saw several riderless horses and a Bulgarian colonel galloping furiously in her direction. The colonel hauled on his steed's rein. He should not have done so. The horse leapt the rock, but it had been wrong-footed. It stumbled on landing; the colonel was flung head over heels at her feet. In a moment, the Serbs had a gun at his head. It was quite unnecessary. The Colonel had been so badly winded that he could not move.

A second later, the *deus ex machina* that had caused this phenomenon appeared, in the form of a French flying machine, unsteadily piloted at a low altitude from the ground by a man in flying goggles and a British military jacket. It was greeted with cheers. Winner could not hear them, but he could see the men waving. It was, however, a mistake to wave back.

The two trees, which, now somewhat blasted, had given their name to the spot, stood by themselves, roughly a wingspan apart. When Winner looked ahead, they loomed with unexpected suddenness before him. A more experienced airman might have evaded them. Winner took the view that he could just about get through the gap. He nearly did. It was almost wide enough, but not quite. The craft stuck in what was left of the branches.

"I am falling," he thought. "I have done this before."

He hit a shattered branch. "The last time I had a parachute. Buttonhooks."

Pine needles scratched his face. "Taking off is always the easy part."

Something that was not a twig snapped.

He passed out.

Forty-Three

Isabel lay in the same ward as Sister Muir. Her arm had been painful, there was no denying it. But more painful was to see Sister Muir. When Isabel swam back into consciousness after the bullet had been removed, she had a dim impression of being under machine-gun fire. It was the shaking of Sister Muir's bed. Beneath a heap of overcoats and blanket, she was shivering uncontrollably. The iron bed frame rattled.

After a while, Sister Muir began, quite suddenly, to throw off the heavy covers, and for the rest of the day she lay squirming as though on hot coals. She made fish mouths as she gasped for air, revealing a yellowish tongue. Dr Aitken took her pulse and looked grave. "Her temperature is 105 degrees and the pulse is bounding," she observed to the nurse.

"Is that bad?" asked Isabel.

"It's what happens at this stage. We've seen so much of it. Usually they recover, if we give them enough quinine, and go home. But it will start again there, worst luck."

The tent was now quiet, in the delicious cool of early morning. A nurse walked up to the bed and sat on the edge, uninvited. It was Goody. "Darling, thank goodness you're here," she said.

"This is early for you, isn't it?" Isabel replied.

"Early," Goody giggled. Her cheeks were flushed and strands of her bobbed hair uncombed. "Or late. They couldn't find the coffee in the cook house, and I couldn't go straight into the dinner tent with the others. I thought you might know where I could get some. I'm desperate for it."

"Goody, what do you mean 'late'?" demanded Isabel. "You haven't?"

"What else could I do? They were divine, the French flying men. My one especially."

"But you left here in the afternoon. I saw you go."

"We went right into Salonika and out the other side. They showed me the camps — they go on forever, tents lined up as though they were on parade, soldiers saluting us everyone. One of the boys was a Major — *imagine, comme on dit en français!*"

"A Major?"

"He said he was. It was very hot and dusty, so of course we had to go to Molho's for a little refreshment. Then dancing at the White Tower."

"You've been out all night, then."

"Mmm. There was a tremendous show outside the White Tower. Not a theatrical show. A little Greek man was there. He's setting up a provisional government. Bands playing, everybody shouting and waving."

"Mr Venizelos? Did you see him? I should like to shake him by the hand." Eleftherios Venizelos was the Prime Minister who had invited the Allied armies to Greece; King Constantine, married to the Kaiser's sister, had sacked him.

"It was the motoring back that I enjoyed the most. We flew through Salonika, in what seemed like the middle of the night, but the shops were still lighted and simply crowds still out, furious arguments underway on all sides."

"About politics, probably."

"No idea. You know how the new streets are, they could be Regent Street, or anywhere — dazzling electric light. Then the mysterious, romantic Old Town. Goodness knows what would happen to a girl there if she didn't have an escort. And then — well, I don't know what to say."

"Neither do I."

"It was heavenly. He said he would marry me."

"They do, I understand." She thought of Petrović.

"As soon as he's able. When the war is over. Talk about the *entente cordiale*. He lives on the *Champs-Elysées* — can you imagine? With his father, who is fearfully rich, but rather puritanical, surrounded by hundreds of housemaids. I bet he's had them all." Her eyes were dreamy with romance.

"Goody! Won't you be late for the ward? I mean, when you report properly."

"Nonsense. I'm simply going straight on duty. Why should anyone know, unless someone snitches. But they won't snitch will they?"

"I can only answer for myself."

"Snitch if you like. It was worth it."

Goody skipped off, leaving Isabel to her reflections.

How easily some people took life. Decisions came with more difficulty to other people. The proposal from Captain Petrović was undoubtedly the most exciting ever to have happened to her. But she was still not sure how to reply.

That evening, Sister Muir's pulse rate returned to normal, her temperature fell, and she broke out into a profuse sweat. Her grey hair was plastered to her scalp like a wet flannel. She fell into a deep sleep.

The next morning, late, she woke feeling better. "I'm sorry to have been such a nuisance."

"I didn't mind a bit. I mean as regards the arm. It was just one of those accidents."

"I'd forgotten about that. I meant, being a burden on the nurses. But your arm, does it hurt very much?"

"I can feel a distinct tingle. But they say I'll survive. It could have been worse."

"I don't see how."

"You might have hit Hugh."

"Who's Hugh?"

"Hugh the Hoopoe. We sound like a couple of owls. I've tamed him. I showed you the cage, remember?"

"Cages are cruel," announced Sister Muir unexpectedly.

"Pretty creatures do sometimes lose their liberty, though? I think I read that in poetry once."

There was a pause; Isabel thought that Sister Muir had perhaps gone to sleep, and her mind wandered. Out of nowhere, Sister Muir said: "The gilded cage. It was a song."

"I suppose we'll sing it on the boat home."

"Will we?"

"If you can remember the words."

"Will we go home?"

"I don't suppose we'll be much use here. They'll probably pack us off."

"Not me. I'll die here."

"Whatever for? You don't want to be buried here. You belong in Argyllshire. What would Gordon say?"

"Oh Gordon. He'd go and fish for another salmon. His way of mourning. His way of celebrating. His way of everything. I wouldn't want to trouble him by dying at home."

"But you won't die. Malaria isn't fatal, not usually."

"I think I will. You feel these things sometimes."

"Not more than once."

Sister Muir, weary of talk, closed her eyes. Isabel worried that her last comment had been flippant.

Sister Muir was right. They gave her copious amounts of quinine, but the malaria had affected her heart, and she died the next day.

Isabel looked past the rolled-up sides of the tent, at the lapwings on the stubble fields. The wind turned to the North-East. Suddenly it was winter.

Forty-Four

They left the staff car in the shade of a fig tree. It wouldn't have been much use in the village, whose only streets were made of beaten earth. "Can one ever get used to Macedonia?" wondered Sunny. "The filth of it."

Simple peered myopically about. "It would never do in Letchworth, but we aren't in Letchworth. You'll find villages like this all over the Balkans and the Middle East. Where's the mosque?"

"There." Sunny looked at Winner's sketch. "We aren't far away."

They made their way past hens, picking morsels out of the rotting vegetables and horse manure on the ground. A mule laden with sacks of flour, fresh from the mill, crossed the otherwise empty square; on top of the flour sacks sat a farmer, with a switch in his hand. Simple addressed him in Turkish. He waved them towards the edge of the village. They came to an old wooden gate in a rough wall. Without opening the gate, they could already see the courtyard beyond through the cracks.

They pushed the gate open, until it stuck on the rough ground. The courtyard was empty except for a large dog on a chain. Rakes and hoes were propped against the walls of the courtyard, at the back of which was a verandah. The barking of the dog summoned the man of the house, who wore a turban wound around a red fez, the tip of which remained visible, like, Sunny thought, a cherry on a meringue. The end of the turban formed a flap which protected his neck. The man's skin was dark from work in the fields. He greeted them with dignity. Simple exchanged what sounded like courtly salutations and he and Sunny were beckoned into the farmhouse.

They entered a large low room, with a ceiling made of rough beams. Strings of onions hung down from some of them. Storage jars made of dark earthenware stood around the mud walls. Between them were divans, scattered with carpets, which looked as though they functioned as beds at night. Their host urged them to sit on one of them, which Simple did, lounging comfortably. Sunny attempted a compromise between a seated and recumbent posture; he did not feel it was successful. He was wearing shorts. The carpet tickled his bare knees.

Simple talked; the farmer talked. Sunny's eyes explored the room. It was clean; mud walls would not have done in Warwickshire but seemed serviceable here. There was an attractive vegetable scent, which reminded him of an apple store. Veiled women flitted to and fro on the verandah. A tray with little, long-handled copper pots of gritty, scalding coffee were brought. Apparently, Simple had made a friend. The farmer's leathery face creased into a smile. The thick beard parted to show his strong teeth. The eyes, dark as squid ink, sparkled.

Simple gave him a resumé of the conversation. "Terrible harvest, but then, which farmer has ever said he's had a good one? The war has made it difficult for him to move his flocks. His wife made the carpets, of course. She is an accomplished woman."

"Good. Have you raised the matter in hand."

"No. We'll get there by and by."

Their host had gone out of the room as they were speaking. When he returned, he draped a towel on Sunny's shoulder.

"They're going to give us a meal," observed Simple.

Water was poured over their hands. "Honey," exclaimed Simple appreciatively. "What a delicacy."

Sunny eyed the dishes suspiciously. "Curds," interpreted Simple. "Those small cubes are cheese — salty, I should think. Eggs cooked with spices. We've been invited to begin." The spoon is for the curds only. They eat digitally."

"I thought that was poisonous."

Simple leant forward to demonstrate, dipping a scrap of brown bread into the honey. He smiled his approval. Sunny had an awareness of honey trickling down his stubbly chin.

Simple was now deep in conversation with the farmer. After the everlasting bullybeef that was the staple of the British Salonika Force's diet, the freshness of the Turkish food spoke to Sunny's palate.

"Our host," interpreted Simple, "has made a radical suggestion that I, for one, would be happy putting to the Foreign Office. He would like Great Britain to take over the whole country. Then they would have peace, honest government and prosperity." Simple chuckled. "I said that they would also have efficient tax collectors who could not be bribed. He wasn't so sure about that." They bade courteous adieus, and the Englishmen walked out again onto the verandah. "I think I've been bitten by something on the calf," observed Sunny.

"Delightful," remarked Simple, not hearing him.

"He told you about the store?"

"That lot of drums that Winner drew? No. I suspect he knew about them though."

"How?"

"Didn't you hear the noise at the beginning of the meal? It sounded very much like somebody beating on one of them as a dinner gong. They don't have oil drums as a matter of course in Macedonia. They don't have motors."

"It could have been a drum for olive oil."

"They use jars. Besides, it would have had a different sound."

Sunny was triumphant. "Winner's keen observation has paid off. You'll arrest the man?"

"It would be a shame to."

"After that nice meal?"

"No. I would like him to lead us to the man behind this operation. Our friend isn't the sort of person to manage a smuggling racket. He's a countryman — happy to get his crops in, his animals to market and make what he can from the land, including a bit on

364

storing oil drums. If he is to be believed, he doesn't own the farm."

"Should we believe him?"

"On this point, I don't see why not."

"So who does own the farm."

"He wouldn't say. His answers were so vague as to be useless."

"I might be able to help there."

"Really?"

"Yes. Once my eyes had got accustomed to the dimness of the room, I made a study of it. While you and he were talking: there was enough time. There was something by the door; a visitor must have left it."

"Of any help?"

"It could be. It was a silver-headed cane."

Forty-Five

"What's happened to the geese?" Jones Twofour's Welsh voice rang through the camp. "Every one of them has gone."

There was consternation. The whole camp knew about the geese and had been hoping for a taste of them on Christmas Day. If not a taste, because eight geese would not feed a camp that now contained well over a hundred soldiers, a smell would have been something. They could have enjoyed the spectacle of goose flesh being eaten, if only by somebody else.

"Human hand, you say. Whose human hand?"

"The one which left us this." Twofour produced Exhibit A, a tin of Daily Mail Christmas Pudding.

"Some joke. I was taking it to show Captain Southall. He will be devastated, he will."

"What happened to the guard?"

Twofour produced a bottle of whisky. It was empty.

"Hankie Lawn." Hankie had been found asleep at his post. His weakness for strong liquor made further explanation redundant.

"You know what this means?"

They exchanged significant looks. "Those cheeky buggers from the Medics." The medical corps had established a hospital near Camp Follies. "Fishy must have told them about the geese when he had his boil lanced."

As predicted, Sunny took the news badly. "What a perfectly Hunnish thing to do. We have been hard at work, producing a theatrical success to packed houses. The whole Division talks of nothing else. Yet they steal our poultry; they mock us with Christmas puddings. I shall drive over and tell them what I think."

"You'll not take Snowball, will you, sir?"

"Certainly I shall take my sheep."

"Do you think she would be safe?"

Sunny was aghast. "Surely, not even that bunch of heathens could . . . But perhaps you're right. Snowball, if seen in the flesh, might present a temptation that those goose-stealing blaggards couldn't resist. Get my winter warm." The last remark was addressed to his Shakes. A cold wind blew from the mountains.

The medic Captain looked, to Sunny, hardly old enough to hold a knife and fork, let alone a scalpel. He was one of those men who, clean shaven and well-soaped, would look baby-faced into their fifties. His attitude, today, was one of complete innocence. "I know nothing of your geese, Captain."

It crossed Sunny's mind to suggest that he would make an exceptionally good bint, but this did not seem the occasion to mention it.

"They were not my geese. My men's geese. The geese have gone and all we have in their place is a pudding."

"The pudding could have come from anywhere."

"You are not suggesting divine intervention, surely. A human agency was responsible. The same agency that stole the geese."

"Quite possibly. I am not Sherlock Holmes."

"But you have geese here."

"I haven't seen any."

"They are in the cookhouse. I can smell them."

"Very little in the world smells better than roast goose," remarked the medic, heartlessly, with what Sunny would have been inclined to describe as a smirk. "Yes, we have geese. You're not the only people to have — or to have had — geese, Captain. They can also be bought for ready money from farmers and stallholders throughout Macedonia. I am not informed of the purchasing arrangements of the cook house, but I rather think you'll find, if you ask cookie, that these are, so to speak, commercial geese, to which we have good title. They are not, in the sense of stolen goods, 'hot', although it does seem," the Captain sniffed theatrically, "that they are being made so in the oven." The Captain's cherubic lips parted in a wicked smile.

"You maintain, in the face of all evidence to the contrary, that these birds are legit?"

"Evidence? Pure supposition. Circumstantial at best. You bring a prejudiced mind to the case. You had decided the rights and wrongs of it before you came."

"Very well," concluded Sunny rather less strongly than he might have wished. "I see I have no alternative but to return to my men and my sheep."

At Camp Follies, he summoned the keepers of the goose flock, with the pointed exception of Hankie. "They have the geese, I'm sure of it. They're roasting them."

"Our goose is cooked, sir, you might say," summarised Chelsea Bunn.

"Cooking," he corrected. "Not on the table yet."

"If you're proposing a stunt, sir, we'd be on for it."

"We can't go around openly appropriating geese that other men claim to be theirs. We have to answer guile with guile. I see that you, Twofour, are dressed for the rehearsal. You look most fetching, if I may say so. They've done wonders with the make-up."

"Who needs brimstone and treacle, sir, when you can plaster your face with this stuff? Inches thick it is."

"The other bints are similarly attired?"

Twofour nodded.

"Get them together. It is time to put your acting to the test. Corporal Bayley, we'll need cauldrons."

There were various popular explanations for the acronym, RAMC. Run Away Matron's Coming was one of the more popular. But in its state of moral outrage, Camp Follies preferred the alternative: Rob All

368

My Comrades. Yet the winter sun shone as much on the temporary hospital as it did on the entertainers. The RAMC appeared to be untroubled by matters of conscience as they went about their morning duties, which included, for the orderlies, laying a large luncheon table in the dining room. Peace reigned over the camp.

It was only broken when a flustered sentry ran between the tents looking for Captain Ellison-Kerr. "What do you need him for, Sandy? Are we under attack?"

"Women," replied Sandy shortly. "Real crackers too. There's a whole load of them asking to come into the camp."

"Well, invite them in."

"Not without the Captain's say so," replied Sandy, hurrying off.

The news that a contingent of the opposite sex had appeared at the gates of the camp had an extraordinary effect on the inhabitants. Slowly at first men started to stroll, as though drawn by an invisible magnetic force, in the direction of the gate. The stroll became a bustle, the bustle became something akin to a stampede. Anybody who could move did so. Patients propelled themselves in wheelchairs and on crutches. Word did not initially penetrate the cook house where the kitchen staff were perspiring over their cookers and field ovens. "Might as well put back dinner, you know," said a soldier, sauntering casually into the tent. "There's a party of women at the gate. The whole camp's gone up to see them."

"That's women for you," said one of the cooks. "Always turn up at the wrong time, they do." He wiped his hands on his apron. "These birds are ready."

"Leave them on the top of the stove, Wilfie," advised another cook. "They'll keep hot enough." With those words the speaker disappeared from the kitchen with the speed of a bullet. Within a few seconds the tent was empty except for the soldier who had brought word of the females at the gate. That soldier was Bill.

"Well done, lads," said Sunny an hour later. "A most effective raid. The objective was achieved to the letter. Rather more so, in fact. Our cauldrons overfloweth. We not only accomplished the repatriation of our geese, but were also able to capture a large quantity of roast potatoes."

"Not to mention gravy and cabbage, sir."

"Gravy and cabbage as you say. A superb effort by the chorus line. Our goose-loving rivals realised the deception, I dare say."

"It took them a while, sir. Parsley was awfully good, sir."

"You see, Tennant. I knew you could do it."

"Then they twigged and it didn't matter, sir. They were as happy to see men dressed as woman, as woman themselves. Almost, at any rate. Blushing with confusion, as you might say, sir. We put on a number — Fishy on the mouth organ, sir — and you should have heard the encores. Then we thought we'd better scarper, sir."

"Meanwhile, Bayley had galloped back with the cauldrons. I hope Storm served you well."

"Such a horse, sir, it was a pleasure to ride him. I had one cauldron tied up behind me, sir, the other in front — some horses wouldn't have liked it. I roped the lids on tight, sir."

"Bravo. Cookie, carve the geese."

"Good Lord, sir, here comes Captain Ellison-Kerr. He doesn't look too happy."

"Cookie, serve the geese quickly. And," he added brightly, as Ellison-Kerr came within earshot, "lay another place for our guest."

"Don't think that I shall eat with you," huffed the Captain. "I am appalled that my unit is camped next to such a gang of bandits as yours."

Sunny, his cheeks bulging with goose, waved his fork. It was some moments before he could speak. He then addressed his men. "I hear we shall have more balloons. Kite balloons," he added for Ellison-Kerr's benefit. "It may not be long before I surrender command of this camp and return to my Section."

The other diners cried "Shame."

"Until then," Sunny continued, "until then . . ."

He turned a smiling face on the Captain and lifted his glass, "Merry Christmas."

Forty-Six

Isabel picked up her pen. It was not easy to write a letter in the BWH. She might have sat on her bed, but it was too low: it would have meant resting the paper on her knees and the ink would have spilt over the bedding. The cook house was greasy. The only other possibility was the common room, or common tent as it should more accurately have been called, but that was shared with other nurses, and she had a very particular letter to write. She had postponed the decisive act on a number of occasions, on the excuse that the common room had been busy. It was winter. Usually nurses crowded there for the warmth, but this evening had it to herself.

She dipped the pen in the ink, but before applying it to the paper she rehearsed her reasoning in her mind.

She had always said that the Serbs were fine. Captain Petrović had seemed specially and nobly fine. Furthermore, he had proposed to her.

She was unquestionably drawn to him. He was young — a few years younger than her — and tragic. He had identified his destiny with that of his country: that was fine. It was what good people did around Godalming. In the case of Godalming, that country was, admittedly, Britain. His was Serbia. It went without saying that Britain had the highest interests of humanity at heart and always acted with decency, honour and compassion. Serbia was being bullied. It was the underdog. It was fighting bravely, its struggle personified by the slender, doomed figure of Captain Petrović. She had seen enough of Macedonia to know that standards of behaviour differ. But Petrović's rules, the ones he was fighting by, were so very far different from those of the Surrey Hills. Her own standards were part and parcel of her very being. She would not

372

change; neither would he. She had seen what that meant.

Isabel had not stayed long in the sick ward. She had reported to Mrs Stalwart-Dousing at the first opportunity. She knew how few nurses there were. "How is your arm now?" she had asked.

"Garshly wound," replied Isabel.

"What's that?"

"An expression. I am perfectly able to take over Sister Muir's duties, if I may."

The Serb army was fighting, the last battle, they said, of that fighting season. "Someone," said Mrs Stalwart-Dousing, "has to bury the dead. You must take a detail of the walking wounded."

The men were a ragged bunch. The Serbs never quite looked like soldiers to British eyes, their uniforms being too rustic to meet military expectations. Besides, the wounded had often lost parts of their uniforms, and had their heads in bandages and their arms in slings. Instead of rifles, the burial party shouldered shovels. Isabel saw them march off. She herself followed in the pony cart. She did not need to be told where they were going. Over the mountains, vultures were circling as they waited their chance to gorge.

Dr Aitken had set up a field hospital in the hollow bole of an immense ash tree. Wounded men were being treated as best they could and, if they had a chance of survival, sent back to the main hospital encampment. Isabel wondered where they would be put when they arrived there. In their early days in Macedonia, the nurses had been inclined to collude with the soldiers who prefer the calm and female ministrations of the hospital to returning to their units. They could not afford such sympathy now. Wounded men were turfed out of their beds as soon as they had been patched up, in order to let others take their place.

"I've brought some men with spades," Isabel announced to Dr Aitken.

"Well, you'll have plenty to do," she replied. "I believe that the dead are being collected. There's an officer on the battlefield now. I've only seen Serb casualties."

"So the Bulgarians must have won."

"They say not. Victory went to the Serbs."

Isabel walked out onto the scene of horror. The bodies of the dead lay in ungainly attitudes. Some had already been heaped together. The wounds were often terrible. But the scene was strangely quiet. Occasionally she heard a crack, as of a whip; but there was none of the moaning that she had steeled herself to expect. Groups of Serb soldiers were moving across the battlefield, looking for wounded.

She heard the crack again. It was a pistol shot.

"Dead, dead, dead," cried Molem Vas. "All Bulgarians dead. Good."

She saw a Serb officer in the distance. He was bundled into a coat, with a scarf wrapped around his head. In his hand was a revolver. "An outrage is taking place," she cried with impulsive anger. Her tone was that she had used — it seemed so long ago — to the farmer who beat his mule in Salonika, the first day she had arrived. Only this was not a matter of animals.

The officer turned to her. His eyes were blank with weariness, incomprehension and possibly indifference. He was as yet some distance off.

The man focused his gaze on her, as though with difficulty. He seemed puzzled. "Isabel?" She saw that it was Petrović. She walked quickly, almost running, to meet him.

"My dear guardian angel," he said on seeing her. "Whatever brings you to this place of death?" He called out and the soldiers who were with him came running. "You shouldn't be here. These men will escort you home."

"I do not intend to go home. I'm here to bury the dead."

"That is not work for a woman."

"It is work for me. And I am pleased I am here, because it means I can tell you that some of your men have actually been shooting the wounded."

Petrović looked at her with patronising forbearance. It was not a look that she liked. "Not all the wounded," he said. "Only Bulgarians."

He was exhausted. He made the observation without thinking of the effect that it would produce on the Englishwoman. It appeared so simple to him, a matter of pure fact. He soon realised his mistake.

She could not think of adequate words to express her disgust. "You must tell them to stop immediately," was her first articulation of it.

"Don't worry. They can take you away from here."

"I shall not go until I hear that the practice has stopped."

"It cannot stop. It is the rule of war here. It has been throughout the centuries. We aren't fighting a civilised, gentlemanly war. We aren't sportsmen, like your soldiers. It's winter. We have to conserve what supplies we have for ourselves. We can't take prisoners. They can't take prisoners. I don't ask my men to do what I won't do myself. It is I who have the responsibility."

"You?" She looked at his gun. She could scarcely comprehend the enromity to which he confessed.

"My duty."

"Is that what you're doing now? Your duty is to humanity."

"I know my duty."

She recoiled from him, as though a door into his soul had been opened and she saw it running with blood. "But, Captain Petrović, why? The BWH would take them."

"You women?" he laughed bitterly. "Take in Bulgarians? Nobody but a naïve English lady who should not be on a battlefield would suggest it."

Isabel was not used to this tone. "Why shouldn't we?"

"Because you would be murdered," he informed her. "Or the other thing. Or both." Then, as though to clinch the argument, he said slowly and clearly: "They are Bulgarians."

Petrović looked at her, aware that it was across a gulf of incomprehension. He very much wanted this woman to be his wife. To him, she epitomised the sweetness of

376

life. She ought to have been shielded from man's work; and yet she had come here. She too had seen the horror of it.

For the moment, his love for her had to be put on one side, while this war was fought to a conclusion. There would be all the time afterwards for him to resume the life of a cultivated young architect. She would help him recapture his old self. Through his love for her, he would soar to greater heights. But for now, as an officer, his duty was clear. It was an iron duty, and now he was tired — too tired to comprehend that he was losing her.

"There is nothing I can do. I'm sorry. I am not the one who makes the decisions. I have my orders."

"If you don't stop, I shall indeed leave." She did not mean simply depart, but something more final.

"I am fighting for my country," he replied. For Petrović, it said everything.

The burial party was digging pits. There were not, however, enough men for the task. She drove the pony back to find more. She held herself erect as she left the battlefield; but the journey was a long one — too long for her not to think of what had passed. A void seemed to have opened up in her heart. On the way, she passed a mule.

Mules were not unusual in themselves but this one had Winner, his leg stretched out stiffly in front of him, sitting on a chair attached to the side. In front of the mule walked Elsie. "Back again," he said, smiling wanly.

"You're back, too, Elsie?"

"Yes."

"You must stay here. The battlefield is no place for an Englishwoman."

"Do you know, Miss Hinchcliff, I believe I shall. Someone will have to nurse the Lieutenant."

The other, easily touched by romance and horrified by what she had seen on the battlefield, smiled her approval. She was glad to have her friend back. Mentally she took a step back: but yes, that is what Elsie was. In Macedonia, the divide between them, shaped by the circumstances of their early lives, had closed. "It's really time you called me Isabel," she said.

Winner and Elsie transferred to the pony cart, hitching the mule behind. The pony trotted on.

It was now evening. Isabel dipped her pen in the ink. She knew now what she would write with it.

For a moment, she thought of Petrović as she had conceived of him until — until, when was it? This morning. He sat well on a horse. He also spoke French. He had conviction.

And — or should that be but? — Serbia was not Surrey. Captain Petrović had been, for Isabel, a stirring dream of high ideals. With him she would have gone to live somewhere that was not Godalming — somewhere with beehives, painted wooden houses and proper peasants, and no motorcars or plumbing. It was a thrilling thought.

Isabel was not by nature adventurous, and the surface of her life had, for the most part, been placid. Her parents had seen to that. They had enough money. She had never heard her father raise his voice, much less swear. They were surrounded by beauty, took a compassionate interest in the village — the Hinchcliffs helped pay for the reading room — and had people from the better houses to luncheon. They lamented the changes that were overtaking the Surrey Hills, although some of them made their own lives more convenient and comfortable. Isabel's twenty-nine years had been spent in cotton wool. The war made her realise that life had other colours. Blood, suffering and horribly mangled bodies, and diseases that were more than colds, which actually killed you if you were Sister Muir; where you might work until you were exhausted, with water sloshing around your possessions — and then for no reason get shot with a revolver. She wasn't sure she could go back to Surrey, and her parents' comfortable house.

Serbia would be pre-comfort. It would be difficult, but in a romantic way. She liked that. It would be an Arts and Crafts world without the need of a movement to reinvent it.

But the escape from materialism came with its own price. She wanted the primitive; she did not want primitive values. Sunny had blown up an airman but was troubled by it. The Serbs and the Bulgarians butchered each other without qualm. Petrović was too much of a Serb not to do likewise. The otherness could not be bridged.

Goody came into the common room. Isabel tried not to notice.

Isabel would have liked to marry him, poor boy. She yearned to. It was not wholly out of love. She did not know if she loved him. How could she know; she had hardly seen him, and then only in extraordinary circumstances. But she loved the idea of him. The real him had been revealed on the battlefield — unless it was another aspect of the idea, beneath which the real him had been lost.

She wiped the pen and began, in neat script, Dear Captain Petrović . . .

Goody threw herself into a chair next to the desk. "I do feel ill, you know, specially in the mornings. My clothes seem to be tighter. Do you ever find that?"

Looking up from her letter, Isabel said that she didn't. "I wonder what it could be?"

There were some things, thought Goody, about which an educated woman could be remarkably stupid.

Spring 1917

Forty-Seven

It was a warm spring day when, Ratty walked out of the camp towards the gypsy caravan which dogged the movements of his company, always appearing in some pleasant meadow at a distance of half a mile or so from the gate.

The previous evening, Ratty had ridden over to the BWH. They had caught the rage for shows. "We open with a Greek play," Mrs Stalwart-Dousing had announced, "written specially for us by Miss Parkes, a professor at Somerville." The stage was filled by maidens, wearing the sort of flowing, pleated draperies seen variously on the Parthenon marbles and Miss Isadora Duncan. Isabel played a muse. Given the state of her arm, it was a largely static part. The effect of the whole was a cross between the Elgin marbles and a village fete. A very large audience of officers had arrived to admire the display of femininity, but it could only be described as chaste. Ratty had hoped to see Nurse Goodman. Apparently she had been sent home. He was glad he had married the gypsy.

The Serb pipers who were supposed to end the evening refused to play, in support of their famously brave leader Colonel Dimitrijevic. He had, apparently, been arrested.

Ratty enjoyed his state of matrimony. His wife was young and smooth-skinned, and if soap had been more readily available, he would have had nothing to complain about in terms of her outward form. Other married folk might have envied the mutual incomprehension that they had of each other's language. The caravan was, he thought, in a terrible state, clothes and bedding strewn anywhere. But it did not worry him. He had to sleep in his tent. The caravan was simply a convenience. It had been one of his better investments.

Ratty did rather wish that she would refer to him as something other than Johnny. Frank or even Ratty would have been nice. And her inability to speak English, and his ignorance of the Romany tongue, did not prevent communication of a kind. She made it very clear that she expected her worth to be demonstrated, each time he came, with a present. He had already paid her brothers more than he thought the bargain demanded, and yet she still asked for money, expensive food or trinkets, the last being impossible to obtain except in Salonika. If she was in a good humour, she expressed her desires teasingly. If in a bad one, she did so sulkily, or angrily, or with menaces. There had been more bad moods than good.

But he still looked forward to his conjugal visits, and not only for the obvious reason." They were a break from routine. She was a challenge, in the same way that a young horse, to a keen rider, would have been. Occasionally, he found a pot steaming on an open fire: that was a change from the cook house. He had become not just accustomed to her, but fond of her. They were both, for a moment of time, in Macedonia together; they were both young — she was very young — and they could sometimes laugh together; laugh in the face of the war.

384

And yes, there was the obvious reason too.

He sprung up the steps of the wagon and pushed open the yellow door. Inside it was in order — or in the same disorder as usual. He turned away, disappointed. He called her name. In response, her brothers ambled round from the back of the cart. "John-ee," said one of them, smiling with golden teeth. "You want jig-jig."

"Yes, I want jig-jig."

The brother whistled. Ratty's bride walked into view. She looked worse than usual, not as regards her scowls — he was used to those — but something else. He rather thought she had been crying. He felt suddenly protective and strode towards her. It meant passing one of the brothers. It was only when he was almost upon him that he saw the knife.

Shortly after the War, a naturalist who had been serving with the British Salonika Force published a book about the wildlife of the countryside. In it, he explained how the vulture's bald head is the product of evolution. The bird is sometimes forced to stick its head into sticky or putrid places to extract a morsel of food. He gave, as illustration, the case of an English officer whose body had been found in a remote gully. His skeleton remained within his uniform, even thought it had been picked clean by vultures. Their beaks could not penetrate cloth, but they could get at the neck; through the thorax they removed lung, heart and intestine. In the process their heads must have become pretty messy; just as well they didn't have a headdress of feathers.

The author did not mention the identity of the corpse. Simple knew, however. It belonged to Captain Frank Sewell. When the body was found, he asked to see the effects, and removed a small diary from one of the pockets. Applying the magnifying glass, he could read the few notes that Ratty had scrawled, in a violet pencil. "Showed wife the hat of boy crushed to death in Goody's Grave. She confirmed my suspicion — it is typical gypsy. She seemed upset."

August 1917

Forty-Eight

Simple was standing beside a well in the garden of a house in the Jewish quarter. Beside him was the Winner. Both men peered into the depths of the shaft. Intently watching them were the tall, robed figure of Mr Pinheiro, father of Rachael, the beautiful chocolatière, and Moise, the beautiful chocolatière's intended. "I have to say it's interesting," concluded Simple.

"You mean anybody could be down there?" queried Winner?

"No, that the well could have been built in the Roman period, and nobody has been down to investigate." It did seem awfully deep.

"They believe it's haunted," observed Winner.

"Then perhaps the noises are being made by the ghost."

"They say they are different noises. They came to me because I've bought seeds from there for the Otter."

"Public Anemony Number One." It was rare that Simple permitted himself a joke.

"Seeds," said Mr Pinheiro in confirmation.

"Do they still use the well?"

Moise came forward. "If you will permit me to say, they used not to use it. Now they do."

"Why now?" asked Simple.

"There is not enough water in Salonika for everybody. Rachael is here sometimes. She draws the water."

"That is Biblically appropriate. Has she heard anything?"

"No. She says never. But I have heard it."

"Heard what?"

"Singing."

"Pleasant singing?"

"Pleasant enough."

"It could have been your imagination." Although the local population had done very well from the presence of the Allied Armies, the overcrowding told on their nerves.

"My esteemed future father-in-law has also heard it. A man's voice."

"Very well," declared Simple, tying a rope around his waist. "I'll go down."

He climbed nimbly over the wall and swung himself down, his feet on the internal surface of the shaft. After a hundred feet, he took out an electric torch and lit it.

"Is it very deep?" called Winner.

"I'll only know that," replied Simple, "when I reach the bottom."

With the torch in one hand, he went slower. He descended another fifty feet, then another: one foot, then the next, until, suddenly, the wall was not there any more. They had said that there was a tunnel going off it. It was tall enough for a man to crouch in, but not to stand upright. The vault appeared to be lined with thin bricks. Simple concluded that it must have been very old, possibly, as they had suggested, Roman.

He walked, stooping, along the tunnel for fifty feet or so, and then, to his astonishment, saw light filtering through. That could only mean that somewhere was an opening. The tunnel opened into a chamber. There was the light: it descended from a fissure that ran up to ground level.

Simple was entranced. It appeared to be a cistern of some kind; or another structure which had been turned into one. Columns stood in ranks, supporting the roofs. Carved columns with capitals, only sometimes the capitals were not at the top but the bottom of the shaft. Beneath them was a pool of clear water. Simple shone his torch into it, wondering if there could have been fish. If so, they could only be albinos. As he flicked light into the corners of the pool he noticed something else. It was a human foot. He elevated the beam. The foot was attached to a body. The body belonged to a young man. He had huddled in the far corner of the space to avoid being seen. In his hand was a gun.

Simple stepped swiftly back into the tunnel.

The young man spoke to him in Greek. Simple replied fluently. It served the purpose.

"I am Ahmed," said the young man. "People know me as Aaron."

In the calm of the evening, Simple and Winner sat on the Otter's verandah. "It's a good thing that it was me you asked to go down the well," he observed to his host. The scent of oleander drifted towards the bench.

"Who exactly did you find down there?"

"Aaron, our murderer."

"I know that." The Otter leant on the railing of the verandah, inwardly enjoying the garden. "But you said that wasn't his real name."

"Thank heavens the Provost Marshal didn't get hold of him," reflected Simple. "He would have done it by the book."

"The boy killed someone."

"Yes, Vassilis. The world is a better place for it."

"What about putting him on trial?"

"Nonsense. The boy's a hero."

The Otter tore his eyes from his plants. "You're getting soft."

"Not a bit of it. He didn't kill him out of love for Rachael, although that came into it. Friend Vassilis was blackmailing him. He wanted him to join the courier network. They've been running information to the enemy. There had been losses recently. Aaron — or as we should call him Ahmed — refused."

"Vassilis wouldn't leave it at that?"

"No. He threatened to expose him."

"Expose him as what?"

"It's true that he's in love with Rachael. Who wouldn't be? That's why he found the job at Molho's. To be near her."

"But she didn't even notice him."

"That's what she said. They are in love. Delightful, isn't it? Ahmed was worried that he would be revealed as a non-Jew."

"What was he doing in the well?"

"He had to hide. She had heard about the tunnel. It was the safest place they could think of. There was also the advantage that they could communicate. She sent down notes when hauling water. Sometimes he climbed up to the surface. He'd been down there for weeks."

"You're lucky not to have been killed." The Otter considered that it was not for the first time.

Simple brushed away the suggestion. "He didn't want to kill anybody."

"He killed Vassilis."

"Yes," conceded Simple. "He hated Vassilis."

If it had not been for the smell of an incinerator operating from without the garden pale, the spot would have been idyllic. The men smoked their cigarettes in silence. After a few contemplative minutes, the Otter asked: "What next?"

"I don't know. Amhed is *Dönmeh*."

"That's a Jew who pretends to be Mohammedan, or a Mohammedan who's a Jew underneath, isn't it?"

"Something like that. There are quite a number of them in Salonika."

"Yes, and Rachael's father is determined that she should marry the rabbi. She prefers Ahmed. He is an enterprising young man, as we know. His family is rich. But there is the obstacle of the father. Shakespeare could have written about it. How fortunate one is not to have children."

"Where is he now?" The Otter carefully extinguished his cigarette: he did not want to spoil the neatness of the path by throwing it over the railing.

"In my office."

"For safety's sake, I suppose."

"My dear Otter, he's there because I haven't found out nearly enough about the important piece of archaeology in which he was hiding. He knows more about it than anybody. Together we shall write a letter to the Royal Institute of Archaeology."

"You and me?"

"Ahmed and I. I am looking forward to the collaboration."

Forty-Nine

Some days later, the Otter looked out from the same verandah; it was a view that usually gave innocent pleasure, but now his expression was glum. The Commander in Chief had insisted on being present when the new kite balloon was sent up, but was far too busy to run down to the plains. It was therefore decided to find a site within the Birdcage, where the Allied armies were encamped. There was no clout of flat land that did not have a tent, cookhouse or hospital on it. Except one. When the Birdcage had been in its infancy, not more, metaphorically, than two pieces of bent wire and a cuttlefish bone, the authorities, knowing that supply would be one of the great questions of the campaign, had treated the commissariat with generosity. The store keepers had been some of the first to arrive at Salonika. They could take their pick of locations. They looked ahead and secured plenty of space for future operations. Since then, the Otter had defended his quite substantial demesne with determination. He took it to be his duty to do so. Against brother officers, he had been tenacious, unaccommodating and — usually because they ultimately moved upcountry while he never did — successful. But he could not prevail over a fixated C in C. The new balloon bed was his garden.

It had been almost too painful to watch the immense slug being inflated. But since his pergola, his paths among the flower borders and his sweet-selling tomato plants had disappeared beneath several acres of oiled canvas, he had found little else to do. The kite balloon had now risen above the earth and floated at its tethers, like a giant blight. Beneath it lay what the Domesday Book would have described as "waste".

Beside the Otter, in an easy chair, his polished field boots on the baluster, lounged Sunny. "I don't like the look of it, you know," he confided.

"Neither do I," moaned the Otter. "The trellis has been smashed like matchwood. They've even brought down the latrine screens."

"Your garden, you mean? Well, the tennis courts will be all right. I was thinking of the weather."

"What about the weather? There's not a cloud in the sky."

"I wouldn't say that. That high-up streak of vapour is often the prelude to something. They've had storms on the Struma. The ascent is scheduled for oh eight hundred hours. I may be wrong, but it could have become blowy by then."

"Good heavens, man. You're not thinking of putting it off." The Otter was desperate. Once the monster balloon had made its maiden flight, it would be hauled off to a more strategically useful sector, leaving the

Otter to survey the horticultural damage, mourn over his battered borders and begin to replant.

"This is about the most inconvenient day in the year. The Follies are opening in Salonika tonight. But," he said heroically, "I am not thinking of myself. I wouldn't want to risk the balloon unnecessarily. We may have to avail ourselves of your hospitality a little longer, I'm afraid."

The Otter turned and walked heavily into the building. "Excuse me. I have some chits to attend to," he lamented.

There was not much in the way of positive cloud by the time the C in C's staff car arrived at seven-fifty. But the sky had turned the colour of a boiled dishcloth, and the wind had begun to gust. Sunny had an impression of white moustaches and a lot of braid. "*Bon sang!*" exclaimed the C in C, in a tone of wonder. "She is very big, that girl." Sunny observed that it was the same size as the other girls had been. "Yes, one forgets. Well, you had better get her into the sky."

"I was wondering if that would be wise, sir. The weather is blowing up a bit."

An ADC took up the point. "We've had a meteorological report, sir."

The moustaches twitched. "What's wrong with the weather? This is a military operation, we can't stop every time somebody opens an umbrella — and it isn't even raining yet. I'm very busy. We have a timetable. We must keep to it."

"They used to say that on the Somme," mused Sunny to himself. Still, nothing much could go wrong: a quick up and down was all that was needed. He said aloud: "Very good, sir. How high would you like me to go?"

"Until I can't see you any more," laughed the moustaches, in humour again.

"I'll go to five thousand feet. Your staff have given me a camera, sir. They've also found some film. Never used it before but I should be able to photograph Salonika for you."

The moustaches signified the acceptability of the idea, and Sunny vaulted into the basket. "Let her out, Ramsgate," he called, "if you would be so kind." It was good to be back. The winch was a new one. It did not creak so much as purr. He began to assemble the photographic apparatus, looking out the box of wooden frames into which the film had been inserted. He adjusted the tripod, twiddled some brass screws on the mahogany box of the camera. It was a big bit of kit, with a long lens.

As the kite balloon floated upwards, Sunny looked out over Salonika, hidden, possibly like a jewel, otherwise a forgotten carrot, at the bottom of the deep sack of the Gulf. There was a small armada of ships on the sea. A seaplane was taking off. On the curve of the bay, the new quays built by the Allies — rectilinear, vice-like — looked alien and out of scale. The city itself scrambled up towards the castle in the vermin-infested, stinking wooden curiosity of the old town. It looked amusingly ramshackle from the air. Around it were the would-be boulevards, palely borrowing reflected light from Paris. The morning sun bathed his face. The gathering wind brushed it.

Sunny shifted to the other side of the basket to see the Birdcage. "Nothing much to report, sir," he told the telephone. "Tents of course, in their hundreds, all in neat lines. I can see the marshes of the Vardar, and the river delta — looks rather like the roots of a hyacinth bulb, if you've ever grown on top of a glass vase. Hyacinth, sir. Flower with a powerful scent, sir. I was saying that the Vardar delta reminded me of its roots. Very good, sir; no poetry. To the East is the British line, linking up with the two lakes. From this height, barbed wire and machine gun posts remind me of — I beg your pardon, sir. Poetry almost reared its head."

It was as though the detritus of a very large tinkers' encampment had been strewn across the dusty landscape. A road struck out through the French sector, crossing the Vardar, towards Monastir, where God, in making the mountains, had a momentary failure of invention, leaving eight miles to provide a pass into Serbia; this was the Monastir Gap. Another road headed north, beside the Vardar, to the British front line in front of Lake Doiran. Another wound its alarming way, through an intestine of vertiginous hairpin bends, past Lake Langaza and onto the Struma Plain. All three roads bore a ceaseless burden of artillery limbers, cavalry platoons, mule wagons and motor lorries. The spindly railway tracks might have been the veins in a piece of fish. Camp Follies stood, in eccentric isolation, on the Struma Plain. To the North

398

came mountains, in a chaotic, incomprehensible heap; on top of which sat Johnny Bulgar.

What most occupied Sunny's attention, however, was above the ground, not on it. From three thousand feet, he could see the dark storm clouds that had been predicted, sweeping over the Struma Plain. The charcoal smudge beneath them showed that it was raining there. Every so often they flickered with lightning. Sunny spoke to his ground crew. "We'll give it another thousand feet, I think. Then straight down again."

The air, which had been hot and clammy at ground level, was cooler now. A buffeting wind rocked the basket. There was a fascination in watching the storm approach, like a firework display. But Sunny wanted to be on the ground again when it struck. Suspended beneath a mountain-sized sack of hydrogen, attached to the ground by a wire hawser, was not, he reflected, a good place to be during a thunder storm. They had stopped letting out the wire. He felt that he had enjoyed the view for long enough. "You can take me down now," he told them.

The voice on the other end was Ramsgate's. "Very good, Sunny. Shall we put on a show? The new winch reels in at five hundred feet a minute."

"Quick as you like. There's a bloody great thunder cloud coming and we could all go up like a puff of flash powder. Tell the C in C to get his camera out. Oh no, I have it."

"Robert," said Ramsgate.

"Bugger Robert," muttered Sunny. "Just get on with it."

Sunny felt a tug on the nose of the balloon and it began to descend like the lift in the Woolworth Building in New York. Sunny's ears popped and he felt his stomach being left behind. He helped the balloon on its way by tugging at the gas valve. The ground was approaching fast. He grabbed the rip cord to deflate on landing.

The balloon landed in what had been Otter's rose garden at such a speed that Sunny was flung onto the other side of the basket by the collision. The rip cord jerked out of his hand. The basket bumped off the ground, pursued by the men the Basket Detail whose job it was to make safe. Bill Bayley was first. As the basket came to earth for the second time, he caught hold of a rope; but as he ran his foot got caught on the stump of a rose bush and he fell, still holding the rope, and in a moment he was enveloped in what he took, for a moment, to be something from a Chinese laundry.

It was the parachute; the rope he had been holding had deployed it. He struggled up through the meringue of white silk to find that the silk was moving rapidly away from him. The balloon was rushing back into the air. It was already a hundred feet above the ground, with the wind carrying it out over the Birdcage. Sunny appeared above the rim of the basket, having previously been on the floor; he rubbed his cheek where an angle of the mahogany camera had struck him. Below, the now fully extended parachute billowed like the sail of a galleon. He could see Bill looking up in dismay.

Bill was shouting something. "Yes, I know the hawser's come off," muttered Sunny. It must have been the bumps that detached it. Without the heavy weight of the steel rope beneath it, the balloon had raced into the air, its nose now pointing upwards and the basket next to the side. It was an unfortunate display for the C in C, but could not, Sunny reflected, be helped. He now had to get the thing down.

The pyrotechnics of the storm came closer. The basket was jerked about as though it were a cork on the end of a string. Sunny took hold of the rope that led to the gas valve and tugged; somewhere above him he heard the familiar "plonk" and knew that it still worked. He looked for a landing site. He was over the hospitals now. Nurses were scurrying from tent to tent, beneath umbrellas. He saw a spur of the fortifications, sticking down from Lake Langaza towards a mountain. He would land short of it. Only most of the intervening ground was too rocky to make a comfortable descent; he needed a patch of English greensward, or failing that a river bed. A nice flat muddy estuary like a cushion. There was one coming up. He tugged on the valve.

The valley beneath him was sheltered. It was the ideal spot, or would have been; but he could see two lorries in it. One of them had what appeared to be a giant oil drum, turned on its side, on it. He recognised this as a British military tanker. Next to it was an unmarked vehicle, covered in turquoise-coloured canvas. There was a pipe going from the tanker to the other lorry. The scene caught his attention. Two people stood beside the lorries, beneath the umbrellas. As he flew past, they looked up. One of them, instantly recognisable from his red cummerbund, was Gazmend. He gazed into the sky with astonishment, his mouth gaping, without a thought of attempting to conceal his identity. They could hardly have expected a huge kite balloon to descend like a hideous vengeance. The other man glanced upwards but was quickly hidden again by his umbrella. Plonk — Sunny shut the valve again, but it was too late to stop the balloon from landing.

Lorries should not be parked in valleys, with pipes going between them. Sunny was far from sure what sort of reception he would get from the petrol smugglers. The basket hit the ground at speed.

Gazmend seemed to have been frozen to the spot. The other man walked purposefully to the cab of the lorry. The balloon bounced back into the air. Sunny thought he recognised Gazmend's companion but it was too improbable. Feeling that his presence in the valley was already *de trop*, he heaved a sandbag over the edge of the basket. The balloon, which had been descending, began to lift. Another sandbag went the way of the first. The ascent gathered pace. Sunny looked back on the scene below him. The second man was waving. No he was not waving; he was putting up his arm, and attached to it was a rifle.

There was a crack as a bullet snapped through the flimsy wicker surround. Sunny quickly tossed out the last of the ballast. The balloon rose further into the stormy sky. He would be going over the mountain after all. But that could mean crossing the enemy line.

Sunny was blown onwards by the wind. There was the lake. It was surrounded by the usual machine gun posts and barbed wire, in case the Bulgars tried an amphibious attack. He would land on the shore, or in the water. He opened the valve; the tail of the balloon touched the surface of the lake and he tugged at the ripcord — once to release the slack, twice for the last of the slack, and the third time to open the side of the balloon. The gas bag, minus gas, sank into the water with a kind of sigh. Sunny scrabbled out of the basket, so as not to be caught underneath. The camera slid into the lake.

The storm clouds parted and a shaft of sunshine lit the earth.

Fifty

An Italian band was playing on the square outside the *Cercle des Etrangers*. "This is the music for me," announced Bigot, the Editor of the *Balkan Gazette*. He had become thinner. He looked like a small, if sickly boy dressed in his grandfather's clothes. "One thirsts for the passions of grand opera in this absurdity of a town." He coughed.

"A drama of some sort is unfolding right here." It was Ivory, the dentist.

"A human tide," returned the journalist, "complete with flotsam and jetsam. That old man with the beard . . ."

"All the old men have beards. Be more specific."

"The old man to whom I refer can be identified by the bedstead he's got on his back. With bedding."

Bent beneath his burden, the ancient figure could hardly lift his eyes sufficiently to pick his way through the crowd that had assembled in the square. Hung about with cooking pots, he resembled a one-man band. The frame of the bed projected above his head like the ladder of a fire engine. Brightly coloured blankets added a note of gaiety that seemed woefully inappropriate to the wretchedness of his state. For most people in Salonika, the bed was their most sacred possession.

"Look at those women," observed Ivory. "One has a sewing machine, one has a grandfather clock. Salonika, I ask you! Is this one of their religious festivals, padre?"

"They may be taking them to the synagogue."

Eggie came onto the balcony. "There's a fire, you know."

"I thought there must be," said Bigot. "You can smell it."

"It started somewhere in the old town. They're going to the harbour to get out of its way."

The grand boulevard which the Turkish governor Sabri Pasha had aligned on the distant peak of Mount Olympus was now called Venizelos Street. A procession of miserable, risible figures was now making its way along it to the seafront.

"Those wooden houses. I'm not surprised," said Ivory. "Insanitary and dangerous. Perhaps they'll all burn down and we'll get something new." Eggie seconded that hope.

"Is the Club going to be safe?" wondered Bigot.

"The Club? Are you crazy?" scoffed Ivory. "The fire is in the old town. It will never get here."

"You aren't proposing to miss dinner, are you?" queried Eggie.

"I merely wondered whether we should take steps towards the Club's preservation, seeing how much our comfort depends on it. I was one of the founders, you know."

"There'll be time enough for that later," returned Eggie. "Shall we go in?"

Sunny walked stiffly into the square. The Italian band was playing but not even the sublime *bel canto* lilt of *Casta diva* could, on this occasion, retain the attention of the crowd, which was restless and thinning, as it mingled with the fugitives from the fire.

Eggie was right. You could smell it. In fact you could taste it. What had been an inconspicuous cloud to Isabel, entering Molho's with Winner and Elsie at tea time, was now more like the emission from a volcano. A dense volume of black smoke was billowing upwards, lit up, from time to time, by sparks. It was in the old town.

Sunny's intention had been to go to the Club. While he had succeeded in getting back to Salonika, it had been by riding on the back of a mule cart. He wanted to change his clothes. Mentally, he could picture himself reaching for a glass of iced wine, and the image was good. But the Club was out of the question now. He had to investigate the fire.

As he walked towards the Hagios Demetrios, the church whose soldier-saint was the defender of Salonika, he had to thread his way through a mass of people heading purposefully in one direction. Many of them were women, heavily veiled and usually shy of appearing in public. They all carried possessions that they had removed from their houses. A boy went past, wheeling a bicycle that was piled high with a carefully balanced load of clothes, jugs and baskets of food, with a birdcage perched on the top. There was, for once in Salonika, little noise, wailing, lamentation and appeals to divine providence having been replaced by the unfamiliar calm of resignation — unless it was shock. A sailor was shouting to the men, who put down their bundles and formed a line. After a few moment buckets of water began to come up. The line must have gone all the way to the harbour. It was a human chain, passing the buckets from hand to hand. But they might as well have spat into the flames, reflected Sunny, as thrown buckets of water into it. As he pushed on, the smoke became denser, the people fewer. Presumably most inhabitants had left.

The noble men of the Salonika fire brigade were at work. They were equipped with the sort of apparatus that Sunny had seen in British country houses. It consisted principally of a water tender on wheels, much decorated with brass. Water was gushing from the flanks of the hose, leaving only a thin stream to be directed onto the fire. It would have been just as effective, Sunny considered, to lay the hose side on, and let the water dribble onto the flames.

The fire had taken hold: that was obvious. Sunny cast his eye down the smoke-filled street. The houses stood shoulder to shoulder. Many of them had balconies with shutters leaning out over the street. Everything that he could see was made of wood.

A man was throwing bottles of wine out of a wine shop, not caring whether they smashed on the cobbles. Barrels were opened, and a stream of wine ran into the gutter. Sunny kicked at a Russian soldier who flung himself onto his chest to lap it up from the street.

Now the hose of the fire engine was being energetically reeled in, and the vehicle turned around. Men were pushing at the wheels to get them to start moving over the cobbles. The tender had run out of water. The engine clattered back to the harbour, to be recharged. Nearby came a sound like a giant intake of breath, and a dancing glow appeared behind a new set of windows. Another house was ablaze.

In the quartermaster's compound, the Otter looked up from the *mimosa pudica* that he was proud to have cultivated. The seeds had been sent out from home, by his mother. He liked the name, *pudica* — a bashful flower, maidenly: the exact antithesis of the British army, in fact.

It was twilight, and he could not see very much; still, it was worth revisiting this delightful bush, as a corrective to the strains of that terrible day. In fact he was happier not seeing it. He knew that, although not actually underneath the kite balloon, it had been trampled by the crew as they had launched it. But he could smell the blooms. He wondered what had happened to Sunny. He hoped he returned safely to the ground. He would share these blooms with him, to restore his equilibrium. It would do Sunny good.

It was difficult to make much out in the dark, but he did not need to. His bashful virgins were waiting there, to yield their sweetness to his nose. Oh dear, that was not, perhaps, an analogy that he would pursue with mother, but his lips parted in a harmless smile as he gazed towards the skyline above Salonika. An orange halo had appeared over the town. Something was up there. Something generally was. He would go to mess, then return to the garden and say goodnight to his flowers. A last sniff before bed.

When the Otter made his nocturnal tour, the halo had turned into a flare. Salonika is on fire, he thought to himself. Flames are eating the heart out of the town. I might be Nero, watching Rome burn.

"Sir, there's only one way of stopping the fire spreading now," said the engineer. "We'll have to clear the streets in its path." He was in the Birdcage, reporting to his commanding officer. From the time of the Great Fire of London, city fires had been stopped in the same way.

The CO objected: "But that will mean blowing up houses."

"Yes, sir. Water won't do any good, sir. Besides, there's no water."

"It's not a job for us, you know," replied the CO. "The responsibility lies with the civil authorities."

"They're overwhelmed, sir."

"Then, the French will have to do it."

"But they aren't doing it."

"You see, there's the protocol to consider. Then the matter of compensation. I'm not sure that we can go around blowing up somebody else's town. We're not an army of occupation. We're here at the invitation of the Greeks, don't forget. Notionally."

"Notionally, sir. Meanwhile, Salonika burns."

"I'm afraid it does."

It was around nine o'clock. As the engineer turned to leave the room, the window was lit up from outside. A giant fireball, made up of blazing material from the upper floors of a house, blew past the building. "Great heavens, it must have travelled two miles," exclaimed the CO. "What the devil will become of our ammo dumps? Lieutenant, start blasting the adjacent streets. Clear a fire break immediately."

"Is it me, or is the air getting thick in here?" wondered Bigot.

"I'll have my savoury," replied Eggie, "then investigate the fire. By the way, where is my savoury?" The last was addressed to the Club waiter.

"Very sorry, Major Eglinton, no savoury."

"No savoury? Then I'll have cheese."

"Very sorry, Major Eglinton, no cheese."

"Some apple pie then."

"Very sorry —"

"For heaven's sake, what can I have?"

"Very sorry, Major Eglinton, no cook."

"Where is he?"

"Gone, Major Eglinton." The waiter made a gesture as of rising flames. "Fire. Whoosh. All go. Now I go, please."

"Very well. Go. We'll take coffee in the morning room."

"Very sorry, Major Eglinton . . ."

"Yes, yes, I understand. No coffee."

Eggie and the other diners walked out onto the balcony, from which, only a couple of hours previously, they had watched the Italian band. The passage of people hurrying towards the harbour, their possessions on their heads, on their backs or in wheelbarrows, had the appearance of a rout. Only it was not enemy cavalry who were herding the people of Salonika towards the sea, but fire. Smoke gusted across their view. "Blast," declared Eggie. "It can't reach the Club, can it?" It seemed too great an outrage for even Salonika to perpetrate.

"Doesn't look promising at the moment," opined Bigot. "A great opportunity for a journalist. I shall compose a front page special from the safety of the White Tower."

"But you haven't seen a thing."

"Do I need to?"

As night fell, the first of the explosions was heard. People were not sure whether they came from the attempt to clear a fire break, or whether the fire had reached some of the dumps of weapons and ammunition that existed around the town.

Sunny had a matter of personal importance to attend to. The Follies had retained their old base in Salonika.

Among the various objects that it contained was his ocarina. Out on the harbour, a great mass of flame was floating on the water. It was an oil barge that had caught fire and was being towed out to sea, away from the ships there. With a shattering detonation, it splintered into a thousand fragments, each of which was snuffed out by the inky blackness of the sea.

Sunny reached the street. He let himself in. It was dark, but he was able to feel his way to the shelf until the triangular instrument was safe in his hand.

Sunny's eyes stung. His head ached. To be alone in the room was, for the moment, a pleasurable relief. He found the ocarina. He put it, instinctively, to his lips. The rippling sounds spilled into the air like a rill of cool water. He stood by the window and looked out. The fire had formed itself into a great semi-circle within the city walls.

He looked into the street. It was not a main thoroughfare; most people had gone. But there was a man coming out of the building opposite. He seemed familiar — of course, it was Ivory Filler, leaving his dental surgery. Sunny supposed that he had gone there out of the same motives as himself. He had a large sheaf of papers in his grip. Ridiculously, out of habit, he turned to lock the door. He dropped the papers he was carrying.

As Ivory picked them up again, Sunny noticed that one of them was an envelope. A big envelope. It was yellow. It was very like an envelope he had seen before.

Fifty-One

From outside the town a solitary church bell rang. Sunny set out to explore the devastation.

By the harbour, the railway line was twisted, the iron rails rearing up like snakes that had somehow been frozen in time. The sleepers were charred and still smouldering. The sea was grey with ashes. To Sunny's ear, it seemed to sob against the piles, in mourning for the ruin of Salonika. Sunny had passed a line of houses roughly two hundred yards long which still stood. Beyond them, desolation. A counterpane had been placed over the head and upper body of a dead man, leaving his feet to protrude from the knees.

Sunny walked towards Piccadilly Circus. To either side, the buildings had been reduced to silhouettes. Some were only one storey high. In the centre of the street was the engine, wheels and steering wheel of a tram car; all the rest of the structure — wooden — had gone.

Here and there stood a French picket to guard against looting, although the shops had been so completely consumed that there did not seem to be much to loot. A few civilians picked over the ruins of what might have been there homes, or the grocers shops from which they had fed themselves, looking for whatever scraps they could find. "Bread, Johnny, bread," called a small boy. Sunny had no bread to give.

A British soldier stood guard over a pile of straw hats. A small, carefully dressed man with a close-cropped beard was offering a drachma note, of small denomination, to relieve him of the merchandise. "No bon," the soldier was telling him. "Don't you understand the lingo? No bon." He caught sight of Sunny and saluted. "I wouldn't go any further, sir. Nothing but ashes, blackened walls, heaps of rubbish. They're trying to damp it down, sir, but fire could break out again."

"Where have the people gone."

"Refugees now, sir. They've set up tents, but there won't be enough, sir. Couldn't be."

In Venizelos Street, Sunny met Winner. He was sketching the devastation. "Isn't this where the bazaar was?"

"Yes, all those cheerful little shops. Not a shred of them left now." There was little to suggest that this had been the best street in Salonika.

Nearby the fire brigade were spraying water into the ruins that were still smoking. They walked on together, towards Hagios Demetrios. It was near there that the fire had started. The front of the basilica had disappeared, along with the roof. In one street, there was nothing left of the houses at all, beyond a single metal gate. The smell of charred timber made their throats dry.

Part of Winner was entranced by the strangeness of what faced him. "It's as though Salonika has been flayed. The flesh has all gone and we're left with the bones. It's truly terrible." He opened his sketchbook again; his charcoal made rapid marks.

Sunny walked on. A notice read, "*Dangereux. Défense de passer.*" He ignored it, turning his feet, as he so often had, towards Molho's. It had been reduced to two walls and a heap of rubbish, amid which he could distinguish the glint of broken mirrorglass. Outside it, on one of the surviving Thonet chairs, sat one of the Molho Frères, peacefully smoking a cigarette. He rocked backwards and forwards.

On seeing Sunny he leapt up and bowed. "What can I offer you, captain?" he asked ironically. "Take a table on the terrace, if you like. We have plenty of space today."

"I'm sorry."

"Don't be sorry. This is Salonika. It has an earthquake, it gets a pestilence, it burns down. Look to history. It is what has been happening since my family came here in 1492. We shall begin again. Or our children will. Personally, I take it as a judgement of God. We opened on Saturdays."

Sunny walked northwards. The fire seemed not to have burnt with quite the intensity that it had done around Hagios Demetrios. Houses stood black, ruined and roofless, but generally two or sometimes all four walls remained upright. There were scavengers here. Like him, they were prepared to risk the possibility of being trapped beneath falling beams. One of the French pickets was positioned outside the facade of one structure: perhaps it contained a safe. Further along, Sunny heard a door, charred, like everything else, and off its hinges, being kicked open from the inside. From the darkness behind it emerged a figure whom he knew. It was Ivory. He was clutching a heavy metal box.

Sunny moved towards him. The picket barred his way.

"Arrest that man, he's looting," demanded Sunny.

414

Ivory looked towards him. The picket saw the metal box and called out angrily. Ivory ignored him. He began to walk away, when the picket called out again.

"It's mine. *C'est la mienne*," Ivory called over his shoulder. The picket broke into a run and put his hand on Ivory's shoulder. "It's mine. It's from my house. I used to live here," protested Ivory.

Sunny drew his revolver. "I shall take charge of that, Mr Fuller. I would like its contents to be examined by the intelligence officer. You, sir, are a spy."

"You, sir, are a fool. But if you'd like the box, take it." He threw it at Sunny's chest. It was heavy enough to knock him backwards; then it fell, gashing his shin. Sunny's gun spun out of his hand. Ivory ran down what was left of an alleyway. The soldier followed him. Sunny calculated that he would head up the hill, towards the old Turkish streets that had lain out of the path of the wind. He ran to cut him off.

The fire had opened some views, obscured others. Taking a street that lay parallel to the ally down which Ivory had disappeared, Sunny had to jump over fallen timbers. They were too hot to put a hand on. Under foot were tiles, glass, scraps of twisted iron. He could see nothing of Ivory. He listened. He wondered if the soldier was having better luck. There was a shot, followed by a cry for help. Ivory ran across the mouth of the street. Sunny waved to another picket. "*Vite, vite. Un soldat blessé*," gesturing in the direction of the wounded man. He ran after Ivory.

Ivory had doubled back and was now making for Salonika's new *quartier*. Some of the tall Frenchified buildings still stood there, externally intact although their guts had for the most part been consumed. Men in white suits and boaters eyed the wreckage impassively, as though it were the most normal thing in the world, while they considered how to reconstruct their lives. Ivory dodged among them. He disappeared into the street beside the Post Office, scrabbling over the fallen roof tiles and other debris. Sunny stopped beside a family whose trunks and bedstead were being loaded onto a cab; the mother had her sunshade up. The three children were neatly dressed. It might have been the beginning of a holiday rather than the end of domestic life as they had known it. He nearly collided with the father, who reproved him in Ladino for his lack of manners.

He ran on but the argument had delayed him. It was just as well. In front of him, the facade of a commercial building unexpectedly leant outwards, wobbled and collapsed in a heap of masonry, enveloping what had been the street in a dense cloud of choking dust. Sunny pulled a handkerchief out of his pocket and held it to his nose. He blinked; grit was in his eyes. It became impossible to see anything. He felt as though he were flying and had entered a storm cloud. He quickly retreated to where the family was now packing itself into the cab. He took another route to get round the obstacle that had suddenly appeared. But he had lost Ivory.

He strode towards the *Place de la Liberté*, as the French called it. What had been the *Cercle des Etrangers* was reduced to a single chimney stack. Only

416

one building — tall, aggressively modern — had been untouched by the conflagration. In front of it he saw a stiff backed figure. It was Eggie. "Ah Sunny, what do you make of it?" he called out. "I've just seen Ivory. In a tearing hurry, for some reason. Positively ran off towards the quay. I say, stop a minute." Sunny did not intend to converse. He was in Venizelos Street now. Two minutes took him to the quay.

There was no sign of Ivory. Nor had Sunny any thought as to finding him. Nearby, sailors filled watercarts with seawater to douse the smouldering wreckage of the town. He realised he was thirsty. A boy sold him a slice of watermelon for ten times the usual price.

The skin factory, where they turned hides into leather, had been destroyed. Architecturally, it was nothing but a shell. Inside, though, the contents still smouldered, wafting a smell of charred flesh across the street.

Sunny threw the rind of the watermelon onto some embers. Ahead he heard a commotion. "Monsieur, monsieur." It was the expostulation of an excited Greek. A man was attempting to seize his gig. The remonstrations stopped suddenly. Ivory had presumably shown his gun. There was a crack of a whip and the gig leapt away along the cobbles. Sunny walked to the place that the confrontation had been taken. He could not use his revolver without the risk of hitting a bystander. The Greek was waving his arms, his vigorous gestures supported by a torrent of words. The group that had gathered stared after the departing gig. They saw the driver raise his whip. But the Salonika roads, rutted at the best of time, were now strewn with rubble.

A wheel hit a lump of masonry. It spun the light vehicle onto its side. Ivory was sent sprawling across the street.

Sunny took up the chase again. He reasoned that Ivory must have been hurt in some way. He would be winded at the very least. He would not be able to run far or fast. Sunny reckoned he had him.

Ivory turned into a building. Sunny approached it with caution. "You aren't to go in there, sir."

"Never mind, Sergeant."

"Strict orders to allow no one in, sir. Very dangerous, sir."

"A man has just entered."

"Then he shouldn't have done, sir. That was a dump, sir."

"It's a dump now."

"An ammo dump, sir. They don't know how much of the ammo survived the fire. Some, presumably, or what little is standing wouldn't be. That ammo will be volatile, sir. Very."

"I'll take it upon my own head, Sergeant, and approach with care."

"You may take it on your own head, sir," muttered the sergeant as Sunny approached the building. "In which case you'll need a bloody big helmet."

"Ivory," Sunny called. He picked up a stone and threw it through the blackened frame of a window. A shot rang out from the shattered building.

Sunny kept close to the wall. He edged his way along it to the side of the building. At the back of it, he found a fire escape. It was buckled but intact. He could not run up it — the clatter of his boots would have given

418

him away. But he could climb up the outside. On the first floor he stepped through a gap in the wall that had previously been a doorway but was now a void. Parts of the floor were intact but he did not trust them. He could see a beam and lightly ran across it until he reached the staircase. At the bottom of it he saw Ivory. He was winding a bandage around his leg.

Sunny wondered what he might do. He rested his hand on a piece of fallen wood. Still very hot, it collapsed, bringing a shower of other embers on top of it. Smoke swirled from the debris.

Sunny clutched his hand; it had been painfully burnt. He tried to wince, rather than curse, but all the same Ivory spun round. For a moment they stared at each other.

You can't get away," said Sunny.

"Why not? It's one to one. I'm armed, but I notice you're not holding your gun." It was true. Sunny's revolver hung from the lanyard around his neck but his hand was too damaged for him to hold it.

"The sergeant out there knows I've come in. Shoot me and the whole of the British army will be after you. There's no transport out of Salonika. If you don't shoot me, I have only to inform the authorities."

"You've nothing to tell them."

"I know about the film. I know about the couriers. I know about the petrol."

"You found out about that eventually, didn't you?" Ivory laughed. "We thought you'd rumbled it earlier. That was why your balloon was shot down. Not the one with you in it, the next one. The other officer. A name like Sparrow. Wren, that was it. Should have been you. We didn't know you'd come to Salonika for a jolly with those nurses. Our man heard you talking about gasoline at Molho's — thought you were onto something. Then we realised you were a fool and left off."

"You're a disgrace to your country."

"Which country would that be?"

"Canada. Britain. We're the Mother Country."

"You know, Sunny, I've always rather liked you. You're a simpleton. Your innocence is touching. Oh yes, I've lived in Canada. You all believed me when I said I was Canadian. My family moved from Constantinople when I was a child. I grew up in Canada but at heart I'm a Turk." He laughed. "You thought that the Turks were dark and swarthy, didn't you? But we're not Arabs. You lump all foreigners together but we're pale-skinned, like you." He stopped to draw breath, then continued: "My sister was beautiful, but died too young. She lived in Germany where my brother was in the diplomatic service. She married a German. You may have heard her name, Countess von Erfurtwege."

"Mrs Earwig?" exclaimed Sunny.

"The boy in the *Albatros* was my nephew. That was a dirty trick. I tried to have you killed for it. You had nine lives. I reckon you've used all of them up, though. Beloved Turkey. Not that I am specially proud of my birthright. There's no future in Turkey, unless, like this place, it's destroyed. The only modern country in the world is the one you're fighting. Germany. It's bound to win, you know. It will be the great European power of the twentieth century. I want to usher in that era."

420

"Is that why you do it?"

"I am an idealist, Sunny. Yes, I want a more perfect world. That is now possible to achieve. We live in an age of progress. Rat warrens like Salonika have to be cleared away. In their place will come straight roads, proper drains and street lighting. We have to blow up the British Empire. No more absurd traditions. Mankind will then fulfil itself. The world will be beautiful. We can eliminate the poor and the sick. Breed humans like racehorses, so that everywhere is only reason and beauty. What a world we'll have then. It's only a pity you won't live to see it." Ivory hauled himself to his feet and limped towards the staircase. He climbed up it. Sunny saw the revolver in his hand and drew back. He retreated to the fire escape.

Lightly he ran up the fire escape to the second floor. He could hear Ivory coming after him, one leg dragging. The noise of his boots was harsh against the metal steps. Sunny dodged into a room. Keeping to the wall, he edged his way into a corner, behind a fallen beam. The beam had collapsed from the ceiling and went from the top of the room to the floor. He did not risk putting his hand on it, but touched it with his boot. It moved. The building seemed hyper-charged with destructive energy.

"Sunny." It was Ivory calling. "Where are you? Let's continue the talk. I want to share some more ideas with you."

Sunny said nothing.

"I could tell you about Sewell. I didn't kill him. The gypsies did."

Sunny continued to keep silent.

"It was your fault. You killed the runner. The boy in the tomb." Sunny could hear Ivory moving around, feeling for him. "He was their brother," Ivory continued. "They didn't like it when Ratty showed them the hat."

Sunny almost exclaimed: "So that's where the hat went," but stopped himself just in time.

"They figured Ratty was on to them. Not that he had a clue about anything. His body will wash up somewhere around the Gulf. Or be unearthed by jackals." Eventually Ivory stopped talking.

Sunny strained his ears for a sound but there was none. That could only mean that Ivory had stopped in the doorway, by the fire escape. Sunny reached his pocket. Out of it he produced the ocarina. He blew into it. The eerie, disembodied notes crept through the shattered building. Sunny heard Ivory move. He stumbled, perhaps against something charred that lay across his path. He swore. More notes of the ocarina drifted into the ether.

At last Sunny saw what was left of the door to the room being pushed very gently open. He put his foot against the beam. Ivory came into the room. Sunny kicked the beam. Ivory swung round and fired, but the shot went wide. He leapt back and the timber missed him, crashing instead into the partially collapsed ceiling on the other side of the room, which now seemed to be kept in place by little more than a tangle of telephone wires. Sunny had hoped he would be struck, lose his balance or at least drop the gun. Instead Ivory levelled the gun at his chest.

"History will be written by the victors," explained Ivory. "Germans in this case. I shall be proved right. Not that it will matter to you. You'll be dead."

At that moment there was a voice from the doorway of the room. "Buttonhooks."

It was Winner. Ivory wheeled round.

"Sorry," said Winner instinctively. Then he explained: "I cut myself." In one hand was the scalpel that he used for his charcoal.

"Two of you," sneered Ivory, but I'm the only one who's armed."

"I saw you running, Sunny. I thought I'd better follow."

Ivory laughed shortly. "Science is about to eliminate two of the biggest imbeciles I've ever met." He pointed the gun at Winner and cocked it.

Winner looked not at the gun, but at the ceiling. "Watch out, it's coming down," he shouted.

Ivory laughed. "I'm not so easily fooled." At that moment, a lump of plaster about three feet across, bound by horsehair and as heavy as concrete, descended next to him. With his scalpel, Winner had cut the telephone line on which the ceiling's suspension had depended. More of the ceiling crashed down in massive blocks, dislodging the floor joists. Half the floor collapsed. Ivory stepped swiftly back, but behind him there was only a void. He disappeared into it, falling to the floor below, where he hit a joist, then crashed to the basement.

Sunny peered down through the building. He could see Ivory lying on a heap of cinders, debris and charred and glowing wood. He and Winner went out to the fire escape and hurried down. The fire escape did not go all the way to the basement, and Sunny did not intend to risk tackling Ivory on his own. He was probably knocked out, but might not have been. He called to the sergeant. "There's a man in there, he's got a gun and he's very dangerous. I'm arresting him as a spy. I would like you to come with me."

The soldier looked uncertain. "You're sure, sir? My orders were to stay out of the building."

"I know, I know," replied Sunny. "But how dangerous can it be?"

Barely had he spoken when the building was rocked by an explosion. The walls blew outwards and then in, as though they were the canvas sides of a tent. They then collapsed into a heap. The soldier grabbed Winner and swung him out of the way of a slab of falling masonry. All three men dived to the ground.

Ivory was dead.

Fifty-Two

The *muezzin* climbed the stair of his minaret. In his hand was a glass of water. The smoke would make his throat dry. Stepping onto the platform at the top of the stairs, he looked out over the ruins of the city. "Allahu akbar," God is great, he said softly. Five years ago, shopkeepers had taken down their Arabic signs and replaced them with ones in Greek letters. The churches that had been turned into mosques, centuries before, became churches again. The fez had all but disappeared: even before the war there had been a fez boycott, when the Young Turks were angry with Austria, where the cloth was made. Now fire had consumed the Jewish and Christian quarters of the city but not the Turkish. The faithful had been spared. He took a sip of water and cleared his throat.

The sound of the *muezzin's* distant voice fell like a dew on the army tents, some of which contained the company of the Salonika Follies. After his wont, Bill Bayley was already stirring. "Our wish was granted," he said, brushing a fly away from his face. "We saw Salonika. Now it's gone."

"I wish we were bloody gone," observed Twofour, "I dreamt I was in Wales, and it was r-r-raining," He spun out the word luxuriously. "Oh it was lovely."

"Remember the swallows and martins flying around the barracks at home, diving and skimming," reminisced Bill. "How they'd swoop over the fatigue parties when they was scything the grass. Why aren't there any here? We've got enough flies."

"You've got the tortoises?" asked Parsley.

They watched the tortoises lumber, in different directions, over the parched ground. The race was a classic. 'Orace beat 'Ercules by a nose, Harthur coming up a poor third. Chelsea Bunn counted his winnings.

Bill returned the tortoises to their stable. His sweaty face was irresistible to the fly population. "Pass me that towel, will you, mate?" he said grimly. Having passed

425

the towel over his forehead, he took it in one hand, flicking an end towards the dense agglomeration of flies at the apex of the tent. Dead and stunned flies were scattered in all directions. He stamped on those that he moved on the floor. The slaughter continued until he was satisfied that the buzzing had been significantly reduced.

He lay down, his ears for once untroubled by undue buzzing. "At last," he declared. "Harmony with Nature."

The cry of the *muezzin* — a different *muezzin* — also drifted over the ruined streets of the city. It was a week since Salonika had caught fire. Across the city, buildings still burnt or smouldered — they would continue to do so for another ten days. Seventy-two thousand people had been made homeless; nearly ten thousand dwellings had been destroyed. Sunny's adventure had left him with concussion and some nasty scratches. It had not, though, been an entirely bad week. If anything the reverse. In hospital he had been tended by Isabel. Isabel had stayed in Salonika to help with the relief work. It was, thought Sunny, a good arrangement. Winner had told her of Sunny's encounter with Ivory. She called it "fine". He intended to propose to her that afternoon.

Now he was fortifying himself at the Club. For there was still a club: not the *Cercle des Etrangers*, whose building had been consumed, but the *Club des Intimes*, which fared better. Although most of the building had disappeared, members could sit on the pavement at

426

metal tables. Some familiar characters were gathered around one of them.

"You see," Sunny explained, "Ivory's fall must have rekindled the fire. It was already pretty hot in there. The fire hadn't really gone out. When Ivory crashed into the bonfire, so to speak, the impact stirred up the embers and it flared out again. Like poking the logs in a grate."

"I still don't believe it," insisted Eggie. "I saw the man practically every week. What he did for my teeth can't be too highly praised."

"Which day did you go?" wondered Sunny.

"I used to go on my way back from the harbourmaster's office. His surgery was en route. A convenient arrangement."

"And you carried with you certain documents?"

"I might have done. I couldn't possibly tell you about them. Classified, you know."

"They might have included details of shipping movements. Charts — that sort of thing?"

Eggie looked wary. "Always safely shut up in my bag."

"And he would give you gas."

"Look here, just what are you saying. So what if I had gas. Ivory said it was the modern way. I can take pain like the next man. There's nothing I would rather do than lead my battalion into battle. I'm just a bit squeamish about teeth."

Sunny did not pursue the matter in that forum. Instead he had another bone to pick. "Does anyone," he wondered, "know what happened to our landlord? I should say, the landlord of our former building, in the days when it was a building."

"That Turk who kept showing up," fumed Eggie. "No idea."

"Nobody does," observed the Otter. "Perhaps he went up in smoke."

Bigot laughed; the sound could have come from a pair of rusty bellows. "Like a djin."

Eggie was not interested in Gazmend's fate. He expanded on a previous theme. "I'm pressing headquarters for a really big show. This is the third year we've been out here. Without any leave whatsoever. I'm damned if I'll go home without having taken part in a show. We've got to have something make our time seem worthwhile. We'd be a public laughing stock otherwise. Can't let the Serbs have all the action."

"Pity that we had to execute their leader." Simple had arrived. "A drink? Yes, thank you. I need one in this heat."

"Which leader?" asked the Otter.

"Colonel Dimitrijevic. The King hated him. Their king, not ours. The Black Hand, I ask you — the Slavs love their melodrama."

"Weren't the Black Hand behind the assassination in Sarajevo?"

"Wretched Serb nationalism. Yes, Dimitrijevic kicked the whole thing off. Good soldier, though."

"Politics," scoffed Eggie. "All I ask is . . ."

"For the chance to lead the battalion into battle?" Simple completed his sentence. "You may get your wish. I've arranged for you to be posted upcountry. Permanently. Now, I must get back."

Bigot turned a yellow eye on him. "Back where?"

"To the refugee camp. Have you seen it? Hundreds of families, all homeless."

"The wailing!" Bigot put his hands to this ears.

"They don't wail, Bigot. The Jews are used to rebuilding their lives. You know," he continued, in a burst of untypical lyricism, preceded by a slight cough, "when you cut down trees in an old wood, bluebells appear. One person has been made happy by the fire. Rachael Pinheiros."

"Do we know the lady?" asked Sunny.

"She makes the chocolate at Molho's. Made, I should say." There was a general quickening of interest. "Her father wanted to marry her to a rabbi. She has used the opportunity of the fire to run off with her beau."

"With the blessing of the father?"

"Not exactly. But since the fire destroyed everything he owned, he could no longer afford a rabbi as a son-in-law. And as the young man's family is quite rich, he may come around in time."

"But is the inamorato a Jew?"

"A *Dönmeh*. So Jew-ish."

This statement perplexed most of the company. "I shall miss him. I had hopes that we would write a paper together, 'A Paleo-Christian Chistern in Salonika'."

"Did they ever discover what caused the fire?" asked Sunny. Having been in hospital, he was not abreast of the news. "Sabotage?"

In the fire's immediate aftermath, people had indeed assumed it to have been deliberately started; they remembered how a German plane had flown overhead. But the Otter gave a resume of current opinion. "Theories differ. A pan of fat in a kitchen going up in flames. A careless cigarette. A pile of hay catching a spark from some mule's iron shoe. A boy collecting eggs from a dark cellar and lighting a match to find his way. Straw as dry as anything in this heat and whoosh, up it went. The hot wind from the Vardar blew straight down Venizelos Street, which might have been specially built as a funnel."

A wheeze and a cough indicated that Bigot was about to speak. "I suspect two clandestine lovers who wanted to pursue their illicit courtship in darkness, and threw a lamp out of the window." He paused to pass a handkerchief over his brow. "But I've always been a romantic."

Winner had a different idea. "Salonika has been packed to the gills since the Allies arrived. This city is another casualty of war."

Eggie would have none of it. "Nonsense. The city was merely waiting to burn down. Wooden and rotting. Did you observe the inefficiency of the civil authorities on the evening of the fire? Completely hopeless. Probably corrupt, though that goes without saying. The French weren't much better. Good riddance to the lot of it. A new, clean city, properly planned with up-to-date sanitation, by British architects even, will take its place."

430

"That's more or less what Ivory thought," observed Sunny.

Prayers finished and the street began to fill with worshippers returning from the mosque. Sunny noticed a straw boater floating over their heads. He removed his revolver from its case and ran into the crowd. "Here is the other villain," he announced, producing Gazmend Effendi at gunpoint. "Ivory's accomplice."

"Where?" asked Simple, peering around. His weak eyes identified a red cummerbund. "Ah, Effendi," he said, making a *salaam*.

"I can tell you something about this man," Sunny told the others. "He has a farm in the Struma; he stored petrol there."

Simple looked amused. "Do put that gun away, Sunny. Effendi, can I order a cup of coffee? Petrol," he laughed, adding to Gazmend, "You would have needed it, eh?"

"What for?" Sunny was bewildered.

"For the *Komitadji*. I think you would call them guerrillas." Gazmend smiled blandly. "We have been conducting some operations behind the lines. The Berlin to Baghdad railway is a most tempting target. We have to get our supplies from somewhere. What we don't use, we can sell for money. It is difficult to go through the usual channels. Officially the *Komitadji*, as a unit of the British army, don't exist. The quartermaster would be horrified." He bowed to the Otter. "No chit."

"But you tried to shoot me," complained Sunny, hesitating as to whether he should lower the revolver. "When I was in the balloon."

"Did you see me?"

"I saw somebody — Ivory, I presume — with a gun. The shot went past me."

"It was indeed Ivory, and he was a very good shot. A child of the prairies, you remember. He would certainly have killed you, if I hadn't at that moment happened to trip over and jog his arm."

Eggie found the conversation difficult to follow. "Do you mean to say that you're on our side? You're a Turk."

"People assume that. I reply that I am — I was — an Ottoman. The Ottoman Empire was not run by Turks. My family were loyal to the sultan. That all changed; the sultan lost power the year after Salonika became Greek. But we were certainly never Turks."

Simple chuckled. "Gazmend comes from Albania."

"With a Greek grandmother and a Bulgarian great-grandfather." Beneath the bushy moustache his unexpectedly pink lips shaped themselves into an almost coquettish smile. "I've always said that I'm a spy." With that he bowed and walked unhurriedly away, tapping his silver-headed cane.

All but one of the men around the table were lost for words. "Invaluable fellow, that Gazmend," Simple murmured.

The Otter reopened the conversation. "Do you know what a Greek said to me? The charred basements of Salonika have made a place for criminals, tramps and lovers. They will keep warm in the embers. So some good comes out of it. I mean as regards lovers. Admittedly not much. But here we have Gazmend:

432

white after all. And thank heaven my garden wasn't burnt."

"Yes, good comes," bubbled Winner excitedly. "My Last Judgement is destroyed. I shall paint a Resurrection. I have something to announce. Miss Fox and I are engaged. She wanted a cause. She will make one of me."

"Congratulations," said Simple. The others joined him. Sunny's brow furrowed. How should he best put the question to Isabel — and what she would say when he did so? Simple continued: "You should receive a medal, you know."

"For marrying Elsie?"

"For that magnificent piece of flying, which herded an enemy colonel across the Serb line. In the heat of battle, too."

"Two medals," took up Sunny. "One for that little assistance you gave me in respect of the late Ivory. But," he continued, considering Winner's marriage, "I can quite imagine you need looking after, and there is your genius to consider." He raised his beer to his lips. "But before anything of that kind can progress, remember your duty to the Follies. New sets."

"They'll have them. Joyous ones."

Eggie groaned despairingly. "Those wretched Follies. Wasn't the theatre destroyed?"

"It was," replied Sunny. "Lost the props, everything. This insubstantial pageant faded. But you know what they say in the circus." He leant forward and took his pipe from his mouth. "The show must go on."

"I propose a toast," cried Winner. They stood up and lifted their glasses. "The show must go on."

A thin smile crossed Eggie's face as he thought of another show, the one round the lake that the British army had been trying to bring off since it arrived. Upcountry, against those wretched Pips held by the Bulgarians.

He got to his feet. "The show," he said, "must go on."

Envoi

On 18–19 September 1918, the British army fought the Battle of Lake Doiran. Troops attacked uphill, in sweltering heat. They wore masks over their faces and sucked the air that they breathed through the rubber nozzles of respirators. Johnny Bulgar had had three years to prepare his defences. Nearly eight thousand men were killed for no appreciable gain. Eggie's show had gone on. It made little difference to the outcome of the War and is largely forgotten except by visitors to the fortifications on Pip Ridge. The latter were so strongly built that, a hundred years later, many of them are still there.

Finis

A note on sources and names

Nearly everything in this book could have happened. Many of the incidents have been inspired by letters, diaries and memoirs of the period.

I have, however, taken some liberties for the sake of my story. The timeline has in places been slightly altered. For example, the Serb army was not fighting around Prilep in 1916, and the *Albatros* fighter biplane with the two machine guns on the upper wing would not have shot down an observation balloon in the spring of 1916; it entered service that August. But I liked the name. Besides, the German ace Rudolf von Eschwege was flying an *Albatros* D.III when he was blown out of the sky by a ruse in November 1917.

I have changed all the names except one: that of General Gay. I have not, however, researched the character of General Gay, only borrowed his name. May history forgive me.